D1519369

NELLY'S CASE

A NOVEL

ANDY SIEGEL

ROCKWELL PRESS | NEW YORK

Rockwell Press
New York, NY
info@rockwellpress.com

Interior design by Renata Di Biase
Cover design by Faceout Studio, Charles Brock, www.faceoutstudio.com
Tug Wyler Mystery Series logo by Andy Siegel and Rebecca Cantrell
Author photographs by Michael Paras

ISBN 1981553347
ISBN-13 9781981553341

> *"I'm only left with shreds of sensation*
> *as to what my life once was."*
> —A young client who was run over by a bus

I dedicate this book to those inflicted with personal injury from an unexpected instance of negligent conduct. I've seen how after this traumatic event there is often no return to the normal existence once taken for granted. The courageous way these survivors have coped with their life situations has inspired this work.

Although The Tug Wyler Mystery Series is meant to be entertaining, I am well aware there is nothing humorous about being the victim of personal injury or medical malpractice.

Seriously, who doesn't hate going to the dentist?

Anyway, in my business, things are set in motion by an unfortunate event, much of the time a preventable one. Let's see how this one plays out . . .

NELLY'S
CASE

THE UNFORTUNATE EVENT

The door opens. In walks Dr. Grad. He's tall, lean, mid-sixties, with a thick head of salt-and-pepper hair, baby blues, and a strong chin. The knot of a dark-red tie, visible beneath his pristine dental smock, contrasts perfectly with his crisp white shirt.

"Hi, girls," he says, his manner engaging, yet professional.

"I'm Dr. Grad. And you," he says to the one reclining in the dental chair, "must be Nelly Rivera."

A timid nod reveals her as nervous. Shifting his attention, he speaks to the other girl. "And, young lady, you are?"

"I'm Nelly's sister, Jessie." He extends his hand.

They share a smile, but then it's back to business.

Looking down at Nelly—wearing a Yankees cap she bought just down the block at the stadium—Grad turns serious. "Let's have a brief talk, shall we?"

"Sure."

"Great. So I've reviewed Dr. Meyer's films," he says in a measured way. "And this is a routine procedure that can be done by numbing the area locally. Cavity work is quite simple and doesn't require anesthesia. So, before we begin, I'd like to suggest that you reconsider and allow Dr. Meyer to do the work. He's a good dentist, and I'm confident that, with your sister's support"—he acknowledges Jessie—"you can overcome this."

What he's talking about is Nelly's dental anxiety. Grad encourages these patients to address their fears before committing to going forward with anesthesia. Most of the time it's a losing battle and, therefore, why they've come to him in the first place.

"But he's not the Painless Dentist, is he now, Dr. Grad?" Jessie's teasing reference is to the ads Grad regularly runs in *Time Out New York*.

"No, I guess he's not," Grad answers. He's in a familiar scenario, one where he knows every move. It's his business, after all.

As he heads toward the IV pole, Nelly grabs the bottom of his smock, giving it a playful tug. He turns, looking down at her. There's no trace of a smile left on her face.

"Yes, dear?" he asks, his voice comforting.

"You *promise* it's not going to hurt?"

"Not even a pinch," he reassures. Nelly looks to Jessie, sitting at her right, who gives an "I told you so" nod of encouragement. The catch phrase of his ads is the line he's just used. That's why they're here.

He opens a cabinet and takes out two solution bags, hanging them on the pole. After accessing an arm vessel, he starts the flow of the larger one, dripping Ringer's Lactate hydrating solution. He then connects the much smaller bag to the drip line. He reaches up and slightly adjusts the mechanism that controls the flow of this anesthetic.

Nelly feels a chill where the fluid enters her arm, then warmth all over.

"Just relax and enjoy the peacefulness," he urges soothingly.

Her lids close as the drug takes its immediate effect. Grad observes her for several moments. He knows well what to expect. Her face wears that familiar tranquil expression he's induced so many times. He looks to Jessie, giving her a reassuring smile, then back to his patient, whose eyes are open just a slit.

"How are you feeling?"

"Drowsy," she's able to respond.

"Good. That's the place we want you to be. Drowsy but not out. That's how conscious sedation works. Now relax." He reaches up to the control mechanism and adjusts the flow of anesthesia. Then he maneuvers a curly plastic suction device under Nelly's tongue and rests the tubing on the protective blue bib covering her clothes. Glancing over at Jessie, he whispers, "Keep an eye on her, like a good big sister." After disposing of his sterile gloves, he slowly turns the knob, then leaves the room, carefully shutting the door.

Jessie smiles tenderly as she looks at Nelly lying there helpless. Here is the girl who once stood up, all alone, to a gang of boys who tried to steal her sneakers back in third grade. It hadn't been easy growing up in the Bronx, where the streets were a daily education all their own. Yet her sister—tough as Jessie knows her to be—still is scared to have a cavity filled.

A few moments later the door opens. Sensing someone's presence, Nelly manages to shift her head ever-so-slightly to the left. A woman enters. It's Rita, the dental assistant, who'd ushered them into the room. She walks to the pole and checks the flow dripping from the two bags at different rates. She looks over Nelly, who gathers the strength to flash an acknowledging smile. After smiling back, Rita disappears just as quickly as she entered.

Nelly, with great effort, slowly repositions herself. Her head tilting left. Deeper and deeper she falls into a restful, anesthetized state.

The door opens again. Or maybe not. Nelly can't be sure at this stage. But she believes she sees Debbie, the young receptionist Nelly saw being reprimanded earlier for wearing denims to work day two on the job. As Debbie moves toward the pole, a cardigan button comes into focus. Then this figure disappears too.

Now standing over her—for some reason—is Jessie.

Though Jessie, who's watching her, can't know it, Nelly is tumbling deeper and faster, deeper and faster, with every drop of the infusing anesthetic. What Jessie can see, however, is that her sister's chest is rising and falling in slow, rhythmic fashion. The infiltrating drugs, like all anesthetics, are respiratory depressants causing hypotension and rapid shallow breathing.

"Keep an eye on her," Dr. Grad had told Jessie when he'd left the room. So she's doing just that.

If we could ask Nelly, we'd learn that she's now at peace without a worry in the world, never having imagined a dental procedure could be so relaxing. Deeper and deeper she drops into that place where you go when anesthesia perfuses your bodily systems and centers of consciousness.

Her chest rises in a measured fashion. Just as slowly, it falls. Up and down, in rhythmic motion. Yet subtle changes occur as Nelly enters a more depressed physiologic state. Jessie, without quite realizing why, is feeling a sense of unease. What's happening?

Her sister's chest movements are difficult to register. Its expansions and contractions are hard to perceive.

Slower. And slower. Until—

"Help! Somebody! Help!" Jessie screams. "My sister stopped breathing! Help! Help!" she yells at the top of her lungs, bolting from the room. Two nearby exam doors pop open. Grad and Rita spring into the hall.

"Help! Please! My sister's not breathing!"

They jostle past her into the room. Nelly is ghost-white. Cadaver-white actually. Grad yanks out her IV. He lifts Nelly from the chair—exhibiting strength uncommon to men his age—now laying her flat on the floor.

"Move back! Move back!" he shouts to the crowd gathered at the door. He puts his ear to Nelly's chest. He cocks her head back, creating an airway. Sealing her mouth with his, he gives two quick breaths, raising her chest. Ear again on sternum. He looks up to Rita.

"Call 911! Call 911!"

"Debbie did!" she tells him. Her voice breaks.

He continues working on Nelly, alternating breaths with chest compressions. Nothing. Repeats for three more minutes. Nothing.

"Oh, my god! Help her! Help her!" Jessie cries out. "Don't let her die!" she yells. Grad continues his cardiopulmonary resuscitation, employing it with efficiency and skill.

But five minutes into arrest, there is still no response.

He checks her pupils. Fixed, . . . doll's eyes, . . . not good. He goes back to work, forcing air into her. He won't stop until she's officially pronounced dead by someone with the authority to do so. That's the protocol.

"Move! Move!" a firm voice commands from near the door. "Out of the way!" orders the emergency medical technician. "Move out of the way!"

Grad, Rita and Debbie, plus two curious patients, scramble out of the doorway, then jockey for position to watch the events. One EMT applies an oxygen mask and ambubags her. The other—with his fingers on her carotid—looks up at Grad.

"How long? How long!"

Grad checks his watch. He depresses the chronometer, angling its face toward him.

"Stop playing with your watch, goddamn it! How long?"

"Nine minutes, forty-three seconds."

"What did you give her?" Nodding toward the dangling lines.

"Midazolam."

"Reversals?"

"No," Grad replies.

"Move out of the way!" commands the EMT to the doorway spectators. His partner, now at Nelly's feet, counts, "One, . . . two, . . . three," and they lift, whisking her in one fluid motion from the room and onto a waiting stretcher.

"Oh, my god!" Jessie repeats. Then says, "Please don't let her die!"

They wheel Nelly down the hall and exit as fast as they can. The entourage of onlookers follows suit. All watch somberly as the stricken young woman is loaded into the ambulance. A throng of city sidewalk bystanders stops to spectate too.

"Let's go!" Grad orders, pulling Jessie's arm. Moments later they enter his car parked at the curb and pull out right behind the siren-blaring ambulance.

It's a race against time. Fighting city traffic.

Jessie turns to Grad, now drenched in sweat.

"Do you think she's going to live?" She can't help but ask.

He answers, keeping his sight fixed on the road. "She'll make it. She's young. She's strong."

But Jessie's not convinced. His tone lacked the certainty she had hoped to hear.

"Dr. Grad?" she asks, in a tone seeking answers.

"Yes, dear?" His concentration doesn't waver.

"After you started the anesthesia . . . "

"Yes, dear, go on," he encourages. "After I started the anesthesia, what?" He glances over the way drivers do. For just an instant, they lock eyes.

"Why did you leave the room?"

1.

t's five after nine in the morning, and I'm sitting outside Judge Wilson's courtroom, waiting for my clients. Her Honor had cautioned me not to be late while I packed up yesterday. I'd been the last one to leave, at which point she began in on me. "We are starting at 9:30 a.m. on the button tomorrow, Mr. Wyler. Not 9:33, not 9:32, and not 9:31. Nine thirty on the button. Do you understand, Counselor?"

"Jeepers, I sure do, Your Honor," I replied, the way Dennis the Menace responds to Mr. Wilson after a scolding. But, let me say, if anyone were a menace here, it would be Her Honor.

The thing is, today will be my big-ass cross-exam of defendant's expert, Dr. Baker. He's a world-renowned gynecological urologist, or so he testified from the witness stand. It's not a specialty I know much about, but still the guy looked familiar—and yesterday I realized why. It's because my mother—a long-term cancer patient—had once consulted him. He'd said to her, "All seems fine down there." Mom's response: "That's because I don't use it anymore."

Yesterday Dr. Baker had told the jurors, at the end of the hysterectomy performed by the surgeon I was suing—on whose behalf Dr. Baker was making an appearance in court—there'd been no perforation through my client's bladder. According to him, had a hole been there, the defendant would've seen it and repaired it with two simple sutures.

My claim is that such an injury to the bladder is a textbook risk of the procedure when removing a woman's uterus. But, if the perforation occurs while dissecting the uterus off the bladder, then it's malpractice not to identify the hole and repair it prior to closing the patient. In effect this is a simple case of failing to see what was there to be seen.

Chucky-boy—aka Charles Lawless—the defense lawyer, knows he cannot win the case if the hole was in the operative field before closure. Therefore, he made use of a lawyer's prerogative—the art of creative legal thinking. His ploy of choice was to propose that the hole had undoubtedly developed after closure. If it hadn't been there to be seen prior, then no malpractice could attach, as there was nothing to see and thus fix. Bizarre.

But clever.

Now let's hear Dr. Helpful: "It is my opinion that no hole existed in her bladder before closure. This is based on conjecture with an assumption, the hypothesis being, in theory, that the hole developed two days later. I have read about this happening during experimentation with laboratory animals. What is speculated is that an arc of electricity jumped off the cauterizing instrument—used to separate the fascia connecting the two anatomies—and onto the nearby bladder wall, causing a compromise to the tissue. At that stage, there was no hole. Yes, the hole developed when the tissues gave way later after the patient was closed. Unavoidable risk."

Bullcrap, buddy.

But, in the spirit of a courtroom litigator committed to the art form, I must say I loved it when he offered that testimony. Because it was so out there I couldn't wait to cross-examine his fabricating fat ass.

As a matter of legal procedure, I made a motion at end of session to strike his testimony as speculative. However, as expected, Judge Wilson denied it. She was angry that I "wasted the court's time" in making the application. I told her I was sorry, but I was preserving my client's rights for appellate review. That's how an attorney says f-you to the trial judge. So, of course, it angered her more. But who cares? She's been giving me the business since opening statements.

Despite my support for the lawyer's prerogative to exercise the art of creative legal thinking, I'm still ticked off at Chucky-boy and Dr. Baker because, me, I have great respect for the legal system. That's why, when a witness under oath bases his testimony on "conjecture, assumption, hypothesis, theory, and speculation," something inside me churns. Those five words are inconsistent with truth; at least that's what the Court of Appeals has held. The term used? "Voodoo medicine." Meaning, the opinion isn't based upon generally accepted principles of medicine. Put simply: it lacks scientific validity.

Judge Wilson dislikes me. That fact though doesn't make me special. She has it in for all plaintiffs' lawyers. Since it's 9:10 a.m., I believe I hear her marching approach from around the corner now. *Fee-fi-fo-frass, I hear the steps of a judicial ass.* I love rhyming nursery stories with legal references. Yep, I'm right. Turning the bend, she comes. I can't wait to say hello. The meaner she gets, the nicer I become. She loathes me even more for that.

"Hello, Your Honor," I say, as she walks by. "Top o' the morning to you. Might I add that you look just wonderful on this auspicious day? A bright ray of sunshine even."

"Counselor—" she says sternly.

I interrupt her, suggesting as I have before, "Call me Tug."

"I will *not* call you Tug, Counselor! I could have you locked up for attempting to curry favor with the court."

"Locked up? As in jail?"

"Yes, as in jail."

"Why would you ever want to do that?"

"Because I *can*. I will see you inside. I expect you to be done with defendant's expert, Dr. Baker, within an hour. He's a very busy man. Do you hear me?"

"My questions will be direct and to the point, Your Honor. I can assure you of that."

"Good." She starts to go, but I feel the need to poke just the tiniest bit more.

"You know, Your Honor." She turns back. "My mother consulted Dr. Baker. It's kind of creepy cross-examining him, given he fiddled around with my mom's privates. Don't you think?"

She gives me a piercing glare. It looks like Judge Wilson—for the first time in her life—is absent a response.

I'll help her out.

"Too much information, Your Honor?"

"Yes, Mr. Wyler, too much information."

I bet she stays up late imagining new ways to make the plaintiffs' bar miserable, which is why I enjoyed giving her that rise. Yet her inappropriate and partial presiding doesn't affect me, not personally. Her conduct severely compromises my clients' rights, a couple who've waited five long-suffering years for their day in court.

You see, that hole in my female client's bladder leaked urine internally where it should never be. And because urine has corrosive properties, it burned a fistula—an abnormal tunnel connecting two anatomies—between her bladder and vagina. Thus she's undergone seven failed corrective procedures to close the space created. Forced to live with a surgically implanted catheter that drains urine into a bag taped outside her abdomen, she must also wear diapers because, at times, she leaks.

I apologize for such clinical descriptiveness. What you need to understand is, being an injury lawyer is a misperceived profession—the stale old "ambulance chaser" tag is a hard one to shake. The reality is, the victims I represent are real people exactly like you and me, going about their business and not planning for catastrophe. Yet, out of the blue, their lives and those of their families have been suddenly and tragically compromised.

Forever.

I hear more steps approaching. Around the bend come the Clarks, Nancy and Harold, my clients. They take a seat next to me on the hard bench.

"Good morning, Mr. Wyler," Harold Clark says. He's the injured plaintiff's husband who also has a claim for the loss of his wife's services.

"We had to pick up our daughter yesterday afternoon," he explains, "which is why we rushed out of here."

But I can tell something else is on Harold's mind. I wait.

Adjusting his apologetic expression, he assumes another one—half-aggressive, half-aggrieved. "We don't like that doctor comparing Nancy to some lab animal."

"I agree."

They both look relieved.

"The judge abused her discretion by failing to strike his testimony, leaving us with an appealable issue. Please don't worry—I'll do what needs to be done here."

"We trust that you will," Harold responds. Nancy stays silent. "But she seems to really be coming after you."

"I agree with you there too."

"Can't you fight back in some way?"

"Harold," I say, using the soothing tone a lawyer employs when about to impart the best trial strategy available in a less-than-fair courtroom, "the jury is taking note of her continued abuse. I don't like playing that card, but, if I fought back, they'd have to choose sides. So I'm just going to sit here and take it on the chin. It's our best option."

I now hear more footsteps.

Hickory, dickory, dock, sounds like the steps of a schlock. It's none other than Charles Lawless, the attorney defending the surgeon responsible for Nancy's unfortunate condition. No joke, his name's Lawless. But, to me, he'll always be Chucky-boy.

Over the years I've watched him go from fairly good guy to kinda-sorta asshole. Now I'd describe him as a beaten-down old attorney who's come to terms with his place in the legal world. He's been my adversary on four different cases, giving me a window on his devolution. I've also had his two ex-partners against me—one time each—but they'd been plain old assholes from the start, without having to pass through any stages.

Anyway, in the heavily populated arena of New York City personal injury litigation, it's rare you'd wind up in court against the same guy twice. Finding Chucky-boy on the other side again, number four, was completely against the odds.

He stops and turns toward me. A brief snapshot will suffice: turkey neck, bad hair swoop, and soft around the gut. I call his style frumpy. I wait as he blows his nose in a dingy hankie. *Yuk.*

"I got the letter," he tells me, folding away the used handkerchief after glimpsing his creation. *Double yuk.*

"That's funny," I respond. "I didn't send you one, unless of course my paralegal misaddressed an envelope." It's only a mild witticism, but it doesn't matter. He never thinks I'm funny. Whether that's a good thing or not, it's definitely been an ongoing feature of my occasional relationship with this decomposing defense attorney.

"Your retention as trial counsel on the *Simone* matter," he continues, ignoring my disavowal. "I mean, why would you want to get involved in that case? It's going nowhere."

Despite having never heard of *Simone*, my first thought is: *Hmm.* Why would he say that, given every case I've ever had with him has gone somewhere.

"Chuck, all I can tell you is, I have no idea what you're talking about. I don't know of a *Simone* case."

He shrugs. "Suit yourself. And for the last time," he says frustratingly, "it's not Chuck or Chucky-boy or Charlie. It's Charles."

"Well, what did I call you?" I ask, knowing full well.

"You called me Chuck."

"Chuck? Are you sure?"

"Yes. Positive."

"I'm sorry." But he can tell, of course, that I'm not. He walks off.

I turn back to my clients. Unexpectedly Harold now hands me a dirty, crumpled envelope marked Photos. It looks like it's been sealed for a long time. I look at him questioningly.

"I went through some of our records last night and found this. Photos I once took that show Nancy's injuries."

"I didn't see any photos in the file from your referring attorney. Did you ever give them to him?" They look at each other. Yet the fact that the envelope's sealed says it all.

"I don't think so," Harold replies. Then Nancy adds, "I didn't even remember we'd taken them."

"Then I won't be able to get them into evidence. I mean, there are judges who *might* let them in, but Wilson never would because they haven't been exchanged pursuant to the rules of court. Maybe I can manage it if we say they were just discovered after being lost. That makes for an exception to the rule, giving the judge discretion. Here, let me look to see if they'd help."

I open the envelope quickly, curious to find out what's inside. I love photos. Juries love photos too. I mean, who doesn't like a good photo of a horrific injury? I remove four snapshots. The first three show Nancy in a T-shirt and thong. I hadn't pegged her as the thong type. Above her pubic area is the implanted tube leading to a bag half-filled with urine taped to her right flank. Harold leans back, peeks, then turns to his wife and gives her a comforting rub on her back.

The fourth picture is different. In this last one, you see Nancy's body above the waist and thus above her catheter. And . . . she's hiking up her shirt, showing her boobs. Exposed are extremely wonderful-looking forty-three-year-old breasts. They're faultless. Good for you, Nancy, given all you've been through.

"Well, what do you think?" Harold asks.

I consider answering—but only for a moment—"Your wife has nice titties." Of course I recognize such a rejoinder is patently inappropriate on many different levels. Still it's the thought that instantly came to mind.

At least I admit it.

But what's clear to me is, the Clarks are not aware of the treat captured in good ol' picture number four.

"*Um*," I answer, "those first three depict the injury very clearly." I look at Nancy, who's wearing her usual innocent-victim face. "But—"

I'm interrupted by the sound of noisy footsteps in the distance. Not just any footsteps but the empathic heel strikes of a man whose cowboy boots are a necessary adjunct to his aggression.

In short, it's the sound of trouble approaching.

Benson!

Yet I hear a lighter *tap-tap* as well. Who's with Henry? There's no guessing—he's too unpredictable—so I wait. In seconds all will be revealed.

"There he is!" Henry announces. He marches over with a twentyish Latina trailing a half step behind. She's wearing large silver hoop earrings, a loose-fitting leopard-print top, and tight jeans.

Henry stops in front of us in his customary authoritarian manner. Then again he'd have to work hard to be anything but commanding. He owns that.

"I'm Henry Benson," he says to the startled Nancy and Harold. "I'm sorry to interrupt like this, but an emergency has arisen involving Mr. Wyler. I'm certain the court will understand."

He turns to me. "Come on," he urges. "We need to leave this minute!"

"Henry, slow down." I look to my clients reassuringly. "I'm in the middle of a trial. This is Harold and Nancy Clark. Harold, Nancy, this is Henry Benson, one of my esteemed colleagues." I love using the phrase—"esteemed colleague"—even if it's hard to work in when your colleagues are lawyers.

"Nice to meet you, Mr. and Mrs. Clark," Benson says, carefully making eye contact with both. "I'm very sorry, but, you see, this is a matter of life and death. This young woman is Jessie Rivera. . . . Jessie, these are the Clarks."

Jessie takes her cue. "Nice to meet you both."

"Dear"—Mrs. Clark points—"be careful. Your phone's going to fall out."

Looking, Jessie responds, "Thanks. That actually happened the other day." She forces her phone deeper into its shallow outside pocket. Dissatisfied, she removes the phone and places it into her pocketbook. "It's a new bag," she adds, implying she's not used to it yet.

Henry continues. "Jessie's sister was the victim of an anesthesia misadventure, and we don't know if she'll pull through. It's an extremely touch-and-go situation. Come on, Tug! We have to get to the hospital. *Now.* Let's go!" He steps forward and takes my arm as if to help me up.

I resist. Subtle defiance but genuine nonetheless. It's not what he's used to, and he's not happy.

"Henry, I can't leave right now. It's an important matter for the Clarks."

Shrewd as ever, he changes tack. "Oh, yes, but of course. How insensitive of me. I apologize completely. I'm just too single-focus right now. Energy runs high in life-or-death situations."

At this instant the sound of yet another pair of footsteps can be heard approaching. A female in cheap shoes is my guess. *Right again.* Mere moments later I see what strikes me as an uptight insurance adjuster in her fifties. She passes us, trying her best not to make eye contact. The fact that she's with the bad guys is a no-brainer because they never feel comfortable looking you in the eye. She enters Judge Wilson's courtroom, and, when the door shuts, we pick things back up, though not where we left off.

"Are those photographs?" Henry asks, pointing to what I'm holding. Like I said, everybody loves photos.

I nod. "Potential evidence."

"Let me see those," he requests. But after, not before, he's plucked them from my fingers. Typical.

"Henry, they're confidential."

He looks to Nancy and Harold, holding the pictures down at his side to emphasize he hasn't peeked.

Yet.

"Mr. and Mrs. Clark, I'm one of the, if not the most well-respected lawyer in the state. Right, Counselor?" he asks, looking to me.

"Yes, Henry." As if I had options here.

"Your lawyer and I have worked together on many cases, and we've been a very successful team. Wouldn't you say, Tug?"

"Yes, Henry."

"Therefore, I'd like to think my input might, in some small way, contribute to the excellent outcome I know your lawyer will soon bring to you and your case. That said, may I have your permission to view these photos?"

"Um, yes, sure, you can look at them," answers Harold as Nancy nods.

Henry looks at them one by one, first trying up close, then far away, revealing his obvious need for a pair of readers.

"Yes, I see. How horrible that you should have to live this way." He arrives at the last one—number four. Viewing it, he keeps his cool, only giving a quick glance at Nancy for a positive ID. She offers him a smile. He returns it, then puts on his serious face.

"This last, I judge, is a bit too much even for a Bronx jury." Opening his lapel, in a twinkling he's tucked it in his pocket. "Take these back," he says, handing me the three others. "I'll hold this one so it doesn't get inadvertently mixed in when you offer them into evidence."

Before I have a chance to react to Henry's little maneuver, a voice issues from the courtroom door. "Inside now," the court officer summons. "Judge Wilson is waiting for you." Here's the moment to mention my observation that, much of the time in the judicial system, the court staff take on the persona of their assigned judge. "Now!" he orders.

"Let's go," I say to the Clarks. "We'll pick this up later." We enter the courtroom. Uninvited, Henry follows with young Jessie, who's been keeping a low profile. I'm not happy about this, nor can I possibly be heartened by the fact that we're the last ones in.

And I mean, *very* last. Not good.

2.

M y clients sit in the first row as instructed—closest to the jury—while Henry and Jessie sit behind them in what's known as the audience seating. On the other side of the courtroom is the cheaply shod insurance company tool. Next to her is the doctor sued, otherwise known as the defendant. He must've gotten here before me. In front of them is Chucky-boy, sitting at the counsel table to my left. In the courtroom, seating is always "us" against "them." Dr. Baker's in the witness box, and, to my great surprise, the jury's already seated.

The trouble is, these good jurors now believe they've been sitting here waiting for me. It's simply a sneaky judicial trick to seat them before all counsel are present—more crap from Wilson. And I'd thought I managed to make the first strike this morning. She set me up for this yesterday, is what happened.

"I told you 9:15, Mr. Wyler," she reprimands. "You're late."

In a medical malpractice case, the cross-exam of the defendant's expert is the pivotal point between winning and losing. Which is no doubt the reason for the judge's deception and an explanation as to why there hasn't been a plaintiff's verdict in her courtroom in four years.

"My apologies to the court, your staff, worthy defense counsel, and to this most patient jury, Your Honor. It was my understanding we were starting at 9:30—not 9:31, 32, . . . or even 9:15."

"Cross-examination, Counselor!" Judge Wilson snaps. "Make it quick!"

"Yes, Your Honor," I say. But what I'm thinking is, *Screw you, Judge, and your inappropriate agenda.*

As I stand, Henry whispers to Jessie, "Make it quick? What kind of judicial instruction is that?"

I'd like to tell him to shut the hell up, but I have an impatient jury staring at me. I take a few steps and stop in front of their box. I need to get them back on my side. It shouldn't take long. No beating around the bush.

Q. Dr. Baker, did I hear you say yesterday that the basis of your opinion was experimentation findings on lab animals?

A. Yes, you did.

Q. And its application here is based on theory, hypothesis, conjecture, and speculation, resulting in an assumption you yourself have drummed up? Is this correct?

A. Yes, that's correct.

Q. And that's because the delayed development of a bladder hole has never been reported in humans?

A. Yes.

Q. Just in lab animals?

A. *Um,* yes, I just said that.

Q. So Nancy would be the first human instance in the history of modern medicine where an arc of electricity jumped off a cauterizer and onto the

```
bladder wall, causing the delayed
development of a hole. Correct?

    A.   Correct.

    Q.   Yet it's never been heard of in
medicine prior to this moment. True?

    A.   True.

    Q.   Rather convenient, don't you
think?

    A.   Convenient?

    Q.   Yes, that this discovery should
come to the surface in a courtroom in
which said revelation also happens,
rather tidily, to be the defense in the
case.
```

The jurors lean back as a group, exhibiting the reaction I was hoping for: disbelief. Good. They're again on my side. Time to move on to the fun stuff.

```
    Q.   Were any of these lab animals
undergoing the procedure known as
hysterectomy at the time? Were they
having their wombs removed, in other
words?
```

"Objection," states defense counsel, rising clumsily.

"Sustained. Move on, Counselor. No foundation made for that question."

Okay, Your Honor, I think. *If you want foundation, then you'll get foundation.*

```
    Q.   Doctor, what kind of lab animals
are we talking about here?
```

    A.   Rats and rabbits.

    Q.   Let's start with the rabbits. Were these big white fluffy rabbits, like the Easter Bunny? Or those tan rabbits that you see on the side of the highway as you drive upstate? Or were they the fluffy long-eared variety with black and orange spots for sale in pet stores?

"Objection!" yells defense counsel as Dr. Baker blurts out, "The tan ones."

"Sustained. I instructed you to move on." Judge Wilson glares at me.

Before I have a chance to state my legal argument that I've now established foundation, a loud, unexpected throat-clearing comes from behind me.

Henry! Rising to his feet!

"Why are you sustaining that objection, Your Honor?" he asks. "Why are you ordering counsel to move along?"

Oh, crap! But I have to say, by the look on the jurors' faces, they're siding with Henry.

"I'm sorry," Judge Wilson responds, her anger mixed with disbelief. "But are you in some way connected to this case?"

No, Henry! Just say no! You and your ego . . . and she and her robe . . . do not mix.

"In fact, I *am* connected to this case," he replies.

Oh, crap, here we go.

The judge turns to her court officer, then gives the gavel a firm, loud bang. "Take these jurors into the back. We have some court business to attend to outside of their presence."

"All jurors, please rise and follow me," instructs her minion.

Once they are gone, Judge Wilson turns back to us with a razor-sharp grin across her face.

"Let's do this off the record," she says, looking to the court reporter. That's how judges protect themselves when they're about to unload in ways highly incompatible with the dignity of their robes. "Sir," she now addresses Henry, "you are to keep your big mouth shut while in my courtroom. Do you understand?"

"No, Your Honor, I don't. You instructed counsel to make it quick before he asked his first question. You directed him to move along off an important point, and you improperly sustained objections without legal basis. Your bias is clear."

Oh, shit! Henry used the *B* word. You never accuse a known partial judge with an indisputable agenda of bias. That's rule number one! Her prejudicial bias may be as plain as the nose on your face, but saying it aloud is, like, career suicide.

I turn and give him the shut-your-goddamn-mouth look. He completely ignores me, and, not done with the game, he continues.

"And I'm not even addressing the fact that you allow medical testimony based on hypothesis, theory, conjecture, and assumption to stand on the record. Are you not familiar with the *Dauber* or *Frye* cases which hold that sound scientific basis must exist for medical testimony to be admitted into evidence?" He gives her a contemptuous stare.

I can't believe the amount of control Wilson's managed to display up to now. But, ready or not, it's about to break down.

"Listen to me carefully. I don't know your connection to this case," she erupts. "But, if you say one more word, I'll have trial counsel"—nodding to me—"thrown in jail for contempt of court."

Me? Why me? Throw Benson in jail!

Henry and I lock stares. I give him my second shut-the-fuck-up leer. Yet, as he sees it, it's more like an invitation. Oh, no . . .

"I dare you."

Judge Wilson's response is what you might call triumphant.

"Back on the record," she says, looking down at the court reporter. "Let the record reflect," she continues, "that, during an off-the-record discussion, Mr. Wyler, counsel for the plaintiff, and his unknown-to-this-court associate each acted in a manner unbecoming members of the bar to such a degree that I have no choice but to declare you, sir—which is to say, Mr. Wyler—in contempt of court."

She sneers at me with satisfaction.

"Officer, cuff the prisoner." *Bang* goes the gavel again as the smile on her face widens.

The officer approaches as I hold out my hands. He guides them behind my back as I peer over my shoulder. Henry's unfolding a fancy pair of antique silver reading glasses and casually slips them on. After cuffing, I'm marched toward the exit. On my way to central lockup, I look behind one last time. The Clarks and Jessie wear looks of disbelief. And who can blame them?

As for Henry, he now, I see, has the photo of Nancy in hand, carefully examining the picture, turning it at different angles, so as not to miss any important detail.

The Tombs

"Go over that again," I say to Quintavius.

"Yeah, so I'm waiting to order a Big Mac, ya understand?"

"Yes. I understand. You're waiting in line at McDonald's to order a Big Mac. Go on."

"Yeah, so the mofo in front of me turns around, ya understand?"

"Yes, Quintavius, I understand. The mofo in front of you in line turned around."

"Yeah, so he kind of looks at me the wrong way, ya understand?"

"And . . . ?"

"So I sez to the mofo, 'What the fuck you looking at?' Ya understand?"

"Yes, I'm pretty sure I do. You said to the mofo, 'What the fuck you looking at?' Did I get that right?"

"Yeah, now he sez, 'Nothing.' Ya understand?"

"Meaning, he kept his mouth shut? Or he said the word 'nothing'?"

"Exactly."

"Well, which one is it?"

"Which one is what?"

"Let's try it this way. You said, 'What the fuck you looking at?' and he answered, 'Nothing.'"

"That's what I'm talking about."

"Okay," I say, "go on."

"So I sez, 'You calling me a nothing, mofo?' Ya understand?"

"Yes, Quintavius. You asked him what he was looking at, and he answered, 'Nothing,' and you took that to mean that he was calling you a nothing."

"Yeah, so do I have a case of libel or slander or some shit like that?"

"No, Quintavius, I have to say you don't."

"You sure?"

"Pretty much so. Now be clear on this next part again, which is to say, the reason they arrested you. I want to confirm I'm giving you the right legal advice."

"Yeah, so this mofo puts his hands up and sez, 'I don't want no trouble, man,' so I punched him in his face and knocked him out. Ya understand?"

"Yes, Quintavius. The guy tells you he doesn't want any trouble from you. He puts his hands up, so as to say, I surrender, and you knocked him out cold. Did I get that correct?"

"Yeah. Self-defense, right?"

"I have to say, Quintavius, as your jail-cell lawyer, I'm on your side. It's just that the applicable law concerning self-defense is a little tricky. I can't say for sure if you're going to get off, but you got a good shot at it."

"Why can't you say for sure, man? Don't ya understand?"

"I understand. But he was, like, giving in, you know? Like saying he didn't want any part of you. And then you just out and punched him square in the face when he raised his hands in surrender."

"Yeah, you got it now. Self-defense, right?"

"Pretty much so. I just can't say for certain."

"I don't get it. Why not? Why can't you say for sure I'm gonna get off? That mofo raised his arms at me. Yo, Chauncey!" he says, signaling over another one of our cellmates. "Get your Vanilla Ice ass over here!"

As Chauncey complies, I wonder why a black dude would go by the name Vanilla Ice. So I ask, "Quintavius, is he named after the rapper?"

"What rapper?"

"Vanilla Ice."

"Who's that?"

"Why did you call him Vanilla Ice?"

"Because he likes vanilla ice cream, why else?"

"S'up?" Chauncey asks upon arrival.

"You been listening. Self-defense, right?"

"Sounds like it to me, Quintavius."

"See?" Quintavius says, turning back to me. "I told you so."

"Yes, you did, Quintavius," I say, making sure not to raise my hands in surrender.

Just then a corrections officer arrives at our cell.

"Wyler."

"Yeah, that's me," I respond. Again, making sure not to raise a hand.

"Come on. You're out."

I turn back to Quintavius. "I need to go, man. Good luck. Stick with that self-defense thing. You got a good shot at it." I look to the rest of the gang, eleven angry fellows in all. "So long, guys. I wish you well. I'll never forget these six hours we've shared."

They give me a wave. I exit the cell, and the corrections officer directs me to walk in front of him.

"You're lucky to know somebody important enough to get you sprung without having to spend the night. There's a one-night minimum here at the Tombs."

He means the Manhattan Detention Complex, which takes its name from its way-below-ground-level cells.

"Yeah, I feel lucky right about now. And, by the way, Officer, I had detailed conversations with each detainee, and, believe it or not, they all vehemently deny committing the crimes they're being held for. Could you make a note of that?"

"Duly noted, Counselor. Come on. Benson's waiting."

"Oh, you know Henry?" I ask, turning back to him.

"We all know Henry down here. Keep walking, Counselor, keep walking."

I'm not surprised. Henry Benson is a famous criminal attorney, after all. Which distinguishes his legal practice from mine, which involves civil matters. Just so you know, we first met when he hand-selected me to take over twenty-one injury cases he was handling or, should I say, mishandling. Our skills are different but, in our ongoing relationship, they're complementary. It's our styles—or should I say, his—that makes for the craziness.

Henry's injured criminals—or HICs as I refer to them—present definite challenges, one of which is figuring out, each time I take on a case, if the client's claim is, in fact, legit. If Henry himself knows, the problem is, he's not telling.

Because I have no wish ever to position myself as an accomplice, my ethical commitment to the system has, at times, interfered with my ability to represent zealously the HICs who are sent my way. Yet I have no problem in allowing—even maneuvering—fake cases to be dismissed by the court. In the interests of justice of course.

Anyway, these HICs are a rough bunch—which may be one reason Henry carries a firearm—and I've found myself in various life-threatening positions. Looking back at just a few, I've been run off the road, locked in a car trunk, hospitalized in a coma, shot in the back of my head excising a section of ear, tied to a chair with a large needle lodged in my spinal canal . . .

Even I gotta say, it makes me sound like a pretty brave guy. But my own view is that I never had much choice, not once Henry starts in, doing his usual number on me. So why do I keep working on Henry's referrals?

The money, the whole money, and nothing but the money, so help me God.

At least I admit it.

The officer escorts me upstairs. I'm signed out by a clerk, given back my possessions, and taken to the lobby, where waiting are Benson and Jessie.

"Good night, Henry," the officer says, as he turns to leave.

"Night, Victor," Henry responds, then adds, "Hey, Victor, I put a twenty down for you on Prancing Pony, and he came in." Henry removes a wad of bills from his pocket, plucking a C-note off the top. "That was your lucky horse," he says, as he hands the officer the bill.

Victor slips it into his front pocket with an appreciative smile, turns, and leaves.

This is my cue. "Thank you very motherfucking much, Henry."

I now look over at Jessie. "Sorry there."

She nods.

"Aren't you thanking me for settling the *Clark* case?" Henry wants to know.

"Huh? What are you talking about?"

"Just what I'm saying."

"Henry! How could you do that? You didn't even know what it was about. Besides, Chucky-boy kept insisting it was a no-pay. I think that carrier is his last remaining client."

"Yes," Henry responds confidently. "Well, I didn't settle the case with him. In fact, he was against it. That woman sitting in the back was the adjuster. Apparently our Mr. Lawless had failed to report that the basis of his expert's opinion was rabbits and rats. I had a little sit-down with her in the hall, and we discussed the legal ramifications of a medical opinion based on theory, hypothesis, conjecture, assumption, and speculation. In short, she was understandably upset with her attorney."

"What did you settle it for? If the answer to this question is under two million, they'll be bringing me back down."

"Two point one mil. I might also report your clients were happy. Come on. You've kept us waiting. We're going to the hospital to see Nelly, Jessie's sister."

I look toward Jessie, take a deep breath, then say, "Sorry I kept you waiting."

3.

W e're riding in Henry's red Jaguar to Lincoln Hospital in the Bronx. It's a two-seater so Jessie is riding sidesaddle across my lap. But I'm not complaining. I figure this is how newly released prisoners feel upon a first encounter with a beautiful woman. That I, Tug Wyler, happen to be a newly released guest of the New York City Department of Corrections doesn't escape me. Yet it's all become easier to take since Henry's shenanigans—the ones that got me hauled away—produced a $2.1 million payout.

As Henry weaves through traffic, Jessie and I are rocked about. Again I'm not complaining. I don't get much opportunity to have attractive young women sit on my lap. And by "much," I mean never. So, yeah, I'm enjoying the ride.

At least I admit it.

So far we've been cruising along in silence. I'm digesting my jail stint; Henry's fixed on the road, and Jessie's got her own worries for sure.

However, it's time to break the silence. I need to understand what's happening here.

"Jessie, I think you realize I'm along for the ride for a reason— and not just because Henry won't take no for an answer. Why don't you start filling me in? Okay?"

"Okay."

It's not a very comfortable position for either of us to have a conversation, but it's the only one we have. "Go on," I encourage her.

"Well, it was because we decided she should try the Painless Dentist."

"Don't know about him. Tell me what he does. Why's he call himself that? I realize it's about getting more patients into that seat, but he must have a gimmick behind the moniker."

"He offers anesthesia," Jessie says simply. "That's his thing."

"Anesthesia? You mean nitrous oxide?"

"No. Nelly gets nauseous and vomits from that."

"Then what kind?"

"He calls it conscious sedation. Nelly has seriously horrible dental anxiety. Anyway, he overdosed her."

"How do you know?"

She sits up as best she can in these cramped circumstances, putting undue lateral pressure on my special place. After she rotates her upper body, we're eye to eye, inches apart.

"Because I witnessed it."

"I see."

Benson adds his two pennies. "I knew Nelly's parents. Fine people. And fine clients too. I was really broken up when they lost their lives in the fire. Yes, Jessie," he says, glancing over at her, "your father was a good man."

That's it. Though I haven't a clue what he's talking about, I'm going to have to deal with it. Typical Henry. One thing though, his word choice was curious—he'd said "Nelly's parents" and "your father," offering the impression that we don't have a traditional family structure here.

"That's a lot for a young girl to deal with," I respond. "And now you're faced with more." I'm kind of winging it, but what else can I do?

"Thank you, Mr. Wyler," she says. "But the truth is, my father wasn't such a great guy. Or a good dad—at least not to me. Nelly's another story."

Having made her correction—evidencing her daddy issues and sibling jealousy all wrapped up into one—she cuddles into me. What I feel is the warmth of her cheek against my chest.

Henry looks over, raising a brow, as if to say, "What's going on?" I raise mine in return, indicating, "You got me."

But I like it.

Of course I could've lived without the "mister" part.

We go straight to the Intensive Care Unit. I hate ICU. It's my least favorite area in any hospital. Too often, for my clients, whatever it may promise, it's less the ICU and more the IDU— Imminent Death Unfortunately.

As we approach Nelly's bed, I note a few points of interest. Foremost, an anxious-looking woman stands there. Nothing unusual about that. Undoubtedly it's the mom. But why is there a Derek Jeter poster taped to the wall, with the Yankees' season schedule right next to it? It's not as if the obviously comatose young woman lying there can see either of them.

As we march forward, I turn to Jessie. "Who's that?"

"My mom."

"I see. Same father, different mothers. You're half sisters."

"Elementary, my dear Sherlock." Henry rolls his eyes.

I ignore him. And it'll just be more of the same if I next deduce Nelly's a hard-core Yankees' fan.

"Hi, Mom," Jessie says. "Thanks for coming. I hope it wasn't too hard to find someone to help at the restaurant."

"Juanita," Benson begins reasonably enough, "this is Tug Wyler. He's the lawyer Jessie will have told you about."

"Thank you for coming," Juanita says softly.

I note her firm grip as we shake hands.

"I'd have been here sooner," I explain, glancing over at Henry, "but a judge wanted me elsewhere."

Now it's Henry's turn to ignore me. Henry addresses her in

a serious tone. "In matters like this, counsel needs to become involved as soon as possible. It's just what must be done." He and Juanita lock gazes, and a measure of tension seems to exist between them. Good thing I don't need to figure out what it is right at this minute.

I do note though that Jessie's mother is an attractive woman.

"Jesus, not again. I just can't believe this," Jessie says, looking at her sister. Her lips tighten in distress. *Beep-beep, beep-beep, beep-beep* is the most prominent of the several mechanical sounds filling the air.

I lean into Henry and whisper, "What did she mean by 'not again'?"

"Nelly was hospitalized before, after the fire that took her parents."

Suddenly Jessie begins to cry; Juanita gives her a comforting embrace.

Just then I notice an actual paper chart recording Nelly's medical progress, or lack thereof, attached to the bedpost. What a lucky break. They're being phased out of most hospitals, replaced by digital records.

When I reach for it, my companions stare at me, with the exception of the patient herself, of course.

"Oh, shit!" I hear myself blurt out.

"What?" Jessie asks.

"Nothing. Let me finish reading."

It's bad. The patient carries the diagnosis of hypoxic-ischemic encephalopathy. That's global brain damage from deprivation of oxygen. Other diagnoses are listed as well, but all arise from the brain injury.

I hear the urgent-sounding approach of sneaker squeaks from my right. We've been joined by a newcomer. A young nurse who, spotting me, places her hands on her hips.

"Hang up that chart! It's confidential!" she snaps at me.

"I know," I say. "But I'm the family attorney. I have authorization to look at it."

"Where is this authorization you speak of, Counselor? We get a lot of lawyers in here, some looking for new business."

I point at Jessie. "I'm here at the request of the patient's sister."

"Listen to me. This patient is eighteen. Has she"—the nurse motions to Jessie—"been appointed guardian?"

Crap, she knows her legal stuff.

"Not formally," I reply. "But she is the proposed guardian. And, in the State of New York, a proposed guardian has the same authority to act as a duly appointed one during the pendency of the guardianship application. It's the case of *Arthur Herbert Fonzarelli v. Officer Kirk*. New York Supp. 2d CH7AT8PM, 1976, would be the formal citation."

"I wasn't aware," she says. "Go ahead then." She walks away. Henry and Juanita both wear startled expressions. Jessie, like the nurse, I figure, is too young to get it.

Wrong.

"Um," she wants to know, "isn't Arthur Fonzarelli the Fonz from *Happy Days*?"

"Yep, Jessie. Channel 7 at 8:00 p.m. was when it originally aired, exactly as I cited it to that nurse. But let's just keep this little episode of creative legal thinking between us."

I can see she's now wondering if her new attorney is a nutcase.

I hang up the chart and turn to them. "Listen, I have to do something that, at this moment, may appear repulsive, but, when this case comes to trial, you'll thank me for my actions."

Henry acknowledges my little speech with the barest of nods. Jessie and Juanita, for their part, have no idea what I'm talking about.

Henry now nods again, this time in a go-ahead kind of way.

I take out my phone and hold it up. "I need to make a video of Nelly."

As I expected, Jessie and her mom look troubled by this idea.

"What you both need to understand," I tell them, "is that Nelly's in a bad way. I hope and pray she comes out of this coma, but I'm certain you know she may not. I need to have documentation of what her life was like during this critical period. Pictures simply supply more evidence to a jury than words ever could. You can describe her condition here, but each juror will form different images in his or her mind, all the while assuming the attorneys embellished the situation for the worse, motivated by large dollar signs. If we show them video on the other hand, they'll all have the same image in their mental file."

Whether or not they're entirely on board, both women nod.

"And, if Nelly regains consciousness, I expect to be taking video at every milestone she reaches. That way, the jury knows exactly what she went through on her long road to recovery. Understood?"

"Understood," Jessie answers. Juanita nods again.

They move aside to allow me the angle I need. I hold up my iPhone, hit the Record button, and begin yet another documentary of the type I often find myself shooting. When I've about finished filming all I believe necessary to capture here, my pal, the bossy nurse, charges back in. She's seen us on Patient-TV, I guess. Not the television fame I'm always hoping for.

"No, no, no!" she admonishes. "No video allowed in here, proposed guardian or not. That's a firm hospital policy. And, listen to me, I can't tell you how offensive it is that you're videoing this poor girl while in coma."

I continue to hold my iPhone steady on Nelly as I move closer and closer to her lifeless face.

"I'm documenting something here which will never be capable of duplication. Please! I'd appreciate you bending the rules a little bit. It's critical I capture this on video."

"No! Shut it off! Now!"

"I'm sorry, really. But I'm unable to do that until I finish what I started. Go get security," I say, knowing that, by the time she returns, I'll be done.

"You have three seconds to turn that off, and then you and I are going to rumble." I look down to where she stopped just inside my personal space, even as I continue to keep the video rolling. I'm a foot taller than she is, standing at six one. This morning I hit the scale at 241. There's no physical match here.

Yet she has every advantage because my self-defense plea will never hold up in court, despite it being on video. And the only attorney I'd ever trust to keep me from behind bars is Henry, despite my having been incarcerated this morning because of him. Unfortunately every judge in the state would disqualify Henry, because, for any charges arising from this impending incident, he's also an eyewitness.

"You win, Nurse," I say, as I lower my phone. "Let's scram, guys."

As we take our leave, she keeps a watchful eye on us. I don't blame her.

On our way into Manhattan, our journey again is minimally conversational. In fact, nobody has said a word. Near my drop-off point, Grand Central Station, Henry pulls to the curb.

"I believe this is your stop, Counselor."

Jessie, gazing out the window, has the look on her face of a person who's just woken up in a strange place. She rubs her eyes, turns to me, and I sense all her bottled-up questions.

I help her out. "Jessie, the way this works is that, when a person's in coma, they obviously cannot act on their own behalf so I'll have to make an application to the court to appoint you as guardian. Once we've taken care of that, I'll make a request for Dr. Grad's medical records. Then I'll have them reviewed by my medical experts. It sounds as if there's a case here—but in New York you need to get an Affidavit of Merit from a physician before starting a lawsuit."

As if in reply, she reaches in her bag, extracting a folded sheet of paper, which she hands to me. "Here's a copy of his record. He gave it to me the day after he OD'd her. He brought it with him when he came to visit Nelly. I'd asked him for it."

"That's interesting."

"Why?" Jessie asks.

"Well, I've been handling these cases for over twenty years, and never do doctors visit their malpractice victims. They always keep away. It's one of the keys to recognizing malpractice—the doctor stays clear."

Jessie shrugs, then bites her lip. She waits . . .

I open the paper, and it's a photocopy of a four-by-six note card with a few lines of scribble on it. I look at her. "This can't be all of it."

"It's everything," she insists, "and, to me, it's illegible."

I look again. What it contains is Nelly's basic personal information and an entry. "I can read it," I say. "I've become an expert at deciphering doctors' handwriting over the years. Given what I've seen, it's not actually that bad."

"Read it then," she demands.

"Okay." And here's what I see:

Radiographs taken by Dr. Meyer received and reviewed. Tooth number 13 requires a new filling. Patient insists on anesthesia. Dental anxiety relative to drilling. Risks and complications discussed. Anesthesia employed. The patient had an anaphylactic reaction. Transported to Lincoln Hospital.

I look up. "Jessie, do you know what 'anaphylactic' means?"

"No, no, I don't. What does it mean?"

Boy, this is difficult. "It means, there's no case."

$4.$

Despite the documented anaphylaxis—which means, simply, an unpredictable allergic reaction to anesthesia—and, after explaining to Jessie only a few rare instances exist where malpractice can be attached to anaphylaxis, I promised I'd investigate further. At the very least I'll come up with an answer for Nelly's predicament. I've learned the value of truth is immeasurable for closure, malpractice case or no case.

There are, of course, other reasons I'm going forward. First, I want to keep Henry happy since he's my most important referring attorney. Second, regardless of any fault on the part of this dentist, Nelly's injuries could translate into a sizable recovery so it's worth the look. Third, I never take a potential defendant's medical records at face value. Last, I kind of dug the way Jessie crushed my left nut in the car ride.

At least I admit it.

If Nelly did have an anaphylactic reaction to anesthesia, I will likely drop the case. That depends on what Dr. Grad did or did not do after the adverse reaction. So we will just have to see.

Several days later I'm at my office. On top of having Jessie's signature on my retainer agreement, I have learned more about the Rivera family. Roberto, the father of both girls, and Nelly's mother, Stella, together had been prosecuted on five occasions for various crimes of fraud and misrepresentation. Represented by the wily Henry, they'd been acquitted each time. Meanwhile, Juanita, Jessie's mother, had served time for involuntary manslaughter. Here, unsurprisingly, Henry had made it clear that the self-defense argument had failed because she'd not been his client. Otherwise she too would have been acquitted.

Henry also made it clear that he didn't like Juanita or trust her. So these girls are one conviction, five reasonable doubts, and a generation removed from being actual HICs. I'm curious to see what difference this makes.

Lily, my paralegal, buzzes. "Alan Cohen's here. He has two big files in his hands."

"Send him in."

"Send him in," she repeats mockingly. Lily's a Latina with attitude, which I alternately appreciate and endure. Alan is another referring attorney. Like Henry, who introduced us, he's a criminal lawyer; but unlike Henry, he's an incompetent and less-than-honorable one.

Alan has referred five cases to me. Two are about to come to trial, and the defense counsel on both has assured he'll settle. But not until after I'd reworked and repled them properly. In a medical malpractice case, the plaintiff is required to serve a pleading called a Bill of Particulars, the purpose of which is to particularize what the doctor did wrong and state the resulting physical injury.

What you need to know is that Alan manages to get the descriptions of the injuries right by simply copying them straight from the medical records. Unfortunately he lacks the skill set to put the pieces together, which is to say the ones necessary to arrive at what the malpractice has been. This means, he's always appearing at my office door with a file that necessitates an amendment to the Bill of Particulars.

It's also a clear indication that trial is right around the corner. How do I know this? I know this because Alan likes to hold on to a case until the last possible moment, attempting to settle it. When no money is forthcoming, that's when trial attorneys, like me, get the call that will force Alan to relinquish a portion of his fee.

But let us move on to the matter of his dishonor.

The other three cases he referred were settled. But not by me. Within two weeks of showing up with the files, Alan took them back. What's important here is, during that interval, I'd sent letters to the defense for each, giving notice I'd been retained as trial counsel. Also in the letters they were put on notice to expect a motion to amend the pleadings with a statement making clear the actual malpractice of the cases.

In response, each defense counsel bypassed me, calling Alan directly, telling him they'd settle as long as he kept me out of things. So that's what this sniveling, drug-addicted, talentless schmuck did. He took my hard-earned reputation and my analyses of the files to effectuate settlements, cutting me out. Is it clear I was not happy?

Nonetheless I've tolerated his conduct because you never know when he'll walk in the door carrying the big one. Maybe today I'll take a stand. We'll see.

"Hi, Alan," I say. It's apparent he's unable to tell whether I intended that as a greeting or an inquiry.

"Hi," he replies, leaving me to decide between the two.

I smile. I like to think it's unreadable.

"Listen, Tug, you'll be interested in this. A brain-damaged baby case." He slides the files onto my desk as I think how I hate the term "brain-damaged baby case." First brought into play, no doubt, by a group of insensitive personal injury lawyers.

Me, I prefer to think of such claims as a "brain-injury baby case," since, as far as I'm concerned, the word "damage" connotes a lesser human value, like "damaged goods."

"The child's name is Adora," Alan continues. "The mom, Maria, is expecting your call."

"Thanks for thinking of me. When's the trial date? Tomorrow?"

"Very funny," he says. "No, you have plenty of time on this one to do whatever it is you feel needs to be done."

"Did you make a demand for settlement?" A demand is made by the plaintiff, which gets negotiations started.

"It's all in the file. But I've got to go now. Someone's waiting to meet me."

Naturally I don't like this dump-and-run business. But then, as he turns to go, he adds a suggestion. "I'd start with their expert response."

Telling me what to do doesn't improve matters here. "I'm not taking this file if you're going to cut me out again after I rework it. I'm done with that, especially on a childbirth brain-injury cases."

He just looks at me, then walks out the door.

The expert response to which he's referred is a legal document that's supposed to reveal what the defense is, usually touching the issues of liability or fault, and a statement that whatever malpractice we claimed did not cause the injuries alleged. I say, supposed to, because oftentimes these responses are just filled with boilerplate legalese, stating the doctor did nothing wrong and that there's no causal connection between the doctor's conduct and the plaintiff's claimed injuries.

Still I'm curious.

I pull it out, noting the plaintiff's name. Simone. *Hmm*, rings a bell. Then I get it. What do you know about that? It looks like Chucky-boy and I are going to tango again after all. This is that case he mentioned in the hall. But it's a pretty messed-up situation when the defense counsel knows you're the lawyer on a case before you yourself do.

I read through the expert response. What I see is that the defense's position regarding liability is a routine one. Adora was the product of a normal spontaneous vaginal delivery without event. But, on the issues of causation and damages—the other two elements a plaintiff must prove to make out a prima facie case— the response is direct and clear, leaving no room for interpretation.

Adora sustained her brain injury as a result of contracting herpes from her mother during childbirth. Maria was the sole proximate cause of Adora's irreversible brain injury because she concealed from her medical providers the fact that she had vaginal herpes. Had the defendants been so advised, they would've scheduled a cesarean section, and Adora would never have been exposed to the virus during the birthing process.

Hmm. It sounds like a pretty goddamn good defense to me.

I'm certain I won't be seeing Alan in the next couple weeks, and you know what? Chucky-boy may finally get his opportunity for revenge.

————

Okay, it's two days later. And I'm still replaying what I know of the *Simone* case in my head. Alan has claimed Adora's brain injury was due not to the herpes virus passed on by her mother but to perinatal fetal hypoxia/asphyxia suffered during childbirth. That the labor failed to progress, that Adora showed signs of fetal distress, that her cord was around her neck, and that they failed to perform a timely emergency C-section. This is pretty much your standard garden-variety brain-injury baby claim during childbirth, if we accept there is such a thing.

I've gone over Maria's labor and delivery record to see if any of that made sense. It didn't, other than Adora having been nuchal times one, meaning the umbilical cord was wrapped around her neck. No signs of late decelerations showed on the fetal heart-monitoring strips, consistent with fetal distress or hypoxia, and no prolonged second stage of labor. Nothing documented during delivery could have caused her cerebral palsy and spastic quadriplegia, these being conditions rendering her wheelchair bound and dependent for all her activities of daily living.

What did stand out were Adora's Apgar scores. Apgars are a system devised to quickly assess the health of a newborn. The score is determined by evaluating the infant's Appearance, Pulse,

Grimace, Activity, and Respirations on a scale of zero to two, at one and five minutes after birth. A cumulative score below three at the second taking indicates a risk that the child will suffer permanent neurological damage.

Adora scored perfectly, with tens at both intervals. Completely inconsistent with an infant who'd suffered asphyxia during the birthing process, causing resultant brain injury.

The other thing I noticed was that the Infant Feeding Notes for postpartum days two through seven were missing. By this I mean, *completely* absent from her infant chart. The feeding note from her date of birth—just one entry, because of the late hour of her arrival—is there. And the feeding notes from the neonatal ICU where she was transferred on day eight are present.

Yet no records are in the file from that critical slice of time—from day two to seven.

And, if one—meaning, Alan—did not review such hospital records for a living, one—again meaning, Alan—would never notice their absence. And, even if he did realize they were missing, he'd never attribute the fact any significance. Though he'd be an idiot not to.

Naturally I would humbly suggest, the above does not apply to me.

Despite Chucky's previous—if unauthorized and unofficial—notification of my retention as *Simone* trial counsel during the *Clark* trial, I had Lily send off this *official* one:

> Hey, Chuck—when you're right, you're right. We do battle
> again. So send me over the nurses' feeding notes you
> held out, and we'll keep this monkey business between us.
> Enclosed is my formal Discovery and Inspection, specifically
> identifying the documents requested.

A D&I, just so you know, is a legal document where the serving party is requesting the exchange of information within the exclusive custody and control of the other side.

My guess is, Chucky's response will be to play the denial game.

However, before leaving to meet my new clients—which is where I'm heading now—I made a quick call to my friend and medical expert, Dr. Mickey Mack. He simply confirmed the possibility of a newborn's contracting herpes of the brain during childbirth, which is all I needed to know before meeting them.

I should add too that, finally getting Alan on the phone to help me with background on the Simones before I headed out, I learned he'd only met them once. And that was the day he'd signed them up. Moreover he'd spoken to them only a single time thereafter. Instead a small clutch of per diem attorneys had been handling the *Simone* case. Such an arrangement is completely unacceptable on any case—but especially on a brain-injury case. I can't help shaking my head in disgust. I don't know how a lawyer can practice this way and sleep at night, or how any client could ever accept such a lack of commitment from their attorney.

Yet it happens.

All the time.

Anyway, the Simones live in Dyker Heights, a Brooklyn Italian neighborhood. If I'm lucky, I'll have a chance to score a Meat Lovers' slice later. But, before then, the job that falls to me, a complete stranger, is to inform this poor woman what the opposing side intends to put forth as its defense. Which is to say, that she gave Adora herpes, and that this, tragically, was the unfortunate reason for the devastation to the newborn's brain.

As I pull up to the Simones' house, what jumps out at me is their front door. It's one long steep flight above street level, absent a wheelchair-access ramp. That means, Adora, now a girl of eighteen, must be carried up and down. At the top of the stairs, I'm a little winded myself.

I ring the bell.

Quickly the door swings open, and I'm greeted by a woman who looks to be in her late fifties or even early sixties. Her hair is in a bun, and she's wearing a long black skirt with a white apron. Because she's leaning on a cane, I assume she's the grandma.

"Hi, I'm here to see Maria," I say.

"Yes," she says softly, "I'm Maria. Nice to meet you."

Boy, am I taken off guard. From her records I know she just turned forty-four. Therefore, I didn't expect her to look like the *nonna* on the label of an imported tomato sauce jar. When I read about the herpes defense, I imagined this Maria to be, well, more of a MILF. Sometimes I'm just ignorant like that in my stereotypes and profiling.

At least I admit it.

"Come in, please. Come in, Mr. Wyler," she says.

I enter, and another stairway is right in front of me. *Wow. Double trouble.* Adora, I must hope, sleeps on this floor.

"I'm sorry I couldn't come to your office," she says, "but, when you asked to speak with me without my husband, Joe, there were no options. I can't leave Adora alone with him for too long, and bringing her into the city is just a big production. And the cost of travel, parking, and then—"

"Not a problem, Mrs. Simone, not a problem at all," I interject.

"Please, call me Maria. Unless Joe's around, then it's better if you call me Mrs. Simone."

"Okay, Maria. How much time do we have?"

"I had Joe take Adora to the park, so a couple hours."

We take our seats across from each other in what I'd describe as their living room. It's immaculate. Not a spot. Around me are low-budget furnishings reflective of their financial stature. Homey cooking smells issue from the kitchen five feet away. Peering over, I observe that the oven is likely decades old. When I look back at Maria, she's wearing a timid, slightly uncomfortable yet encouraging smile.

"Maria," I begin forthrightly, "the date of malpractice was eighteen years ago. I'm new in this territory. To be up front, I've never handled a brain-injured baby case where the baby was an adult at the time of trial. Is there a reason you waited so long to hire an attorney?"

I can quickly see that I've pressed a button. One I didn't know was there.

She's already showing more discomfort—and that was only question number one. Since this is anything but a social call, just wait until we get around to the real purpose of my visit.

"Well, you see," she says, in an unmistakably sincere tone, "Joe and I are simple people. We never had any intentions of bringing a lawsuit. I'm responsible for the circumstances we find ourselves in, and we take care of our responsibilities. But, when Adora was approaching ten, the medical staff changed where she goes, and she was assigned a new occupational therapist. She insisted we had to meet with Mr. Cohen to discuss how this happened. I believe they're business associates."

"I see."

In New York, the time limit within which to bring a claim for a birth injury is ten years. I saw Alan had started the lawsuit only three days before the statute of limitations ran out on Adora. This new OT, I'm sure, was on Alan's payroll. Meaning, he greases her palm as a thank-you for the referral.

It's illegal. But Alan does it, and other PI lawyers do it too. They regard it as merely a simple bit of useful business.

The fact of the matter is, such a tragic situation demands the retention of an injury lawyer. When I'm brought in—and I know it may sound corny—my dedication to securing the best outcome is about my passion for justice, a commitment that exists apart from any greed I might acknowledge. I love to win. I even live to win. And I'd be crazy not to exult over the monster awards.

There's just more to it, that's all.

"What do you mean by your statement about being responsible?" I'm back in the moment.

"Well, she's my child. I gave birth to her so I accept full responsibility."

Oh, man. This is going to be even worse than I thought.

"Are you aware of the claims Mr. Cohen has made on your behalf?"

"Years after we signed that piece of paper, he told us it had been the doctor's fault. You know, the brain injury. But I don't believe that's so," she states with confidence. "It was a normal delivery. My mother was a midwife in Rome where I grew up, and I often helped her. This is just the way Adora was born. Acts of God happen in the best of medical hands."

"Do you remember the delivering physician exhibiting a sense of urgency to get Adora out?"

"No. I remember he said the cord was around her neck, then he slid his finger under and released it. She came out right after. No problems. She was small, you know, a little premature."

"Yes, I saw she was premature. Nothing else?"

"Nothing."

That's what I was afraid of. I just don't see an obstetrical case here. Not from the records and now not from the mother's own account of events. A mother who's saying it was an act of God and that the doctor did nothing wrong. The only thing that doesn't make sense is why she ever went forward with the lawsuit.

Here's the truth: I despise nothing more than involvement in a medical malpractice case that lacks merit. Doctors work long and hard to become physicians, and they deserve enormous respect for all the good they do. I mean it. So, what I'm saying is that, if, after my thorough investigation, there's no case, I'll make sure this matter is discontinued with prejudice so it's gone forever.

That said, it's time to get down to the difficult communication I came to Dyker Heights to impart. So here goes.

"I asked to speak to you privately, Maria, because the business I'm in operates by a set of conducts. And one of them is that the defense inevitably has a distinctly different version of the story from ours. Your case is no exception. Sometimes, I have to say, the defense's position is legitimate, but often it is not. Right now, sitting with you, I need to make some sense of the defense put forth here."

NELLY'S CASE / 45

I pause to get myself ready but, at the same time, realize I really need to get a handle on our claim before addressing the defense.

"Go on," she says. And gives me another of her shyly encouraging smiles.

"Okay, well—"

Suddenly a kitchen timer dings.

"Oh, just a minute," she interrupts. Into the kitchen she goes, where immediately she picks up a wooden spoon. This she uses to taste the simmering sauce I've been smelling. Stopping to slip on oven mitts, she picks up a big pot next to the sauce, moving it over the sink. Its contents get poured into a strainer with a hot *whoosh* of rising steam. What I'm watching come to life is a heaping plate of spaghetti and meatballs. The finishing touch is a wedge of hardened cheese grated atop. Next thing I know, she's set it down on the coffee table in front of me.

"Eat," she says firmly, then walks back to the kitchen. She takes out a label-less bottle of red wine and pours a full glass. "Joe and I made this. It's good. Drink."

I take it from her. I look up at Maria, then down at the plate. It looks incredible. I'll eat and drink first, I tell myself, then ask whether she has genital herpes. Please excuse my immature crudity, but she didn't cook this shit with her vagina.

After stuffing me with a second plate and a glass refill, we find ourselves in the position we were in right before I downed the best spaghetti and meatballs of my life.

"Now," she says, "go on."

"Okay, Maria, but this isn't easy." I'm feeling my stomach churn just a bit.

"Please, Mr. Wyler."

I plunge in. "The defense is Adora contracted herpes from you during childbirth, and that's what caused her brain injury."

My companion freezes.

Shocked. Speechless. Her jaw drops. Her eyes shut for a second or so. Then, as if in a quick change of emotion, she opens them and gives me a curious look. "How could that happen?"

"It's simply a medical fact that it can occur, the specifics of which I'll know more about after meeting with my expert."

"No, what I meant was, it couldn't. I don't have herpes."

Now it's my head that's tilting.

"Joe's the only man I've ever made love to, and that was only a few times just before I became pregnant with Adora. We haven't had intercourse since she was born. We haven't done a lot of things since Adora was born. But one thing's for certain, I don't have herpes."

"I see." I pause. She waits.

"If it is a defense tactic as I'd thought," I continue, "meaning, one without any actual merit or basis in fact, then there are ways of preemptively dealing with it. First, though, I'll need you to go to your doctor—no, scratch that—to a doctor I'll select for the single purpose of screening you for the herpes virus. A negative result will put this defense to rest."

"How much will it cost?" I can see she's still trying to take it all in.

"Don't worry. It's my treat."

I should explain that the reason I'm paying cash for Maria's herpes screening is because that way there'll be no documentation of it in her medical insurance records, should it come back positive. Sneaky, yes, but completely legal and above board in the interests of justice and good lawyering.

After I left Maria's, I drove straight home. And when I walked in the door, I made sure to embrace each of my kids. They didn't know where it was coming from when I wouldn't let go—the three of them doing their personal variations on "Okay, okay, Dad"—but I did. For sure.

5.

N ow I'm on a crowded subway thinking about my new clients and their grievous situations. I can fairly say my mind was racing with the responsibility I already felt for each of them—Maria and Adora, Jessie and Nelly—and the emotional mayhem their families are feeling.

I surface at Wall Street and walk toward my destination, the defense counsel's building where I'll be conducting a deposition. I get there five minutes late, which means I have five to burn before heading up. I like to hope the malpracticing doctor is waiting uncomfortably with the court reporter staring at him, wondering what the guy did wrong. Maybe the doc is even squirming a little, if only in what passes for his conscience. It's my practice to arrive fifteen minutes late for this very reason, to enhance the squirm factor.

Standing in front of the building, smoking as usual, is Jimmy Broderick. This guy is a serious Old-Timer. By which I mean, a group of lawyers who've been defending these cases for so long they've become completely jaded. They no longer believe any plaintiff is really injured and will "defend to the end." That's their motto. I've known this guy since the day I passed the bar, and over these two decades I've watched him, like Chucky-boy, biodegrade a little more each year.

"Hey, Jimmy, what's up?"

"I'll tell you," he answers emphatically, not skipping a beat, as I watch the gob of spit in the corner of his mouth string up and down. "You know that case we got together?"

"Which one? The head-trauma case?"

"Head trauma, *schmed* trauma. No, not that one, the other one," he says, barely getting out his sentence as he spirals into a cough. He takes another sustaining draw as if the tobacco were laced with oxygen.

"You mean the foot-amputation case?"

"Yeah, that one. But it ain't no amputation."

"Jimmy, a doctor took a saw and cut off the front half of my client's foot. In orthopedic circles, they call that a midfoot amputation. She's left with a stump at the end of her ankle."

"That's ain't no amputation, I'm telling you."

"Sure it is, Jimmy. A transmetatarsal amputation, to be specific."

"She's got half a foot. And that's plenty to get around on. Just like I said, that ain't no amputation."

"Okay, Jimmy, let's hear it." I know my lines just the same as he knows his. I also know his story will take up the exact amount of time I need to kill before stepping into the elevator.

"All right, if ya really want to know," he says, "I'll tell ya." I can't wait to hear this one. After taking another long draw and looking at his cigarette the way smokers do when measuring remaining puffs, he begins.

"I was defending a case once," he starts out reasonably enough, "where the shovel edge of my client's backhoe pinned some guy against a wall and cut off the poor son of a bitch's legs just below his hips." He winks, takes a last drag, throws the butt to the ground, mashes it out, looks back up, and says, "Now that's a foot amputation."

"When you're right, you're right, Jimmy." I check my watch. "See ya, wouldn't want to be ya."

In today's case, my client's uterus had been perforated during a diagnostic dilation-and-curettage procedure to investigate abnormal vaginal bleeding. That's a risk—similar to the perforation of Nancy Clark's bladder during hysterectomy—but we've learned, if you're going to cause a hole, then right away notice what you've done and repair it. Maybe these surgeons should be required to have their vision checked as part of their medical license exam.

Anyway, this guy missed it, and a horrible infection set in. Next thing my twenty-one-year-old client knew, she was having a hysterectomy.

When I enter the conference room where I'm expected, the only person there is my court reporter.

"Hi, Sam," I say. He manages a grin. Sam doesn't speak much. He's been doing depositions for me for ten years, and the only time he talks is when someone asks for a read-back of testimony. I like it that way. But I'm more than a little disappointed that the defendant doctor isn't in the room, having a reflective moment.

I take out my MacBook and open to the video of Nelly I shot at the hospital. It's my first view, having downloaded it this morning. She is lying there, comatose. The footage is short, and I play it again. Halfway through viewing number three, the defendant doctor walks into the room with his attorney. I momentarily look up, then back at my screen, trying to figure something out.

They take their seats. I close my MacBook; the doc is sworn, and they look to me to begin.

But I don't.

"Can you guys give me a sec?" I ask. The doc looks to his lawyer, who nods assent. I flip back open my MacBook, go to the video, and hit Play. I watch it five more times.

Holy crap!

When the Yankees were mentioned by that nurse, Nelly's right eyebrow lifted up, just a tad, hardly noticeable. I was so preoccupied with said nurse and completing the video I didn't notice.

"Listen! I've got to get out of here! Now! I have a client in ICU who the hospital thinks is in a full-blown coma, but she's actually locked-in." I start packing up.

"Wait a minute! The doctor's here," the lawyer comes back at me.

"Duly noted, Counselor. Duly noted. This is an emergency."

"What's the emergency?" he counters. "She's in a coma."

"That's the point," I snap back. "She's not. Locked-in syndrome is a condition in which a patient is aware but cannot move or communicate verbally, caused by a complete paralysis of nearly all voluntary muscles in the body except for the eyes."

I bolt out of there . . .

————

I run into the hospital and race up the stairs to the second floor, where I now assume a more normal, careful pace as I proceed to the foot of Nelly's bed. I don't want to create a disturbance in ICU, that's for sure. Hey, she's breathing on her own, having been taken off the respirator. That's a good sign, given that it's nine days after the event.

A very good sign.

I place my hand on her ankle and give it a squeeze. No response. I give it a harder squeeze, reproducing what medical professionals like to call "a painful stimulus test." No response. I walk to the head of the bed and look at her motionless face. Her eyes are closed. She seems peaceful. Such a pretty girl. Think *Sleeping Beauty*.

I whisper in her ear, "Nelly, can you hear me?" No response. I raise my voice. "Nelly, can you hear me?"

Still nothing.

I stop to think. *Hmm*. I have an idea.

I lean in and whisper, "The Yankees suck."

Her right eyebrow raises the tiniest bit. *Wow*.

I excitedly rush to summon a nurse. Fortunately the first one I see is not the same as on my last visit.

After I explain my relationship to the patient, I say to her, "Watch her right eyebrow when I give her the word. Ready?"

"Yes."

"The Yankees suck."

Up goes the right eyebrow.

We look at each other. An ICU is no place for a high five, but we do it anyway. I see her name is Kelly—first or last, it doesn't matter. "Nurse Kelly," I say politely, "it might be a good idea to get a doctor from neurology in here." She nods.

I step out of ICU and give Henry a call. He picks up on the third ring, as is his unvarying practice. "Are you almost here?"

"Parking now. What's happening?"

"A lot. Is Jessie with you?"

"Right by my side."

"Come on up. This is crazy."

"What's going on? Let's not play games."

I find Henry's choice of words noteworthy given what I'm about to say.

"Another Yankees' miracle," I tell him.

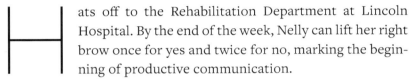ats off to the Rehabilitation Department at Lincoln Hospital. By the end of the week, Nelly can lift her right brow once for yes and twice for no, marking the beginning of productive communication.

Following the next week, she responded to verbal commands by moving her head to nod yes and no. She was also able to maintain visual focus. She seemed to understand that I was her attorney for something bad that happened at Dr. Grad's office. However, she was making only minor progress with her mobility below the neck, and I admit I wasn't all that happy with her assigned physical therapist.

Therefore, I made a recommendation.

After hearing me explain, with Henry offering support from the sideline, Jessie set about putting into motion the transfer of Nelly to Rusk Institute of Rehabilitation-Medicine in Manhattan. It offers the best brain injury recovery program in the entire country. It took a week for Jessie to pull the trigger; however, she needed the kind of comfort level with such a decision that comes only with time.

As I'm sitting at my desk, thinking about all this, Lily buzzes.

"I just opened the mail. We got a response to the Discovery and Inspection for the nurses' feeding notes on the *Simone* case."

"Bring it in."

"Do I have to make a special trip? Or can I give it to you when I see you?"

"Forget it. Just tell me, do they deny having the notes or not?"

"So, you want me to read it to you? Is that what you're asking?"

"Yes, please."

"I will just this one time, but only if you promise not to tell anybody."

"I promise. Well?"

"They deny."

"Is the response verified by Chucky-boy?"

"Jesus. Give me a sec . . . yeah, it is."

"Can you get him on the phone for me, please?"

"What?"

"Can you get him on the phone for me?"

"I'm sorry. Can you speak up?"

"Lily, you heard me."

"I wasn't sure that I did. I thought you asked me to dial a phone number for you. That's what you asked, is it not? After asking me to read to you. Is that what just happened here?"

"Yes, Lily, that's what just happened."

"That's what I thought. I wasn't sure. Is your phone broken? I don't think it is because we're speaking on it."

"No, it's not broken."

"Your dialing finger broken?"

"No."

"Sprained?"

"No, not sprained."

"A hangnail then?"

"No, no hangnail."

"So, you just want your people, meaning me, to call his people to get him on the phone, so your people, meaning me again, can tell his people to get him on the phone, so when he does pick up, your people, meaning me, can tell him to hold one minute for Mr. Wyler, like we're running some kind of Hollywood studio over here?"

"Forget it," I say, defeated.

She clicks off.

Here's the thing: Lily is smarter, more efficient, and more dedicated than anyone I've ever known. She's run my one-man practice like a precision instrument for more than a decade. So the trade-off is, she can smart-mouth me all she wants while I admire her, shall we say, decorative attributes.

More important, I can sleep at night without the worries of a small businessman. Most of them anyway.

I dial Chucky-boy myself.

"Lawless and Associates." It's the voice of an elderly woman, whose identity I'm well aware of.

"Chuck, please."

"No one here by that name." *Click.*

I dial back up.

"Lawless and Associates."

"Yes, hi, I just called a second ago and asked for Chuck. Is he in?"

"His name is Charles," she says in a corrective, if not exactly protective, manner.

"I understand that," I respond, "and I also know no associates work there. But you don't see me correcting you on that, do you?"

"One moment," she says, ignoring my retort while whispering "Asshole" loud enough for me to hear before she hits the Hold button.

I guess I'm not the only one with a Lily. But at least she's not my mother, who Chucky's receptionist happens to be.

"Hello."

"Hi, Charles. It's me."

"I figured."

"How so?"

"My mom gets upset when people don't call me by my proper name. You know that. But it never stops you."

He's right, of course.

"Listen, I received your response on *Simone*—and, Chuck, I'm really disappointed with you."

"Counselor, stop calling me Chuck. My name is Charles. Please, I'm not going to ask you again."

"Okay, but I got a big problem with your response—especially since you verified it by signature to be the truth. I know these records were generated and exist. So, either the hospital pulled them from the chart before they sent you copies or someone from your office pulled them. Not you of course. I know you wouldn't do that, given the many cases we've had together. You lose with honor."

Ignoring my jab, he answers, "I called the hospital and spoke to Risk Management. Shelly there pulled the original and went through the entire chart page by page. There are no Infant Feeding Notes for days two through seven. And you're right. I wouldn't pull them, and I'm the only guy left in the firm, partly thanks to you. Why are you making such a big deal about feeding records? The girl contracted herpes during childbirth from her mother. We did nothing wrong here. This is the one."

"Charles, we both know that, in a malpractice case, a single entry can change the entire complexion of things. The point here is, I'm missing one whole area of Adora's care and treatment. And I'll need those records for no reason other than for the sake of completion. No stone unturned. Do you get me? Are you in your office this afternoon?"

"I am."

"Would you mind if I popped by and showed you something?"

"Suit yourself." *Click.*

For the record—attorneys like that phrase—I'm not even partially responsible for the demise of Chucky-boy's firm. They did it to themselves. One partner, during trial, failed to offer me the money that the insurance company had directed him to offer—a sum I would've accepted—and then the jury, as it turned out, gave me ten times that amount. As for his other ex-partner, I had nothing to do with the guy's coronary. Slab bacon and juicy steaks, maybe; big belly, possibly; the stress of courtroom battles, definitely. But only happening to be his adversary on the day he dropped dead, I'd submit not. It was just his time. So Chuck need not thank me. It was the handiwork of someone closer to home.

————

I arrive at Rusk Rehab for my weekly visit to Nelly. Since her transfer here, she's made remarkable progress. I know this because I've been visiting her every Thursday afternoon, and some weeks I've seen her twice. Her recovery can be bullet-pointed as follows:

Week four after injury. A speech pathologist was holding a letter board in front of Nelly, and she'd identify a letter by looking at it, spelling words out this way, one letter at a time. It was a laborious process. But certainly, further progress. And she could now move her right arm and leg side to side.

Week five. To my surprise, Nelly was sitting up in bed for the first time. She was also able to lift up her right arm and move her right leg. Her left side was not functioning. The medical term is hemiplegia. At this time, they also removed the feeding tube sewed into the side of her gut and were teaching her how to swallow, using liquids.

Week six. She was using a spelling board by herself. It was basically a typewriter keyboard on her lap, and she'd struggle with her right hand to point to each letter. She was also trying to say the letter each time she pointed.

These are only a few of the many challenges of recovery traumatic brain injury or TBI survivors face on their way to maximum functioning level. Simply put, it's most likely Nelly will experience a future of ongoing coping and problem solving.

Anyway, I can't wait to see her latest progress. I like trying to guess how far she'll have advanced each time I visit, and I continually underestimate her. The truth is, she's reached such milestones because of her eight-hour-a-day commitment to different modes of therapy.

I exit the elevator and walk to the nurses' station.

"Good afternoon, Counselor. Those flowers are beautiful."

"Thank you. Is she in her room?"

"No, rehab."

Right away I run into Ernie, there in the hallway in his wheelchair. He's taken a liking to me. Unfortunately his brain injury—visible in the form of a horseshoe-shaped scar on his right temple from a craniotomy—has left him with clear limitations. As I approach, he beckons me over. When I'm within range, he slowly reaches up with great effort, grabs my lapel, and draws me closer.

"Hey, sonny boy," he says. "Always keep your eyes on the cash register. You got that? Never take your eyes off the cash register. Every time it opens, you got to watch. Never trust the people at the register. You got me?"

He lets go, having made his point. I step back.

"Ernie, so what you're saying is that I should watch the cash register?"

"That's what I'm saying, sonny boy."

"Got you, boss."

His eyes now shut.

It's the same each time I pass him. But I don't mind.

When I get to rehab, Nelly's lying on a mat, looking up at the ceiling, with a therapist stretching her left arm. I'm able to detect minor voluntary movements of her left leg. Which is a first. I sit down on the mat at her feet, without her noticing. Whenever a guy in a suit sits on the floor, he looks like an ass for some reason. Don't you think? The therapist folds Nelly's arms across her chest and raises her into a seated position by pushing her back forward.

"Hi," I say.

"Hi," she replies.

"You can talk!"

"Y-yes." Her eyes flutter a bit.

"Does Jessie know you can talk?"

"N-no."

"Listen," I say, eager to spread the news, "you finish here, and I'll wait for you in your room."

In the hall, I get Jessie on the phone.

"Oh, hi," she says. "The letter showed up. You know, the deposition date. I thought I was supposed to go on one day and then Dr. Grad would be deposed on a different one."

"Yes, I know that's how I explained it to you. I was surprised too that they wanted to conduct both on the same day. Defense attorneys usually never want to do that because then they have limited time to prep the doctor—or dentist as the case may be. They also don't get to bill for a second day. But defense counsel said Dr. Grad is eager to get out his side of the story, which is why this case is moving so quickly. Also there's not a lot of questioning for either of you, since the malpractice occurred over just a few minutes. Nelly will give her testimony on a different day."

"I thought you said they'd waive it, given the difficulty of her having to spell each word one letter at a time."

"Not if she can talk."

There's a moment of silence on the other end of the line. I'd call it quiet shock. "What do you mean?"

"She's talking. A few minutes ago I just spoke to her, and she answered back."

Jessie doesn't reply. So what I say is, "Hey, why don't you come over here and have a talk with her? I'm sure she'd like that. You know, to see you a bit more."

"I—I . . . of course. Oh, my god! I'm so happy for her. I'll drop by tomorrow. I gotta go." *Click.*

That was strange. I've been having a hard time figuring out where Jessie's coming from, at least since Nelly's been in rehab. In my line of business, I've had every opportunity to learn what a wide range of reactions and coping mechanisms you see following a loved one's catastrophic injury. Some step up to the plate, like Maria Simone, and others, like Jessie, are stuck in the dugout, despite getting the nod to pinch-hit. Hey, what I mean is, I just wish Jessie was more involved in Nelly's care and that she visited more often.

Crap. Here comes Nurse General. No joke, lots of them are tough cookies, but this one's four-star at least.

"Hey, Counselor," Nurse Rodriguez says, pointing at my phone, "need I tell you again that you can't use your phone on this floor?"

"*Um*, I wasn't using it."

"You're full of *mierda, abogado.*"

"Thank you," I reply courteously.

She suddenly softens. "So, I'm curious." She pauses. "Do you give all your clients this kind of attention? You know, visiting them in the hospital, bringing flowers, and decorating their rooms with Yankees' stuff, like you've hung on every inch of Nelly's walls."

"The truth?"

"Yes, Counselor, *la verdad*. I understand that may be challenging for you."

I smile. "No."

"So why her?"

"I can't explain. Maybe it's because she lost her parents in a fire and landed on her feet. And then this happened, and, for reasons I'm not understanding, her sister isn't being supportive enough. Or maybe it's because she has this force of will she's calling upon to get better, working triple time in therapy and making progress beyond anyone's expectations. Plus all of us go to the dentist and, when we leave, immediately resume our lives." I pause. "I guess it's a combination of all that. Nelly, mainly, makes you just want to root for her."

Nurse Rodriguez nods. Then says, "I'm not big on her sister."

"Half sister."

"Whatever."

"What makes you say that?"

"Like you said, she should come more often."

Now it's my turn to nod. "Here's what I'm thinking."

"Go ahead."

"Take Ernie over there. . . . You know him pretty well, right?"

"Yeah. He spends half the day watching the telephone switchboard, thinking it's his cash register."

"Yeah, well, he's gonna be in that wheelchair for life, right?"

"Seems pretty clear."

"Well, would you wheel him to the foot of a stairway and ask him to walk up?"

"Of course not."

"Why?"

"Because I know he can't do it."

"So, you understand he lacks capacity."

"Yes."

"Well, does that make you not like him?"

"Of course not."

"Why?"

"'Cause he just can't do it."

"Right. So maybe Nelly's sister is the same way. Maybe she just lacks the capacity to be supportive to the level that you and I deem acceptable under these devastating circumstances. I'm sure people have let you down on occasion, *verdad*?"

"*Sí, es verdad.*"

"So do you get my drift here? And I am in no way defending her sister's lack of support."

"I get it, Counselor," she says. "But that doesn't change my opinion."

"You're tough."

"You've got to be if you want to survive working on this floor."

Suddenly my attention's diverted to Nelly coming our way. As she's wheeled toward us, she keeps her upper body balanced. The term is "trunk control." She's also able to keep her head up and focused on me all the while. Major progress. The orderly brings her to a slow rolling stop in front of us.

"Th-thank you f-for waiting."

Wow. "I'll take her from here," I tell the orderly with a polite nod.

Everyone we pass, both patient and staff, looks approvingly at her. I guess I'm not Nelly's only fan. Once in her room, I allow a few beats for us both to settle down. Then, watching Nelly's face, I can see her exhaustion.

"So, how are you feeling?" It's what I always ask first. In such a situation, it covers a range of meaning. And it's pretty amazing that I can now pose it to Nelly. But I'm not prepared for her response.

"Burns?" Unexpectedly she answers me with a question of her own, kinda gazing past me.

"Burns?" I ask. "What do you mean?"

"F-from the fire? Is my f-face burned?"

My heart sinks. She's looking at me for a reply. An explanation. She thinks she's here because of the fire she was in. Do I correct her? Do I get a doctor? What do I do? I don't want to compromise the mental and emotional aspects of her undoubtedly still-fragile recovery. Yet my curiosity has been sparked. What's hauling this up to the surface?

"Mom . . . Dad? W-why haven't they c-come to visit me?"

Oh, man!

"Nelly, I know you must have many questions running through your head, and all of them will be answered. But, for now, why don't you get some rest?"

She very slowly shakes her head. Instead of being elated at her progress, she appears simply miserable.

I try again. "It's just you've been through so much, and there's a well-thought-out plan for your recovery. The medical professionals here will have to field your questions. But, to answer your first one"—her gaze suddenly disappears—"no, you don't have any burns on your face."

Nelly tilts her head in response. "Why would I have burns on my face?"

7.

Now standing on the street in front of the hospital—knowing it's likely I'll be reentering soon—I make the first of two calls.

"Hey, Jessie, sorry to bother you again. It's just that something started happening with Nelly that, on my own, I can't make sense of."

"Okay. Let me hear it."

Her tone seems only curious. I wish I could read her better.

"So," I say, "your sister thinks she's here because of the fire. What can you share with me that you think I should know?"

She doesn't reply.

"Hello?" I prompt her.

"Um, first, can you tell me what she said?"

"She wanted to know if any burns were on her face and how come her parents haven't come to visit her."

More silence.

"Jessie, you there?"

"I'm here. It's just that, it's . . . upsetting, that's all. Did she say anything else?"

"Nope. That's it."

There's a small sound. I think she's cleared her throat. Which is a cue for me to take a deep breath. Man, I wish I knew what was going on.

"Jessie, help me out here, please. What do you make of this?" I want to be considerate, but, you know, it's suddenly as if the script is getting an unauthorized rewrite.

"I'm not sure," Jessie begins. "This is all new. She never had any memory about the night of the fire. I mean, like, absolutely none. The doctors at the time had a name for it—post-traumatic amnesia. The only thing she ever recalled was coming home from the hospital. She was admitted for one week for severe smoke inhalation, and they wanted to observe her. She was in shock. No surprise really." She hesitates a second. "Who wouldn't be?"

"I see. Well, I'm going to talk to her doctor about this. I think he should be made aware."

"That's a good idea. I'll talk to him too. What's his name again?"

"Dr. Furman, Steven Furman," I remind, peeved she doesn't remember his name.

"Oh, yeah, right. It's hard without Nelly . . . " She sighs. "I need to go." *Click.*

I can't make up my mind whether that conversation was actually satisfying. I think not. That's the second time she had to go. Go where? Although I did learn something. Post-traumatic amnesia. *Hmm.* Poor Nelly. And how does that affect—if at all—the malpractice case I'm on board for?

I make call number two.

"Benson here." After the third ring.

"Henry, we need to talk."

"What's up?"

"Listen, Nelly's made pretty amazing progress since I last updated you. She's actually able to speak."

"You're right. That's amazing. Now she'll be able to testify about her damages."

"I guess that's one way to look at it."

"Tug, I appreciate that may have sounded a bit insensitive. But, believe me, I do have a place in my heart for Nelly and Jessie. After all, I've known them since they were little girls. Unfortunate, that fire."

Henry's heart isn't an organ I like to think about. If he claims one, fine; I'm not arguing.

"Yes, the fire. The problem is, she was under the impression her parents are alive and that she's in the hospital because of the fire."

"That's a bit alarming."

"I agree. Obviously I need to speak to her doctor, who'll be making his rounds soon. I'm at the hospital."

"The hospital? Again?" His tone turns questioning, edging toward disapproving even.

"That's right."

"You're not getting into one of those situations where the lawyer falls in love with the young, beautiful, injured, and highly vulnerable client, are you?"

"No, Henry. This is real life, not daytime TV. I'm just filling in until Jessie steps it up a bit more, that's all. Listen, what do you know about that fire?"

"What's to know? The house caught fire and burned. Her dad died, and her mother—who was suffering already from terminal cancer—lived a few days longer."

"How old was Nelly at the time?"

"It was two years ago, so she was sixteen, making Jessie eighteen."

"Whom did Nelly live with after her parents died?"

"Juanita."

"And Jessie too, I assume."

"Yes, of course. Jessie had split her time between her parents before the fire. Nelly had more adjustments to make. Jessie believed Roberto favored Nelly. And Juanita agreed. Truth is, he once told me he had trouble dealing with Jessie because she reminded him of her mother. He despised Juanita, and the feeling was mutual."

"That's unfortunate for Jessie."

"Yes. But it's my belief everyone tried their best, to the extent they were capable. After her release from prison, Juanita even moved to Yonkers, where the girls were living when their dad moved them out of the Bronx to get a better education."

"When did they move from Juanita's house to their apartment in East Harlem?"

"Not long ago. After Nelly graduated high school."

"You got anything else for me?"

"That's about it. Those wheels are turning, Counselor. They're audible over the phone. What's up?"

"Nothing. It's only that Nelly seemed to regress so bizarrely. I was pretty floored. If I know a little more about the circumstances, it all might make a bit more sense. And I'd be better equipped to field her questions."

"Sounds reasonable."

"Yes, I'm a man of reason." *Click.*

Heading back into the hospital and returning to Nelly's floor, I exit the elevator and bump into Dr. Furman, catching him off guard. His medical specialty is rehabilitation and physical medicine.

"Hi, doc. I need to discuss what just occurred between Nelly and me."

"By your tone, it sounds serious. I'm listening."

As I tell him, he proves to be an empathic listener. "So," I conclude, "what do you make of this?"

"Post-traumatic amnesia is not uncommon. Sometimes it's organic, meaning the brain from a physiologic perspective has lost the memory forever. And sometimes it's a subconscious repression of a bad memory—a defense mechanism, if you will. So then Nelly suffers this second traumatic event, and whatever happened in that dental office somehow triggered the surfacing of her repressed memories."

"I get it. But, if she brings up the fire again, what should I do?"

"I say, don't push her. Don't ask questions leading her to a deeper place. Be a good listener."

"Understood. But how about handling questions, like why her parents haven't visited her?"

"That's a tougher one. Until she's out of the woods and the

neuropsychologists have had an opportunity to evaluate her, just deflect things as best you can. She's been through a lot, and there's more ahead. It's a wait-and-see situation."

"Okay. What about the eye expression I caught?"

"Sounds like the gaze some of our hypnotherapy patients take on. It's known to occur during a reflective moment."

I nod. But, as I leave, I ask myself, what next?

Litigation Games

Arriving at Lawless & Associates, the first thing I notice is that the sign on the door has been altered. Removed are the names of Chuck's former partners, both the one who died after our trial and the guy who withheld an offer, costing the insurance company millions and his firm the account. A bunch of little holes remain where the drilled-in letters were taken off. This sight can't be reassuring to clients.

The place needs a paint job; the carpet's splitting at the seams, and the magazines on the coffee table are way outdated. On the other hand, maybe they're collectibles.

I approach the elderly woman sitting at the desk, who I assume to be Ma Lawless.

"Excuse me, I'm here to see . . . " I hesitate for a second, trying to decide if I'm going to say Charles, Charlie, Chuck, or Chuckyboy. I opt for a moment of kindness. "Charles Lawless." I get a nod, like my life was just spared.

"I'll see if he's available." A minute later the man himself appears.

"Come on in," he greets me. "Mom, hold my calls."

"Okay, Chucky."

Hmm.

As we enter the conference room, he points to the table. "There's my copy of the hospital record. Suit yourself. I'm going to grab water. Want?"

"No, thanks." As soon as he's out the door, I go to the exact place where I know Adora's feeding records are missing from my copy and wait. Two minutes later he returns, and it's time to get down to business.

"I'm here because I wanted to show you something." I put my finger down on the hospital record. "See this, Charles. It says Infant Feeding Notes. That's the heading of the page, and all the feeding entries are supposed to be documented thereafter. As you can see, the sole feeding entry for Adora's date of birth reads:

WB, six ounces of formula taken, RGD, SKT.

"Given her late hour of birth, this would be the only entry for that date. But, when you turn the page," I say, flipping it over, "it goes right to the Vitals Chart instead of being a continuation of her feeding record for the next day."

I flip back. "This is the only feeding entry through postpartum day seven, the morning she was transferred to the neonatal ICU. Once transferred, the feeding entries pick up as they should." I turn to the ICU notes and indicate the designated place for listing feedings. "See what I mean?"

"No, I don't."

"What do you mean, you don't?" I'm annoyed. "I just showed it to you."

"I'm telling you, I don't see it," he repeats stubbornly.

"Charles, right here!" I say, jamming my finger down. "Right here it says Infant Feeding Notes. There's one entry for the day she was born, and the next page is the Vitals Chart. But there should be the continuation of the feeding record for each and every day up to transfer to the ICU and then the Vitals Chart. Come on, you know that."

"I see the Infant Feeding Note you're pointing to, but that comes to a natural conclusion. It's a complete entry. There's no arrow to signal the note is continued on the next page. The word 'continued' does not appear to indicate it goes on, and the sentence, as written, is full and complete. So, no, I don't see it."

Chucky-boy must be playing dumb because I know he's not. Disheveled, bad breath, big gut, high-water pants revealing white tube socks, absurd defense tactics, yes. Dumb, no.

"Chucky, I'm not talking about that particular note. I agree it's complete. But no other entries appear for the following days until transfer. There should be at least eight feeding notes per day for a newborn. That's SOP. And the only reason there's just a single entry for day one is because the child was born late in the evening," I say, for, like, the third time. "Get me?"

"Can't say I do. Listen, maybe they didn't keep a daily feeding record way back then after a normal initial entry. Heck, I don't know. The point is, I don't understand why you got yourself involved in this case. Cohen is a criminal attorney and doesn't know what he's doing. The mom has herpes and passed it along to her kid. Horrible situation. She should've just told her doctors." He gives me an emphatic look, one that's meant to help convince me.

"Answer me this, how do you know Maria has herpes? On what basis?"

"Because she tested positive for it, the antibodies."

"What do you mean, tested positive? When?"

"At her independent medical exam."

"Why did she have an IME if Adora is the injured party?"

"I sent Cohen a Notice of Physical Exam for Maria, and his office set it up without objection. Why don't you ask him?"

This catches me off guard, but I don't let him see. "Listen, I must've overlooked the IME report when going through the stuff Cohen gave me. You happen to have a copy handy?"

"Sure." He picks up one of the files on the table and thumbs through it. "Here," he says, handing me a folder.

I open it, and inside is a narrative medical report, detailing a physical exam performed on Maria by an infectious disease doctor retained by Chucky-boy, to whom it's addressed. Above all, a narrative report was not in my file, the very file this scumbag Alan

Cohen delivered. I take a moment to read the report and the lab testing attached thereto, then look up.

"I appreciate your position in more concrete terms now. Could you have your mom make a copy of this for me?"

"I'll make it myself," he responds, grinning.

"Thanks. But that still doesn't mean those feeding notes weren't pulled, Charles."

"Call me Chuck," he says, offering an uncharacteristic bit of playfulness because of having scored off me.

He can be as funny as he likes—but I know a cover-up is in play. Because my asshole's tingling. Okay, I know it sounds crazy—and, yes, I was wrong once, that time being hemorrhoids—but otherwise it's a specific sensation that happens to be superaccurate in signaling intentional suppression of evidence. And I'm lucky to have developed such a useful cue early in my career.

As soon as my wingtips hit the sidewalk, I aggressively whip out my phone. Alan picks up on the first ring. There is something to be said for a person who picks up on ring number one.

"You settle my case?"

"No, Alan, I didn't settle your case. Furthermore it's not likely that it will ever settle."

"Why's that?"

"I'll tell you why. But first I want to apologize to you."

"For what?"

"For saying you're a motherfucking scumbag who compromises his clients in every which way and whose fucking law license should be revoked for incompetence if there is such a ground."

"What? What? What did I do wrong?" he nervously shrieks.

"You served Maria up for an IME inclusive of a blood test for the herpes antibodies. That's what you did wrong!"

"I thought they were entitled to IMEs?"

"They are, but only of the injured plaintiff—Adora! And of Adora only! You gave them something by law they weren't entitled to, and it completely blew up in your face.

"Or don't you already know that by now?"

"You mean, uh, their infectious disease report?"

"Yeah, that's what I mean. And the herpes screening. Where the fuck is it? Because it's certainly not in the files that you gave me."

"Oh, I have it. I was going to get it to you," he explains, not exactly convincingly.

My blood pressure's skyrocketing. "You were *going* to get it to me? That's nice. When were you going to get it to me?"

"*Um*, soon."

"Soon. Good. That's nice, too. Is there anything else that you held out that you intend to give me soon?"

"No, that's it."

"So the only document you withheld was the one which explains, in detail, the defense in the case as confirmed by blood test of mother and daughter."

"*Um*, yeah. I don't know why you're so mad. Their expert response, which I told you to look at first, says the same thing."

I count to two. "No, it didn't. It said Adora's brain injury was caused by herpes contracted from her mother. A specific assertion, yes, but accompanied by objective testing results to support the claim, no. There was no mention of confirming blood tests. The infectious disease narrative lays it all out—the confirmed source of the herpes—with scientific validity." I count to two again.

Then I tell him, "I'd send you this file back right now if I didn't have plans to go to Maria's for spaghetti and meatballs, and to discuss the results of the herpes test. The test I sent her for, which was obviously unnecessary. I don't understand how you could withhold from Maria the finding of her blood test or of the conclusions of this infectious disease doctor hired by defense counsel."

"Well, it's just that I thought it'd be better if you told her. And I didn't know you would send her for a herpes test of your own. That was pretty smart thinking."

"Alan! This is not a game! It's someone's—no, three people's—lives!" *Click.*

8.

The depositions of Jessie and Dr. Grad are today. It's the first time I've ever handled a malpractice case where I've had an eyewitness to the events in my front pocket. But it's time I hear Nelly's version, which is why I'm passing the nurses' station at Rusk.

"Hi, Nurse Rodriguez. How are you today?"

"Fine, thank you." She looks as if she might ask how I am but then thinks better of it. "Nelly's waiting for you but don't ask me for my permission to see her before visiting hours again."

I nod as I start down the hall. To my surprise, the patient is sitting up in bed, fully dressed.

"Hey. You look great." And I mean it.

"Hi," she says, looking up from her iPad. She's wearing her Yankees' cap.

"How are you feeling?"

"Better every day."

"That's excellent. And with the progress you've been making, Dr. Furman anticipates you'll be ready for discharge sooner than expected. That's exciting news."

"I know. But they're so nice here, I wouldn't mind staying longer."

"That's funny. I can't recall a client of mine ever wanting to stay in the hospital longer than necessary."

"It's just ... I'm not exactly eager to go ... home." The last word seems to stick in her mouth and not because of any problems with her physical speech.

She adds, "I miss my mom and dad. They're dead, you know."

"Yes, I know. Losing your parents, especially tragically, is never easy. You know you have my deepest sympathy." I take a breath. "But the thing is, right now we need to have a serious conversation ... "

"You mean, about the l-lawsuit?" That little blip revealed her stutter is still there, even if on its way out.

"Yes, about the lawsuit." Suddenly I notice that she has a mild left-sided facial droop.

"Okay. I understand. I knew we were going to need one soon."

"Yes, well, that's good. But, in fact, Dr. Furman only recently gave me the go-ahead. Still, I believed in proceeding slowly, for your sake. However, in a couple hours, I'm going to take the deposition of Dr. Grad."

"The Painless Dentist," she offers. I hear a note of sarcasm.

"Yes. The Painless Dentist. And Jessie's giving testimony then too. So I need to know what you recall about that day to complete the picture."

Nelly sighs. "Dr. Grad's a n-nice man." And now there is a different, gentler tone.

"He may, indeed, be. Although I appreciate how difficult it's likely to be for you, I have to hear everything you recall about that day."

"W-well, to start with, Jessie and I had a fight that morning about money."

I nod. But, of course, I have no idea what's coming. It's all news to me. And starting now is when I'm going to learn it—from the usual multiple perspectives.

"She spends too much. I only have about half of that money left, you know."

"No, I don't know. What money?"

"Insurance money."

"What insurance are you talking about?"

"From the house burning down."

"Oh, I see. There was a property damage payout."

"No. That's not settled. The life insurance, I mean."

"Life insurance?"

"Yeah. I got money from my mom's death benefit. That's how we were able to afford moving out of Juanita's to live on our own. But Jessie spends too much money." She makes a little face here. "I can't stop her."

"I'm sorry that's a worry of yours. But let's try to focus on what you remember about your visit to Dr. Grad's office, okay?"

"Y-yes, I know. But you asked me what I remembered from the day I went to Dr. Grad's office, and our fight is the first thing I remember."

"You're absolutely right, Nelly. But, from this point forward, I want to focus on the dental care."

She nods. "Well, I remember Dr. Grad p-putting something in my arm, a needle. Then he connected it to a b-bag on a pole."

"An IV drip?"

"Yes. I remember f-feeling really relaxed. Then somebody came in and checked the pole, not once b-but twice. I'm certain of that. Then, right after the second check, I remember being unable to breathe. It was scary . . . but familiar."

She looks toward the ceiling, and suddenly a blank expression comes over her face. With her head tilted, she gazes just off to my right, as if something's caught her attention. When she resumes speaking, her delivery's a monotone.

"The smoke started filling my room, and I couldn't breathe. I tried to open my door, but it was stuck. I was crying and calling for help. It was getting harder to breathe. I was trying my best, but the smoke . . . It was thicker and thicker. I couldn't see. I heard sirens and banging. The next thing I remember, I was on the front lawn. Jessie was there. Safe. They saved the house . . . " Her voice breaks, and she gasps at the memory. Her face is confused and sad. "But not my parents," she finishes.

She begins to cry. Looking straight at me now, she is refocused but obviously exhausted. "I-I'm tired. D-do we still have to talk about Dr. Grad's office?"

"Of course we don't," I reassure her.

On the 4 train uptown I can't stop thinking about Nelly. She's caught in a messed-up space between the worlds of two traumatic events, with the only prognosis right now being Dr. Furman's cautions to "wait and see."

Now as I approach the office building where the depositions are to be held, I see Jessie waiting in front as arranged. But she's not alone. Her companion is a good-looking Latino guy with a backpack slung over his shoulder. Spotting me, she gives him a good-bye peck on his cheek and sends him on his way.

I greet her, saying, "He seems like a nice fellow."

She grins. "Not really."

"Good to know. Listen, I saw your sister earlier, and she's making really startling progress. No one anticipated it."

"I know. I can't wait for her to come home. I miss her."

"Well, I'm sure she misses you too. Anyway, you need to know that the confusion she's been exhibiting is still present. It's really strange, these sudden shifts."

"I don't understand it," Jessie replies. "Nelly never had any recollection of the fire, so it's got to be more a product of her imagination than about actual memories."

"I don't know as much about this as you do—but what she conveys, as to her emotional relationship to your family's fire, is pretty intense. And very real."

Then the young guy she just dispatched saunters back, breaking up our curbside exchange.

"I'm gonna see you later, right?" he says to her.

Jessie nods.

He stares hard at her for a moment, then turns, and leaves—for the second time. As he does, I hear a clanking sound. Like a pocket filled with change. Looking, I note the source to be the chain of nunchucks dangling off his backpack. Really?

"Anyway, right now we need to move on. Defense counsel will be asking a lot of questions about what happened at Dr. Grad's office. Just go with what you've told me. You don't need formal prepping." I pause, then zero in on a critical point. "Whatever we know Grad did, I'd like to ask you not to display anger toward him."

"Why? I am angry." She bites her lip, then lets out a big sigh.

"I understand. Just don't show it."

"Why?" Her expression is tense.

"Because his attorney will be writing a deposition report to the insurance carrier, and I want him to say what a lovely girl you are, and how you and your sister have been wronged by this malpractice. It makes resolving the case easier down the road. You never want an angry plaintiff. Jurors hate angry plaintiffs, even if they're badly injured. The role of wronged victim is the one to go for."

"That should be easy." She now makes a mock-cheerful face.

The lesson here is, no one wants hospitals or lawyers in their life, but it's usually not a matter of choice.

Entering the deposition room, Sam, my court reporter, is already seated. I recognize Dr. Grad from his website, but I don't know the defense attorney. In fact, I don't know his firm either. Their office, where we've just arrived, is slickly expensive, designed to impress. But all I can glean from their website—since you research the enemy before you're to sit down on their territory—is that they claim no expertise in medical malpractice. They must be new to the game.

"Jessie," Dr. Grad says from across the table, where we've seated ourselves on the opposite side.

"Doctor," his lawyer breaks in, "I did say to you that it is inappropriate today to engage Plaintiff."

Grad turns and gives the man representing him a stern look. "Well, the plaintiff has a name, and it's Jessie. And I already told you not to bother me with your silly lawyer formalities. Please settle down, or I'll have my insurance carrier hire a different attorney." This last is pronounced with a firm look.

The lawyer makes a face with which I'm familiar, that of defense attorney surrender.

Now Grad turns back to us.

"Jessie," he says, "I hope Nelly is recovering. I had to stop visiting her at the hospital after I gave you a copy of my chart on strict instructions from my carrier. They said it would interfere with my defense and that, if I went to see her again, they'd disclaim coverage for noncooperation. Ridiculous."

He pauses, then adds, "And I just want to tell you how sorry I am about all this."

Sam and I look at each other—the way two people do to acknowledge and confirm they heard the same unlikely thing. I look at Jessie who doesn't know how to respond.

I do.

But I'm going to do it nicely, with an accusation formed as a question, because it looks like Grad actually might be a nice man.

"We appreciate your sincere concern, Dr. Grad," I begin. "This is a terrible situation all around. May I ask, by saying 'sorry,' are you admitting you did something wrong?"

"Don't answer that!" orders his lawyer, placing his hand on Grad's forearm.

The dentist shakes him off, then turns his focus back to me. "No. I'm not admitting I committed malpractice. I simply feel horrible that a young person was injured, that's all. Showing concern for a fellow human being by saying you feel sorry has nothing to do with admitting malpractice."

"Got ya, doc. We appreciate your empathy and concern." I look over at Jessie. "We're starting with you."

She nods assent.

Jessie's deposition is short and uneventful, with the substance as follows:

```
(1) Grad came in and initiated the
anesthesia, then left;
(2) An assistant named Rita came in,
checked on things, then left;
(3) Then Nelly slipped into
unconsciousness while they were left
alone in the room, unattended.
```

That's it.

I have to say, it's pretty hard to hide the anger I feel at a doctor administering an anesthetic and then leaving the room. The only inconsistency between Jessie's testimony and what Nelly told me earlier is how Nelly had believed she was checked twice after the anesthesia had been started.

The defense attorney proceeded to do an excellent job focusing on time intervals, trying to establish that Nelly had had her cardiopulmonary arrest exactly consistent with the triggering of an anaphylactic reaction. He was thorough on the damages sustained too. They, however, speak for themselves. There's no question but that Nelly suffered a brain injury. Its magnitude though still remains to be seen.

During the brief lunch break, Jessie and I sit in the salad bar downstairs. We, by unspoken agreement, don't discuss the reason we're here. I'm now attuned to the chip on her shoulder, even if its origins are unclear.

As we head back up to the conference room, she stops suddenly to say, "Listen, I really appreciate all you've done for my sister. The nurses have told me how often you've visited. Thank you."

This catches me by surprise. But it's a gesture appreciated. Even if it doesn't explain anything.

9.

Now it's time for Grad to be sworn in. And so I begin my questioning.

Q.   Did you employ an anesthesia technique known as "conscious sedation" on Nelly?

A.   Yes, I did.

Q.   Please define that term.

A.   Conscious sedation is the administration of drugs which produce a state of depression of the central nervous system and an altered level of consciousness, while still allowing a patient to respond to verbal commands. It preserves protective reflexes while maintaining an unassisted airway.

Q.   Is that also known as "light anesthesia"?

A.   That term is also used, yes.

Q. What was the purpose of employing conscious sedation on Nelly?

A. Pain and anxiety management were the paramount consideration in her case.

Q. On the date you gave Nelly anesthesia, were you licensed by the State of New York to employ conscious sedation anesthetic drugs?

A. No. I have to say I was not.

Q. Were you aware when you undertook treatment of Nelly that, to employ such anesthesia, the State of New York required dentists like yourself to be licensed?

A. No, I was not.

Q. But, since then, you have come to learn of this fact?

A. Yes.

Q. What was the source of your knowledge?

A. My attorney advised me. But, I have to say, it made no difference.

"Off the record!" calls out the defense lawyer. "Doctor, I told you that you are to answer only the questions counsel poses. Please, do not be gratuitous. And certainly do not repeat conversations that we had which are privileged in nature."

Grad looks at him again scornfully.

"May I continue?" I ask. Defense counsel, I know, will be rolling his eyes at my next question. But Grad opened up the door.

"Yes. Sorry for the interruption."

Q. Can you explain what you meant
when you said it made no difference?

A. Of course. I had been employing the
same anesthetic drugs in the same manner
for thirty-six continuous years prior to
the date of this occurrence. And, I might
add, without incident. The law requiring
dentists like myself to become licensed
came into effect some six months before
my treatment of Nelly. So you see, I was
qualified, in fact had taught courses on
employing anesthesia of this nature. But
I just wasn't licensed because of the
temporal relation of things, the enacting
of the law, that is.

Q. Would you drive a car without a
license?

A. No, I would not.

"Objection!" calls out defense counsel. "Don't answer that
question."

I counter, "That's a late call. The basket counts."

Q. Can you tell me the types of drugs
you used on Nelly and in what dosage?

I'm interested to hear his answer because his office record—
or, should I say the scrawled sixth-grade note card documenting
Nelly's care—is silent on the topic.

A. Certainly. Dosing of medications
that produce conscious sedation is
individualized, and I implemented
the standard minimum regimen for the

continuous infusion of 5mg/ml formulation
of midazolam, also known as Versed. I
used a loading dose of approximately 3
mg infused over several minutes until I
achieved the desired level of sedation,
then adjusted it down to 50 percent of
that for the maintenance of the sedation,
which I found to be the minimum effective
infusion rate for Nelly.

Q. Is that regimen in conformity with
the manufacturer's dosing guidelines?

A. Exactly. It's actually their
minimum dosing for this drug.

Q. How was the volume of anesthetic
controlled during administration?

A. I set the flow-controller clamp
for the midazolam IV bag on the minimum,
that's how.

Q. Was this an electronic flow
controller or a manual one?

A. A standard manual wheel-type flow-
controller clamp.

Q. How did you know when you reached
the sedation level that you desired?

A. I assessed her.

Q. How?

A. Her speech was slow or thick, and
her facial expression mildly relaxed—
meaning, she didn't have slack jaw. Also
her eyes were glazed and less than half
shut, indicating she was mildly sedated.

> Q. Is monitoring the patient's vitals during conscious sedation the standard of care?
>
> A. Yes, it is.
>
> Q. Were you monitoring Nelly's vitals beginning at the initiation of the drugs?
>
> A. Yes, I was.
>
> Q. Can you tell me how?
>
> A. Yes, she wore a finger clip from a pulse oximeter machine set on the counter and . . .

"That's a lie!" Jessie shouts, rising from her chair. "She didn't have anything on her finger, and there was no machine!"

I stand and ease her back down, saying, "It's all right. Please let me ask my questions."

"But he's lying!" she insists.

"I understand. It will all come out in the end. It always does. But, for now, I need you to sit and keep quiet. The court reporter is taking everything down."

She looks at Sam, whose hands are above the keys, ready.

She's right of course. Grad was lying for sure. I could see it on his face. A nice man and a caring one. He just happens not to be telling the truth.

> Q. Do you still have this pulse oximeter machine?
>
> A. Um, yes, I do.
>
> Q. Do you have one or more than one of these machines?
>
> A. Just the one.

I pause and make a demand. "I call for production of the pulse oximeter machine, inclusive of the make, model, manufacturer, purchase receipt, and serial number."

"Please put all your requests in writing, Counselor," replies the defense attorney.

I give him a nod.

> Q. Did you keep an anesthesia log that documents the start time of the procedure, as well as when the anesthetic drugs were given and their amounts?
>
> A. No, I did not.
>
> Q. Did you document her BP, respirations, and heart rate at the start and at five-minute intervals thereafter by using a standard anesthesia graph?
>
> A. No, I did not. I relied on the pulse oximeter.
>
> Q. Can you tell me how long it was after the initiation of anesthesia that you became aware there was a problem?
>
> A. Just over five minutes.
>
> Q. And on what do you base this five-minute interval if you weren't keeping a running anesthesia log with spaced five-minute entries?
>
> A. Well, um, you see this watch I have on here? It's a Tag Heuer. Tag Heuer for many decades was the supplier of official Olympic timing instruments. I use the subdial of the chronometer to gauge time frames. And such was the case here.

"Okay, let the record reflect that the doctor has pulled up his left sleeve and removed a wrist watch, placing it on the conference table. He has now depressed the top of the three buttons." I look over to the opposing counsel. "So stipulated, Counselor?"

"*Uh* . . ." he says but hesitating. "So stipulated."

      Q.   Doctor, you can put your watch back on. Now were you in the room when you became aware there was a problem?

      A.   No, I was not.

      Q.   Were there any medical professionals in the room at the onset of the problem?

      A.   No, there were not.

      Q.   Can you tell me where you were when your patient was under anesthesia and ran into trouble?

      A.   I was treating a different patient.

      Q.   Where was this other patient?

      A.   In a different exam room.

      Q.   Can you tell me whether you were treating only one other patient or more than one other patient at the time you became aware there was a problem with Nelly?

      A.   Including Nelly, I was treating three patients.

      Q.   Was each of these patients receiving conscious sedation at the same time?

A.   Yes, they were.

Q.   Was anybody else in your office
assisting you with these patients?

A.   Yes, that would be Rita. She's a
sedationist.

Q.   Is she licensed to employ
anesthesia in the State of New York?

A.   No, but she's a licensed
sedationist and is qualified to monitor
patients under the effects of anesthetic
drugs.

Q.   Was Rita in the room when Nelly
got into trouble?

A.   No, she was not.

Q.   Was she with you?

A.   No.

Q.   So she was with the third patient
under sedation?

A.   Yes, that's correct.

Q.   How were you monitoring the two
other patients under the effects of
anesthesia if you only had one pulse
oximeter, and I assume you were wearing
only one Tag Heuer, both being used for
Nelly?

A.   *Um, uh,* there were no incidents
with the other patients.

Q.   I understand. But, how were you
monitoring the other two patients?

A.   Visual monitoring by checking

their facial expressions, eyes, chest
motion. Visual.

Q. I see. But, if there were two
medical professionals, you and Rita,
monitoring three patients under the
effects of anesthesia at the same time,
would it be fair to say that, at all
times, at least one patient was left
alone, unattended?

A. Yes, that would be true.

Q. And in this instance that would be
Nelly. Correct?

A. Correct. But her sister was
watching her.

I look to Jessie. She can hardly contain herself, seemingly ready
to explode. I turn back to Grad.

Q. Are you suggesting you were
relying on Jessie over here to monitor
her sister?

A. No, I'm not saying that.

Q. Let's move on. What or who notified
you that there was a problem?

A. I heard Jessie scream, so I came
running.

Q. Was the infusion of the anesthetic
still at half the initial dose when you
became aware something was wrong?

A. Yes. It must've been.

Q. When you entered the room, did you
assess Nelly?

A. Yes.

Q. What was your assessment, and what were your findings?

A. Well, first I stopped the infusion by pulling the line out of her arm. On assessment, she wasn't breathing but was white and motionless. I felt for a pulse, and there was none.

Q. Did you know how long she hadn't been breathing as of this moment?

A. No, I did not.

Q. What did you do next?

A. I lifted her out of the chair and began giving her mouth-to-mouth.

Q. Are you certified in Basic Life Support?

A. No, I am not. But I learned how to give mouth-to-mouth in the army.

Q. Wonderful. Did you have oxygen available?

A. No.

Q. Well, did you have a fully stocked crash cart in your office to properly and adequately address adverse reactions to anesthesia drugs?

A. A formal crash cart? No, I did not.

Q. Well, have you heard the term "reversal agents" relative to the use of anesthetic drugs?

A. Yes, I have.

Q. Define for me what a reversal agent is.

A. A reversal agent is a drug given to reverse the effects of a particular anesthetic drug. Each drug has a specific reversal agent. What they do is reverse the respiratory and cardiac depressive effects of the anesthetic drug employed, bringing the patient back to consciousness.

Q. Midazolam, being a respiratory and cardiovascular depressant, causes hypotension—meaning, low blood pressure and bradycardia—which is to say, a slow heart rate. Correct?

A. Correct, by definition.

Q. And reversal agents address this, am I right? They aid in bringing the blood pressure and heart rate back to normal, true? And the patient back to consciousness, true?

A. Yes, those are true.

Q. Did you have the reversal agent for midazolam in your office on this date?

A. No.

Q. What is the reversal agent for midazolam?

A. I don't know.

Q. So would it be fair to say that you did not give Nelly reversal agents after she stopped breathing?

A. I did not.

Q.   Are you aware that in the absence
of giving a reversal agent, all the mouth-
to-mouth in the world would never make
a difference because of the physiologic
effects of the anesthetic drug on the
cardiac and respiratory systems?

A.   I did not know that.

Q.   Did you depart from good and
accepted dental practice by giving
anesthetic drugs to Nelly without having
at your disposal reversal agents in the
event of an allergic reaction?

"Objection!" blurts defense counsel. "Don't answer the question."
"Mark it for a ruling, Sam," I instruct.

Q.   Was Nelly in respiratory and
cardiac arrest before the ambulance
arrived?

A.   Yes.

Q.   Meaning, full cessation of function?

A.   Yes.

Q.   How long was she not breathing,
beginning at the moment when you became
aware something was wrong?

A.   Nine minutes, forty-three seconds.

Q.   Tag Heuer?

A.   Yes, Tag Heuer.

Q.   I noted on your record for Nelly
the word "anaphylactic." Can you define
that term for me?

A. It means an allergic reaction. That's why I hold that I did nothing wrong. You cannot guard against that.

I move to strike the unresponsive portions of that last answer. Which means I'm preserving my right to have a judge strike from the record the self-serving aspect of his answer. Then I resume my questioning:

Q. So it is your opinion with a reasonable degree of medical certainty that the cause of Nelly's cardiopulmonary arrest was an allergic reaction to the anesthetic drug you gave her?

A. Yes.

Q. What is the basis of your opinion?

A. The event occurred within the expected time period for an allergic reaction. And I gave her the minimum standard dose that would not cause an arrest in the absence of an allergic reaction. Making it the only explanation I can think of.

Q. Is that what you told the ambulance crew?

A. Yes.

Q. And is that what you also told them at the hospital?

A. Yes.

Q. And did you see them document your diagnosis of an anaphylactic reaction in her permanent record?

A. Yes.

Q. The first entry on the note card that is your office record includes the acronym PMH. Does that stand for prior medical history?

A. Yes.

Q. Then the entry next to that is a circle with an *A* in the middle and a diagonal line striking through it. What does that mean?

A. That she has no history of having been under anesthesia.

Q. Thank you for coming here today, Dr. Grad. I have no further questions.

There, that's done. All that's left is for me to escort one extremely upset young woman from the room to the elevator and out of the building.

Uh-oh. Who'd have imagined it? Here comes the Painless Dentist himself. Why isn't he conferencing with his attorney, as he should now be? Given he's such a nice fellow underneath all his incompetence, he shouldn't be stepping onto the elevator with Jessie and me.

The word "insensitive" comes to mind. I look away from him and up at the floor numbers, trying to decide whether he has the brains to avoid conversation at least.

Nope.

"Do you live in the city?" he asks me.

But I'm prepared. "Flumazenil," I reply as the doors open.

"Excuse me?"

"Flumazenil," I say again.

"Is that in Tribeca?" he asks.

"It's the reversal agent for midazolam."

10.

was proud of Jessie for not starting a cage fight in that elevator. It showed tremendous restraint. Would I have been able to do the same? I'm not sure. We parted ways just outside the building after only the briefest of recaps. I was okay with it. She's a young woman who has already had her fair share of family tragedy.

However, right now it's three days later, and I still haven't heard from her. In the ordinary way of things, I get a post-deposition call from clients usually within twenty-four hours.

Anyway, I have three tasks today: First, settle the *Scott* case. Then meet with Mick, my renegade expert. And finally to set off on Trace's Big Adventure. This last item though depends on whether I settle the *Scott* case. All or nada. I'll get to Trace later.

Now you may be wondering what the *Scott* case is. But, for the moment, the important fact to know here is I hate it.

Stopping for a coffee on my way upstairs, I'm just paying for it when my phone goes off. Jessie.

"Hi. I've been expecting this call from you," I tell her.

"I had to digest things. So how do you think Grad's depo went?"

"How do you think it went?"

"To me, it didn't sound right."

"I'm listening. So let me hear what you took away from it."

"No license, no monitoring machine—despite his lie—no log,

leaving the room, working on three patients at a time, not certified to perform CPR, no crash cart, no oxygen, no, what did you call them? Oh, yeah, revival agents—"

"Reversal agents," I help her out.

"Whatever. All of it just doesn't seem right."

"Want to know why?"

"Because it's not," she answers, beating me to the punch.

"Correct. A true malpractice case is like a slap in the face. And what you heard the other day was the sound of a giant *smack*. Your assessment nailed every act of malpractice this guy committed, except one—the major one—the one I'm going to use to settle the case when the time is right. I have to say, if he'd been in the room, he would've seen her slipping away, allergic reaction or not. And, if he'd had the reversal agent and given it to your sister as she started to slip, it would've saved her from the brain injury, left-sided paralysis, or any other injury we find out she sustained from this. It's criminal conduct. Nonetheless they'll pay an expert to say it was anaphylaxis and that reversal agents wouldn't have made a difference."

"Criminal?"

"Yes, criminal. Grad could be charged with a crime, in my opinion."

"So what do you think this case is worth?"

Gosh. I can't help thinking that here was a speedy shift. "Too soon to tell . . . but a *lot*."

"Okay, well, I've got to get to the gym and relieve some stress. Bye." Just like that, she's gone.

I realize I'm slowly shaking my head. Let's back up. I mean, I have to question why she didn't ask what the major malpractice I alluded to might be. I'm also not happy with her already focusing on the money.

Upstairs in my office I make that *Scott* settlement call. Less than a minute later, we're done. The adjuster offered twelve thousand dollars, saying it was a gift. She said, if I wanted a penny more, I'd have to give her copies of my client's medicals from his three prior lawsuits. That's because she admitted to a sneaking suspicion that my client, Mr. Scott, had claimed the same injuries to the same body parts in those other cases. I told her I was unaware of any priors—which is the truth—and that I'd speak to him.

I dial him up. "Mr. Scott?"

"Who's this?"

"Your lawyer."

"Yes, Mr. Lawyer Man. I spoke to Trace. He said you'd have some good news for me. My sue-money."

"Well, he was right. I got you twelve thousand."

"That ain't hardly enough. I thought you were good."

"I'm pretty good."

"Twelve K ain't pretty good. Shit, twelve K sucks."

"I know it may sound light, but it turns out the insurance adjuster knows all about your prior lawsuits. Which, I might add, you kept from me. Anyway, it's a big problem if you now claim injury to the same body parts as in those cases. So, did you?"

"Nah, man. Back then I hurt my knee and neck."

"Okay. But, in our case, you're claiming you hurt your knee and neck too."

"Really?" he asks, surprised.

"*Um*, yes, Mr. Scott, really. And you *really* ought to know what you injured, not to mention you should tell your lawyer about prior accidents and injuries when, as I did, he asks you this."

"I thought I did tell you." He clears his throat. Or is that a chuckle? "My bad."

"No problem. Listen, was it your right knee that you injured in your prior case or cases, as the case may be?" Pun intended.

"*Hmm*. Is it my right knee I'm claiming I injured here?"

"I got my answer. Listen, the insurance adjuster said she wouldn't pay a dime more unless we gave her your prior records. If we give her your prior medicals, she'll verify it was injury to the same body parts, and she'll pull the twelve thousand off the table. You don't want to shoot yourself in the foot by being greedy, do you?"

"Nah, man. Been shot in the foot before. That shit hurts."

"Good. I'll mark the case settled." *Click.*

I hate that my name is attached to this piece-of-shit case. But I had to take it because Mr. Scott is related to a close friend and business associate who I'll be calling in a minute. Handling a case like that isn't why I became a lawyer. In fact, it goes against the very grain of my legal existence. I'll definitely feel guilty taking a fee—but, I'm ashamed to say, not for long.

At least I admit it.

I dial Trace. Trace is the right-hand man and visible presence of a guy named the Fidge, a mysterious fellow who takes care of things around the hood. The hood would be Brooklyn, the Bronx, and certain sections of Queens and Manhattan. He's a community leader of sorts. Everybody seems to know of him but few have met him, except for the upper echelon of his peeps, as Trace likes to call them. These peeps, I might add, are a group of highly accomplished people. I met Trace when I was handling the matter of little Suzy Williams, another Benson referral.

After Suzy's case, Trace opened a storefront law office in the heart of Brooklyn with my name on the shingle. I've been there twice. He sends the walk-ins directly to my city office. My deal is, I take a reduced legal fee and donate the difference to some charitable organization the Fidge set up. I was a little leery at first but was presented with hard evidence that certain political figures in high places were listed as contributors.

"Trace," he answers in his deep commanding voice on ring two.

"*S'up*, Trace. It's me."

"*S'up* don't work. Stop trying. Good job today. Pick you up at eight."

"You spoke to Mr. Scott already?"

"Cousin. Black sheep. Eight."

"Okay, but I have a meeting before, out of the office. So can you pick me up there?"

"2-1-2?"

"Yes, downtown."

"Text me. Be curbside."

"I will. Do me a favor?"

"What?"

"Don't send me piece-of-shit cases like Scott again, cousin or no cousin. It's a matter of principle."

"Done." *Click.*

After spending the rest of the day doing law office housekeeping, I head down to Jingles Dance Bonanza to meet my medical expert and buddy, Dr. Mickey Mack. Or, more accurately, my pal Mickey Mack who no longer has a license to practice medicine. But it doesn't mean I can't use him as a sounding board and consultant. His medical expertise covers countless specialties, and he has a firm grasp on the medical-legal game, so his advice is always invaluable. He reads medical files with a Talmudic intensity, and it doesn't hurt that we meet in a gentlemen's club. One time in fact, I even picked up a new client, Cookie, at Jingles.

"Thanks for going over the *Simone* stuff I sent you. Now, is my adversary's defense legit? I mean, is it really possible that, during childbirth, Adora contracted herpes from her mother that ravaged her brain?"

"To answer your question, of course it's possible. Anything's possible. But is it more probable than not—what you lawyers call a preponderance—that's the question, no?"

"Yeah, yeah, good use of legal lingo. But go on, I'm listening."

"Well, I'll speak in generalities. This matter involves genital herpes, not oral. But you knew that already. Next, there are different contraction periods for the mother. 'Primary' would be a first encounter with the virus—but then there's 'long-standing' as well. These different periods bear on the mother's ability to produce antibodies to fight the virus, which is a consideration here. And, at last, we must also assess whether the mother was in an active outbreak during the pregnancy and at delivery."

He pauses. Which is a chance for me to head for the bottom

line. "The thing is, I got a brain-injured child, and the defendant is claiming the kid contracted herpes from her mother during childbirth, making it an existing virus which, as far as I'm aware, the mom was ignorant of. I believe her and so would you if you met her. What I want is for you to tell me the stuff I'm up against. Please. Because, if I were on the jury and heard testimony that Maria concealed herpes from her delivering doctors, together with the positive HSV tests, I'd toss them to the curb. That is, if this defense had medical merit."

"Okay, but I wasn't finished. The fetus can contract and be infected with neonatal herpes during gestational development from the virus crossing the placenta. Next, if the delivering physician uses fetal scalp-monitoring electrodes on the child's head to check the baby's heartbeat during childbirth, the tiny scalp punctures may serve as portals of entry for the herpes virus. Last, an active outbreak during delivery can also infect the child."

"Doesn't sound good for the good guys."

"Not true. That only speaks to the merits, meaning whether it can happen. But it's got weak legs, let us say."

"Keep going."

"First, there's a proof insufficiency for both parties to the lawsuit."

"Why's that?"

"We need to remember here that Maria's HSV test was done nearly eighteen years after Adora's delivery, so it's impossible to determine if it was a primary herpes infection, meaning her first encounter with the virus, or one that was long-standing as of the time of delivery."

"Keep going."

"As with most viruses, when the body encounters one, the natural response is to build up antibodies to fight it. So, if this was a first encounter during the pregnancy or birth, there was little defense because there wasn't enough time for Mom to build up the antibody immunity. But, even in that case, the statistical chances of the transmission are low."

"How low?"

"Very. I'd venture under 20 percent. And, if this was a long-standing virus, then there's less than a 1 percent chance for the child to have contracted herpes under any scenario because the antibodies circulating in the mother's blood protect the baby during pregnancy. In fact, the antibodies can even be transmitted to the infant through the placenta. Understand?"

"Here's what I think you're telling me. The bottom line is that we'll never know if, eighteen years ago, Maria had a primary outbreak of herpes during childbirth or whether it was long-standing because no one did an HSV test at that time which could provide us with this information."

"Correct."

"Okay. And I get the rest—primary versus long-standing. I'll just give the jury both scenarios and argue the unlikelihood of the event from a statistical point of view. But it still sucks."

"Why?"

"Because jurors prefer simplicity and lean toward the obvious. Both Maria and Adora have positive HSV tests, which translates into a verdict for the defense. That's simplicity. Plus one other factor goes against me."

"What's that?"

"Maria told me Joe, her husband, was the only man she'd ever had intercourse with. And that was just before she got pregnant, which puts us into the primary exposure category."

"Yes, but then there's still only a 20 percent chance of contraction."

"I understand. But jurors favor all or nothing. If Maria had it, then she gave it to Adora, despite the statistical improbability." I look at my watch, 8:00 p.m. "Listen, Mick, I'm sorry to pick your brain like this and run off, but I got to hop."

"Where to?"

"I have a job to pull tonight."

11.

walk outside, realizing I hadn't taken in any of the lovely sights Jingles has to offer. Waiting is a 1962 black Impala SS 409 bubbletop. My ride. The stainless steel curb feelers are an inch from the sidewalk's edge. The car, idling with a rip-roaring hum, is showroom immaculate, Armor All tire shine included. As I approach, the smoked-out driver's side window descends.

The man behind the wheel—a big black fellow—has a shaved head and dark plastic wraparound shades. I don't think I've ever seen Trace without them.

"In." He commands. The window rises. Just as I pass the midway point of the polished steel grill, he gives his baby some juice, causing me to spring back.

I get a bit jumpy when I'm about to commit a crime.

"Hold tight," Trace tells me, as I engage the buckle. Before I know what's happened, I'm thrown back from the g-force, looking to grab something as he does his signature peel out. We hit fifty, then come to a pinpoint stop for a red light three seconds later.

"I see the accelerator and brakes are working well."

"They work," he says, staying focused.

"So do we have a plan?"

"Stay close."

"Sounds like a good plan."

We arrive at the Kings Medical Center, the defendant hospital where Maria gave birth to Adora. Trace drives by the front entrance, slowlike, window down, and gives a nod at a young guy standing there. Which sets this fellow into motion and he enters the building. Trace now pulls a right, then another, then a third one, halfway down the block. At this point we're in a back lot where medical refuse is hauled away from the hospital.

"*Um*, Trace," I say, "is it really a good idea to park at the scene?"

In response, he opens his black leather jacket to reveal an automatic tucked into his jeans. He pulls it out, checks the clip, then tucks it back in.

"What's that for?" I ask nervously.

"The unknown." He's calm and collected.

"We're not robbing a bank, Trace. Leave that here!"

"Let's go."

"No."

"You want them records, right?"

"Right."

"Then come on now."

Shit.

I follow him. Closely. We enter from a delivery bay, walk down a ramp, and find ourselves in a dark basement. How he's able to see in here wearing those shades is a true mystery. I hear a metal sound I recognize as the noise of a fire door opening. We proceed into what appears to be the hospital laundry room.

"Yo, man," says some superskinny kid waiting here. He and Trace nod at each other. This new guy takes a step back and looks me over. "Who the fuck's this?"

"The lawyer."

"Yo, man, we don't need no lawyers around to witness the deed."

"Nah, man. On retainer. Privilege. Necessity."

"Oh, I got ya. Cool. Come on."

We head to the third floor, where our mission's set to begin. People stationed at a variety of checkpoints greet us. The next thing I know, we're standing in front of a glass door, which tells us that inside is the Medical Records Department. *Hours 9-5*, in case you're curious.

Mr. Yo Man now takes out a split ring with no less than twenty-five keys on it. Giving it a quick thumb through, he selects one, jabs it into the slot, and twists. Before entering, he looks down the hall to a figure at the last checkpoint where the intersecting corridors meet. Who happens to be looking the other way. So our companion funnels his hands around his mouth, then birdcalls *koo-koo! koo-koo!* The dude turns and calls back *ka-ka-ka! Ka-ka-ka!* Stealth moves.

We leave the exotic bird sanctuary and enter Medical Records after Yo Man assures us there's no video surveillance.

"What's the name?" he asks. Trace looks at me.

"Maria and Adora Simone."

"Come on, the *S*s are over here."

I spend the next five minutes thumbing through files. Nine medical records are labeled "Simon" but not one "Simone." I look through the Simon files one by one, thinking they may have left off the *E*. But, in the back of my mind, I know it's a futile effort. Their name was spelled correctly in my copy of the records.

"It's not here," I say.

"Yo, man, it's got to be here."

"Well, it's not." I look over at Trace.

"The case is in litigation, right?" our escort asks.

"Right," I answer.

"Then it's here."

"Well, it's an old chart, eighteen years ago."

"Don't matter. If it's in litigation, it's here. Hospital policy. At least until they finish the conversion to digital, that is."

"Do they keep records in any other place?"

"Nah, man, this is it," he says confidently, yet perplexed.

Then it comes to me. "Shit! It's in the Risk Management office."

"Oh, snap," he says. "That's possible. But we ain't set up for that."

"Then get set up," orders Trace.

"It ain't like that."

"Then make it like that." In response, he gives Trace a "Come-on, man" look, followed by an expression of "Don't make me do this." Trace stares at him.

"A'ight," he says, "wait here. I'll be back." The kid walks out, and I hear the birdcalls again.

"Trace," I say, "we can abort and come back when they're properly set up. In every movie I've ever seen, when the plan fails and they go for some spontaneous alternative, it always goes wrong."

"This ain't the movies."

As we wait, the quiet makes me more unsettled. I can feel tension building, anxiety. Maybe we should have hit the hospital pharmacy for some chill pills before doing this. Several minutes later our guy comes back.

"We good. Come on. But I got no idea if they got cameras in Risk Management." Now it's up to the tenth floor. "Stay close to me," our Sherpa from the hood warns. "The guard on this floor is one bad cracker. No offense," he adds with a grin.

The hall we're in is empty of just about everything, including exotic birds. As we walk, the sound of my own footsteps is the only noise. We arrive at an intersecting hallway, but, before making the turn, the kid instructs again, "Wait here." He disappears around the corner.

Trace looks down at me. "Next time wear sneakers."

"Next time?"

Our escort returns. "Follow me," he says.

Halfway down the hall we arrive at a door marked Risk Management. Now the key ring makes its second appearance. At try-number eleven, he looks up and explains, "It's got to be one of these, just was never in here before."

Three keys later, I hear the tumbler *click* of success.

"Listen, T," he says, looking relieved. "You on your own from here, too risky for me. The cracker's a hothead. Thinks he's some kind of sheriff. Shot three people when he was a cop, one for smiling. They kicked him off the force, and he landed here. He's called Timmy. Timmy the Terrible."

"We good," Trace responds. Our pal now walks away, after giving us instructions on how to leave or escape.

"Here, take this," Trace says, handing me a black stocking.

"What's this?"

"What's it look like?"

"A stocking mask?"

"Right."

"Really?"

"Put it on," he says. "No arguments. In case of security cameras."

As I comply, I'm dying to look in a mirror, then shake the thought as the seriousness of what we're about to do sets in. We enter to find the layout a large common area with eight separate flanking offices, four to our left and four to our right. File cabinets are everywhere.

Crap.

"Never gonna happen," he says, nodding to what we see.

"Never say never, T. First things first," I say. "See if the name 'Shelly' appears on any of the door nameplates on that side. I'll check this side. I remember the defense attorney mentioning her name."

He takes three steps, stops, and turns. "Here. Door number one."

It was meant to be. We enter.

Shelly's file drawers are alphabetized. I open the drawer marked *S-Z*, flip though a few folders to where it should be, and there it is. *Simone*. I take out the thick chart and go to the spot where I know the missing feeding notes should be and strike gold. The missing records—days two through seven—are exactly where they're supposed to be. *Fuck you, Chucky-boy*, I think. Or fuck this Shelly if she's the one who withheld them. Or fuck both of your conspiring asses. And speaking of asses—the tingle was right again.

"Trace, did you see a copy machine in here?"

"Affirmative."

After waiting five minutes—which seems like fifty—for it to warm up, I make copies. I would've simply snapped a shot with my phone, but I don't need self-incriminating digital evidence against me should things go wrong. On my way to replace the record, I take a yellow Post-it off Shelly's desk and write a little message for her, affixing it to page two of the "missing" records.

Before leaving, I give the place the once-over, making sure it looks undisturbed. Trace opens the door so we can make our get-away, and I walk out and stop. Trace closes the door behind him. Turns. And stops.

Standing in front of us is a large security officer with his gun drawn. It's aimed at us. His name tag—Timmy. Crap! The crazy cracker.

"Take off your masks." We do as told. He tosses his cuffs to Trace. "Your right wrist to his left."

"I don't do cuffs," Trace responds. Naturally this enrages Timmy the Terrible, making his red face redder. He keeps the fire-arm trained on us. Removing his walkie-talkie from his belt, then depressing the button, he reports in.

"I got a situation at Risk Management. Bringing two unauthorized mask-wearing men down to security." He reholsters. But only his communication device. "What are those papers in your hand?" he asks me, using the nose of his weapon as a pointer.

"Copies of medical records that this hospital pulled from my client's chart. Since they wouldn't give them to me, I had to come here and get them."

"You a lawyer?"

"Yes."

"You're breaking the law."

"Technically I'm not. You see, I provided a duly executed authorization, signed by my client for the release of these records and—"

"Shut your face. Give them to me." I step forward and hand him my unburied treasure. He turns to Trace. "Cuffs," he says, point-ing. Trace responds by tossing them back at Timmy the Terrible, who darts to his left, catching them, off balance, with his free hand two inches from the floor.

I instantaneously realize the following three things:

1. Trace's throw could have caused an unintentional discharge of a weapon pointed at my chest.
2. We just blew our only chance for a mad dash, having put Timmy off guard.
3. Timmy has high-level hand-eye coordination, important information under the circumstances.

"Let's go," Timmy instructs. "You two first." We walk to the freight elevator, and he takes us down to the basement. "Make a right," Timmy says as we get off. We approach a metal door that announces Hospital Security. About ten feet from our destination, Trace stops and turns around.

I do the same but with much less authority.

"We're going to leave now," Trace states. "We entered through the laundry back entrance, and that's where we're going to exit. But before we do, give him those papers back."

"I don't think so," Timmy responds, now raising his gun so it's pointed at Trace's face.

Trace takes a giant step forward, closing half the distance between them. That was ballsy. Timmy locks his jaw in response. Trace inches his hand to his belt line where his own weapon's waiting.

No fucking way. I'm not letting this go down. Before I have a chance to say anything, Timmy retargets the barrel of his gun—at my face.

"Take another step, big man," he says to Trace, "and I'll shoot his fucking head off."

It's time for me to make my contribution here. "Trace," I tell him, "don't take a fucking step! We're talking about some stupid medical records here. I don't sign on to die for my clients! Committed legal representation, yes. Death, no."

Trace looks at me. "It ain't about that now."

"Yes! It is! That's exactly what it's about. Chill-lax!"

"Nah, man, Mr. Barney Fucking Fife got into our business. That ain't acceptable. Violates certain codes I live by. Besides, he don't got it in him. He can't pull that trigger."

"What the fuck! What the fuck?" I scream out, in a high-pitched voice. "Don't fucking test him! It's a fucking lawsuit we're talking about here! I don't want to die for that!"

"It's a matter of principle," Trace responds. "He got into our business, and he ain't pulling that trigger."

"Principle?" I'm screeching now. "That's Timmy the Terrible! He can! And he has!"

"I'm stepping," Trace says, in a determined voice. "If he can't cuff, he can't shoot."

"Fuck man!" I scream, noting everything coming out of my mouth is falsetto. "Please, Trace, don't take that step!" I look to the hand holding the gun. It's getting ready to squeeze, moving the way a trigger finger does before applying pressure.

"I'm stepping," Trace responds. "Close your eyes if you're scared."

I look at him. He's as serious as serious can be. I can't believe it. I close my eyes, like the little sissy I now realize I am. Warm liquid trickles down my leg into my left shoe, reaffirming I hang left. I listen for the bang.

But instead what fills the air is a trio of laughter.

I open my eyes.

Trace has his hands on his knees, laughing so hard he can barely hold himself up. Timmy is holstering his gun, shaking his head the way people do when they just pulled one over on somebody. Next to them stands our young companion, pointing at my crotch and cackling like a hyena.

"Oh, man," Yo says, "you got him good, Trace."

12.

'm not looking forward to today. It's early in the morning, and I'm on my way to Maria's house to discuss the herpes issue. For the life of me, I cannot figure out what's going on here.

But, whatever it is, it's not good. By now she must know it was me who, in effect, brought it to her attention. And I was so unhinged by the boyz' little prank last night that I left the copies of the withheld medicals in Trace's car.

It would've been nice to review them before coming here. At least that way there'd have been good news along with the bad.

As I pull up, I see who must be Joe and Adora. They're getting into their car. I exit my vehicle and approach them.

Adora's confined to a wheelchair and looks like what a brain-injured baby looks like when eighteen years old. I know that might not sound right, but it is what it is. The truth though? I've never handled such a case where my client was older than six at the time of trial. Still I know what I know.

Her ankles are locked into the wheelchair's leg braces. She has minimal trunk control, and her neck thrashes back and forth. Her eyes are crossed, and drool seeps from the corner of her mouth. Her arms are bone thin, as are her legs. She can't weigh more than ninety pounds.

She looks like Maria, only in a severely disabled, retarded kind of way. And, of course, I know the word "retarded" is politically and socially unacceptable these days. I'm in the business, for Christ's sake. Still I'm pretty sure that's the word which comes to mind when people of my generation catch a glimpse of her.

At least I admit it.

Yet only to myself.

The one thing that sticks out about Adora, above all, is the smile plastered across her face. Like it's stuck there. I'm not sure it's a "real" smile, but, at least for Joe's and Maria's sake, Adora exists with the appearance of continual happiness.

Joe is a short, stocky guy with a full thick head of hair held perfectly in place with some shiny hair formula. You can tell by the worn look on his face he's been there and back again, several times. The strain on a parent raising a child like Adora is unimaginable, not to mention the effect it puts on the marriage.

I feel embarrassed pulling up in my fancy SUV, thinking today I should've driven my vintage Eldorado. I think Joe would've gotten a kick out of it.

"Hi," I say, "I'm—"

"I know who you are, the lawyer. Our new lawyer—until you dump us too. We never should've done this." I completely understand where those salty words are coming from.

He's busy picking up Adora, so I forego a handshake.

I watch his careful handling of her and observe his patience. When he turns to me, I begin again.

"Listen, Joe, I'm your lawyer to the end. And, as far as this undertaking is concerned, you did the right thing." He doesn't acknowledge me. He just keeps on getting his daughter ready, the way he's accustomed to. And, even though I said those words, I'm not really sure I believe them at this point. It may be easy for some of my colleagues but not me. Possibly Joe senses this.

"You need to think about Adora's future when it comes to this lawsuit, when you guys aren't around to take care of her. I know you understand that—and I know it must worry you."

Huh. When I said her name, Adora's smile widened. She defi-nitely knows her name.

"Yeah, well, but this is killing my wife," he says, as he shuts Adora's door and turns to me.

"I appreciate that."

"I don't think you get what I'm saying exactly."

"Go ahead, Joe. I'm listening."

"Look, I'm not a very sophisticated guy," he starts out. "But the way I see it, up until the time we met that lawyer, Maria took responsibility for what happened here. She was okay with that. She knew not every kid is born perfect, so we just accepted and dealt with it as best we could. Then this lawyer tells us that Adora's con-dition was caused by something the doctors did and that gave Maria an emotional break. She stopped punishing herself in the hopes this might be true."

He pauses. "Now suddenly you get involved, and she's become all torn up again. Worse than ever. Can hardly get her to talk or do anything. I don't know what's going on, but it ain't good. So tell me, . . . how long you want us to stay out for?"

"About an hour," I answer, grateful the conversation's ending here. He gets into his thirty-year-old Cadillac Fleetwood, where Adora's now settled. The well-kept car is humming, the same tune as my Eldo.

I give him the signal that I have one more thing to say.

"Yeah?" He leans out.

"Can you put down Adora's window for a sec?"

He looks back at her, then to me. "Sure."

She doesn't even twitch in response to the window going down. Not good. I scrunch my head in. "Hey, Adora," I say, causing her to turn my way. A quizzical look crosses her face. That's good.

"I'm your new lawyer," I say. "I can't make you better, but I can certainly make sure the hard road you've been on softens up."

She gives me a bigger smile. "Maybe only just a bit, but I know every little thing counts in the battle you and your parents are fighting. You understand me, little one?" Her smile again seems to widen.

I return to Joe's window. "She's pretty responsive, isn't she?"

"I suspect she knows more than people give her credit for. But the doctors say that ain't real."

I look back, then move to her window again.

"Adora." She inclines slightly toward me, and the smile appears bigger again.

Back at her father's window, I ask him, "You believe that's a real response, don't you?"

"I know it is."

"Me too." I step back.

He puts the car in Reverse, then suddenly stops and pulls forward with his window on its way down.

"Yes, Joe?"

"Thanks for coming out here. I appreciate your help. Things are just tough, you know?"

"Yeah, I know. Hang in there."

Time to deal with Maria.

I ring the bell. No response. I try again. Nothing. I lift the well-polished solid brass door knocker and try that now. Still nothing.

What's going on?

Suddenly the door slowly opens. Maria looks like a wreck. She says hello but so softly I can barely catch it. How I feel is like the bull in the china shop I already know I am. I follow her into the living room. Where to begin? I look around. It's a mess. She looks at me. Still silent . . . but expectant.

She's waiting for the ax to fall. I decide to play for time.

"*Um*, I see you're not using a cane today. That's great. I was meaning to ask, why do you have one?"

Without looking up, she answers, "I herniated a disc in my lower back carrying Adora up and down the stairs. She's just too heavy for me now. I need spine surgery to fix the problem—to take the pain away—but I don't have the time. It's a prolonged recovery."

So much for beating around the bush. Might as well get on with the necessary stuff. "What's going on here, Maria?"

"Don't you know?"

"Not really." But maybe. "You haven't returned any of my calls."

"You know. Why do you want me to say it?"

"The testing?"

"Yes, the testing. I have herpes." She breaks down crying, putting her head in her hands the way one does when ashamed.

There's nothing I can say, and I just don't feel comfortable consoling her with a forced embrace. So I'll wait it out.

Maria looks up and takes a deep breath. As she exhales, she pushes her hair to the side the way women do when they're gathering themselves. I watch her take another deep breath.

"So," she says, in a sad, defeated tone, "I guess we should drop the lawsuit."

"Not so fast. We have a lot to talk about."

"What's to talk about? I have herpes—which I never knew I had—and I gave it to Adora."

"We don't know that. That's just the defense allegation."

She looks at me as if I'm crazy. "Well, the doctor you sent me to said I have it! And what's curious is, Joe doesn't."

"I thought you didn't want him to know about any of this yet. Why'd he have to leave today?"

"He didn't, and he doesn't. I had our primary care doctor test him at his annual. He didn't even know. I explained the situation to Dr. Marks, and he said he'd do it, but, if it came back positive, that he'd have to tell Joe. He's negative."

"Interesting." I sit for a moment without saying anything, cupping my chin like Rodin's Thinker.

"I'm glad you find all this interesting."

"I'm sorry. I didn't mean it that way. But, wait a second, you told me Joe is the only man you've ever slept with."

"Yes. That's what I said."

"Well, did you question Dr. Marks or the doctor I sent you to as to how on earth you could've contracted genital herpes if Joe's negative?"

"I didn't have to."

Oh, boy. Here we go . . .

"Talk to me, Maria, I have your lawsuit to win here, and lack of knowledge is the enemy."

She breaks down crying again. But I'm not getting up. I know maybe I should at least attempt the comfort thing at this point, but I've got business to do, and this is a tough-love situation.

After a while she looks up. "I was raped."

Crap! This ain't gettin' better.

"Is that how you became pregnant with Adora?"

"No!" she screams. She stops for a moment. "Joe's her father. I was raped when I was eleven. That was the only other man who was ever inside me. And it was then I must've contracted herpes." She starts crying again, hard.

Time for an educational intervention.

"Listen, Maria, I highly doubt you gave Adora herpes of her brain. Do you hear me? It's extremely unlikely."

"Why?"

"Because the statistical chances of that occurring are near zero."

"Oh, please, save it," she says, the way one does when everything's over and defeat is all that looms ahead. "What's so hard to understand here? I was raped, got herpes, and gave it to my daughter. It's black-and-white, and this lawsuit has brought it to the surface. So why are you saying that?"

"Because, according to medical science, you only could've given it to her if you were having a first-time outbreak. That obviously was not the case if you'd contracted it when you were eleven. And, let me ask, have you ever had an outbreak?"

"No. Or at least not that I know of."

"That's probably because you had it when you were too young to know better, and, since then, your body has built up immunity to it. This long-standing immunity makes it near impossible for you to have given it to Adora insofar as it could be responsible for her brain injury."

"If all this is true, then why will they be throwing this at me?"

"They can say anything they want in way of a defense if they have a basis, along with a medical expert to back it up—and they do. Adora's birth records note she developed little pustules on her belly just after childbirth."

"I remember that," she says. "It was a red rash all around her stomach. But they told me it was nothing."

"And it was nothing, most likely little pink pimples, otherwise known as neonatal acne. But a first-year resident penned—in one entry, mind you—a question mark next to the word 'herpes' as a differential diagnosis. I'm sure Chucky-boy saw this, concocted the herpes theory as a cause for her brain injury, and then got lucky with his HSV testing."

"What do you mean his HSV testing?"

"The blood test they performed on you and Adora supported the defense and—"

"You mean, you knew I had it before you sent me for your test?"

"No, actually I didn't. That's the truth. Unfortunately our Mr. Cohen did not provide your entire file. But the point is, now that there's a lawsuit, they're trying to make something out of nothing."

"All this from a rash?"

"Yes, that's what I believe. Their whole legal defense is based on a harmless rash common to newborns. It wasn't even cultured because they knew it'd go away, just as it did. But, since no definitive pathologic diagnosis was ever attached to it, anyone can say it's anything as long as there is a medical basis. And their expert's claiming the rash was herpes pustules which Adora had contracted at delivery from her belly sliding across your birth canal. That's about it."

"That's about it?" she repeats. "It sounds like a lot to me."

"At this moment it's a defense that's grounded in medical science. At the same time it's with very little statistical chances of having occurred."

"So, if not herpes that caused Adora's brain injury, then what did?"

"I'm hoping to come up with that answer soon."

"Soon," she repeats sarcastically. "It's been eighteen years, and the trial is around the corner."

"Yes, I know."

13.

eading back from Maria's, my phone goes off as I pass Brooklyn Law School, my alma mater.

It's Lily. "*S'up?*" I say.

"That's a lawyerlike greeting. Listen, Nelly's on the line from the hospital. She wants your cell number to speak to you right now. I told her you were in conference with another client outside the office, but it sounds urgent."

"She has my number. I inputted it in her contacts. And wrote it on the back of the card I gave her and on the bottom of the poster of the Yankees' schedule for that matter."

"Do you want me to give it to her or not? I'm busy, and she's on the other line."

"Yes, please give it to her."

Click.

That was her *click*, not mine, as I had a question about our court calendar. My phone goes off again.

"Nelly?"

"Hey. Where are you?"

"Where am I? I just left a client's house in Brooklyn."

"Great. Come pick me up."

"What do you mean, come pick you up?"

"Which word didn't you understand?"

"I understood the words, just not the message."

"I hope you don't have this problem in court. I've been discharged."

"That's unbelievable. Congratulations. Can't Jessie make it?"

"Jessie flew down to South Beach with her boyfriend. She'll be there for a week. How soon can you get here?"

"I'd say a half hour."

"Good. Hurry up. I'm dressed and ready. Do you know anybody with Yankees' tickets?"

"Yeah, that's not a problem. But I'm surprised they're letting you out. I thought you had another week?"

"I did. But Furman cleared me on certain conditions."

"What are they?"

"I'll explain them when you get here. Hurry up. I can't wait to get out of this place."

"On my way." I pause, remembering something. "But, listen, weren't you saying not long ago that they were so nice there you wouldn't mind staying longer?"

"I never said that. What, are you crazy? I'm in a brain injury rehab ward. Hurry up." *Click.*

Making premature *click* number two.

I'm certain she'd said that the last time we discussed her proposed discharge. She may be experiencing short-term memory problems; the possibility doesn't make me exactly jump for joy—as she herself now seems to be—over this proposed discharge.

———

Nurse Rodriguez passes by as I exit the elevator. "You never cease to amaze me, Counselor," she says.

"*Uh*, thanks. What do you mean?"

"You know what I mean." She walks off, giving me a thumbs-up. As I make my way, a few more of the staff who I pass—the speech therapist, another nurse, and the physical therapist—all give me smiles too. I roll with it, puzzled, as I make my way to Furman, who's standing at the nurses' station.

"Good afternoon," I greet him. "I'm here because Nelly tells me you're discharging her. She sounded pretty thrilled at the news when we just talked."

"Couldn't do it without you."

"Don't you think you're giving me a little too much credit? I only helped when I could with the PT and OT. Really it's the work of your dedicated people who deserve all the credit and recognition."

He looks at me with interest. "Yes, of course. But if you hadn't volunteered to take her to your home, she'd have to stay here until her sister got back."

Dumbfounded, I play for time. What was going on here? My house? "What exactly did she say?"

"She said you agreed to all the terms."

Taking a deep breath, I say, "Just go over these terms for me. I want to make sure I have them all down." He shoots me a questioning look. Which, of course, is a close second cousin to disbelief.

Slowly he begins to pronounce the list of my upcoming responsibilities. "That you'd administer her medications in the morning, make sure she doesn't do anything too strenuous, have her keep up with her home therapy exercises and"—he pauses before finishing—"you'd not leave her unsupervised for too long a period of time."

What am I hearing here?

"Right. It's all coming back to me now." Am I more than a little irritated? "And you're sure she's good to go?" I ask with an incredible restraint that passes muster as careful concern.

"I do feel confident releasing her to you, most especially given the amount of time you've put in overseeing her progress."

I take another deep breath, then nod. "Oops," I say, glancing at my watch. "I just remembered a call I need to make. I'll be back in a sec."

I find the only place on the floor where I can make a private call without being busted by Nurse General—inside a large janitor's closet.

"What's the matter?" says my wife, picking up.

"Nothing."

"Then why are you calling me? You know I'm about to step onto the court."

"Yes, well, sorry about that. But it seems I'll be bringing home a house guest, and I wanted to let you know before I left the hospital with her."

"A house guest? From the hospital? Who? Why?"

"My client Nelly Rivera—"

"The girl who was overdosed by the dentist?"

"One and the same."

Just then the door opens. Crap!

"Hold on a sec, hon." I bring my phone down as she starts in on me.

"Wait!" Tyler yells. That's right: Tyler Wyler, my wife.

Meanwhile, who's at the door but good old delusional Ernie. "Hey, boss. What's up? I'm on a call."

"I didn't know this was a phone booth," he says, surprised. "I've been looking for one. You see, I left the store to make a deposit with Mr. Whipple at the bank and forgot to tell Maggie to watch the register."

"I gotcha, Ernie, buddy. But right now you need to let me finish this call. Then the booth's all yours, okay?"

"Seeing it's a cash register emergency, I need to make the call now." *Jesus.*

"Honey." I've returned to the phone. "Can you hold on for a second? A friend of mine needs to make a quick call."

"What on earth were you two talking about? Who's Ernie?"

"Humor me, honey. Please."

Silence.

"Hon? You still there?"

"I don't know what the hell is going on, but under no circumstances should you ever have one of your clients as our house guest. I can't think of anything more unprofessional."

"No disagreement there. But it's only for a week, and I don't have a choice."

"Sure you do. You're just making a bad one. I need to warm up." *Click.*

She's right again. But I'm past the point of no return.

After making sure Ernie's comfortable in the booth, I head back to Dr. Furman. At just this moment Nelly's walking up to him. She's wearing a Yankees' jersey with jeans and her low-top Converses. She looks hot. Hotter than Jessie, which I wasn't able to fully appreciate before now. Maybe I had a transient creepy-old-man crush on the wrong sister.

At least I admit it.

She's come a long way in her rehab from complete left-sided paralysis to weakness or hemiparesis. Her limp is hardly noticeable, with the left foot revealing only a bit of visible problem coming up and moving forward. The plant seems about right, but her push off goes out to the side. The paralysis of her left arm too has progressed considerably. Visually it droops ever-so-slightly from the shoulder, while missing about 50 percent of its preinjury strength across all muscle groups. But at least she can use it now. In fact, she is wheeling her overnight bag with her left hand.

What seems to have recovered best is her facial palsy. You can hardly notice her lips slant down on the left side, and the way she applied her lipstick with a tiny rise at the corner makes up for it.

That sums up her physical recovery. However, the degree of acquired weakness from her brain injury in the way she thinks, feels, and acts—cognitive, emotional, and behavioral—is still not fully known.

After Furman goes over her meds—stressing her antiseizure pill as the most important—we head for the elevator. Everybody on the floor, both staff and patient, is aware of her discharge and line the hallway, as if a parade were passing. I register to what extent she's familiar with the names of the folks bidding her good-bye. It seems to me one positive indicator in the matter of her occasionally problematic short-term memory.

But, wait a minute, here's Ernie. Nelly's face lights up.

"I remember," she says to him, "always keep your eye on the cash register."

He grins.

"You know," says Nelly softly to me, "Ernie caught his sister stealing money too."

I give her a quizzical look. "What do you mean by that?"

"Just that Jessie used to steal from my mom's wallet," she says in a confiding tone. "To buy cigarettes. Pot too." She pauses. "The fire wasn't electrical, despite what they say. And now she steals from me."

As I'm trying to take in this unexpected sharing—but then everything at the moment is unexpected—she returns to the present just as fast as she'd left it.

"What are we waiting for?" she demands. "Let's get out of here." Her mood is excited, cheerful.

"Do you mind waiting a few secs? I'll be right back . . ." I blurt out. Without waiting for a reply, I scoot into a room, politely borrow a chair, and set it in the hallway, leaving her seated. And impatient.

My brain's on overload. First I learn, to my total surprise, that I'm taking home a client. Against every bit of my better judgment, as well as against legal advice. Did I ever mention Tyler's a retired lawyer? But wait; next I learn sisterhood's not all it's cracked up to be. And what was that about the cause of the fire that killed her parents? Oh, yes, something other than apparently determined.

Furman sees me bearing down on him. "Is there anything wrong?" A reasonable question, I think.

"Listen," I say, "are you sure she's ready for discharge?"

"Pretty sure."

"Is that answer supposed to instill confidence in me?"

"No. But it was an honest one. What's troubling you?"

"She took on that gaze and started in on the fire thing again just now and how her sister poached money from her mom's wallet. I'm not trained to handle this shit, so I'm asking, . . . are you sure she's ready for discharge? To me?"

"No worries, I promise. She has a little confusion, a little relapsing into the event of the fire and into some stuff from her past. But keeping her here isn't going to change that. Over time we're hoping such mental digressions will fade. So listen to her but try not to engage. The human brain is both fragile and capricious. She's shown how resilient she is."

"Okay," I tell him.

But I'm not happy.

———

As we fight traffic on our way crosstown—with Nelly peering out the window—she suddenly breaks the silence we've been keeping.

"Pull over right here," she directs me.

"Where?"

"Over here . . . just double-park."

Okay. I figure this is when we'll have the chance for her to tell me what's up.

Instead she bolts from my SUV, like a six-year-old who just saw the ice cream man, leaving the door open.

"Hey, where're you going? I'm suppose to keep you under observation."

She stops. "I want a slice! Now. You can 'observe' me eating it when I get back in the car. Want one?"

I get it. She's OD'd on hospital food and now has to assert her independence from it.

"Here! Don't forget you need cash!" I remind her.

She laughs and takes a twenty from me. It's not as if I don't already have a daughter at home, not to mention two sons. For all us Wylers, pizza's a food group.

So here we are, munching our slices. For my part, I'm thinking about my family and what their reaction will be to meeting one of my injury clients for the first time. Most particularly on my mind is my highly advance-notice-preferring wife, who's already weighed in on this completely awkward situation.

"On the topic of food," I say, breaking what turned into pizza-eating silence, "what's your favorite home-cooked meal? I'll ask my wife if she can whip it up for dinner to celebrate your discharge."

"What do you mean? I'm not going to your home. I'm going to my apartment."

"But Jessie's in Florida," I remind her.

"Yes, and that's exactly why I'm going there. I'm moving out while she's gone."

"Listen carefully," I now say. "I'm responsible for you until she comes back. That's what I told Furman, and that's how it's going to be. From my office, we can swing by your apartment to pick up any necessaries you need, but you're coming to my house, end of story."

She thinks about this and isn't happy. I watch her as she chews her lip, pondering. "Will I have my own room?"

"Yes, the guest room."

"What will I do all day?"

"If my wife can't watch you—and she has a full schedule with her tennis, yoga, personal trainer, aerobics class, mah-jongg, Candy Crush addictions—did I say tennis?"

"I don't remember. I have short-term memory loss."

"Really? You didn't remember I just said—"

"Tennis." Her tone is teasing.

"Yes, tennis. But don't do that," I warn.

"Do what?"

"Mess with me."

"Mess with you how?"

"Stop that, Nelly. I mean it."

"Stop what?"

"Stop pretending you can't follow our conversation."

"Follow it where?"

I give her an exhausted look.

"Okay, I was just kidding around." She laughs. "I've been cooped up for a long time, is all."

"Thank you," I say. But my relief is short-lived.

"For what?" she wants to know.

"Nelly! Please!"

"Gosh, just kidding. Give me a break, okay?"

"Well, I've represented a great many TBI survivors, and what you just were doing, being cute, can actually signal problems. So I need to keep what's fact and what's fiction clear enough to be able to assess your progress. Is that *clear enough?*"

"Over and out," she shoots back.

WB, RGD, and SKT

In my regular parking lot, Oscar the attendant gives Nelly an interested look as we exit the vehicle.

"What's up?" I ask him.

He only grins. No point in explaining. Let his fantasies go where they may. More fun for both of us.

As we make our way to my office, Nelly's lack of stamina becomes increasingly obvious. Then, when I hold open the door and she steps in, she sniffs. Loudly.

"What's up?" I inquire, knowing what stimulated her olfactory nerve.

"It smells like pot in here," she tells me.

"I don't know what you're talking about."

"Yes, you do." She giggles. From being her lawyer and protector, I've morphed into a walking punch line. And it's not a transition I'm enjoying.

Just then a fellow—all right, a fairly obvious dealer type—walks out of the door from my inner office.

"Want to explain?" she asks. He passes us as if we're not here.

"Not really. Let's just say, I have a colorful subtenant."

The next order of business is to introduce Lily. Although uttering her name doesn't guarantee I'll get her attention, I make the attempt and somehow succeed. "You need to know," I tell her, "that, as of right now, I'm Nelly's unofficial temporary—which is another way of saying, interim—guardian. That means she'll possibly be coming into the office with me until Jessie returns from Florida." I pause. "So I'd like you to do your best to adjourn any court appearances I have during this period. Understood?"

"Yes, sir," she says—mockingly of course. The two females share a laugh. I can see this is going to be fun—not for me—for them. "Oh," Lily adds, turning back to me, "Trace dropped off those feeding notes you'd left in his car. I put them on your chair."

"Thanks. Come on, Nelly. It's time to play lawyer." She follows me into my office.

"What are those?" she asks, referring to the feeding notes my gaze is fixed on.

"Medical records for a case—or actually a handful of missing records."

"What do you mean 'missing'?"

"They were pulled from the chart by the people who were sued so I wouldn't know about their existence. Sneaky, huh?"

"Jessie's a sneak" is the reply she chooses to make.

Shit. For a guy like me—a licensed member of the inquisition business—the most natural thing in the world for me to do now would be to ask what exactly that means. But Furman warned against such engagement. Therefore, I'll resist in the interest of Nelly's mental health.

"*Um*, okay."

"You always have to watch out for her. She'll stab you in the back."

"Here's what I think, Nelly. Right now I'd rather not talk about this."

"Okay, but y-you said she's my guardian. What I'm wondering is, who's going to g-guard me against her?"

It's a reasonable question. Yet any context is definitely missing. And I'm not going to let her bait me.

Instead I read the missing medicals while she sits in the guest chair on the other side of my desk. The first page is labeled Infant

Feeding Notes and is identical to what I already have. It's the single feeding entry for postpartum day one. I turn the page, going to the next note, which constitutes the first entry of what was withheld.

In felt marker print it reads:

> WB, infant took six ounces of formula, sucking reflex
> healthy. RGD three ounces, SKT.

"What are you reading?" Nelly interrupts.

I lower the papers again.

"Medical records, I just told you that." She shakes her head. As if she doesn't remember my telling her that less than a minute ago. This time she's not being playful.

"*My* records?"

"No, not yours."

The trouble is, I really do need—no, *want*—to give my full attention to these feeding records. Nelly, to her credit, senses this and subsides temporarily. Besides which, more than ever, she's running out of steam.

The three other feedings penned by the night-shift nurse for postpartum day two read the same way—verbatim—with the WB, RGD, and SKT acronyms. I do a Google search for them but can't find medical words or phrases out there on the digital superhighway that reveal what they mean. I sigh.

I look across my desk, and Nelly's nodding off. We need to leave soon. But only after I reread what I have here, through postpartum day seven. What I can tell is that the handwriting for postpartum days one through six are from two different nurses—a day-shift nurse and a night-shift one. The entries of the former are all similar. They read basically: baby fed, observed, and attended. The night-shift nurse offers near identical observations, all neatly printed in marker. Each starts with WB, indicates in ounces how much formula Adora took, then offers up those two other mysterious acronyms, RGD and SKT.

However, the handwriting of the nurse who made the one and only entry for postpartum day seven is different. This sole entry is the last note in the Infants Feeding Notes before Adora was transferred to the neonatal ICU from the premature baby nursery.

It reads:

> Child fed and resting comfortably. Child found in crib, blue, cyanotic, and not breathing. Code called. See code record for details.

Hmm. I look up, and Nelly's rubbing her eyes.

"We'll be leaving soon," I say. "I promise. I only need to think a bit more. Okay?"

"Okay. But don't forget I've got to pick up my stuff."

"I won't."

"And I need to change out of these clothes."

"Fine."

"And take a shower."

"You can take a shower when we get to my house." She nods.

On the drive home—after stopping by the girls' apartment on 138th Street—Nelly's pretty much zoned out next to me. And it's a good thing.

She's had a long day.

Me, I'm still focused on what I've just read and reread.

What the heck does WB, SKT, and RGD stand for?"

14.

When Nelly and I arrive at my home, my kids are playing basketball in the driveway: Brooks, age ten; Connor, age nine; and Penelope, who's seven. They're seventeen months apart, which just happens to be my suggested way to space three children.

Anyway I had Tyler prep the kids not to ask Nelly about her case.

I park, and Otis, our large Labradoodle, bounds over to greet us. He's all wags. Tucker, his younger, goofy Goldendoodle playmate, is right behind him.

"Oh, my god, a puppy!" Nelly bends down to let Tucker lick her. He's happy to oblige.

As Connor and Penelope run up, I can see they're making a race out of it, as usual. Close-in-age kids can share a higher level of competition and rivalry, and that's the way it is with these two.

"I win!" Penelope declares.

"No! You had a head start!" Connor retorts.

"No!"

"Let's stop it right there, guys," I tell them. Surprisingly they do.

"Look, Dad," Penelope says, "Tucker really likes her." I turn. He's humping Nelly's thigh.

"Down, Tucker!" I command. "That's no way to greet a house guest."

"It's okay," Nelly says. "I love dogs."

"I think he loves you too," Brooks, my eldest, quips.

"Nelly, these are my children"—I look around, as if for other candidates—"I think."

"Dad!" Penelope protests. "You know we're your children!"

"Just kidding. Anyway, Brooks, Connor, and Penelope." I point in turn.

"Great to meet you. I love basketball. Can I play?"

"Yeah, yeah!" they cheer as Penelope grabs Nelly's hand, pulling her toward the hoop.

"No, guys! That's not happening. Nelly knows better."

"Is that because she hurt her brain?" Penelope asks. So much for their mom's briefing session.

"You weren't supposed to say anything," Connor reprimands her.

"Yes. That's exactly why," Nelly casually answers. "But I can play a quick game of Around the World." She looks to me, as do the kids.

"Not happening!"

"What's that blue stuff?" Penelope asks, pointing to the fabric over Nelly's jeans zipper.

"Not sure," Nelly responds.

"It looks cool. I like it."

"Yeah. Me too."

"Jessie was wearing the same brand of jeans the day I met her," I add.

"These *are* Jessie's."

"Well, it's nice that you guys share."

"Share?" is her sarcastic response. "Jessie's not a good sharer. I asked to borrow them the day we went to Grad's and was met with a firm no. That she was going to wear them. And I'd told her not to buy them in the first place. They're too expensive. But since she didn't take them with her to Florida, they're fair game."

I nod.

Avoidance is the best policy here.

A while later we find ourselves at the dinner table.

"Dad?" Connor begins.

"Yeah, son."

"Does Nelly have a good case?"

Here's the thing about Connor: When I put him to bed, he likes to hear about the case I'm on. Though I edit anything I tell him for the sake of his nine-year-old consumption, still his comments can be surprisingly acute.

"Connor, you just reprimanded your sister for asking an out-of-line question. Nelly's here to get some rest and relaxation."

"Okay, Daddy, but what happened to her?"

"I was in a fire," Nelly responds. My wife, knowing otherwise, shoots me a confused look. Nelly notices it and says, "Oh, I'm sorry. That was something else. What happened now is that I was in the hospital for a long time after a dentist gave me bad care."

This seems like progress to me. It's the first time she's caught herself confusing the two events.

"Pass the ketchup, please," I say to Connor, determined to change the subject. Thankfully I successfully do.

After telling the kids good-night, I check on Nelly, knocking softly so the dogs don't go crazy downstairs.

"Come in." She's lying on her side in the fetal position, arms wrapped around her knees, pressing them against her chest.

"Everything okay?"

"Does this house have a fire alarm?" I can see her face is tight. Her expression is anxious, voice strained.

"Detectors. You'll be fine. Get some sleep."

"She did it, you know," she murmurs.

"She did what?" *Oops.* I had my orders from Furman. Too late.

She yawns. Then seems to relax a bit. She's saying something, but I need to lean closer. "If she knew I knew, she'd be angry" is what I hear.

She's closing her eyes. "I could never tell her, . . . and you can't tell her."

"I won't. I promise." I turn off the light as I walk out the door. I'm pretty concerned here but don't really feel sure what to do. I've never had a situation like this before.

"Good night, Nelly."

"Night," she replies.

Once in the sanctuary of my den I stretch out in my recliner and open my MacBook. I enter *Rivera*—the sisters' last name—and *fire* into Google. It's time for me to learn more about this fire.

Five million five hundred twenty thousand search results pop up. But, when I scan through the first ten pages, there's nothing close. So I refine my next search by adding the word "house" before the word "fire."

Eight hundred forty-seven thousand search results this time—much better. Let's see: **Man and Dog Displaced after House Fire**. *No.* The **Rivera House Nursing Home** has zero as the total number of fire safety deficiencies. *No.* **Mount Armonk Resident, Jane Rivera, also Known as J.T., Faces Charges after House Fire**. *No.*

But I'm getting warmer.

I now add the word "Yonkers," the town in lower Westchester County, New York, where the girls were raised after leaving the Bronx. Hey, here it is. An article from the Yonkers *Daily Herald*. It's titled "Orphaned by House Fire." The article reads:

Tragedy strikes two local sisters, Nelly and Jessie Rivera, ages sixteen and eighteen, respectively, whose father Roberto, age sixty-two, died in a house fire, along with Nelly's mother, Stella, age fifty-four, who was married to Roberto.

The blaze started in the master bedroom on the second floor of the house and quickly burned through to the downstairs where the girls slept. The Yonkers Fire Department arrived on the scene to find the elder sister, Jessie, a high school senior, semiconscious just outside the front door of the house.

A heroic act by fireman Stevie Ledbetter saved the life of Nelly Rivera, found not breathing under her bed, overcome by smoke inhalation. She is in serious but stable condition at St. John's Mercy Hospital. "Nelly's lucky to be alive," said Ledbetter.

Roberto Rivera was at home in Yonkers on bail, pending trial for the attempted murder of a Queens man. His attorney, Henry Benson, persuaded the court to release Rivera on bail, citing his wife, Stella Rivera, was suffering from terminal cancer.

Not only was Roberto her primary caregiver, Benson explained, but Roberto also had been taking care of Jessie and Nelly, owing to his wife's advanced illness. Benson further argued that Mr. Rivera was not a flight risk, given the gravity of his family's situation.

Jessie is captain of the debate team and runs the school's Young Business club. Nelly, a sophomore, is the starting point guard on the varsity basketball team.

Police Chief John Dickson reports the cause of the fire has not been conclusively determined, but the fire department states they believed it to be electrical in nature.

15.

s I ready myself to leave after an unusually uneventful day at the office—though still second-guessing having left Nelly in Tyler's charge—I get the call I've been expecting.

It's my pal, Chucky-boy. I'm certain he has a new beef.

"Charles, how's it going? Did you get the Notice to Admit and the Discovery and Inspection demands I served on you?" I, of course, know he did, since it has prompted this call.

The "notice" asked Charles to "admit" that the Infant Feeding Notes for postpartum days two through seven that I enclosed are true and accurate copies of Defendant's original hospital record. The D&I asked that Charles identify the names of the three nurses whose signatures appear therein.

"Where'd you get those records from?" he demands to know without any preliminaries.

"That would be privileged under the guise of attorney work product, Chucky-boy. You know that."

"Don't call me Chucky-boy, Counselor."

"Well, you said I could call you Chuck."

"I take that back. Privilege has nothing to do with these hospital records."

You wouldn't be wrong if you said he sounded extremely upset.

"Now where did you get them?" he repeats.

"Work product, bro. Can you say 'work product' ten times fast?"

"Listen, I have a mind to call the police. Shelly, the hospital's risk manager, tells me the originals were tampered with. You wouldn't know anything about that, would you?"

"Why, of course not, Charles. Do you understand the implications of what you're saying?"

"I sure do. Do you?"

"Why don't you tell me why Shelly feels they were tampered with?"

"A note."

"A note?" I pause. "You mean someone broke in and left a note. Not too smart. What kind of note?"

"Well, a Post-it actually. Left on the file."

"Interesting. What did it say?"

"'Game on.' Now what do you know about this?"

"Not a thing, Charles."

"Then it looks as if what I need to do is get those two words analyzed by a handwriting expert against your signature. Who'd be laughing then, Counselor?"

Time to get serious.

"Do whatever you want, Charles. You're the one with dirty hands. Just answer my Notice to Admit and the D&I. That's all I care about. Then we'll be square."

A moment of quiet follows. "Well, I admit those are the records that we were both missing, and I emphasize the word *both*."

"Fine. And what else?" I ask.

"As far as those nurses are concerned, one's dead, one still works there, and we're unable to identify the signature of the last, the nurse who found the girl not breathing."

"Well, keep asking your people until you find out who she is."

"It happened eighteen years ago. Nobody's around other than the people I've already spoken to who might identify a signature from that long ago. Which is perfectly understandable."

"Well, keep trying, Charles. That's all, keep trying. Now, are you going to voluntarily produce the nurse, the one who still works there, for oral deposition?"

"If I didn't, you'd make a motion to compel it, right?"

"Right."

"That's what I thought. I already spoke to her. She was the evening-shift nurse and doesn't remember a thing from that long ago. Still, you're more than welcome to waste your time asking her questions."

"Great. I'll have my paralegal, Lily, set it up."

"No need. Given our impending trial, I can have her in the day after tomorrow if your schedule permits."

"It permits. Bye, Chucky-boy."

"Don't call me—"

Click.

I'm Caught in the Middle Here

"She went into one of those trances" is how my wife greets me.

"You didn't entertain it, did you?"

She looks at me. Unrepentant. Nothing new here.

"I told you her doctor advised me not to."

"Well, he didn't tell me."

I'm not going to win this battle. "So what did she say?" I'm obliged to ask.

"Nelly said she knows how the fire that killed her parents was started."

"Really? Well?"

"She couldn't remember."

"I don't get it."

"It's odd. She's sure she knows how the fire started. The problem is, she can't remember what she knows."

"You mean, like, it's in the vault?"

"Yeah, like that. But gradually more comes back to her, so she gets better able to distinguish between the two events."

At that moment I hear Nelly at the top of the stairs.

"Honey," I whisper. "Please don't experiment with my client anymore. I appreciate your interest and your concern, but a lot of stuff is going on."

She interrupts me, hissing back, "Did you know Jessie's mother stabbed some guy and went to prison for murder?"

My eyebrows shoot up as my wife—having had the last word again—heads toward the sink as Nelly comes down the last step.

Benson had told me it was involuntary manslaughter, the difference between that and murder being that the death occurs unintentionally.

But, as I greet Nelly to ask about her day, my phone goes off. It's Jessie. Excellent. I've left five messages for her since Nelly was discharged, without a return call until now.

"It's your sister," I say.

Nelly shakes her head.

"Hey, Jessie," I answer. "How's Florida?"

"Is she with you?" Her tone is hostile.

"Why, yes, Nelly's here. What do you mean?"

"What do you mean, 'what do I mean?' How was I supposed to know? I just called the hospital, and they told me she'd been discharged into your custody yesterday. Don't you think you should've consulted me on the matter? I'm her court-appointed guardian. But I guess you know that already because you appointed me."

"Just hold on there, Jessie." I realize I sound defensive. "Nelly told me she spoke to you about this before discharge, and you okayed it." I glance across at Nelly, who quickly turns and looks out the kitchen window.

Crap!

"She never spoke to me, and I had no idea. Why didn't you call me?"

"Well, I did."

"Before she was discharged?"

"Well, no. But, like I said, she told me she'd talked to you and obtained your consent."

"We're talking about my brain-damaged sister who slips into the past, confusing it with the present, right?"

"Yeah, well, she's getting better with that and—"

"Look," she says, cutting me off, "this is a little too loose for me. It's okay that she's with you because it got her out of there sooner. I understand that. But she's my sister, and I'm responsible for her, so I don't want anything like this to happen again. Okay?"

"Yes, Jessie," I say thinking when was the last time I'd been reamed by a twenty-year-old.

"Good. Now tell me, what do you mean, she's getting better with her confusion." I now stroll from the kitchen and into my den, closing the door.

"It's seems she's growing more aware of the distinction between the two events."

"Is that it?"

"Basically." I hesitate. "It's just that she's told my wife that Juanita stabbed and killed someone."

"She did. But it happened during a mugging. My mom wrestled the knife from the guy's hand, they fell to the ground, and he landed on it."

"Did she go to jail for that?" I ask, though I know the answer.

"Yes. But she was given reduced time for mitigating circumstances, which were further reduced for good behavior. I was just a kid." She now reverts to her agenda. "Listen to me, what I want to know is if you called Dr. Furman and told him what's going on with her?"

"No." And I recognize it's a reasonable question.

"Well, don't you think you should? Maybe she belongs back in the hospital."

"You're right. But I did speak to him at discharge about this, and my wife just told me what I reported to you only fifteen minutes ago. I plan on calling Furman. Believe me, I'm sorry for the poor communication about her release."

"You were wrong to trust Nelly. It's crazy to believe she's fully herself again, fully recovered."

"You're right," I say again. I'm caught in the middle here, in the wrong for trying to do something nice, and I'm not liking it. Circumstances have brought me closer to Nelly, yet legal authority resides with Jessie.

"Please don't let my tone throw you off. I really appreciate what you're doing for me and my sister, *really*. I'll be back in town soon."

"Would you like to talk to her?" I ask.

"Not this minute. I've got to run. I'll call tomorrow."

"Okay, that's good. Bye."

"Bye."

When I open the door of the den, standing there waiting for me is Nelly. Oh, man. Her expression's hard to read.

"What's wrong?" I ask.

"I told you. I'm scared of her."

16.

W hat's up, Henry?" I'm once again walking into Chucky-boy's building. My phone rings, and it's Benson.

"Are you crazy, man, taking Nelly home with you?"

"*Um,* no. I don't see what the big deal is. Either that or leave her in the hospital for another week or more—depending upon when Jessie feels like coming back from Florida."

"Well, I just spoke to Jessie, and she didn't seem too keen on it."

"Is that what she said?"

"No. She didn't have to. I know her well enough, and she's not happy."

"Listen, I didn't see any harm in it. Besides, Nelly led me to believe that she'd gotten Jessie's consent before we left the hospital."

"She's a clever one, that Nelly. Always was. I guess there's no real harm." *Click.* And, just like that, he's gone.

"Hi, Charlie's mom," I say, upon entering. "Is the witness here?"

"Yes," she says, annoyed. "Charles is in conference with her."

"So he's telling her what to say which he believes will help win his case?"

"Yes. . . . I mean, no. . . . I mean, he's speaking with her."

Minutes later I enter the windowless conference room where Judy Lambert, the nurse I'm here to depose, is seated on the other side of the table. Sam, my court reporter, is seated, ready to go.

"Hi," I say to him. He nods back. I have two goals for this deposition: one involves a state of physical health, the other an identity. So keep that in mind now.

> Q. Good morning. I'll try to be direct and to the point. Did you review anything prior to coming here to give your testimony?
>
> A. Yes, my entries in the hospital record.
>
> Q. Which entries would those be?
>
> A. I was on the night shift in the premature neonatal nursery.
>
> Q. Among other responsibilities, were you responsible for the nutritional well-being of the baby Adora Simone during your shift?
>
> A. Yes.
>
> Q. And, to that end, did you make entries in the Infant Feeding Notes?
>
> A. Yes.
>
> Q. For what days?
>
> A. Postpartum days one through six.
>
> Q. Why didn't you feed this child on postpartum day seven?
>
> A. Because that was my day off. That was the day off of the day-shift nurse too. We went six straight days.
>
> Q. I see. I've gone through your notes for each feeding and find them to be nearly identical. Am I correct about that?

A.   Pretty much so.

Q.   Did you mean the same thing every time you used the same words or letters?

A.   Yes.

Q.   What did you mean when you wrote the letters *WB*?

A.   That stands for "well baby."

Q.   Are the letters *WB* known as a standard and accepted medical acronym in the nursing community? Because I couldn't find it on a Google search if it is.

A.   I'm not sure.

Q.   What do you mean, you're not sure?

A.   I may have made that one up.

Q.   Do you make up medical acronyms often?

A.   Not anymore.

Q.   What do you mean by that?

A.   Well, I had a habit of making up my own abbreviations, but administration called me in and told me it was unacceptable. They said that some of the other nurses were unable to understand what my letters meant and to stop doing it, so I did. Stop, that is.

Q.   So, at the time you took care of Adora, you were still in the habit of making up your own medical acronyms?

A.   Yes, that's correct.

Q.   That was very creative of you.

A. I thought so.

Q. Can you define for me what you meant when you documented *WB* in Adora's chart, which we now know stands for "well baby"?

A. Yes. The infant, for the days I was involved in her care, had a normal sucking reflex, normal appetite, was normal physically, had a strong cry, and was thriving. I just meant that she was well in every regard.

Q. What did you mean when you wrote "child fed"?

A. You're kidding me, right?

Q. I kid you not. Even though it may seem like a silly and obvious question, I have to ask it on the record. Just bear with me, will you?

A. Okay. "Child fed" meant that the baby was fed, that she took her bottle.

Q. What did you mean when you wrote the letters *RGD*?

A. That stands for "regurgitated." That was one of my favorites. Don't you think they should have a short form for that word?

Q. Yes, I do actually. What did you mean when you wrote *RGD*, which we now know stands for "regurgitated"?

A. Just that she threw up.

Q. What did you mean when you wrote the letters *SKT*?

A.   That was another one of my abbreviations. It stands for "suctioned." After she vomited, I used a little device to suction out the vomitus.

Q.   At all moments when you were involved with this infant's care, was she anything but a normal, well baby?

A.   She was always fine.

Q.   And what was the nurse-to-infant ratio in the preemie nursery?

A.   It was one nurse for every two infants—the two infants being placed next to each other.

Q.   And what was the observation criteria in that nursery?

A.   Constant observation.

Q.   Define, please.

A.   That the two infants to which you're assigned should be watched at all times.

Q.   I'd like to turn your attention to the only feeding note for postpartum day seven that was documented prior to the child being transferred to the neonatal ICU from the preemie nursery. Are you familiar with that note?

A.   Yes. I saw it when I was reviewing my notes. That's not my note. Like I said, that was my day off. And it was made by a day-shift nurse anyway.

Q.   I understand. All I want to know is whether you can identify that signature?

A.   Yes, that was Nurse Lucas.

Q.   First name?

A.   It began with an *M*. Monica, I believe. I'm not sure. It was a long time ago.

Q.   Did you ever speak to Nurse Lucas about her entry?

A.   No, I wanted to, but I didn't.

Q.   Why did you want to?

A.   Because the child was healthy, then all of a sudden she wasn't breathing.

Q.   Why didn't you speak to her then?

A.   I never saw her again.

Q.   Do you have any independent recollection of this child? Meaning, in your mind's eye, can you recall the time you spent with Adora?

A.   No. But I remember coming back after my day off and the child being in the neonatal ICU and Monica being gone.

Q.   Thank you for coming here. I have no further questions.

"Come on. I'll walk you out," Chucky-boy casually says to me.

His mother sits at the front desk, writing notes on what look to be birthday cards.

"Good to see you again, Mrs. Lawless," I say politely. She looks at me suspiciously.

"Mom," Chucky begins. But, sensing a reprimand, she gives her son a suspicious look too.

"I told you I didn't want you doing personal stuff in the office."

"Please, I'm your mother. You don't tell me what to do."

He looks at me and shrugs, then opens the door for me. But instead of walking out, I turn to him.

"Yes, Counselor?" he asks.

"Charles, something obviously happened to Adora on day seven because she was perfectly fine until just after that feeding."

"I have two words in response."

"And they are?"

"Incubation period."

"Incubation period," I repeat. The question mark here is implicit.

"Yeah, incubation period. Seven to ten days is the incubation time for herpes to seed and destroy a newborn's brain. Search the Internet. I'm confident our jury will, despite judicial instruction otherwise. Again I don't know why you're involved in this case. It's a no-pay, and that will never change. Both mother and child are positive for the herpes antibodies."

"Yes, duly noted. But that doesn't mean Adora has herpes of her brain contracted from her mother during childbirth."

"Then how did she get positive?"

"It was passed to her from her mother—the antibodies, I mean. It's very normal for the mother to pass on this protective antibody in utero. That doesn't mean the child ever had an active outbreak of herpes—or herpes of the brain, for that matter."

"My experts are of a different opinion." He gives me a confident look. *This is in the bag* is the message.

"Well, you know that note written on day seven by Nurse Lucas, the last one before transfer to the ICU where it reads 'child found in crib'? You know, where Adora was found blue in color and not breathing?"

"Yes."

"Well, if the observation in that nursery is constant, then why would the baby be 'found'?"

17.

elly ended up staying at our home for only four days. Jessie did the right thing and cut her trip short. That was several months ago. And so the patient's been back with Jessie—reluctantly I might add—ever since.

Unfortunately Nelly's fears and concerns about Jessie continue and are growing worse. Dr. Furman has explained that paranoia involving a loved one is commonly seen with Nelly's kind of injury. He noted Nelly's recent brain MRI showed encephalomalacia—brain shrinkage from tissue death—in her frontal lobes. These govern personality.

Given the MRI findings, Nelly was administered a battery of neuropsychological testing to help define her acquired weaknesses and preserved strengths. They revealed limitations related to decision-making and, regarding memory, with dissociation and misconceptions. The results were, however, strong when it came to planning, problem solving, and other cognitive functions.

Anyway, to settle her nerves about Jessie, I told Nelly she could use her medical alert device—necessary for her, owing to risk of seizure—to reach me in an emergency. It's a pendant she wears around her neck, and she's jazzed it up to look less functional and more fashionable. It's decorated with cubic zirconia studs, and a sterling chain has replaced the fabric strap. Neither

Jessie nor anyone else can tell it's anything other than a piece of bulky jewelry, because that's the way Nelly wants it. And I gave the monitoring company special instructions to call me first in case of emergency so I can be aware of the situation—medical, Jessie-related, or otherwise.

As for her flashbacks, Nelly claims these visions of her repressed past have just about stopped occurring. They only surface, she says, when there's a trigger. However, I'm not sure I believe her. I think she's putting her own slant out there, to avoid judgment. When we met yesterday to prep for her deposition this morning, it appeared to me she briefly zoned off to that place. But she quickly denied it. The implication being, she's now fully conscious of the lapses.

Anyway, I've long since stopped talking to Jessie about this issue because most of these turn out to reference her, Jessie, in a very negative way. Whether these perceptions are based on any truth or not, I've learned, among other things, that Jessie was a bully, a thief, and cheated in school.

All this can't help but change my view of Jessie, no matter what I actually know or don't know. And this is because Nelly offers her sisterly defamations with such conviction, great detail, and clarity.

Yet I struggle to withhold my inflamed suspicions, as abetted by Nelly. After all, I'm dealing with a brain-injured client. So I just file it all away for future reference.

I see both sisters approaching me now. I'm standing in front of defense counsel's building where Nelly's deposition is to take place. Jessie moves at a good clip with Nelly lagging, still hampered by her injuries.

Her breathing, I note too, is labored. This means, I need to get her to a cardiologist for a heart workup. In such situations, doctors often are so focused on the brain injury that compromises to other structures, systems, and functions can go overlooked.

"Good morning, ladies," I say to them.

"Hi," Jessie snaps.

"Hi," Nelly says, just as angry, if not more so.

"What's the matter?"

"Jessie won't stop spending my money. It's the only thing we have to live on right now."

"Why do you care? You're gonna get rich off this lawsuit while I'll have to waitress at some dump for the rest of my life."

"Nice, real nice. You're so cruel!"

I have to agree with Nelly here. "Ladies!" I interject in a firm tone. "Please, cut this out!"

This breaks the tension but only a little. They turn away from each other. Me, I'm thinking how I don't want to be caught in the middle of their bickering. But I got a glimpse of Jessie's other side. And it wasn't pretty. We walk in. Silent.

"Hi," I say to the receptionist, "we're here on the—"

"*Rivera* case. I know. I remember you from last time. I'm to show you in. Follow me, please."

I turn to Jessie. "You're more than welcome to sit in," I say. I should have realized asking her to come in support of her sister could easily backfire. "But it's not necessary. I know last time it was a tough day for you, so, if you want, you can wait here."

She looks to Nelly, who still seems angry and upset. "I'll wait out here."

We walk down the glass-paneled hall into the same conference room we occupied for Jessie's and Grad's depositions. This time it's empty. I hate being the first one to the party.

A minute later, counsel for Grad enters, sitting down before the file resting on the table. Next comes the court reporter, who seats herself in front of the waiting steno machine. I shift to the side, keeping both counsel and Nelly in view.

"Miss Rivera," Brad Miller, Grad's lawyer, begins, "do you recall the day you went to Dr. Grad's office?"

"Yes."

I'm watching closely. To me, Nelly appears unfocused. But we'll see.

"I want to take you back to the day in question and go over what you remember. Would that be okay with you?"

Nelly nods. "Yes."

I can't help liking him for treading a bit softly. As revealed at Jessie's deposition, he's a kinder, gentler variety of the usual predator acting for the defense.

"Do you remember what you did that morning when you woke up?"

"Yes," she says again.

"Tell me in a general manner what you did up until the moment you arrived at Dr. Grad's office," he encourages.

"Well, I knew when I woke up that morning it was going to be a big day. We had planned it, . . . Jessie did. I mean, I think. You see my mother was very sick, and my father, well, it seemed he might be going to prison this time."

"I'm sorry to interrupt," Miller breaks in, "but are you referring to the morning you went to Dr. Grad's office?"

"Yes, . . . I mean, I am," she says confidently.

"Off the record for a moment, please."

Uh-oh.

"*Um*, Mr. Wyler?" he requests.

"Call me Tug."

He nods. "My background check shows her parents died a couple years before in a fire." Miller looks at Nelly, who's waiting for his next question.

"Your investigator got it right. That would be the fact of the matter."

"So what is she talking about?"

I lean in toward him, which, of course, is the signal for him to do the same. "Mr. Miller," I say softly.

"Call me Brad."

"Brad, you're aware that we're claiming brain injury here, aren't you?"

"Yes," he whispers, first looking to be sure Nelly can't hear, then back at me. But she isn't paying attention to us anyway. I can see her mind is elsewhere.

"Good. Then continue with your questioning," I tell him.

"Back on the record," he says.

Me, I'm thinking the stress associated with this deposition is one of those triggers Nelly mentioned.

"Go on with your answer, Miss Rivera," he urges.

She turns but gazes past him. Suddenly she's here again, concentrating—but on what?

"Okay, well, we went to school, and it was a day like any other. We came back home after our activities and watched *The Price Is Right* at 7:30 p.m. Anyway, Dad had two glasses of wine, then left for who-knows-where. Mom was pretty heavily medicated because of her pain and was sitting in the bedroom recliner. She had one of those machines that automatically fed her meds through a port in her chest. The thing is, I was getting cold feet about the whole thing. I knew it was wrong, but Jessie wanted to go ahead. I mean, it wasn't her mom anyway."

"Pardon me for interrupting you, Nelly." I can see Brad Miller is trying to stay cool. "But I want to remind you that we're talking about the day you went to Dr. Grad's office for dental care. Are you with me on this?"

"Oh, man. I'm sorry. I just lost track of things. Okay, . . . let me see. . . . Yes, right, where was I? We arrived at the office and sat in the waiting area for a while, chatting with the new receptionist, Debbie. She's my age. Anyway we were taken into an exam room, and Dr. Grad came in. He's a really nice man. He started the anesthesia, asked me a few questions, looked over me, and left the room. Then someone else came in to check on me, and then she left the room. I was feeling really light-headed at that point." She pauses.

"Then I remember Jessie couldn't find her phone. Anyway, someone else came in—I'm not sure at this point if it was a nurse or the receptionist—but I know it was somebody who worked there.

"After that, the fire was burning wild. I could smell it and hear it crackling. I tried to get out of my room, but the door was stuck so I crept under my bed. The smoke filled my room and overcame me. The next thing I remember is being on the lawn and then in the hospital. Dr. Grad came to visit me a few times, . . . but I'm not really sure when."

"Okay, Nelly, let me stop you here," her questioner instructs. He leans in this time, and I meet him halfway. "She's obviously confusing the fire she was in with the care my client rendered to her."

"Really, Counsel? What makes you say that?"

He gives me a look.

"I'd imagine this is something you'd want to report to the insurance company when asking them for authorization to settle this case. Meaning, the fact that she has posthypoxic global encephalopathy with associated time-dementia syndrome."

"Posthypoxic global encephalopathy with associated time-dementia syndrome?" he repeats.

"Yeah, posthypoxic global encephalopathy with associated time-dementia syndrome," I confirm.

"I didn't see that diagnosis in her medicals. I've never even heard of such a condition."

"Well, it appears that's what she has, doesn't it?"

He looks at her, then back. "I'd say so, yes."

"Then continue, Counselor."

He smiles. I like this guy. We settle back into our respective seats.

"Nelly," he says, "are you aware that you're confusing the fire you were in with the care Dr. Grad rendered to you?"

It's hard to read her expression. "*Um*, am I? I didn't think I was. Well, I'm not sure if I am. I know I was doing that for a while. Are we allowed to take a break? I'm getting a splitting headache thinking about all this. I'm sorry."

"Certainly, Miss Rivera."

I liked it better when he called her Nelly. We sit here as Brad

Miller leaves the room. Neither of us says anything, but I look at Nelly encouragingly. Whatever is happening, none of it is simple, none of it easy, and none of it do I yet completely understand.

Defense counsel now reenters, holding a glass of water, and gives it to Nelly. "I thought you might want this."

This guy has to be the most considerate defense lawyer I've ever met. My hope is that he's married to another empathic defense lawyer and they have lots of children, thus creating a new breed, if you will.

After this little break, Brad switches gears from the issue of liability to damages, changing his focus to Nelly's physical limitations. Obviously well-versed on her medicals, he asks specific questions about her physical injuries, along with any compromises to her cognitive, emotional, and behavioral being. He's doing everything he's supposed to except for one thing. Mr. Good Guy never inquires into Nelly's relevant prior medical history.

This is a big mistake if the defense is anaphylactic reaction. And it is.

"Nelly, would you mind undertaking a battery of tests to help define the degree of compromise to your mental facility? We're now several months out from your baseline testing, and I'd like to see if you've made any progress as a result of the cognitive therapy you've been doing."

"Sure, I'd like to know myself."

He folds back his legal pad. Depo over.

"Counselor," I say, "are you done?"

"Yes."

"Completely finished?"

"Yes."

"So, you have no further questions, correct?"

"Correct. What don't you understand, Mr. Wyler?"

"Just making triply sure on the court reporter's record, that's all."

"I assure you, I'm done."

Yes, you are, I think to myself. *You're done.*

"Nelly," I say, as the court reporter packs up, "would you mind joining your sister in reception? I need to speak to counsel for a second."

"Sure," she answers.

Meanwhile Brad is writing a note on the back of his pad about her gait pattern. The guy is thorough, just not complete.

"We gonna settle this case now?" I ask him. Casual but to the point.

"I'm sorry. She's a lovely girl, and it's a horrible situation, but, at this point, it's been marked Defend, despite my personal opinion. The carrier believes this was an anaphylactic event, which takes it out of the realm of malpractice. Doctors are not liable for allergic reactions."

"Is that the final word on the matter?"

"No. You know how it goes."

"Good. I have some thoughts about this anaphylactic defense, which may give your carrier something serious to think about. We'll discuss it at the proper time."

He replies with a nod.

And so, just as he's said, we're done.

18.

gave the girls a lift back to 138th Street after Nelly's deposition. Having witnessed her heavy breathing, I've made it as clear as I can that her subway riding is no longer an option. It's too stressful. Nonetheless the atmosphere in my SUV is still stressful enough.

And the tension elevates when I pull up to their building.

Jessie's boyfriend is standing there.

"I hate that asshole," Nelly comments.

"Too bad," Jessie counters.

I encourage them to be more civil to each other—blaming the unfortunate situation as the root of their troubles—but my words are not well received.

After I drop them off, my destination is Hastings-on-Hudson. Pusska, my investigator, has located Monica Lucas, the missing nurse from Adora Simone's postpartum day-seven feeding. I'm paying her a surprise visit.

While she's likely aware I'm tracking her down, finding her when she's not expecting me is the best way—from my point of view—for us to meet.

Here's how I see it. Litigators, like myself, are extreme egomaniacs and control freaks. My ego leads me to believe that if I, personally, come up here to speak to her, she'll talk to me because

I am who I think I am. Moreover, the control-freak side of me says not to let anyone else contact her because they could mess it up. Then I'd blame them and, next, myself. Bottom line: it's not a situation for delegating.

My GPS then signals I've arrived. What I see is an old ranch-style house. I stop and put my SUV in Park. Just as I do, a large man exits the front door. I decide to keep the SUV running. He doesn't, shall we say, look friendly.

As I open my door, he shakes his head no. So I opt for a less invasive approach. My window goes down.

"Excuse me!" I call out, as he continues his slow approach. "But does Nurse Monica Lucas live here?"

"No and yes." An odd answer.

"No and yes?"

"No, meaning, she's not a nurse anymore. And, yes, she lives here."

"Would you mind if I spoke to her?"

"I would."

"Why's that?"

He continues forward. "You're the lawyer, right?"

"That would be me. Why can't I speak to her?"

"Because she doesn't want to speak to *you*. The hospital lawyer told us you'd try to speak to her. He also advised she has the legal right to refuse. So she's exercising that right."

"Why?"

"Because she put this behind her years ago."

"Put what behind her?"

"Nothing. Time for you to go."

I look past him to an open window, left of the screen door. A silhouette behind the shade revealed someone sitting there, bringing a cigarette up, taking a long draw.

"Monica!" I yell. "I need your help. You're the only person who knows what happened."

"That's enough," he orders, standing next to my vehicle.

But I'm not done.

"The hospital lawyer," I yell, "has experts coming to court to say the infant contracted herpes from her mother during birth which ravaged her brain. But it's just not true, and I believe you know that. Please! I need your help."

This large man could've cut me off or shut me up in a number of ways. But he didn't. I give him a nervous smile.

"Listen," he calmly says, "I let you say your piece. It's time for you to leave. Now."

"Okay," I respond. "But Monica needs to come to court. Judicial closure is the only way this will ever truly be over—for everybody—including you. You want to move on with your life, don't you?"

No response. I continue.

"If a jury believes this herpes defense—which is an outrageous lie—then the life of this mother will be over. Only Monica can set my client free. And herself."

He turns and heads back to his house.

I think I got to him.

———————

I'm now heading toward my next destination. It's in an area of Yonkers that's less urban than the rest of the city. Not too far past the woods of Old Croton Aqueduct State Historic Park, I turn onto a dark road, drive to its end, and park.

Before me now is the remainder of a mostly burned-down house. The Rivera former domicile. It's all boarded up, except for the front door—which is the one thing you'd expect to find secured shut. Like all such remnant places where families used to live until tragedy struck, it's creepy.

Why am I here? Because I'm curious. About what? I have no idea. Just curious.

As I get out to take a closer look, my phone goes off. I check the screen. What are the chances of this? Nelly.

"Hi," I say. "Is everything okay? I mean, with your sister."

"My parents were murdered."

Oh, man!

"You know, Nelly," I begin, walking toward the front door, "the doctors aren't sure what to make of your flashbacks or newly surfaced recollections. So I really don't know how to respond."

"What's there to say? It's done. In the past."

"Death by murder is never in the past. That's the crime's irony—it lives on forever. The only person it's over for is the victim."

"I guess. But it was for the best."

"Nothing about murder is ever for the best. Do you realize what you're saying?"

No response.

I grab the doorknob, turn it, and enter. Patchy darkness mixes with rays of scattered dusk-light coming through the roof holes. "You still there?"

"I'm here," she responds.

"Well? Do you realize what you're saying?"

"She started the fire."

"Who started the fire?"

"I can't remember exactly, . . . but I know that's how she planned it."

"That's how *who* planned it?"

"I can't remember."

"Well, you've already said Jessie 'did it' and that I shouldn't tell her you knew because she'd be angry with you. Is that what you were talking about? Starting the fire?"

No response comes at first. "We weren't supposed to get hurt. But now I know that wasn't her real plan."

"Whose plan? Are we talking about your sister?"

"No. . . . Yes. . . . I'm not sure. *Uh,* . . . she's coming. I gotta go." *Click.*

I pocket my device and leave. More curious than ever.

19.

last saw Nelly six weeks ago. It's normal to have stretches of time without client contact in personal injury cases. And, given the nature of my last interaction with her, I should say the break was more than welcome.

Now we're sitting on a bench outside a courtroom of the Supreme Court in Bronx County, the venue where her case is pending. I've just explained how I'm about to argue her Motion for Summary Judgment.

A summary judgment motion is where you ask the court—not a jury—to determine the issue of liability or fault in favor of one party and against the other. The criteria for granting such relief is that no genuine issues of fact are in dispute between the litigants; therefore, you ask the judge to apply the controlling law to these undisputed facts and render a decision.

Such motions are rarely made in general negligence cases because it's always a he-said/she-said scenario. "I had the green light," says the plaintiff. "No, I had it," says the guy being sued. Motion denied.

Issues of fact are for a jury to resolve. And, in a medical malpractice case, it's unheard of to make such a motion. The he said/she said brings into play battling experts offering varying opinions on the standard of medical care. A plaintiff's expert says the defendant departed from good and accepted standards of medical care during his treatment of the patient, while the opposing side hires a defending expert to claim there was no departure. Motion denied.

But I'm feeling good about my motion.

Nelly's case has been transferred from a civil court judge to Judge Hess, who has a large criminal caseload. That hardly ever happens, but it did here. Judge Hess is known for throwing the book at the convicted. Which is the reason I've asked Henry not to show up. As we enter the busy courtroom, I register the sound of a familiar voice.

"There you are."

Crap! Henry! "I thought I told you to keep your distance."

"No issue of fact there, Counselor." His reply makes allusion to my motion.

"So why are you here? Everybody knows Hess hates you. It was headline news—or don't you remember?"

"Old news. We've made up."

"Still, I don't want you anywhere near me when I argue the motion. I don't want this judicial ass suddenly realizing you have a connection to the case. Besides, the last time we were in court together, I ended up in jail."

"In jail!" Nelly exclaims. "Why'd you go to jail?"

I turn to her. "It's a long story. To make it short, let's just say Henry landed me there as a way of ensuring I begin working on your case expeditiously."

A wide grin crosses Benson's face.

"Stay away from me, Henry. Got it?"

"Nonsense," he says.

Crap!

Since we're the first case scheduled for the day, I'll be arguing in front of the crowd now amassed in Hess's courtroom and awaiting their turn. The 138 other cases are mostly criminal matters.

I make my way to the first row with Nelly. I never bring my clients to court for motions, but, in this instance, her presence is invaluable. It's a dispositive motion involving a young woman who, under the effects of anesthesia, wound up with a brain injury. Oh, yeah, her cardiologic workup for the fatigue I noticed revealed she has heart wall damage from her cardiopulmonary arrest. Not only will brain tissue die if it's deprived of oxygen but heart muscle will too.

Benson follows us, despite my *ixnay*. He asks the guy behind us to move so he can sit there.

Turning, I say, "I just told you I didn't want you near me, Henry."

"And I said, nonsense."

"All right." I scowl at him. "But, at least, sit tight and keep quiet."

Bang! Bang! Bang! "Order in the court," shouts the bailiff with the gavel. "Order in the court! Everybody take seats. If you can't find a seat, then take yourself outside."

We hear the bangs again. "All rise!" orders the bailiff. "God bless America!" he next yells. "Part 21 is now in session. Let the record reflect that Honorable David E. Hess is present and accounted for, and shall preside fairly and justly, upholding the constitution of this great State of New York. May I have a 'Hear, hear!' from the audience, please."

"Hear, hear," we all mumble.

Now, for the first time, Judge Hess wields the gavel. "Order in the court!" he yells. "Listen carefully to my instructions. Alison will be calling the calendar. The moving party shall answer, 'Ready for,' and the opposing party shall answer, 'Ready in opp.' If one side doesn't answer, it will be marked second call. Otherwise both sides approach counsel tables ready to argue. And speak clearly into the microphone."

"Number one," Alison says, "the matter of Nelly Rivera by her legal guardian Jessie Rivera against Defendant Dr. Michael Grad."

"Ready for," I say, rising.

"Ready in opp," Brad Miller calls out.

As I proceed forward, Nelly whispers, "Hey, you left your papers on the bench."

I smile at her. "Don't need them."

I arrive at the gate that separates or "bars" the arguing lawyers from the rest of the audience and hold it open for my adversary to enter. I usually derive pleasure extending courtesies before the execution, but, since I like this guy, it just doesn't feel the same.

We take our positions at side-by-side tables, at which point Hess says, "I'll hear argument from the moving party."

I lean forward, tapping the head of the microphone to check if it's on. A reverberation blasts throughout the room. "Whoops!" I say. But before I get a chance to utter another word, the bailiff whispers something into the judge's ear while looking in the direction of Henry Benson.

Shit!

Hess shakes his head and picks up the stack of papers in front of him pertaining to our case.

"Shall I start?" I ask as Hess puts on the readers hanging from his neck on a cord.

"One moment, Counselor," he says, flipping through my motion. He looks up and resumes addressing me. "Before you begin, I'd like to give you this opportunity to withdraw your motion. What we have here is a medical malpractice case, and every lawyer in this room knows that summary judgment is denied in such matters, as there's invariably a battle of the experts. Therefore, if you choose to go forward, I must warn you that, in addition to denying the motion, I'll be imposing sanctions and costs on you for bringing a meritless motion and wasting the court's valuable time. What do you say to that, sir?"

"Okay."

"Okay, meaning, you're withdrawing your motion?"

"No, what I mean is, okay, if you deny it, sanction away."

The crowd buzzes, and Hess picks up his gavel, giving it three more bangs. "Go on then, Counsel," he challenges. "Make your argument."

"Will you be relying on the contents of my papers when deciding this motion, Your Honor, or just my oral argument?"

"Both. Now go on."

"Did you get that, Ms. Court Reporter?" I ask, ensuring the transcription of Judge Hess's statement for posterity.

"Got it," she shoots back.

"Go on, Counsel," Hess now urges me. "Stop talking to the court reporter. Let's hear argument."

"You want my argument," I tell him. "Then here it. Grad messed up."

"And . . ." the judge encourages.

"And nothing. He messed up. It's in my papers you were just looking through."

"Motion denied," he says, with great satisfaction. "By the powers vested in me, I hereby sanction you five thousand dollars together with costs and attorney's fees to compensate opposing counsel." *Bang! Bang! Bang!* "Step away. Next case, Alison."

I tap the microphone three times, causing the most annoying screech to resound throughout the courtroom. Again. "Is this thing still on?" I ask.

"Don't touch the mike with your fingers again, Counsel," directs Hess.

"You mean, like this?" The screech heard 'round the world issues forth a third time.

"Yes, like that!"

"Sorry, Your Honor."

"Leave, Counselor. I've called the next case so you have to clear the area now. Behind the bar, please."

"*Um*, okay, Your Honor. But you said I'd only be sanctioned if I lost the motion."

The judge laughs, as grins also appear on the faces of his staff. "Counsel," he chides, "weren't you with us? You already lost the motion." He looks to his left, and his clerk starts laughing. Then he turns to his right, and the law secretary joins the chuckle.

"I'm sorry," I say apologetically. Of course, I'm anything but. No one else need know that though. "I just didn't hear anybody argue in opposition, that's all."

"Oh, so you need to hear opposing arguments for such a silly motion?" He makes his left and right nods at his supportive posse, who once more respond with loyal smirks. "Okay, Counsel, I'll entertain you."

Now, turning to Brad Miller, the judge says, "Counsel opposing the motion, state your argument for the record, please." At this my adversary seems a little uneasy.

"Well, Your Honor," he says, "we have no opposition to the motion." If Hess's jaw didn't have a mandibular joint, it would've dropped to his desk.

"What do you mean, you have no opposition?" He scrambles for the defendant's papers sitting before him.

"Well, Mr. Wyler's right. Dr. Grad messed up. He wasn't licensed to employ anesthesia. He didn't keep an appropriate anesthesia log. He didn't monitor the plaintiff's vitals properly. In fact, a sales receipt showed that he didn't purchase the pulse oximeter, which he'd testified that he'd used, until six months after the event. Moreover he failed to be in the room while the plaintiff was under the effects of the anesthesia, and, worst of all, he wasn't up to date on his Basic Life Support certification. Nor did he have or employ appropriate reversal agents. He really goofed up here, Your Honor. Big time."

I honestly am not sure I know how to describe the expression Hess now wears.

"I see," he says in a low tone, understandably embarrassed he hadn't at least glanced at the defendant's partial opposition papers. Reluctantly he continues. "I'll set this matter down for a trial on damages."

"That's fine," Brad says. "But we want the record to be clear that, although we concede Dr. Grad was negligent in his care of Nelly Rivera, it is our position that this negligence did not cause her any harm. We want a jury to determine the issue of causation because it is our opinion that she had an allergic reaction to the anesthetic agents, rather than being overdosed."

"I see. I hereby strike my prior decision, withdraw my order for sanctions and costs, and grant relief of summary judgment in

NELLY'S CASE / 163

favor of plaintiff. This matter is remanded for a trial on the issue of causation and damages."

Hess is now giving Henry—who's visibly excited—a dead-eyed stare.

Bang! Bang! Bang!

No Stone Unturned

Just as Nelly, Henry, and I get outside and down the first three courthouse steps, I say, "Crap!"

"What?" Henry asks.

"You two wait here. I left my motion papers inside."

I enter to hear Alison say, "Case number four, *The State of New York v. Joseph Whatley.*" The two lawyers involved are offering their responses as I head to the first row bench where my motion papers are.

Just as I step outside the courtroom for the second time, an attorney I'd seen approach the bench after my case comes up beside me.

"Hess is an ass."

He catches my attention with that. "Oh, I see you speak my language."

"I know that case of yours—*Rivera.*"

"How so? I'm pretty sure I was retained while she was in a coma."

"I was at the district attorney's office when it happened."

"What involvement did the DA's office have in Nelly's case?"

"You mean, you don't know?"

"Apparently not. Enlighten me, Counselor."

"Sure," he says, eager to tell.

"Well, when 911 was called, EMS arrived, and your client was at death's door. In transit to the hospital, one of the guys called the police department because he thought the matter would involve a death. EMS is instructed to do that. The detectives went to the dental office and undertook a crime scene investigation. I was the assistant district attorney assigned to the case so the investigation came to me. We were contemplating a charge of negligent man-slaughter if she died. When she didn't, we were contemplating lesser charges. The matter's still open—and now simmering again."

"How do you know that?"

"Because I just buzzed the guy who stepped into my shoes."

"Who's that?"

"Jack Herring."

"What did he say?"

"He said he had no idea Grad wasn't licensed and that he'll take another look at the file. He also wasn't so happy hearing about the other acts of malpractice issuing right from the mouth of Grad's own attorney."

"Did your office know there was a civil case?"

"We did. Benson called us to inquire how the criminal matter was going soon after it happened. He said it'd help the civil case if we went forward. I told him my decision to prosecute wasn't motivated by civil matters."

"When you were involved, did my client or her sister, Jessie, know of your investigation?"

"Yes. I spoke to the sister one time while your girl was still in coma. You don't get an eyewitness to a negligent manslaughter too often—but, of course, there was no death. Grad was very cooperative too. I never heard a suspect speak so freely. He came in without an attorney, said he didn't need one, and signed a document stating that his civil lawyer, the guy here today, was not his criminal lawyer. He took the same position on the issue of causation, an allergic reaction unrelated to his care. That's been the stumbling block for us. Our experts said it had merit, even though an overdose was the more likely cause. But the allergy explanation creates reasonable doubt. We don't go forward when there's reasonable doubt built in from the outset. It can ruin our conviction stats."

"Is Jack Herring friendly? Meaning, will he share his investigation file with me?"

"Probably. If you keep it under the radar. But what do you care?

You won liability, and the remaining issue, causation, is pretty clear. You say he messed up causing the arrest, and Grad says she had an allergic reaction. So what's the use of seeing the criminal file?"

"It may have some bearing on proving causation, and besides . . ."

"Besides, what?"

"I conform my practice of law to one simple principle."

"Oh, yeah," he says. "What's that?"

"No stone unturned."

I exit the building to find Henry and Nelly standing exactly where I left them. There also is Brad Miller. Crap! The thing is, I never want defense counsel to have any more than the minimum exposure to my clients—meaning, limited to when the scheduled obligatory examination before trial takes place. The more exposure to and interaction with my client, the more self-certain conclusions the defense draws about the extent of the recovery underway.

I move quickly. "Come on, guys. We've got to go." As I take Nelly by her elbow, Henry grabs my arm, foiling our escape.

"Not so fast."

"Why's that?"

"Counsel here is talking settlement negotiations with us." Crap again!

That's the last thing you ever want to happen—engage in any sort of settlement talks in front of the client. It's a conversation in which a plaintiff's attorney still wants to stress—overstress, if you will—the extent and degree of the harm as much as possible. It's about maximizing the financial recovery. It's how you do it, no exceptions.

At least I admit it.

However, ordinary common sense, not to mention human decency, confirms you can't do that with the client standing there without being hurtful and insensitive.

"Okay, great. We'll continue the conversation another time. Let's go," I say, nudging Nelly's elbow.

"Slow down," Henry says, stopping me again.

I turn on him. "No! You slow down!"

But, hey, it's not good to tussle with the guy who regularly sends you large cases.

"Henry, sorry," I say. "But might I speak to you privately over here?"

"Give me a moment," he tells our adversary, making it clear, with his tone, that he's calling the shots.

"Nelly," I say, "would you mind joining us?"

We step away to a distance I'm comfortable with and huddle. "Listen," I say to them, "talking settlement on the courthouse steps on a sunny morning when Nelly looks pretty great here just isn't what we want to be doing. There's a reason brain trauma's known as the silent injury—because its most devastating effects are hidden on the inside, not visible on the outside—a fact which defense counsel can easily lose sight of. Do you two understand me?"

Nelly nods. Henry starts to say something, then settles for a nod-equivalent.

"Good. Wait here." I walk back to defense counsel.

"Listen," I say, "he's one of those overzealous referring attorneys. I apologize if he inappropriately initiated settlement negotiations."

"Actually I initiated. So, I'm the one who owes you the apology."

"No worries. But why, given all this time now, hadn't you made any such overture to me?"

"Well, as instructed, I called the carrier after Hess ruled on your motion. And, even though we all knew what the outcome would be—once liability was over—as a matter of law, they instructed me to start the talks. So it just kind of slipped out when I saw Mr. Benson with your client, and he told me how she'd been his referral."

"Got ya. Did he make a demand for settlement?"

"He did not. He was trying to get me to say how much I thought the case was worth first."

"At least he knows how to play the game," I say with a grin. "Listen, the formal demand is ten million."

"Sounds way high."

"I've got a brain injury, and I've also got heart wall damage. The two most vital organs of human existence have been severely and permanently compromised in an eighteen-year-old girl. How far off can I be?"

"I was going to recommend four."

"You're a reasonable man," I tell him, patting his shoulder. "You do that, and I'll meet you halfway."

"Seven?" he says.

"That's the number. And you keep that number between you and me. If you tell the carrier my number is seven, they'll think it's three point five. And I believe you know what I mean."

"Yes. I do. This is not my first dance. I'll make some calls." He pauses the way one does just before making their final statement on the topic. "But don't lose sight of the fact that the defense here is anaphylaxis, and you could get zero." He turns and makes his way down the rest of the steps.

I walk over to where I left Henry and Nelly. "We're on the right road here."

Henry's expression isn't quite what I'd call satisfied. "Yes, well remember who he came to first to start the ball rolling."

"Understood," I say, stroking his ego. "He initiated with you. Good job." At this, he offers an affirmative nod, turns to Nelly, and smiles. She smiles back.

"See you later, litigator!" He's looking pleased with himself as he heads off.

I put Nelly in a cab and give the driver her destination and money to cover the fare. As they pull away from the curb, I grab my phone.

"Benson here," he says, picking up on the third ring. Like he always does.

"It's me," I say. And then move quickly to the point. "Why didn't you tell me about the criminal investigation?" I'm pretty used to Henry's shenanigans. Still you just never see them coming.

"Didn't I?"

"No, you didn't."

"Must've slipped my mind."

"That's a pretty major slip." I pause. "It's just that, when they do crime scene investigations, they preserve a shitload of evidence. You know that. After all, you're the criminal lawyer. Maybe it could've helped me."

"You won liability. How much more could it have helped?"

"The issue in this case is what caused Nelly's brain damage. And the fact of the matter is, I didn't have in my possession all available information to explore the possible causes when I questioned Grad at his deposition." I hear dead air on the other end of the line. He thinks I'm making a big deal about nothing. I'm not. I assure you.

I continue. "The answer to the causation question," I explain, "is the key to this case. If I make it clear the malpractice caused this, rather than an adverse reaction, it will increase the case value by undermining their defense."

"*Uh-huh.*" The Benson clock is ticking. His boredom threshold, that is. It's easy to tell.

"Right now, we say 'malpractice,' they say 'anaphylactic.' But maybe it's possible to find the answer right there in the criminal file, from the information it contains. Maybe they have no defense at all, or maybe we have no case at all. Or maybe only God really knows the answer as to what happened here." I wait for his response.

"I gotta go." *Click.*

20.

'm on my way to the Bronx County District Attorney's office but not before making a short detour to Grad's office to view where this all went down. Actually seeing the site of an event helps it be real, which is, in part, why I went to the Rivera home. Upon arrival, I'm startled. Taken aback. It's a street-level office, and a For Rent sign is on the door. I walk up to the window that has an unlit neon sign reading The Painless Dentist. I look in. The place is vacant. No, abandoned.

What to do but phone defense counsel for some guidance here. Insight, let's say.

"Hey," I begin, trying to sound casual, uninterested, and uninformed. "I've been wondering how Grad's practice is going."

"Really? Why's that?"

"Only wondering."

"Well, if I don't tell you, you'll easily find out on your own. So, to cut to the chase, not so well. His practice isn't going very well at all."

"I appreciate your honesty. Is there a more informational chase we can cut to?"

The guy sighs. "He's currently an employee at a cut-rate dental clinic in Chinatown. It's a shame. Grad practiced forty years in the same place, basically taking care of everyone in that neighborhood—generations of families—and lost it all because of this."

"It is a shame." I like Brad Miller, as I've said, and am willing to commiserate. "But, you know, what he did here could be construed as criminal."

I wait for his response. Yeah, I baited the hook and need to see what turns up. It'd be entirely crazy that he wouldn't know about the criminal investigation. But I didn't. Plus Grad told the DA his civil lawyer was not his criminal lawyer. How to figure this? I'm not sure.

"Maybe," he replies.

Now what the heck am I supposed to make out of that? "Listen," I tell him, "call me after you get some real settlement authority on this case." *Click.*

It's truly unfortunate Grad would lose his practice over this. And I feel horrible for the guy. But he really did commit malpractice.

His own lawyer even said so.

I head up the Grand Concourse to the Bronx District Attorney's office only ten blocks away. Time to play forensic investigator.

I walk in, go to the sixth floor, approach the security desk, and ask for Jack Herring.

One minute later, a tall young man, blond and good-looking, emerges from behind a security door. He can't be more than twenty-six, which isn't good for Grad. It's the young assistant district attorneys who need to make names for themselves. What they're about is stockpiling convictions to help them climb the prosecutorial ladder.

"Nice to meet you," Herring says, looking into my eyes while giving what I'd call an inappropriately firm shake. This guy is confident.

"Likewise," I say. "I really appreciate you being a good sharer."

"I like that, good sharer. You share pretty good yourself. Come on. I got things set up for you."

"Hey," I say, "what did you mean, I'm a good sharer?"

"I obtained your summary judgment papers from the court's motion support office. You're making my job easy."

"You going forward against Grad?"

"With the good work you've done for me, more than likely. Got to make an example out of a guy like that. We had no idea he was putting people under without a license."

"Yeah, that bothered me too." We're on our way down the hall. "But given his extensive experience, he was qualified to employ it."

Herring stops and turns. "You're not defending his conduct, are you?"

"You read my papers. Did it seem like I was?"

He resumes walking. *Whew.* That was close. If he thinks I'm in any way soft on Grad, Herring will close up shop before it opens. But the thing is, I feel guilty about what's happening to the Painless Dentist. I can't help it, but I do.

"That's my office," Herring says, pointing into a perfectly kept workspace as we continue on. I note a brown paper lunch bag on his desk. When we've gone twenty feet farther, he grabs a door-knob and says, "In here."

We enter a small windowless room. In the center is a square metal table with a large cardboard box on it. The stark white room with bare walls is perfect for interrogation, except I'm here to see what's inside that box. Hopefully an evidentiary gift.

"That's it," Jack says, pointing to the box. "Have fun. Just don't mess anything up, okay?"

"Can I handle what's in there?"

"Absolutely. Nothing's sensitive to tampering, and we don't have a chain-of-custody issue. Handle it all you want. It doesn't matter. Just don't break anything."

Yep, everything about his manner says: young up-and-coming ADA.

"Got it, sir." I added that last because I knew he'd like it. He did. What my companion really is, I realize, is a junior Henry Benson. Herring will be defending hardened criminals one day, once he realizes that's where the big dough is. He may even refer to me a new set of HIC cases—Herring's Injured Criminals.

"When you're done, come to my office," he orders. "That's where I'll be."

"Okay," I say, foregoing the "sir" this time.

What I find in the box are items in Ziploc bags, as well as loose papers. I pull out the first plastic bag, filled with photos. I open it and take them out. The stack's as thick as five decks of cards, bound together with a heavy rubber band. I flip through the pictures, one by one. They show your typical dental exam room from every imaginable angle.

The most important thing, however, is not what's in these photos, but what's not. There's no pulse oximeter machine. How could Grad lie like that? Testifying under oath that he used one. He's such a nice guy. I just can't understand; it seems out of character. Then again we all lie.

Not all the time. But we do.

At least I admit it.

Putting the photos aside, I take out the papers. The top one is a witness statement taken over the phone from Jessie. Crap. I never knew about this—she never told me. The next page is a standard police report. It parrots the information contained in the responding EMS call report, which I already possess. The next document is a preprinted form, itemizing the physical evidence gathered at the crime scene. There's only one entry. It reads "intravenous infusion set."

But, to me, it says, big-ass stone that needs to be turned.

Onward. I reach in and take out the other Ziploc. It's so large I'm sure you can't buy it in stores, unless you're shopping at a Crime Scene Evidence-Gathering Plastic Bag Shop. I open it and carefully take out the infusion set. I lay it on the table in the configuration it assumes when hanging off an IV pole. The assembly consists of two

NELLY'S CASE / 173

IV bags: one large that contains hydrating fluid and one small that contains a 5 mg/ml formulation of midazolam, the anesthetic.

Attached to the bottom of each bag is a clear round plastic device known as drip tubing, where the drips fall from the bottom of the bag and collect. Attached to that via short pieces of infusion lines are roller-type control clamps to regulate the volume of flow. Coming from them are infusion lines leading to a Y-connector where the two fluids merge into one line and flow to the patient's vessel.

I analyze them.

The most important thing here is the flow-control clamp on the line coming from the anesthesia bag. This device regulated the drip rate of midazolam going into Nelly's arm. I was surprised in Grad's deposition to hear him testify that he used a manual flow controller rather than a more updated electronic device. I imagine soon the standard of care will call for using only electronic ones. Right now, no.

Time to analyze the clamp.

The adjustable regulator works by providing constant pressure across a piece of the infusion line. One end of the adjustment provides shutoff where the diameter of the tubing is completely compressed. If you roll the dime-shaped plastic wheel in the other direction, the pressure on the infusion line decreases, thus increasing the flow rate. If you roll it all the way, there's no pressure, creating full flow.

One doesn't have to look too closely to see that the clamp is in the open full-flow position. It's obvious. And I don't know much about flow-controller clamps at this point, but it certainly does seem odd that it's all the way open. Especially since the flow controller for the hydrating fluid is only half-open. And, interesting, since Grad testified he had set the flow-controller clamp on minimum.

The first thing that comes to mind is, of course, the issue of causation. If this thing really was all the way open, I've got a slam dunk here. I take out my phone and snap photos of the device at every which angle. When I'm done, I pick it up to take a closer look.

I hold it to the light, giving it a careful examination from six inches away. I see tiny fibers around the mechanism's plastic wheel. I look back at the evidence log to see if there's any mention of these fibers. There isn't. *Hmm.* I'm pretty sure these things come out of sterile packaging, and they're supposed to be handled under sterile conditions, so what the heck are these fibers?

I turn the now-empty evidence storage box upside down and see exactly what I need that happens to be holding the box together. I peel off a piece of the clear plastic packing tape, doing the best I can to minimize the amount of cardboard box material sticking to it. I need this tape as pristine as can be. I apply the sticky side of the tape to one side of the clamp and come away with half the fibers. The other side is full of them, so there are plenty to spare. I fold the tape over to seal them in, then stick it in a pocket.

One last thing to do. I check the clamp controller for the hydration fluid. No fibers. Interesting.

Everything I've taken out I return to the box and leave it in the center of the table, just where I found it. I make my way to Herring's office and stop at his door. He has a napkin stuffed into his collar to prevent any soy sauce splashes. With chopsticks in his hand and an authentic wood block in front of him, he's tucking into his lunchtime sushi.

"Looks tasty," I comment.

"Early lunch. Want a piece?" he asks, pointing to what I'd say is a spicy tuna roll.

"No, thanks. That stuff ain't cooked enough for me."

He nods and smiles. "How'd it go?"

"Went fine." *Fine fibers* to be exact. "Thanks. Not really much there."

"What are you talking about?" he says, beaming with the look of a future conviction. "We got photos of the office. There's no pulse oximeter—and you got the guy to say he used one."

"Well, I didn't exactly get him to say that. He just did."

"Yeah, well, if I don't nail him for reckless endangerment or the unauthorized use of a chemical agent, I'll get him for perjury. It's open and shut on that one."

"It would seem so. If you go after him, what's the maximum he could face?"

"Worst case scenario, a couple years."

"Seems like a long time for lying."

"What? Are you soft? He ruined this girl's life."

"True. But she's come a long way on her road to recovery."

"I'm happy for her, but I'm in the criminal justice business. Do we have anything else to discuss?" He's annoyed.

"No, not really. I'd just like to be informed on how you intend to proceed on this matter, given that I represent the victim."

"When I decide, you'll get a call."

"Thanks," I say, patting my pocket to confirm its new contents. These fibers mean something.

21.

ily, did you do that title search?" I'm standing by her desk.

"You mean, the one you asked me to do?"

"Yes. That one."

"Sure did."

"And did you confirm the Riveras were the owners?"

"Sure did."

"And did you find out about this property damage litigation for the fire loss of the house?"

"You mean, the one you asked me to look into?"

"Yes."

"Found that out too."

"Well?" I ask.

"It's still pending, but there's an appeal."

"What for?"

"According to the appellate briefs, Henry Benson claimed—"

"Wait. Are you saying Henry did the appeal?"

"It's in the name of his office, but his appellate lawyer's name is on the papers."

"Okay."

"Anyway Henry claimed the insurance company, Greater Home, conducted an unauthorized fire scene investigation by an unqualified individual."

"Stop there. What does that mean?"

"By the terms of their policy, Greater Home was required to give prior written notice of their proposed inspection and failed to do so. Also the fire investigator—who are usually ex-firemen or trained fire professionals—was neither."

"Go on."

"The lower court agreed, granting Henry's motion to have their inspection findings deemed unreliable and precluded from evidence at the time of trial. In response, Greater Home made a motion to the court for another inspection. Henry opposed it, saying the fire scene was now tainted, and the court agreed. Again. Greater Home appealed. Both decisions."

"How much is the claim for?"

"Five hundred thousand."

"How about the life insurance payout? Were you able to get the numbers?"

"Sure did."

"And did you learn what company it was written by?"

"Sure did."

"Well?"

"Greater Life. A sister company to Greater Home. I also got the name and number of the claims adjuster who handled the file."

"Great. How much did Nelly get?"

"Five hundred thousand. The payout was to Nelly, jointly with an officer of the Yonkers Bank as court-appointed trustee, until she turned eighteen, at which time it became hers."

"Why didn't you just tell me all this from the start?"

"Because, as you can see, I'm doing my nails. If I'd told you from the start, you would've ordered me to stop with the manicure to tear out the sheet of paper from my notebook with the info. Here." She hands me the piece of paper. "So, by dragging it out, I was able to finish my last two nails."

I enter my office and sit down. It's common knowledge that, before paying out a death benefit, an insurance company's claims adjusters will make their best attempts to deny the claim. They should be called "disclaim" adjusters. What I do now is call Trudy Anderson, the life insurance adjuster whose name appears scribbled on Lily's notepaper.

Naturally I get her voice mail but forego leaving a message.

I don't know what I'm going to say when I get her on the phone anyway. Let's see: Hi, Trudy. I'm the lawyer representing the Rivera sisters on a malpractice case. Listen, ever since Nelly came out of her coma, she's had visions of the night she lost her parents in the house fire. The one where you paid half-a-mil death benefit, with litigation pending on the property damage claim? Yeah, that one.

Anyway, Trudy, her visions are now so fact-specific that she thinks someone started the fire on purpose. You know, arson. That's something you'd disclaim a life insurance and a property damage claim on, right? Especially if you found out the arsonist was connected to the beneficiary. Oh, and that makes the death of her mother no accident—as so defined by the terms of your policy—so I guess my client owes you that $500K back. I think the crime we're talking about here is insurance fraud, Trudy, as far as you're concerned. But I guess the real crime is murder.

Yeah, I'm happy she didn't answer.

Lily buzzes.

"What's up?"

"You sound like Bugs Bunny when you say that."

"Thanks for your commentary. Now do you have something to say?"

"Grump. Yeah, Trudy Anderson is on the phone. She said our number came up on her caller ID. I imagine you just phoned her, right?"

"Good imagination. I told you to block that out."

"You need to block it out from your phone. You're technologically challenged." *Click.*

I stare at the blinking light for a second. No, really, what am

I going to say to this woman? I go for spontaneity. "Hello, Ms. Anderson. How are you today?"

"Are you calling on a new claim? Because I don't have your number in my system."

"No, it's not a new matter. It's an old one. You may have to pull your file from archives."

"I don't think so," she says, not snottily but confidently. "I know all my files, cold. Past and present. And I even know the future ones, just not when the insured's going to die. But I pretty much know everything else."

"You sound like you're on your game."

"Why, yes, I am," she says with more than a touch of smugness. "I've been Adjuster of the Year for nineteen out of the last twenty years."

"That's pretty unbelievable. Do you have trophies?"

"Plaques, all plaques. They're identical too. They look beautiful hung in rows of five, but I still need to win this year. This year is important."

"Why's that?"

"I want to fill the empty space at the end of the bottom row. It will look better, more balanced. But, of course, that won't make up for my one loss."

"Well, I'm rooting for you."

"Why, thanks." But now she sounds a bit puzzled. "Anyway, how can I help you? We've been on the phone almost two minutes already. I like to keep calls under four. I'm more productive that way. Go on."

"Okay, well, . . . I'm calling on the Nelly Rivera claim."

My chatty new friend goes suspiciously quiet.

"Hello?"

"Yes. I'm still here. What's your relation to her?"

"I'm her injury attorney."

"Now she's making an injury claim?"

"Yes."

"What do you want from me?"

"Information."

"What kind?"

"Any and all concerning your investigation of the death benefit payout."

"What's your name?"

"Tug Wyler."

"What's this all about, Mr. Wyler?"

"I need to learn more about, shall we say, the family dynamic."

"Why?"

"Her sister is her guardian, and Nelly may come into a large sum of money, so I'm doing some due diligence on her sister's trustworthiness."

"Not over the phone. They randomly monitor our calls."

"Sounds juicy."

"It is. I saw you called from a 212 area code. Listen, I'm coming to the city tomorrow evening. We've got our annual gala. I can meet you before if you like."

"Um, I'm picking a jury tomorrow, . . . but, yeah, I like. Where?"

"Grand Central. That's where my train pulls in. Six thirty in the evening, sound okay with you?"

"Sounds like a plan. I really appreciate you speaking to me."

"Are you kidding?" she responds fervently. "I've been trying to get someone's ear on this one forever. This goddamn claim cost me my perfect record. And more." *Click.*

22.

Okay, so Chucky-boy and I have gotten our jury selection out of the way in record time with minimum grief. But, I have to say, I was a bit distracted thinking about my meeting with Trudy Anderson tonight. Right now though, I'm on my way to Chucky-boy's office to pick up an item I need. The thing is, he never gave me a copy of Nurse Lucas's corrected transcript, and the judge has ordered him to do so before opening statements tomorrow. A witness is given an opportunity to make transcript content corrections after an oral deposition. From there I'll head to Grand Central, one block from his office.

After enjoying my usual repartee with Ma Lawless—who was folding laundry on the reception desk next to a jar of quarters— I'm out of there. After she threw the transcript at me, that is.

I feel the adrenaline flowing as I walk to Grand Central. Too-easy-to-tease Lawless son and mother, they're both sad cases. And they bring out the rascal in me. You might even say, the best of my worst. I just can't help but give my immaturity free rein around them.

At least I admit it.

Once in Grand Central, I go to the lower level and a bench across from Track 110 on which Trudy's train has just arrived. I sit and watch as people emerge from the track area. One woman heads straight for me. She's in her mid-fifties and dressed the part for her evening's event. However, what catches my attention most are her bulging eyes. She's holding a photo-album-type binder with all kinds of papers sticking out of it. She veers to my right and gestures me to follow. The closer I am to her, the crazier those eyes seem. Yet her manner is businesslike.

We take seats across from each other in a café area, and she places the album on the table. I can tell it's in lieu of a greeting. Somehow our relationship has bypassed small talk.

"What's that?" I ask, though I have a hunch.

"My scrapbook."

"I can see. Of what?"

"It's a beneficiary profile scrapbook."

"What's a beneficiary profile scrapbook?"

"It's something I put together on a death benefit beneficiary for a life insurance policy."

"Do you make scrapbooks for all beneficiaries?"

"Nope," she says. And looks at me expectantly.

I take my cue. "So why did you make one on the Rivera matter?"

"Because of the suspicious death of the insured, occurring within six months of policy generation. That's why, among other reasons. So I make scrapbooks to tell the story—if there's a story to be told—and here there was."

"I'm still listening."

She regards me carefully with those slightly mad eyes. But her words are entirely sane. "Let me put it this way. There was a constellation of fact and circumstances surrounding this policy that gave rise to some unease even before it was issued."

"And you, of course, are here to share those points of special interest."

"Correct. I will share them with anyone who'll listen. Anyone but my superiors, that is, since it's already cost me a well-deserved plaque—along with other aggravations."

"I see. But why are you so eager to share them with me?"

"Because, in this industry, one thing I encounter I just cannot tolerate."

"And that is?"

"Insurance fraud."

"I couldn't agree with you more." I pause, to emphasize what I next say. "From my perspective, when representing clients with legitimate claims, when I pick a jury, I incorporate the topic into my voir dire."

"Really? That's surprising coming from a plaintiff's lawyer."

"To some degree, I agree with that statement too."

"What do you tell the jurors?"

"After the preliminaries, I tell them we are here not only on an individual matter but also to test the integrity of the system. And one of the things we will be doing is evaluating if someone is trying to put something over on the system. Therefore, it is their job to make sure that doesn't happen. I imagine you get the picture."

"Clever. They're hearing *you* explain that."

"Clever, maybe, but I really believe in the system and hate abuses of it just as much as you do, I can assure you."

"Oh, I doubt that. I'd do just about anything to prevent insurance fraud."

"You're very committed."

"Yes, I am."

"Why?"

"You really want to know?"

"Sure."

"When I was a kid," she begins, "my father was in an accident. I was sitting next to him in the car. It was just a tap in the rear caused by the guy in front of us stopping in the middle of the street for no reason. Like he was trying to cause the collision. Then this man sues my dad, claiming his back surgery was a result of the accident. For the next two years, my dad was scared we would lose our home because he had minimal insurance coverage. It took a big toll on him, all that worrying. One evening while he was complaining about the situation, he was so upset he had a heart attack right in front of me and died at the hospital later that evening. Then our lawyers find out this guy had back surgery scheduled even before the accident. The whole injustice and emotionality of it just left an indelible mark on me."

"Oh, wow." I shake my head. "That does make it clear where you're coming from."

Neither of us says anything for a few moments. Then Trudy gets back to the business at hand. "First, tell me what kind of injury case you're handling."

"No problem. Nelly was the victim of malpractice. A dentist unlicensed to employ anesthesia overdosed her, causing both a brain injury and heart wall damage."

"And you're sure of that?" she asks.

"Certain. I just won summary judgment on liability. In fact, it was unopposed."

"And you're certain she sustained these injuries?"

"Yes."

"Interesting." She draws out the word.

"Why?"

But she hardly needs my prompt. Her next words come quickly. "Because I don't believe anything is ever the way it seems with that family. They're a band of criminals and no-goodniks."

"When you say 'that family,' to whom, in particular, are you referring?"

"All of them. Stella, Roberto, Juanita, Jessie, and Nelly."

I'm impressed with her name recall. "Why?" I say again.

"It's all well-documented in here." She taps the scrapbook labeled Rivera Claim. "Nelly a bit less," she concedes, "because she has no memory of that night."

"Well, that's changed a bit."

Trudy's face lights up. "What do you mean?"

"Bits and pieces are coming back to her, stimulated by what happened in my case. And I should say, I do know a little about the backgrounds of Stella, Roberto, and Juanita. But you're imposing a pretty harsh judgment on Jessie and Nelly. I mean, they were teenagers when their dad and Nelly's mom died."

Trudy's eyes are now blinking rapidly. She's obviously in the know. About what, I hope to find out.

"Let's get started," she says. "I have to head off pretty soon." She opens the scrapbook, revealing a one-page document taped to the inside cover. "This was the application for life insurance submitted by Stella Rivera. It formed the basis for our underwriting people to decline to issue her a policy."

My attention is immediately caught. Not by the document. But rather by the fact that Nelly had confirmed receiving her mother's death benefit. That's what the girls have been living on. Still, my only job for the moment is to listen.

"Why?" I know my lines.

"Because she made several material misrepresentations in her application."

"What were they?"

"She stated she'd never smoked, that she had no history of medical problems, and that she was not under the care of a doctor for any conditions at the time of application—to name the top three of several."

"How did you find out these were misrepresentations?"

"Good question. We got lucky in this instance—because usually we find out about the misrepresentations after the applicant, or should I say, insured, dies."

"How'd you get the break?"

"This particular type of policy was summarily issued if the applicant checked off 'No' to each medical history question on the one-page application."

"All anyone had to do is check 'No,' and you issued a policy?"

"That's what I'm saying."

"It doesn't sound like a very thorough underwriting process."

"It wasn't, and it didn't need to be, based on our business model.

Internally we called it the No-Pay policy. We were selling a massive number of policies with very little cost associated with the underwriting. All the underwriter had to do was see that 'No' had been checked in all nine boxes, and, *bang*, the policy was issued. Then, when anyone put a claim in for a death benefit, adjusters, like me, were to find a way to deny it. It was quite a financial success."

"Are you proud of that?"

"I wasn't. But, at that time, I was scared of management, like everybody else. Plus the rationale—and we were indoctrinated with it—was that all applicants were dishonest. End of story."

"Sounds wonderful. Go on."

"Okay, the way it worked was, once the insured died and a claimant requested the proceeds, we would review every 'No' answer in the application. We'd be checking them against the decedent's medical records prior to the application date, looking for inconsistencies. Management taught us how to stretch the definition of what an inconsistency was, making finding them easy. So, by checking 'No,' the applicant made a material misrepresentation of their medical condition, thus creating a legal basis to deny the claim. Once denied, most people walked away because they couldn't afford to hire a lawyer to fight the denial, most of which were improper. Of the minority we litigated, each and every one of those claimants ended up settling for a fraction of the policy value."

"This makes me feel a lot better about the insurance industry," I say sarcastically. "Because it confirms everything I've ever thought. So how does all this relate to my clients? If I understand things correctly, you denied her mother's coverage, yet this claim was paid out. I don't get it."

"Let me back up a little. Only 1 out of every 750 of these applications was properly underwritten—meaning, a medical background review was undertaken—even if it contained all the 'No' checks. Stella Rivera happened to be that one. And her history of cancer was not hard to find. So hers was among the few applications that were denied. Like I said, we got lucky."

"I'm still listening but don't understand. Why did you pay Nelly if no policy was in effect?"

"The payout was for the death of Roberto Rivera. He applied too. On the same date. And so a policy was issued insuring his life. When he died, a cross-reference was undertaken, which bore out his wife's denial. The first red flag. That's because, in the industry, spouses are presumed to think alike. Then I undertook the standard approach for these No-Pay policies, investigating whether I could get his knocked out, based on a material misrepresentation. I found several. Not bullshit stuff either—but real material misrepresentations about his prior medical condition. For instance, 'No' was checked next to the box asking if he had any liver conditions, yet his medicals showed he had stage 2 liver cirrhosis."

"I don't get it. So why'd you pay out his life insurance?"

"Circumstances and politics."

"I'm listening."

"Well, even though Roberto Rivera had misrepresented, and even though we believed what happened was an arson event—for which we could deny payment—the case involved disclaiming both this death benefit and a property damage claim to a young girl orphaned in a tragedy that received local media attention."

"Girl or girls?"

"Girl. Nelly was the sole beneficiary."

"Pretty disgusting of Roberto to cut out his daughter Jessie."

"He didn't."

"Go on. I'm still here."

"Stella, Nelly's mom, was Roberto's designated primary beneficiary, the one to receive all the proceeds upon his death. But she died in the fire too. So Roberto's designated contingent beneficiary, Nelly, received the death benefit."

"Well, if Roberto made Nelly—to the exclusion of Jessie—the sole contingent beneficiary, then he did, in fact, cut her out."

"Normally I'd agree. But not in this instance, Mr. Wyler."

"Call me Tug. Go on."

"Review of the policy applications shows that both had been filled out by Stella. The same exact cursive handwriting—Stella's. All Roberto did was sign—first-grader style—where indicated."

"Did you have them evaluated by a handwriting expert?"

"Don't be ridiculous. See for yourself. They're in the scrapbook. All you need do is compare Stella's signature to the handwriting in the applications. In fact, I'm certain Roberto couldn't even write in cursive. Check out his signature. He printed his name in all capital letters."

"Got ya. What were the politics?"

"At the time, Greater Life Insurance Company was being investigated by the New York State Department of Financial Services—the state agency responsible for supervising and regulating all insurance business—with regard to the No-Pay policies. Bad faith—that is, the lack of proper underwriting together with our improper denials based on nonexistent misrepresentations by the policyholders—was the problems under state scrutiny. So an internal decision was made to pay the claim in an effort to avoid further negative press from a double denial in an already bad time."

"Double denial meaning—"

"Our sister company, Greater Home, was in the process of denying the property damage claim."

"I understand the politics. But how does any of this actually relate to my case?"

"I'll tell you how. Out of the vast numbers of policies issued and claim benefits wrongfully denied, this was the one policy where denial would've been proper, just, and indicated."

"Based on the material misrepresentations by Roberto Rivera? Or should I say, by Stella on his behalf?"

"That and the fact that he may have been murdered by an arsonist who was also a beneficiary."

"Are you suggesting Stella killed him?"

"All I'm saying is that, in these situations, the most likely suspects are the beneficiaries, which means the surviving spouse, children, or anyone else with a financial interest in the death of another. That includes Juanita. Especially given her history."

"That's a serious allegation you just made. Especially since the surviving spouse herself died from the fire, and Nelly barely escaped. What do you have to back it up?"

"Just the arson part."

"Go on."

"Residue of a flammable liquid—gasoline—identified where the parents were sleeping. That's what we knew."

"How?"

"My investigation."

"Your investigation?"

"Yes. Mine. I went to the Rivera home myself and did a fire investigation."

This must be the unauthorized investigation Henry had the court throw out.

"You went alone?"

"Yes. Alone. It's all documented in there." She nods to the scrapbook.

"Why would you do that? I thought you were employed by Greater Life, and this was a claim against Greater Home."

"They're really the same company, despite being separate legal entities."

"So you went out there on your own and inspected the place?" My tone is unavoidably one of disbelief.

"Sure did, to preserve evidence. Juanita called in the death the day after, which haste always raises a red flag in my book. So I immediately pulled the files, . . . and, well, you know the rest. I caught some heat for that because they claimed I wasn't 'qualified,' despite having taken a few courses. I think that's what cost me my plaque."

"But I don't get it. Why didn't the local police do an arson or murder investigation?"

"They did."

"So?"

"'So?' I'll tell you 'so.' Henry Benson, the family attorney, advised John Dickson, the local police chief—who knew the Rivera girls well because of their close friendship with his daughter, Samantha—that, if it were established to be arson, Nelly would be denied both the death benefit and the property damage claim. Benson also reminded the guy—who later lost his job for accepting a bribe in an unrelated matter—that Stella was on her deathbed and that the father, Roberto, would have been going away to prison for life had the fire not occurred. So this cop, getting the local fire chief on board too, manipulated the outcome. What happened was an electrical fire determination. Case closed."

"How do you know all this?"

"I know, trust me. I can prove it too."

"This is all pretty hard to believe."

"Not really. It's the kind of stuff people will do in life insurance situations. But I need to get going now. You can keep this for a while." She slides the scrapbook over to me.

"*Um,* this looks like an original. So I'd prefer not to have the responsibility of safeguarding it. Could you make me a copy?"

"Don't worry about that," she says, returning it to me. "I have copies." As she stands, she stops for a moment before speaking. "One thing you could do for me."

"What's that?"

"I'd like to talk to Nelly."

"About what?"

"About what she now knows about the fire."

"Why?"

"Personal reasons. The need for truth and closure."

"I can't do that."

"Why not? There's nothing at stake."

Certainly she must know there is. I'll remind her.

"I can't have her giving statements—oral, written, or otherwise—when there's pending litigation regarding the property damage claim."

"*What?*" Her surprise is genuine.

"I said, there's pending litigation. You know, you mentioned it before. The property damage claim with Greater Home."

"That case is closed. It was part of my agreement."

"What agreement?"

Trudy Anderson sits back down. And she's not happy. "I made a lot of noise about this case. Stella was properly denied issuance, and Roberto's application had clear misrepresentations. I was totally against the payout. It was improper. The fire was an arson event, which would be a complete bar to a property damage recovery. I told you before, the one thing I can't stand is insurance fraud. And this was a prize-winning example—*if* such prizes existed. So, my agreement with management was that I would keep mum to the Department of Financial Services when questioned about our No-Pay policies—which was the only leverage I had—if and only if the Rivera claims were resolved by payout of Roberto's death benefit, with Greater Home getting Rivera to voluntary discontinue the property damage claim. And I was informed that this did, in fact, happen."

All at once her eyes seem to bulge more than ever, almost popping out of their sockets. This is one angry lady.

"Well, it didn't."

"I was told it did!"

"Not what happened. Look it up."

She stands. Seeing how rattled she is, I'm worried about her now.

"You wanted to know if Jessie Rivera could be trusted with Nelly's injury money." She gestures at the scrapbook. "Enjoy your reading." Then she's gone.

What a set of obvious contradictions Trudy presents. I'm on her side when it comes to insurance fraud. Yet she participated in a clear cover-up of the Department of Financial Services No-Pay investigation. Not only that but she actively participated in Greater Life's insurance fraud on unsuspecting policyholders by finding reason to deny death benefits to significant others. Money, no doubt, these men and women were relying upon in times of need. Not all were scammers. Not by a long shot.

You can't have it both ways. Either you're against fraud or you're not.

I sit here trying to digest what I've just heard as it related to Nelly's visions. Not to mention Trudy's statement that someone, maybe Jessie, started the fire and that two people had been murdered. It's very fucked up, is all I can think. Because it seems possible. It's also fucked up because Nelly somehow found herself locked in her room when the door wouldn't open, and so she could've died too.

That way, Jessie would have gotten it all—death benefit, property damage payout, and Stella's estate—as Nelly's only living relative. *Hmm.* And Nelly's scared of her.

Maybe she has good reason to be.

You'd think Henry would've shared some of this shit with me. But since he didn't, I know, if I asked, he'd tell me it's none of my business. The way things are developing, I'm almost willing to admit he'd be right.

The one thing I can't lose sight of though is that Nelly sustained a significant brain injury, which means I just can't accept her assorted recollections at face value. It's sad but true.

I spend some time flipping through the scrapbook, and what I read is absolutely incredible. Two aspects in particular are impossible to ignore. First, it puts Jessie in—shall we say—a less-than-positive light. Second, Trudy Anderson dug deep. Like Grand Canyon–deep.

Time to go. I'm making my opening statement in Adora's case in the morning. Unfortunately now I couldn't be more distracted. To add to it, this may be the first time since I started litigating that I won't be able to stand in front of the jury and tell them *exactly* what happened to my client, including the how and why.

Only Nurse Lucas knows how Adora ended up this way. The

trouble is, I doubt Nurse Lucas will show up tomorrow, despite my efforts to get her there.

I walk over to the Metro North departure screen. The commuter trains. Mine is leaving in ten minutes from Track 112. Good, it's just over there.

As I turn, something bashes the back of my head. I mean hard. On impact, I hear a metal-on-metal noise. A distinctive sound, the kind linked chains make when in motion.

I go limp, falling face-first to the tile floor. As I try to get up, I hear that metal noise again, closing in. Then *bang!* One more whack.

I'm slipping away, and, despite the hustle and bustle of Grand Central, I hear the sound of escaping footsteps fading away as I fall deeper into unconsciousness. The gait sounds so casual. I catch the reverberation of clanking metal in rhythm with each step as they recede into the distance.

Nunchucks, I think. *Badass boyfriend.*

But why?

23.

have a gargantuan headache. When my eyes open, I know it's going to be worse, . . . but I do it anyway. *Ouch!* Photophobia, that's the medical term for light sensitivity. My surroundings come into focus.

My first thought: *Isn't this a role reversal?* Standing at the foot of my bed is Nelly—looking at my chart.

"He's up," she gleefully says, turning left. I follow her line of sight. My wife.

"Hi, honey," I say.

"You're lucky you're here."

"Because I didn't call?"

"Exactly. Now what happened?"

"Someone hit me in the head. I was mugged."

"No. You weren't mugged. They didn't take anything. It was a straight assault. Did you say something stupid when someone tried to cut in the hot dog line again? I told you, your righteousness would get you into trouble. Are you listening to me? Hello?"

Shit! The scrapbook! Crap! Nelly can't know about it.

"Where's my stuff?"

"In the closet," Tyler replies.

"Open it up," I instruct her. Then I realize I'm drawing attention to the one place I don't want Nelly anywhere near.

Even worse, Nelly herself looks to be obeying my command, putting a hand up to halt my wife. "I've got it. Don't move," she tells Tyler.

"On second thought," I say, raising my hand toward Nelly, "forget about it." She stops and turns, focusing on my hanging IV line. I stare at the bag, watch a few drips, and then look at Nelly.

"This is weird," I say.

"Very," she agrees.

"Nelly, could you go out in the hall and call a nurse in here, please?"

"Sure." She leaves.

My head is pounding. I close my eyes for a moment, looking for relief, but I need to act fast. Opening my eyes, I turn to Tyler.

"See if there's a scrapbook with my things in that closet."

"A what?"

"A scrapbook."

"Why would you have a scrapbook? A scrapbook of what?"

"Never mind that, just do it! I'll explain later."

"Why not now?"

"Honey, please, I don't want Nelly to know about it. Hurry up."

"Nelly? How would she know about it?"

"If she gets a glimpse of it when she comes back in."

"Back in where?"

"Back in here."

"Here? What are you talking about? You're in the hospital. Why would Nelly be here?"

Oh, man. My mind is playing tricks on me.

"I'm sorry. I don't know what I was thinking. But can you do me a favor and see if a scrapbook is in the closet?" Reluctantly she complies and peers inside.

"Nope. No scrapbook. Just your briefcase and clothes."

Crap! Maybe that's why Jessie sent her thug after me. Maybe she suspects my suspicions. I mean, Nelly's visions are bringing stuff to the surface. But no way could she have known anything about Trudy Anderson.

"Ouch!" my wife exclaims, as she shuts the closet door.

"What, honey?"

"I broke a nail. You look in there next time."

"Well, when I'm not lying here, I'll maybe take my turn." In walks a nurse.

"Um, are you my nurse?" I ask her.

"Yes."

"Did they X-ray my head?" I want to know.

"They did. No fractures. Just some soft-tissue swelling under the scalp. Your wife told me you were a malpractice lawyer and would have a bunch of questions."

I turn to Tyler. "That sounds like a smart idea, honey, telling my health care professionals I'm a malpractice lawyer." I return my focus back to the nurse. "Well, she was right, but she was also wrong. I actually don't have any other questions. Can you take the IV out of my arm and then bring in a form for me to sign?"

"What form is that?"

"The AMA form. I want to go home. It's almost two in the morning, and I have a trial starting in a few hours."

"You're not going home," Tyler states.

"Yes, I am." If anyone knows the drill here, it's me. And I need to take charge. "Bring in the against-medical-advice form for me to sign. And you can also give me your discharge instructions. But I already know that, if the pain gets worse over the next twenty-four hours or if I become dizzy, light-headed, or have other progressing neurological symptoms, I should immediately come back to the hospital so someone can drill a hole in my head to release the pressure on my brain from a space-occupying bleed. Did I get that right?"

She gives me a look.

"You have it right. I'll be back with the form." And she's out the door.

"I don't think this is a good idea," Tyler says.

"I know you don't, but all I really have is a bump on my head. I have too much invested in Adora's case to let the judge disband my jury. I'm going forward. Besides, I can't let Maria live another day thinking she was the one who hurt her child. I just can't."

24.

For many reasons I wish I had thick hair instead of buzz-cutting the little that's left. But I never thought one need would be to cover up a bump on my head. What's my jury going to think? But I have questions of my own. Namely who the hell attacked me? And why? An officer came to the hospital and left his card with Tyler when I was out of it. So I'm hoping he knows or has a few ideas here.

But right now that's way, way secondary.

As I approach the courthouse, I'm going over what's about to happen. How I frame the Simones' and Adora's story for the jurors is a very big deal. To start with, I'll tell them that some-thing took place after Adora's morning feeding on day seven. That I don't know exactly what did happen will be part of the sad tale. And, despite the fact that I have three well-qualified experts, we're still without a real answer. My neonatologist, pediatric neurologist, and hospital nursery nurse will all testify that the harm involved the nursing staff's failure to properly monitor a high-risk infant in the premature nursery—where the nurse-to-baby ratio is one-to-two.

Why?

Because the nurse whose care Adora was under refuses to talk.

I should tell you that it's improper for me to say such a thing to the jury in my opening statement—that the nurse refuses to cooperate—because it interjects me into the proceeding.

But I'm going to do it anyway. I've got nothing else.

Besides, when the judge asks me to call my first witness, I'm going to stand right up and say, "The plaintiff hereby calls to the stand Nurse Monica Lucas."

Since she obviously won't be there, the judge will then inquire why no one is proceeding to the witness box. At which point I'll explain in open court, in front of the jurors, that Monica Lucas was the hospital employee and nurse assigned to Adora when the incident happened, that she's been subpoenaed to come to court, and that she's choosing to ignore it.

This is when the judge—who has the discretion to dispatch a sheriff to enforce the subpoena but is unlikely to do this—will instruct me to call my next witness.

When I put my process server on the stand, he'll say he personally served Nurse Lucas for the purpose of this trial, which is true. Having heard this, the jury will know I did my part to get the only eyewitness to court. More than likely, the jury will then suspect that it was good old Chucky-boy who's behind her no-show and that a cover-up's in play. That, of course, is exactly what I intend to argue in my closing statement at the end of the trial.

Waiting in front of the courtroom door are the Simones. Maria, who, I note, looks frightened. Next to her, Joe reminds me of the guy in a cartoon, unaware he's standing under a teetering boulder. Not an easy spot to be occupying.

Adora, in her wheelchair, wears a dark-blue Sunday dress with a tiny white flower pattern. She doesn't seem to have a care in the world. Yet it's unlikely that she knows this. It's also unlikely that she's aware that all her care—minute to minute—falls squarely on the shoulders of her parents, all but extinguishing their individual existence, not to mention their marriage. Looking at Adora, what you can't help thinking is how weak and delicate she must be, with her rail-thin arms, legs, and bony torso. The wrist and ankle braces she wears for tendon contractions prevent her hands and feet from further contorting into unnatural resting positions.

On approach, I dread the conversation I'm about to have. I promised Maria I wouldn't tell Joe about the herpes defense in hopes of settlement. But Chucky-boy has made it clear that ain't happening. And I can't let Joe hear it for the first time during opening statements, making me the keeper of that boulder.

I take a deep breath. It won't be easy. But I know I have no choice.

"Joe," I begin, "I need to talk to you about something regarding the defense position in Adora's case."

Naturally he looks puzzled. Maria, meanwhile, is watching me anxiously. Like I say, I feel horrible.

"Okay," he replies. It's already so clearly not a good day for him.

Touching his arm, I lead him off just a few feet away. "You should know," I tell him, "that, in lawsuits like these, some attorneys will do anything they imagine might help to get their clients off. Yours is no exception. What you need to be aware of is that defense counsel, during opening statements, intends to claim—mind you, it's *only* a claim—that Adora's brain injury was caused by transmission of the herpes virus from her mother during the process of childbirth."

"That's crazy. I'm the only man she ever made love to, and I don't have this thing."

Just then the door squeaks, and Chucky sticks his head out of the courtroom. "Better get in here," he tells us. "We're starting."

I look at my watch. "We got twenty minutes."

"Well, the judge is ready to go now."

"Okay, be right there." I turn back to Joe. "Anyway . . ."

Another squeak. "Inside, Counselor," barks the court officer, peeking out. "Now."

"Can I—"

"No, now!" he says, as I mull over whether leaving Joe in a state of complete denial is good or bad. "I'm holding the door open over here, Counselor."

We enter. Donald, my process server, is sitting in the back.

I direct Joe and Maria to sit in the front row, making sure, first, their daughter's wheelchair is nearest the jury box. A courtroom's no place for children, I recognize, but I well know that jurors need to see the effects of severe brain injury to appreciate it. Adora won't be here every day, but her presence is important today. It's opening statements this morning, and, during afternoon session, I put my pediatric neurologist on the stand. His testimony will have the greatest impact if he can use Adora herself for illustration of what injuries she's sustained.

After fifteen minutes of preliminary instructions, the judge looks to me to begin.

"Thank you, Your Honor," I say as I stand. "May it please the court, Defense Counsel, Joe, Maria, and Adora Simone, and Ladies and Gentlemen of the jury." I push my chair back dramatically, then carefully make my way to the jury box.

"Not always, but sometimes, lawsuits can be like mystery novels, where you piece information together as you go along, hoping to solve things in your head before reaching the book's end. And sometimes what's not before you is just as important as what is, thus requiring the drawing of an inference. I'm going to suggest to you that this case may present such a scenario, so I'll be brief.

"All you really need to know as we start this undertaking is that Adora Simone was born a well baby, kicking and screaming much like any other newborn. Maria will tell you," I say, motioning to her, "and the hospital records will agree. What they will reflect is the fact that Adora was not only healthy the day she was born but the day after and the day after that too. The records are clear that, as a newborn, little Adora was a well baby, a healthy and thriving infant, for the first six days of life. These records to which I'm referring, are—to repeat—the hospital's own."

I pause. "One of the hallmarks of a well baby is the instinct to feed. And feed is exactly what Adora did day by day, feeding after feeding, every three to four hours for her first six days of life.

Each feeding note in the record—a normal, encouraging record—reflects this. Nurse Lambert, on evening duty, went so far as to document in each note 'well baby, baby fed, baby regurgitated'—this last means throwing up a little—and 'baby suctioned.'"

I take a long breath, holding it a beat or two to increase the drama and to signal the turning point I'm approaching. "What occurred after that first morning feeding on day seven of Adora Simone's life is the focus of the mystery we are all here to solve.

"This is because whatever happened then changed everything." I shake my head slowly.

I now walk toward Adora, making sure never to give the jury my back. "What happened to this baby who was born well?" I repeat, as I move behind her. "A baby no longer, she's heavier and very inert.

"The mystery of Adora's life—and what event it was that took it away from her before she had a chance to live it—is the mystery we are here to tackle together." As I say those last words, I grasp her wheelchair and slowly roll her before the jury.

Again I pause. "My good citizens of this jury," I continue, "something happened, and you will need to tell us what it was." I stop and look around, bringing my gaze to rest on Adora. "You must tell us what it was because it's unlikely that anyone will arrive here, take the stand, and confess to the responsibility for the catastrophic event that brought Adora's healthy life to a halt. Forever."

The room is silent. Exactly as I want it to be.

"What I hope to provide now," I go on, "is all the information you need to solve this enigma, this tragic puzzle. As I've said, you will be asked to draw inferences—reasonable and inescapable extrapolations—from what is and what is not before you."

I carefully wheel Adora back to Maria, then solemnly return to the jury box. "I should offer, before sitting down, that I have my own opinion on this matter, a strong one. However, I will be holding it back until summation—in order that you have the opportunity to piece together what I believe to be so from the evidence but without my influence. Lastly I should say I've withheld much from you at this juncture, information which you will hear soon from the lips of defense counsel."

Here I rudely point to Chucky-boy. It's a plaintiff's attorney's prerogative, and one I infrequently like to avail myself of. Then, wearing an expression I intend to convey both valor and commitment, I resume.

"All distortions and half-truths shall be dealt with at the appropriate time and in the appropriate manner. That I can promise. Just know that I am aware of the benign antibodies of a viral condition, a medical circumstance that will form the basis of the defense in the case. This argument should be viewed as a red herring, if you will. Don't be fooled. On behalf of Adora, Maria, and Joe, thank you for listening to me."

The judge looks to Chucky after I take my seat. "Mr. Lawless, do you want to begin your opening or take a break?"

"Begin. It's a short one," comes his reply. "I only have a few words to share." My opponent rises, walks over, and occupies the spot I've just vacated. He steadily regards each of them, going down the jury box, taking his time. This maneuver in and of itself creates a serious tone.

"During childbirth, this extremely unfortunate child," Chucky says, looking over at Adora with convincing concern, "was exposed to an active herpes virus. This exposure was via mother to newborn. Once contracted, this viral presence ravaged the fragile infant brain. If it had been known, however, that Mrs. Simone had herpes—had she told her physicians of this—a cesarean section would've been planned and performed. Had that been the case, Adora never would've been exposed to this heinous virus. And her years of suffering, as well as those of her parents, would have been prevented.

"It's important to be open and honest with your doctors, and this case is, possibly, the most tragic such example of information withheld I have ever seen. Of course it is conceivable that Maria

Simone was unaware of her virus. At times, outbreaks can have minimal symptoms. In either event, my client did nothing wrong. What seems a mystery is, in fact, solved. Thank you for listening to me."

Oh, shit. That had been real good. Better than real good. Really, really good. Direct and to the point. Also it was the first time he'd allowed how it was possible that Maria didn't know. There's the winning defense in the case: Maria didn't know. Yet it'd have been great if he had omitted claiming Maria kept something from her doctors. That's a dangerous allegation, which could backfire on him, I have to tell you. But I understand it. Given the symptomatology of the condition, he simply had to make a judgment call and offer both possible scenarios.

The jurors folded their arms and looked at me as if I'd hidden this crucial fact from them—which I kind of did—despite having prepared them for its arrival.

You're always preemptively supposed to offer your weaknesses in these situations. Yet there simply hadn't been any good way to present this one openly and directly, at least not that I could see, given the fact that Maria and Adora each are positive for the herpes antibodies. One choice would have been to explain the half-truth—that both tested positive for the antibodies—while at the same time suggesting that the herpes was not what had caused Adora's condition. But I couldn't do this without having to spend time laying out the relevant medical facts and background. Instead, I wanted the jury to hear this information for the first time from my very credible medical expert rather than from me, the plaintiff's lawyer.

I've never been in such a bad position at the start of a trial. Crap. Yet things are about to get worse, I've no doubt. That's because, in a few minutes, I intend to call the phantom nurse, Monica Lucas, to the stand.

I happen to glance back at Donald. He's trying to communicate something to me, but I can't tell what it might be. Odd, but I'll worry about it later.

"Call your first witness, Mr. Wyler," the judge orders.

"Yes, Your Honor. Plaintiff calls to the stand Monica Lucas, the nurse who fed Adora on the morning of day seven."

"We don't need any ad-libbing, editorializing, or embellishing," the judge admonishes. "Just the name of the witness will be sufficient."

"Sorry, Your Honor." I look around expectantly. Turning back to the judge, I say, "She was subpoenaed for today but obviously is ignoring it. Maybe you could . . ."

"Behind you, Counselor," the judge directs, lifting his chin. I turn and see a woman standing. She was noted to be forty, yet she looks much older, as if she's been through tough times. Much like Maria.

"Are you Nurse Lucas?" I ask. Out of the corner of my eye, I catch Donald's affirmative nod, which answers that question. He personally served her with the subpoena, so he knows this is she.

"Please, Counsel," the judge reminds, "wait until the witness is up here, in the box and sworn, before you start your questioning."

"Sorry, Your Honor," I say again. But at least the jury now knows I've never spoken to her. This is going to be one spontaneous cross-exam.

What Happened Next?

As she makes her way to the witness stand, I'm reminded of what happened to Chucky-boy during the *Clark* trial the day before Henry Benson appeared with Jessie in tow. The case where my client's bladder had been perforated during hysterectomy, the case Henry settled as I sat in jail, owing to Benson's big mouth, and the case in which I never got back from Benson that bare-tit snapshot.

I remember the moment when Chuck violated the rule of thumb that even nonlawyers know. *Never ask a question to which you don't know the answer.*

The exceptions to this in practice—believe me—are rare.

Excuse my backtracking, but I want you to hear this. So that day

Chucky had asked Harold Clark, a clinical psychiatrist—as a man who believed in therapy, who earns his living providing counseling to couples—why he and Nancy had never sought therapy to try to remedy their lack of intimacy.

To this Harold responded with a question, offering Charles an out. "Do you really want to know?"

Too bad. Chucky bit. "I think the jury's entitled to know. If you're asking compensation for the loss of your wife's services, why didn't you mitigate these damages and go for counseling, the type that you yourself believe in and make a living at?"

"Okay," he said, "then I'll tell you. You see, at first, not only was I taking care of my wife but also her live-in elderly mother. Soon after Nancy's third surgery, our twelve-year-old daughter found her grandmother dead upstairs. It was very traumatic for her, and I spent a lot of time helping her through it. Then Nancy's widowed sister was diagnosed with lung cancer and came to live with us. She unfortunately died a slow horrible death six months later after our home had turned into a hospice. I guess the stress of things got to me because I had a massive heart attack the day after we buried her. Following my quadruple bypass, I started having these headaches, and they found a tumor in my brain. I had the best team of neurosurgeons remove it and experienced a fine recovery. This last wasn't so long ago now. So, you see, having therapy to discuss the lack of sex in my marriage hasn't been on the top of my list of priorities over the last several years, especially since my wife feels uncomfortable with that device sewn onto her pubic area. Does that answer your question?"

But onto the no-longer-phantom Nurse Lucas.

"You may inquire of the witness now, Mr. Wyler," the judge says, following the witness's swearing-in.

I look at the nurse. I can tell she's upset and on the verge of tears. I'll need to handle this delicately because the last thing I want is for the jury to be hating the big bad plaintiff's lawyer who made a defenseless woman cry. This is one of those aforementioned rare times when

I can ask questions I don't know the answers to. And that's because I sense she's here for confession: forgive me, lawyer, for I have sinned. A true witness rarity. I mean, why else would she show up? And then stay, after hearing me tell the jurors that it's unlikely anyone will take the stand and confess to any responsibility.

"Nurse," I say softly, "are you frightened right now?"

"Yes." She gives a little nod as she answers.

"Upset?"

"Yes." The nod is more emphatic.

"Well, there's nothing to be scared of and, as far as you being upset, might that be because of the tragedy that occurred?" Let's call this the straight-ahead, no-bullshit approach.

"Yes." She looks down at her lap.

"And did you come to court today as a way of clearing your conscience?" Even I can hardly believe myself. But I'm simply going with my gut.

"Yes," she says. Now her lips are twitching. I worry she's about to lose it. My own head's aching, I realize, from my last evening's encounter. Still, I have a job to do here.

"Bailiff!" the judge calls out. "Get her some water, and hand her this box of tissues." While Nurse Lucas collects herself, I look over at my adversary. Chucky is pretending not to see me, which suggests he knows what's coming.

"You may continue, Counselor," the judge says.

"Nurse, you were sitting in the back of the courtroom during my opening statement, true?"

"Yes, I was."

"So you heard what I had to say?"

"Yes, I did."

"And are you here to help us solve this mystery once and for all?"

"Yes."

At this point I have to make my first tactical decision. I can go straight for the kill or else I can slowly lead up to it. I choose the latter.

"Nurse, did you take care of Adora on day seven?" All of us sitting here—or, in my case, standing—know by now what that refers to. And it's not when God rested.

"Y-yes." Here's a woman who truly looks haunted. She shuts her eyes for an instant, and I imagine her seeing the tiny, burbling, and healthy Adora in her memory's eye.

"Would you mind if I first asked you just a few questions about Adora before that time?"

She hesitates for the briefest of seconds, then replies. "No."

"Was she born healthy?"

"Yes."

"Was she a well baby and perfectly fine for her first six days of life?"

"Yes." Her eyes shut again.

"And, at the moment she came under your care, was she also healthy and in a state of well-being?"

"Yes."

"And did you give Adora her bottle for feeding on the morning of day seven? The first feeding of the day shift?"

"Yes."

"And did she drink her formula like a well baby?"

"Yes."

"And do you remember what happened after that?"

"Yes."

"Tell us what happened."

There it is—the open-ended question—my first ever.

"I was called to the nurses' station." She stops.

What I thought would be an all-out confession requires a comforting nudge. "Respectfully we need more information here." My tone is considerate. My mind, however, is racing. And my head still aches. "Where was the nurses' station in relation to Adora?"

"Fifteen to twenty feet away."

"And why were you called there?" Slowly is the only way to handle this.

"To sing 'Happy Birthday' to one of the night-shift nurses who was about to go home."

"And did you go and sing 'Happy Birthday'?"

"Yes."

"And where was Adora at that time?"

"In her bassinette. When I left her, she was resting comfortably."

"I appreciate that. But, when you left Adora, you knew you were breaching your nursing duties to keep her under constant observation, did you not?"

"Yes." Her eyes now shut, she lowers her head.

"What happened next?"

A sizable pause occurs before the answer comes. "When I returned to her, she was cyanotic, blue, and mottled in color. She wasn't breathing. I started CPR and called a code. It was horrible."

"Do you know what happened to her? Why she stopped breathing?"

"Not for sure," she says. Tears are now falling down her cheeks.

"Well, what do you think happened to her?"

"Objection!" Chucky yells, jumping to his feet.

"No, I'll allow it. Go on," the judge tells her.

"I'm not certain."

She needs more help. "Nurse, did you familiarize yourself with the feeding entries existing in her record when Adora became your patient?"

"Yes," she says, almost inaudibly. She looks over at Maria, then at Joe, and back to me.

"Were you able to read and understand these feeding notes that had been entered prior to your involvement?" I ask. Keeping my tone level and courteous is the only way to go. But both the tension in the courtroom and my own impatience are spurring me to go faster. Yet I must not. Even Tug Wyler can know the call of restraint and discipline.

"Yes." Her voice remains low. Her expression at this moment is blank.

"Even Nurse Lambert's entries which employed her own set of acronyms?"

"Yes." The box of tissues slips off her lap, and she reaches quickly to retrieve it.

"Did you notice a pattern?"

"Yes."

"And can we agree that pattern was Adora took her formula, regurgitated her feeding because preemies have underdeveloped digestive tracts, and then had to be suctioned with a vacuum designed for such an occurrence?"

"Yes."

"And can we agree that the reason one of those little vacuums is used to suction out vomited formula is to prevent the infant from either aspirating or reswallowing it down the wrong passageway into its lungs?"

"Yes," she says, dropping her head into her hands.

"And, if the formula goes down into the tiny premature infant lungs, that can cause the baby to stop breathing. True?"

She raises her head. "Yes."

"Because it mechanically obstructs the exchange of oxygenated air, and the infant begins to suffocate, isn't that so?"

"Yes."

"And if an infant suffocates, what happens is they become cyanotic, turn blue, and stop breathing. True?"

"Yes, that's true," she confirms. She looks at me, and I see despair in her eyes.

I move nearer to the witness box. Now only a few feet separate us. "Nurse," I say, "I know this is a difficult thing for you, but I have to ask."

She nods.

"After you fed Adora and before you went to the birthday gathering at the nurses' station, did she vomit her food as she had for each and every feeding during her first six days of life?"

"No," she softly responds.

"When you came back and found her—that *is* the word you used in your note. Correct? 'Found' her?"

"Yes, that's what I wrote."

"Well, when you found her, was there evidence she had vomited?"

"Yes," she says. She closes her eyes tightly, again lost in the pictures locked in her memory.

"And she choked on her vomit—that's what happened, isn't it?—because you weren't there the way you were required to be to suction it."

"Yes, that's what happened."

"Nurse, thank you for solving this mystery for us."

She looks at Maria and then at Adora, tears flowing from her eyes. Clearly she has one last thing to say. And she does.

"I'm sorry. I'm so sorry."

$$25.$$

y phone vibrates. I pull it out. It reads Alert One. Who the heck is Alert One, and why is their number stored in my address book?

"Hello."

"This is Melissa Freeman. I'm an emergency care coordinator at Alert One. I received an alert from subscriber Nelly Rivera. The special instructions on her account direct that we call this number before initiating standard protocol."

"I see. Thanks. What's the call location?"

"The transmission received from our satellite indicates an origination site of 138th Street in New York City. Do you want us to dispatch emergency services to the address?"

"*Um*, not just yet. I'll get back to you if necessary. Do I ask for you?"

"The same information is available to all ECCs."

"Thanks again, Melissa." *Click*.

I hit the speed dial assigned to Nelly. Half a ring in, she picks up.

"What took you so long? I could've been dead by now."

"Nelly," I begin carefully, not at all sure what might be going on. "Are you okay?"

"I'm fine. I was just checking to see if this thing worked. But what took you so long to call me?"

"I dialed you right away."

"Well, I pushed the button nine minutes ago."

"Okay. I'll have a talk with Alert One. The delay was on their end, not mine. Now don't push that button unless it's an emergency. You got me?"

"It was an emergency. I was overcome with an emergent need to see if this thing worked."

"That's not an emergency," I counter. "So don't push the button again unless it's a real emergency. You got that?"

"No promises."

"What do you mean, 'no promises'?"

"Like I said, no promises."

I'm not getting anywhere here. "Listen to me. You know the story about the boy who cried wolf, don't you?"

"In my opinion, that kid was a schmuck," she states. "And that stupid tale is fundamentally flawed."

"Oh, really," I respond. I'm curious. "How so?"

"Well, I appreciate the moral that nobody believes a liar even when they're telling the truth. But the story's just not believable."

"I'm listening. Go on."

"Okay," she says, pleased to explain. "You mean to tell me the townspeople entrusted all their sheep to this joker shepherd and nobody came running on his third cry for help because the first two were false alarms?"

"That was Aesop's point in this fable."

"Well, it's not realistic. That's all."

"Why not? He'd proved himself a liar."

"It doesn't matter if he was a liar. Too great a loss was at stake for too many people for no one to show up to check on things— you know, the sheep—and help protect them from the wolf."

"Really?" I say, intrigued by this analysis.

"Yes, really." Her tone's mocking, as if I'm an idiot. "Those sheep were their entire livelihood. You'd think at least one of those locals would swing by to see what's up. That's all I'm saying."

"You have a point there. And I appreciate your wanting to share. I'd like to know your opinions on *Snow White* one day too. But, for now, please don't push that button again unless it's a real emergency. You got that?"

"As long as you understand I'm not crying wolf." She pauses. "I'm living with one. Or didn't you get hit on the head hard enough to realize that?"

There's a moment of quiet, as I digest this.

"Are you saying I was clobbered by someone connected to your sister?"

"No, . . . yes . . ."

"Well, which is it? No or yes? Because when I told you about my incident, you sure as shit didn't implicate her then. So . . . pick one."

"Maybe, . . . I don't know. You just better respond quicker next time." *Click.*

Oh, great. The truth is, her concerns about Jessie have gotten out of hand over the last week. Nelly's been calling my office twice a day to talk to Lily, whose patience, as we know, is imperfect in the best of times. Lily feels sympathy for Nelly—a sister Latina, after all—but also cares about maintaining the boundaries of her job. Increased anxiousness and paranoia are behaviors I've seen many times, resulting from brain injury. Nelly also lacks response inhibition and is becoming impulsive as well. Of course she's been phoning me too. And I've been patient with her—except for maybe that "sure as shit" comment—but we're talking criminal conduct here. It's not an easy situation.

On the brighter side, a two-million-dollar offer is on the table from Grad's insurers. I advised the sisters to reject it. Jessie wanted to accept, owing to their dwindling financial situation, although Nelly is willing to follow my legal advice. Yet now— with all that money on the table—Jessie was forced to take a job as a waitress, which is creating a great deal of tension between the sisters.

What you should know is, as attorney, it's my job to get Nelly fairly compensated. The problem is, my collateral concerns require enough concrete answers to enable me to sleep soundly once this is all over. As guardian, Jessie will be the one to control the money, and thus I need to make sure she's capable of putting her sister's best interests before her own. Taking the two-mil was clearly against any such best interests. It was a first offer—and I explained that increasing ones would be coming. Jessie didn't care. She wants the money.

It should be obvious to anyone paying attention to the circumstance here that there's a conflict of interest when anyone who's guardian is also the sole heir in the event of the untimely death of the person they're "guarding."

I'm nervous and concerned about their relationship, which is why I'm making this trip. What I need here is to learn more.

You Mean, Roberto's

So here I am, pulling into Fritzi's Frijoles, Jessie's mother's restaurant. I bet I'm the only one here with an agenda beyond the sauerkraut taco or famed red-hot schnitzel that Nelly speaks of.

As I walk toward the door, what I'm reminded of is Trudy's missing scrapbook. It had clippings with pictures of the restaurant from the local paper after the fire. Truthfully it's hard to place Juanita in all this—my sense of her, up to now, is an inconclusive mix of pluses and minuses.

I enter and enjoy the spicy cooking smells. Spotting me, Juanita heads over. Remember Van Halen's "Hot for Teacher" video? That's what she makes me think of. With her glasses on a chain around her neck, she's a cross between a naughty librarian and an overworked short-order cook. I wonder if any of the regular patrons ever have similar fantasies. She greets me.

"Mr. Wyler, this is a surprise." But her smile says that it's not an unpleasant one. "What can I do for you? Have you time for lunch?"

"I'm definitely here for a bit of your time, if you can spare it. And I apologize for not calling first." I sniff the air and grin. "How about a taste of your signature schnitzel?" She heads to the kitchen.

While I eat, I take in the sights. Fritzi's is a little run-down but homey. Juanita took over the lease of a well-established old-school German coffee shop—adding her own touches to the menu to suit the neighborhood's changing demographic.

"So what's going on?" she asks after she's removed my now shiny plate.

"Wow," I say. "I'm breathing fire. That more than lives up to its reputation."

"Thank you," replies Juanita. "But tell me why you're here and what you need. Please."

"Okay," I agree, after taking another big swallow of water. I look directly at her. "Here's the thing. You know Nelly and Jessie better than anyone else could."

She nods. "I think so."

"Good. So how would you describe their relationship?"

"Well, it's a good one, as far as sisters go. Why don't you just ask them?"

"It's gotten complicated, is all. My concern here is that Nelly keeps having these flashbacks. Memories of stuff that happened . . . things she never had any prior recollection of until after she came out of her coma."

"I've had only hints that this might be going on—from Jessie. But Nelly's been under medical supervision for a good chunk of time in Rusk, a top facility. I think I need to know better what's worrying you."

"Me, I'm just struggling to make some sense out of what could be true and what might be mind games. But what's most important to me at this very moment is learning how you view their relationship."

"Can you tell me why?"

Crap. This is just what I'd hoped to stay away from but knew was unavoidable.

"Because Nelly may be coming into money from her malpractice suit. With Jessie in charge of it . . ." I pause. "That makes for . . ." I stop again. "Issues."

"If I understand you, and I think I do, then I have to ask, does every lawyer show such consideration?" She's staring at me curiously.

Good question, I think. But I sidestep it. "That money is to compensate Nelly for the trauma she went through and the lasting harm she experienced. It's the safety net in the event she can't resume gainful employment. Therefore, you don't want a situation where Jessie spends Nelly's money for the wrong reasons."

"I see." She pauses, considering. "Well, they've had their differences, like any sisters, but Jessie's a good girl and can be trusted. Is that what you're looking for?"

"Yes. But I've managed to learn about a few past episodes that disturb me. For example, back in high school, they had a vicious fight, during which Jessie broke Nelly's jaw with a pan in her face."

Now her attention's commanded by a table of arriving customers who want to place their orders. But, when she returns, Juanita doesn't answer right away. Finally she says, "I remember the girls talking about that fight. Jessie was swinging the pan to keep her sister away, and Nelly tripped on an old torn rug they had up at the house, falling into it midswing. That's the way it was told to me."

"I see." I look at her with what I believe is still a neutral expression. I need to keep going with this. But I don't want her spooked and leaving me in the lurch here.

I take a polite breath. "I hate to bring this up about your daughter, but I understand Jessie was suspended from school for stealing the answers to an eleventh-grade science exam?"

"That's a pretty specific tidbit. How'd you know about that?"

"Research."

She's a mom, after all, and now looks unhappy. "Okay, so I get that this sort of background information might be helpful to you. But since I already know all of it, why are you here bugging me?"

"I understand how you must feel. I'm simply doing my job—to the best of my ability."

She bites her lip. "Jessie always denied that one. She could've avoided suspension by admitting to it, but she refused. Said her best friend Samantha—her dad was police chief—was the one who stole it but refused to give her up."

"That's honorable. Especially given the dad, who might not have taken it so well."

"My girl *is* honorable. Still I get it. There are trust issues here."

"That's right. I'm glad you see where I'm coming from." I steel myself for the next more difficult part. "What do you know about the fire?" I ask. No beating around the bush, right?

"What's the fire got to do with anything?"

"Not exactly sure. But it's part of their mutual history. A shared tragic event. I guess I just want to know what you think the hidden scars are. There have to be some."

"We always thought it was a good thing that she had no memory of the fire." She hesitates. "But this does make sense, as Jessie's given me bits about what's changing for Nelly. Not that I fully understand though."

Obviously I wonder about that chat. Since I can't reveal what Nelly's confided in me, what I now say is this: "So, with regard to the fire, . . . what sort of ongoing influence, if any, has it had on their relationship? I think my position is simply, and needfully, a protective one, regarding Jessie's ability to exercise proper judgment over a large sum of money."

Juanita stares at me now. "I don't know exactly how to respond to that, I'm afraid."

"I'd like to encourage you to try."

She tilts her head. "I can't think of anything."

A quiet moment passes between us. It's her subtle cue that it's time for me to go.

"You've been very helpful, and I appreciate you talking to me so candidly, especially since we're discussing your daughter's character. Is it too much to ask, as a favor, that you don't tell her about my visit today? It would upset her, I know, and, believe me, that's not what I'm trying to do."

"Certainly. I understand completely."

"Thank you for your time." I stand up.

"You know," she continues, "this conversation has reminded me of ones I had with that life insurance lady. Looking here, there—everywhere really—in her determination to deny the payout of Stella's death benefit."

"You mean, Roberto's," I correct her. *Oops.*

"*Um*, . . . yes," she amends but only after a beat. "That woman was crazy, I tell you. She thought she was some kind of insurance avenger, like out of the comics."

"Yeah, I spoke to her too," I remark casually. "She never let this one go."

Juanita's definitely mulling that over as I walk out. She doesn't even hear me say good-bye. I've revealed more than intended. Not the mark of an experienced lawyer.

At least I admit it.

But let's see if this little conversation sets anything in motion.

26.

need to finish what I started. That's why I'm standing at the curb, waiting for Trace. Despite all the street noise the city has to offer, you can always hear him approaching from a block away.

Up to the curb now rumbles his Impala. The 1962 Chevy SS 409 bubbletop was the best that model had to offer in my opinion. Some would argue the 1958 convertible. Naturally passersby slow their pace to stare at this black metal piece of muscle history with its high-gloss paint, shiny steel accents, and menacing engine cowl. The passenger window slowly lowers, and gangsta rap escapes. I lean down, and Trace turns his head ninety degrees.

"In."

As always I obey. Edward, an accountant in my building, watches, perplexed. Here's a white mid-forties lawyer getting into a low-rider driven by a gigantic black man with a shaved head and plastic wraparound dark sunglasses, sporting a Shaft-style leather coat—in June. As he stands there reading the personalized license plate, THEFIDGE, I can see him mouthing the words. A puzzled look crosses his face. I don't blame him.

Trace is doing his signature peel out as I give Edward a thumbs-up.

"I'm still mad at you for that shit you pulled at the hospital."

"Over it," he says.

"I'm glad you are. But I'm still salty."

"No. *You* get over it."

"I will. But that was fucked up."

"Just playing."

"Wonderful. Next time you want to have a playdate, can you make sure no one aims a loaded gun in my face?"

He smiles.

We're on our way to see Fred Sanford of Sanford & Son, in the heart of Brooklyn. Not the sitcom comedian who owned a junkyard; he passed away. However, this Fred Sanford owns a junkyard too, as well as a television repair shop. But being an astronaut is his claim to fame.

I met Trace through June Williams, the mother of little Suzy, an injured child from a prior Henry Benson case. Trace then introduced me to Fred. We've all been friends ever since. Fred served as my expert witness on the *Williams* case. He's, in fact, well qualified to act as an expert in many fields. In Suzy's case, he offered expert opinions in the fields of electrical engineering, immunohistologic chemistry, and forensic pathology. Today, however, he'll be needing to put on a different hat.

I could've made the trip to Fred's on my own, but Trace said he wanted to "see my face." I'm not exactly sure what he meant. Our trip was silent until the moment we pull up. No surprises there. Trace, if you haven't noticed, is a man of few words.

"Oh, by the way," I say, "I settled the case we stole back my client's records on."

"*Simone.*"

"That's right. *Simone.* What they did wrong turned out to be in those missing pages."

"'Course."

"'Course?" I respond, questioning.

"'Course."

What to me is an arrogant display of completely deplorable ethics is just business as usual in Trace's reality.

You do what you can get away with.

Fred steps out of his brownstone as we pull up. He's a black man in his mid-seventies and spends his days wearing the most expensive bathrobes money can buy. Today's is a silk leopard print with an oversize hood. It matches his leopard skin slippers, which are real. He has a scruffy beard—just like Redd Foxx, who played the sitcom Fred Sanford—and has the same moseying-around habits.

"Come on in!" Fred calls out. "But not if you're going to go pee-pee in your pants."

Embarrassed, I turn to Trace. "Is this the face you wanted to see?"

"Word."

"Thanks, buddy."

He smirks, then says, "Here." Which translates as, he'll be waiting here when I'm done conferring with Fred.

Once inside, we head directly to Fred's lab in the back. There we settle ourselves on old bucket car seats welded to heavy metal bases bolted into the floor.

"Tea?" he asks.

"I'd love some, thanks." He gets up and leaves the room to brew up a pot of serious spiked tea. Gazing over at an authentic gas lantern, I feel a smile cross my face as I recall Fred puffing away on his corncob pipe the last time I was here—when he confirmed my suspicions about Suzy's case.

He reenters, holding two steaming china cups. The royal emblem on the side of each reads Buckingham Palace. The last ones we used bore the NASA seal. Fred is quite the honored man. He puts our tea down on a large wooden-cable-spool-turned-coffee-table, the name Con Edison spray-painted across it.

"So," he tells me, "your ear doesn't look too bad." He's referring to the injury I sustained while working on behalf of little Suzy.

"Yep. It healed."

We both chuckle even as we know what a close call I had.

"Well, what have you got for me?"

I reach into my pocket and pull out the folded-over tape containing the fibers from the DA's office evidence box, placing it on the table.

"This."

He looks at it. "*Hmm*, let's see," he says as he scratches his chin. "Ah, yes, it seems to be a piece of clear plastic packaging tape folded in half. Not much of a challenge."

"Very funny, Fred. How much do you want to know?"

"Nothing. I'll figure it out." He holds it up, giving it a once-over as I sip my tea. Its sweet high-alcohol-liquor flavor is delicious. Next he raises the tape to examine it in the glowing light, then puts it back down. Removing his pipe from his pocket, he flicks an old army lighter, and a cloud mushrooms toward the lantern. He's definitely on the case.

His next move is to rise—seemingly annoyed that he has to—and walk to a counter. There he picks up a magnifying glass with an antique carved ivory handle. Walking back over, he reseats himself. Pausing for a swallow of his elixir, he murmurs, "Nice."

Then he sets about separating the edges of the tape, making use of the magnifying glass.

A moment later, he asks, "The fibers?"

"The fibers," I confirm.

Now I watch him work his magic. Carefully extracting just a few of the fibers, he puts them under a crazy-looking vintage microscope, like out of a mad-scientist comic.

"*Um-hum*." I hear this and recognize it for a sign pertinent information's just been scrutinized. So I'm pleased naturally.

His next task is to retrieve ten small shallow, round dishes from his chem lab cabinet, setting them in a row next to the microscope. He looks in the eyepiece while pulling out a drawer underneath it. Reaching in, he produces a large pair of tweezers with a fine-point tip. He plucks fibers off the tape, placing the samples in the various dishes. Once he's retrieved small vials from a cabinet shelf, he drips one tiny drop of clear solution from each into the separate dishes, then waits. Within moments some develop color.

He returns to me now, relighting his pipe. I take in the aroma. Normally I hate pipe smells, but Fred's selection of tobacco is the exception.

"More tea?" he asks.

"I'm feeling all right from this one, thanks."

"How about an aperitif?"

"No, thanks. The tea did the trick." I grin appreciatively. "You want me to ask, or are you going to tell me?"

Having Fred on my side is a great feeling. Not only is he a bona fide genius but he's ingenious in all the best ways.

"First, I have a question for you."

I look at him expectantly. "Sure. Shoot."

"Where'd you retrieve these fibers from?"

"They came off an IV flow-control clamp. It's a . . ."

"I know what it is," he interrupts. "I hold a patent on one I developed while in the army. No time to adjust flow rates with bombs coming in, so I invented one with a standardized flow rate for the pain meds we were administering. In that way we could monitor the hydrostatic height between the supply reservoir and a patient."

"I'm not surprised—even though I have little idea what you just said. But what do you have for me?"

"Where was the IV being administered?"

"In a dental office."

"I see," he says, again scratching the white stubble on his chin.

"Well?" I can't help it. I'm getting impatient. Enough with the suspense.

"This is an interesting one because of the oddity of things."

"I'll beg if I have to. Just say the word." I'm playing my role, right? The clueless sidekick.

"No need," he says.

Whew.

"Yes, well, . . . these IV flow controllers are hooked up under sterile circumstances. But, if these fibers were taken from the controller, then I'd have to suggest such circumstances had been compromised. Although . . . I did isolate synthetic rubber residue on the specimens."

"And so . . . ?"

"And so," he replies, "if the medical professional who used the controller was wearing gloves, then they were not sterile."

"Can you be a little more specific? What did you find?"

"I found fibers."

"I'm pretty sure I knew that before coming here. Please just tell me what you learned about them."

"Yes, well, . . . a fiber is the smallest unit of textile material. It has a length many times greater than its diameter. Fibers can be natural—plant and animal—or man-made. They are the basis of fabric." He pauses. "What I found here was a blended fabric—a mix of man-made and animal. Fifty percent of the fiber was polyester, 40 percent was rayon, and 10 percent was wool."

"Okay. So I'm superimpressed that you could break things down into percentages with a drop of solution. But is that all you found?"

"What did you envisage from a fiber speck?"

"I don't know. Something more."

He smiles. "Okay. I have something more."

"I hate when you do this, Fred," I tell him. "Go on."

"The source of this fiber is very uncommon," he explains. "Not the man-made stuff, the wool. Most wool is sheep's wool, but this isn't."

"Go on. Stop with the games. Please. What kind of wool is it?"

"It's cashmere. And I'd say the goat was from Iran."

"Are you telling me that you know the wool content of that miniscule fiber is from some goat in Iran?"

"That's what I'm telling you. But it's low quality—the cheap kind—recycled."

"You're good."

I sigh though. We've arrived somewhere, but it turns out to be Iran.

"Maybe I am, but this is good for you too."

"How so?"

"These fibers are involved in one of your legal matters, correct?"

"Correct. But you knew that already."

"Yes, well, so I did." He looks at me innocently now. "Can I assume you want to know the source of these fibers or, more specifically, the person who owns the article of clothing these Iranian goat fibers came from?"

"That would be helpful. Go on."

"I'm of the opinion that the identification of less common animal fibers, such as these, at a crime scene would have increased significance."

"Because . . . ?"

"Because they're so uncommon, they give a match a higher degree of reliability. Show me someone from that dental office who wears Iranian goat, and you'll have whoever you're looking for."

27.

enry! Pick up, Henry!" I yell into my phone.

"Three," Trace says, referring to the number of my call attempts. "Busy. Trim time."

"No, Trace. He's not picking up because he knows how badly I want to talk to him. Ego, buddy, it's all about ego with this guy. I need you to drop me off at his apartment."

"Nah, man, too invasive."

"Just drop me there."

"No."

"You're kidding, right?" No answer. Trace never looks like he's kidding.

My phone goes off. I look at the screen. Benson. "Hi, Henry."

"What seems to be the problem?" he asks. "Three calls."

"Where are you?"

"Yankel's Bathhouse."

"When will you be done?"

"I don't do business when I leave here. Why don't you join me?" he says in an encouraging tone. "You sound stressed."

"That's because I am. Where's Yankel's located?"

"On it," Trace interjects.

"Never mind, Henry. I'm on my way." *Click.*

Trace pulls up to a handsome town house. It's in the middle of an otherwise dilapidated block in Alphabet City on the Lower East Side.

"Fun," Trace says, as I reach for the car door handle. I look over at him. He gives me a sly smile.

"I'm a bit uptight for fun," I tell him. "But thanks for the wheels."

He nods. I get out, and he rumbles the 409 as the door shuts.

After I knock and am admitted, I approach a counter at which sits an adorable Asian girl. Standing next to her is a slight man in his mid-twenties, wearing a yarmulke. In front of him is the cash register. My guess would be he's Yankel. Before I say a word, the girl comes around, takes my hand, and leads me away. Two steps in, I stop and turn to the young entrepreneur. He raises his brow in surprise, the inference being everyone comes here for the same thing.

"Hey, sonny boy," I say playfully. "You've got to always keep your eyes on the cash register, okay?"

He grins, taking no offense. "That's sound advice. You go enjoy yourself while I keep my eye on the cash register. Ming," he says to my new companion, "make sure this gentleman gets the royal service. He's Henry's friend."

She bows, then pulls me along. We walk me down a wide circular staircase lit by candles on the wall and step into an open changing area. On a trunk table is a stack of entirely inviting black bathrobes. Next to them is a pile of thick black towels. Both are heavy-weight soft terry. Ming now hands me one of each and leads me straight to a corner dressing—and undressing—room.

"Thanks," I say, as I start to set aside my briefcase.

She intercepts, taking it from me, gently setting it down.

"Thanks again," I tell her.

Now she steps forward and reaches for my tie. "I got it. Don't worry."

A disappointed look crosses her face, as if I've denied her some privilege.

"Go ahead," I say. "I'm sorry."

Her face lights up as she unknots my tie. She slides it off, and, for some reason, the slow way she pulled it around my neck woke up the little guy downstairs.

I go to unbutton my collar, only to see that upset expression come over her face. "Sorry," I say.

I stand there as she undresses me, pouting if I try to help out in any way. So I just let Ming do her thing until I'm just standing here, butt naked. Before reaching for the robe, she looks at my confused dick on the quarter bone and smiles. Aiding me as I don the robe now, she double-pats it, which I have to say is suddenly less confused on the half bone. And rising.

Removing a pair of blue rubber flip-flops off a stocked shelf, she kneels and places them on my bare feet.

But, when she starts to lead me again, I give a little pull back.

"My wallet and watch have great value to me, as does my briefcase with my computer in it. I'm not comfortable with them just left out there in a doorless cubby."

"They are safe," she assures me, offering a smile which tells me my concern is understood but unnecessary.

She leads me down a narrow candle-lit hallway, opening the last door we come to. The fifteen-foot square room is refreshingly scented. In its center is a three-tiered fountain with water flowing down from bowl to bowl. Around it are four white marble-slab beds, one occupied by none other than Henry Benson. He is naked. *Ugh!*

I never imagined when we formed our partnership and I became the attorney for Henry's injured criminals—or HICs—that I'd ever see him naked in a dimly lit chamber with slices of cucumbers covering his eyes. I check out his package, but it's just normal human curiosity. I definitely have more interest in the girl attending him. She's an adorable Asian woman, although Ming, who's still holding my hand, is cuter.

"*Um*, . . . hi, Henry."

Without making a move, he answers, "Lay down and relax. You need this."

I go to lie down, but my escort stops me. Untying the belt of my robe, Ming slips off my protective covering. My first thought as I stand there in all my glory is: *Yep, I'm bigger.* And even if Henry, ever the litigator, would claim diminishment owing to prolonged heat exposure, don't buy it. He might never admit it, but I'm certain he'd notice and definitely register me the winner here if he could see the comparison for himself. Men are ridiculous in this area.

At least I admit it.

I lay down on my slab—which is surprisingly warm—with my head at a right angle to Henry's. My eyes are covered with a warm moist cloth. Ming takes a large copper scooper, fills it with water, and slowly pours the warm liquid over me. Nice.

"Feels good now—doesn't it?" Henry asks, obviously hearing the light splashing sounds.

"Sure does," I say, as the next pour trickles over me. I hear the door open, and, peeking, I see two more adorable Asian women appear. *The relief team,* I think, but I'm way wrong. My number two approaches, wearing a wash mitten, and scrubs the bottom of my foot. She makes her way above my ankle, continuing up to my beef roll, soaping that up too while Ming washes the suds away in synchronicity. I'm hoping and praying I don't firm up again because all this stuff's just fun and games until somebody pops a boner. Even if they're used to it.

I look over, and Henry's girls are involved in the same process. After completing the front side, mine flip me over. When the scrub down's complete, I receive what I can only describe as a four-hand massage. My mind has never had to handle assimilating tactile stimulation from four different sources. But I get used to it real fast.

"Henry," I say, "I agree this is great. But I got a boatload of crap running through my head that needs to be discussed."

"We'll discuss it in the cooldown area. For now, enjoy."

After a further half hour of the same twenty-finger massage, we wind up, fully robed, semireclining on lounge chairs, facing each other, with a little round table between us.

"Go on if you have to. I'm all ears," he says.

I'm a little distracted by the clump of seaweed resting on the top of his head but not so much that I can't say what I came here to say. For the record, I skipped the seaweed and the cucumber, preferring my vegetables on a plate.

"I don't really know where to begin, Henry. So I guess I'll just start with my conclusions."

"Go on. Beginning at the end is never a bad place to start."

I get right down to it then. "I think Jessie may have burned down the family home, killing Stella and her father. She may also have tampered with the anesthesia flow that Grad was giving Nelly, attempting to kill her too."

He just looks at me. I wait for a response, but I'm not getting one. He's definitely thinking about it. He reaches for his glass of lemon water, takes a cool sip, then places it back down on the table. "Have you gone mad, boy?"

"I don't think so."

"Why do you think she burned down the house?"

"First of all, she's not such a nice girl. Which is according to certain stuff I've learned about her past. Meaning, I think she may have it in her."

"Funny, I've always found her to be quite an agreeable young woman—and I've known her since she was a child. But go on."

"Well, I met with the life insurance adjuster assigned to the claim—"

"Trudy, the nutjob?"

"Yes, and why didn't you tell me about the death benefit and property damage litigation?"

"First, because it's none of your business. Second, because I would be in breach of my oath of confidentiality. Third, because it's irrelevant to your pursuing her malpractice claim."

"Anyway," I say, having anticipated his response and understanding the rightness of it, "Trudy shared her thoughts about the investigation with me. She even had made a scrapbook out of it, one bursting at the seams practically, with all her findings and the stuff she turned up about the Riveras. I had it. I saw it."

"A scrapbook, you say?"

"Yeah, a goddamn scrapbook."

"I'd like to see it."

"Well, you can't."

"Why not?"

"Because it's gone."

"Then get it for me."

"I can't. I don't know where it is."

"You've gone mad."

"No, not in that sense anyway. But I am mad. Angry mad. You see, after Trudy gave it to me, I was assaulted, and the book was stolen by whoever conked me on the head. I think the perp may have been sent by Jessie."

Henry looks at me pityingly. "You're working too hard," he concludes.

"No, Henry. Trudy gave me the scrapbook. I read through it, then was smashed in the head right after—and it was stolen. Jessie's the only person with motive."

"So, you're saying Jessie smashed you in the head?"

"No, I didn't see who did because I was blindsided. But I heard a *clankety-clank*."

"Are you saying you're hearing clatter in your head, son?"

"No. The actual sound of metal clanking together. The same sound a nunchuck chain makes."

"So, you're saying Jessie's part of a nunchuck-carrying gang?"

"No, but her boyfriend is."

"Then what you're saying is that her boyfriend smashed you in the head and stole the scrapbook at her command because she knew you were coming into possession of it, and its contents incriminate her in the fiery death of Nelly's parents—one of the couple being, in fact, her own father."

Hearing Henry's summation makes me realize that it all does sound more than a little far-fetched. "*Um*," I say, "well . . ."

"Never mind," he says, "but I'm curious. Is her boyfriend a ninja?"

"Stop playing. Please. I'm serious here."

"Okay, where did this happen?"

"In Grand Central."

He grins. "Grand Central's under video surveillance. Have you seen their video yet?"

"I'm waiting for the call. I spoke to the MTA cops, and they've secured it. The trouble is, they're having technical problems viewing it. However, they assure me it soon will be available."

"Let me know immediately when this happens. But do go on. What else makes you believe Jessie incinerated her father and stepmother other than the contents of this scrapbook which you no longer possess?"

"I'll get another copy. Anyway Trudy Anderson states that she confirmed it was arson. Plus there was financial motive. Jessie is Nelly's only living relative. So, if Roberto, Stella, and Nelly die, then Jessie gets everything."

"I understand that. Anything else?"

"The flashbacks Nelly has been having, they factor in too. I've told you about those. But the kicker is, she outright told me her parents were murdered in that house and that she was locked in her room during the fire. Being rescued—when the fire department arrived—is what foiled Jessie's plan."

Henry gives me a perplexed look. "Anyway, by 'arson,'" he goes on, "I'm certain you must be talking about the gasoline, correct?"

"Correct."

"What I believe," he now says, "is that a crime *was* committed in that home. But not a murder. And not by Jessie. Trudy Anderson illegally entered the premises, and I believe she contaminated the scene with gas herself to avoid a payout."

"Why on earth would she do that?"

"God only knows what her motives were."

I keep silent. But God may not be the only one with that insight. Trudy's motives for combatting insurance fraud run deep into her father's grave.

"And even if we assume it was arson, we can't just jump to Jessie being the guilty party. I was involved with the family during the time frame and I know a lot more than you do. The first thing you should be aware of is that I could give you a list of people who wanted Roberto Rivera dead, beginning with both his wife and ex-wife. Then the names on the witness list the DA gave me, and that's just a start.

"Roberto made a career of making enemies. He was the type of criminal who stole first from people he knew—his friends in many instances. Plus both girls were injured in that fire, to varying degrees, which makes it unlikely that Jessie would've started it. Not to mention that, no matter how much Jessie didn't like her father, it wasn't enough to want him dead. And to include Stella's death as part of the mass murder plan simply seems to me out of the question. End of story.

"Now," Henry says, as if that was truly and finally that, "what makes you think Jessie tampered with the anesthesia and attempted to kill her sister? For the second time."

"Okay." I'm eager to share, knowing that, thus far, I sound like a complete idiot. "I went and looked at the physical evidence the detectives collected at the dental office and what I noticed was that the IV flow controller for the anesthesia drip bag was in the full-flow position. Even the worst dentist in the world wouldn't have the roller clamp fully open. Grad may not have been licensed, and he may be a liar, but he certainly was qualified to employ anesthesia. Then I noticed these tiny fibers on the flow controller, so I lifted some and had them analyzed. They were a mix of different fabric material but the one that stands out is a recycled wool cashmere fiber from an Iranian goat."

"I see. You have gone mad."

"No, I don't think so."

"Well, do you think this goat from Iran is an accomplice or maybe just a coconspirator? Or maybe the goat was in the wrong place at the wrong time. Maybe he had a cavity and needed a filling. I suggest we start out by seeing if this goat has an alibi."

"Very funny, Henry. I'm glad you find it amusing. Me, I'm all worked up about it."

His humorous look quickly changes. Here it comes. "I'm the criminal law expert here, correct?"

"Correct."

"The expert on crime-scene forensics, correct?"

"Correct."

"One of New York's ten best criminal lawyers as selected by *New York Magazine.*"

"That would be you, Henry. Now say what you want to say."

The stern look that had all but vanished quickly returns. He hates being told to do anything.

"Now listen, and listen good," he commands. "This roller clamp could've *rolled* into the open position at any point in time after Grad malpracticed her. Who knows how many people manipulated it between the moment of malpractice to the one when you pulled it from some evidence box? As for the fibers, what we are talking about here is the transfer and persistence of a textile material to the surface of this IV controller. Transfer can be from direct contact or it can be a secondary transfer where the fibers find themselves landing there without direct contact from the article of clothing."

The look I give him is curious. He's on a roll, but it's okay. I'm interested to see where he's going with it.

"That's right," he affirms. "Clothing sheds these fibers as a natural consequence of just being worn. Tightly woven fabrics shed less than loosely knit ones, and the age of the garment affects the degree of fiber transfer too. Newer clothing may shed more because of an abundance of loosely adhering fibers on the surface of the fabric, and so on and so forth.

Those fibers may have been floating around in the dental room from a prior patient, from the nursing staff, or from Grad himself. I also recall Jessie saying that patients from the other rooms came to watch the unfortunate festivities. Emergency personnel were at the scene. The police entered the room. Then the crime scene investigators showed up to collect the evidence. Clearly there can be multiple sources, known and unknown, for the contamination of what we call, in criminal law, 'trace evidence.'"

"Is the lecture over?" I went to law school. I know all about trace evidence.

"It is. But was an abridged one because this topic covers volumes."

"Fine. However, you left out one option."

"What's that?"

"That this trace evidence came directly from something Jessie wore."

"There's no basis to support that," he retorts.

"Really?" I counter. "If the other people in that room were wearing cashmere from Iranian goats, then I would agree with you. But, I don't recall the uniforms of nurses, dentists, ambulance personnel, and police being made from cashmere, Iranian goat or otherwise."

"Maybe not," he says, angered. "But the only way you'd sway me would be if a forensic fiber examiner matched what you removed from the IV controller to an item of Jessie's clothing—and that's just not going to happen. She's your client, and you can't ask her for the clothing she wore that day in an effort to implicate her in an attempted murder. Got it?"

I think for a second. Yep, my gut tells me he's right. I'll give him the answer he's looking for. But this shit ain't over. "Got it."

"Now, would it be fair to say that you haven't told anyone about this?"

"That would be fair," I answer.

"Good. Keep it to yourself, or you'll be in serious breach of our code of ethics."

"You mean, the Rules, Henry?"

"Yes, I mean the Rules," he confirms, meaning the Rules of Professional Conduct. The holy bible of what we can and cannot do as lawyers vis-à-vis our clients.

"I hear you. But such information presents many problems beyond ethics and morals. What we're looking at here is criminal."

"I'm going to remind you of something for the last time," he snaps at me, like a dog behind a chain link fence.

"Yeah, what's that?"

"Jessie is your client! You're the lawyer for both these girls, and your obligation is to them. If you even think of breaching your legal duty, I'll have to ask you to remove yourself from the case. In fact, I'll have the Rivera sisters sign on with a different lawyer if I even sense you have intentions of continuing on with this ridiculous notion. Do you understand me?"

At this moment I realize we're experiencing the first real difference—which is to say, serious difference—Henry and I have ever had. I will give him the answer I know he wants to hear.

"Yes, I understand."

The conversation should be over now, but, like most lawyers, I just can't help myself. "You know, Henry, this has other implications, such as Jessie's ability to act in her sister's best interests as guardian."

"Don't worry about that."

"How can I not worry about that?"

"Because I just told you not to!"

He gets up in a huff, and the seaweed flies off his head, landing on my lap. In his flip-flops, he stomps out, madder than ever. I can hear him muttering about me being an idiot. We both know, of course, that, if it turns out Jessie really did do this, then Grad's off the hook, and that two million dollars, plus whatever else may be coming, is out the window, along with our fee.

This was relaxing.

28.

'm on a Metro North train heading toward the city. It's 8:30 in the morning, and I'm reflecting on a thought I had last night after leaving Yankel's. I can petition to have Nelly declared competent and remove Jessie as guardian. This would prevent her from having direct access to Nelly's money. The problem is, Dr. Furman said he'd only support such a petition under limited circumstances, none of which apply as of this time.

I make the call I decided on last night just before Henry stormed out. I scroll through my address book looking for his code name. There it is—Ethics Lawyer—the ultimate in professional oxymorons. The voice mail picks up.

"You have reached the law office of Roscoe Jenkins, specializing in ethics and conflicts. You should've made this call before you did your deed." *Beep.*

I hang up and try again. This time he picks up.

"Tug Wyler, what a surprise!" he says. "Let me guess. Now don't tell me you have another issue with a Henry Benson referral."

"You're so good at what you do, Roscoe. You got ten?"

"Five. I have to run across the street to the disciplinary committee for a hearing. Give me the nuts and bolts—and let me mull it over. I can see you at my office at one."

"Great, so here it is . . ."

After hearing the salient facts in a condensed version, he offers a one-word summation. "Slippery."

Once in Grand Central, I grab a cup of coffee and sit on the steps leading to the Apple Store and make call number two. "Brad, it's Tug. Where we at on this? Any movement?"

"I was just going to buzz you. They're up to four million on Nelly's case. I told them you wouldn't take it. Still, communicate it to your clients anyway and give me the formal rejection. Like I told you, I've recommended the number we spoke about. Just be patient. It's a process."

"Thanks," I say, reminding myself what I thought already, that he's not a bad guy at all for a defense attorney. "Can I give you a little something to use with your carrier, information that might help them get the rest up a little faster so we can close this out?"

"Sure. Anytime I provide something new, it gives them a reason to reconference the matter and come up with more money. But I can't imagine anything new at this late stage of the game."

He won't need to imagine. I'll go with a piece of intelligence he knows, just to elevate his confidence. After that, what I'm going to drop on him won't be pretty. I saved this for the right time—and the right time is now. And, despite how fond I am of Brad, I'm going to feel good about his fall off the cliff.

At least I admit it.

First, let me lead him to the edge. "Great. Listen, even if we assume it was an allergic reaction like Grad's been contending—rather than an overdose—the issue is his failure to have and use the appropriate reversal agents. This contributed to Nelly's downward cardiorespiratory spiral, arrest, and resultant brain and heart wall damage. So, even if we embrace the allergy-based position, he can still be found liable."

"You must think I'm stupid." He's partially right, but it's not specific to him. I feel this way about most defense counsel.

"How do you think I got them to come up with the four?" he

continues. "I told them how we can lose even if it was an allergic reaction. I didn't just start working yesterday, you know."

"Of course you're right. I'm sorry." Here it goes.

"Can I suggest something else then?" I say, interested to hear his response.

"What else is there in this case?"

"Well, if your defense is that Jessie had an allergic reaction to anesthesia, wouldn't it be important to know whether she ever had anesthesia prior to this event?"

"What are you suggesting? Grad's record clearly indicates she had no prior exposure to anesthesia." His voice rises.

"What if his record is inaccurate?" I propose.

"Well, there's no documentation of any such exposure in her hospital records either." Now he's angry.

"But there is."

"Not in her admitting history or in subsequent histories, for that matter."

"Yes, well. We know Nelly entered Lincoln Hospital in a coma. Her sister would have provided the information, if she remembered. But Jessie was upset, to say the least. And Nelly herself only began to be verbal later, when she was at Rusk. The info to which I'm referring, however, *can* be found deep in the record . . . if you look."

"What appears 'deep' in her record?" he challenges.

We are definitely having a conversation for which he's unprepared. His voice has clouded with a mix of suspicion and uncertainty.

"She had her tonsils out when she was ten," I tell him.

No response.

There's more. "So I obtained those records. Nelly, it turns out, received for her tonsillectomy the same kind of anesthesia Grad employed. No allergic reaction. I'd suggest that's inconsistent with your defense of anaphylaxis. I'll send you a copy."

He offers no response. To me, that is. Instead I hear him say, "Fuck," followed by a *click*.

He's mad—at himself—for not asking Nelly at her deposition about her prior surgical history. He relied instead solely on his client's inaccurate record while neglecting to examine extensively enough the records from Rusk.

Me, I had no duty to give him an authorization for the release of these records because he never demanded such. But, if he decides to read closely the admission record I'm gratuitously going to send him from her tonsillectomy, he'll see they, in fact, didn't administer to her the same exact anesthetics. A close first cousin but not identical. Which can make all the difference in a defense. Sure, I bent the truth just a bit in the interest of justice. Still, in my business, that's called good lawyering.

At least I admit it.

For now though, his ass is on the line because his anaphylaxis defense no longer appears to have any basis. The only alternative—overdose. In the language my friend Ernie understands best, *cha-ching*!

Sock It To Me

I stand and toss my cup into a trash can as I head for the MTA Police Headquarters here in Grand Central. They claim they've ironed out their technical glitch and now have a clear video of my assailant. It's time to see if I can ID this mofo.

Where I find myself is in a large room containing an array of audio-visual equipment. For the moment, the only person with me is the tech support guy. From him I learn that the detective handling the case is due any moment. However, it's now almost an hour later. Finally the door opens and in walks two fellows, one young and one old.

"Sorry to keep you waiting," the senior type says. "I'm Detective Gilman, and this is Officer Parker. He's the responder who found you on the floor."

"Thanks," I say to him. "I appreciate it."

"That's okay," he says, wearing what I'd call an odd expression. If I didn't know better, I'd say he was holding in a laugh.

"Like the phone message I left you," Gilman continues, "from the video it appears to be a random act of violence. Your assailant didn't take anything and just walked away afterward."

"Well, Detective Gilman, actually my assailant took a scrapbook I was carrying."

"Yes, well, I read your email. But we went back over the video and established that she didn't take it."

"She?" I question. "Are you telling me I was attacked by a *woman?*"

Officer Parker lets a laugh slip out. I stare at him.

"Sorry," he says.

"Parker," Gilman admonishes, "collect yourself. This is a serious matter."

"Yes, sir," he says. But his lip is quivering.

"After the crowd dispersed," Gilman continues, "there, on the floor, was your scrapbook. Willie, one of our maintenance engineers, picked it up and threw it in the receptacle he was responsible for. He's been instructed to deliver all such articles to the Lost and Found in the future."

"Oh, good," I say sarcastically. "That helps me out."

"Play the video, Joey," Gilman now instructs the techie who's been sitting here quietly. "Mr. Wyler, look at screen two and let me know if you recognize your assailant—or anybody else for that matter." I see myself standing at the train departure screen, holding the scrapbook in my left hand with my briefcase in my right.

I can tell you one thing: I look out of shape.

As I turn toward my track, a little old lady, holding a white tube sock weighted in the toe, winds up like Mickey Mantle and smashes me across the back of my head. I go down like a ton of bricks.

Parker can't help himself, beginning again to laugh.

"Shut up, Parker!" Gilman commands.

It's the strangest thing I've ever seen—watching myself get knocked out by a geriatric female assailant. I mean, when her weapon of choice hit my head, I went flaccid, dropping what I was holding as I crashed face-first to the floor. As I try to get up, she steps closer and bashes me again, like she wanted to make sure I'd be out of commission for the next week—or maybe even permanently.

Once again I hear Parker laugh. He can't help himself. After looking over me, confirming she got the job done, my attacker casually walks away. A moment later, several people converge on my motionless body. Within thirty seconds, there's a crowd, and this is when Parker shows up.

"Well, do you know her? Would you like to see it again?"

"Yeah, let's see it again," Parker chimes in.

Gilman scowls at him.

"No, Detective. I don't need to see it again," I say. "The thing is, I'm not sure. She looks familiar, but I'm just not certain. Can I mull it over for a day and get back to you?"

He gives me a suspicious look as if I'm withholding information. "Call me tomorrow. We got nothing else to go on. You'd think there'd be one witness or bystander who'd have intervened . . ." He shakes his head.

"You'd think so," I agree.

Once on the street, I pull out my phone. He picks up on ring four. He's a fourth-ring kind of guy. "Hi, Chuck. How're you doing?"

"Not so good. Forced retirement. Adora's case was my last. The insurance company pulled the account and hired other defense firms to take over my remaining cases."

"Sorry to hear it, really."

"Yeah, well, I'm okay with it. I didn't have much left anyway. My mom's a little frazzled though. Funny thing is, she thinks you're the cause."

"Speaking of your mother, you might want to know I just saw a video at MTA police headquarters of her assaulting me in Grand Central with a tube sock of yours filled with laundry change."

Silence reigns on the other end. Then he says, "You're kidding, right?"

"I'm afraid I couldn't be more serious. They have the whole thing on video."

"Ma!" I hear him yell. "Get in here!"

"Hey!" I say. "Charles!" I'm trying to get his attention.

"Give me a minute," he requests. "Okay?"

"No, I don't think so. I'm on my way over. Meanwhile you discuss the matter with your mother." *Click.*

Arriving at his building, which isn't so far from Grand Central, I phone him from the street. He's naturally unhappy-sounding, having extracted the story from the now aptly named Ma Lawless.

Hearing it, I shake my head. Which still aches a bit. It seems that she acted impulsively after hearing from Nurse Lucas that she'd received my subpoena and was coming to court. So Ma Lawless took matters into her own hands, fearing another trial loss would prove decisive to her son's career. She was right.

I inform him now that I'm heading upstairs to his office. There, when I enter, I see Ma, looking unrepentant, sitting behind the front desk. The place is in a shambles, awash in law texts, files, papers, and packing boxes. Chucky-boy stands beside her.

"Well, do we have a deal?" I ask. Our brief conversation of a few moments earlier had included my terms. Dictated and non-negotiable.

"Yeah, we have a deal." He nods to his mother. "Go ahead."

She resists. Her lips remain tight.

He prompts her again. "Go ahead, Ma."

She stays mutinous for a few beats longer, then caves. "I'm sorry I hit you in the head with Chuck's sock filled with quarters. I promise I will never raise my hand to another human being as long as I live."

I nod. "Fine," I say, "I won't press charges. I wish you and your mother well, Charles."

On the elevator ride down, I have to wonder what the two of them are saying to each other now. I also ponder how similar a coin-loaded sock and a nunchuck sound.

29.

On the sidewalk, I take the deep breath I deserve. Mothers. You gotta love them. Just then my phone goes off. The ID reads Alert One. Crap. *Not* again.

"Hello, Alert One, you got the right guy. What's up?"

"This is Melissa Freeman from—"

"Hi, Melissa. I know. I know . . . ."

"As an emergency care coordinator, I received an emergency notification from Alert One subscriber Nelly Rivera. The special instructions on this account direct that—"

"You call me before instituting standard protocol. I don't mean to be rude and cut you off, but I know the drill. Can you tell me where the call's coming from, please?"

"Certainly, sir. Our satellite transmitter indicates the call came from the same 138th Street address as last time, the subscriber's apartment. Would you like me to dispatch Emergency Services?"

"I don't think that will be necessary, Melissa. Thank you." *Click.* I speed dial, and Nelly picks up halfway into the first ring, as expected.

"That's better," she says. "Now I feel a lot more comfortable. Your response time was just over a minute. I guess you straightened them out."

"Yes," I say, "I did. What's up? Is everything all right?"

"It is now, given you've established an acceptable response time."

"Not a problem. But, like I said, you don't want to make your-self into the girl who cried wolf."

"And like I said, that fable's baloney. Those townspeople had too much at stake not to respond. Just like you."

"Duly noted. Only don't do that again."

"No promises."

"Whatever. Listen, I have some news for you. They've upped the offer to four mil on your case. Share that with your sister and discuss it. However, more is on the way, I'm pretty sure. So my recommendation is, hold tight."

"If I take the money, is it mine? Or does Jessie control it, like everything else in my life?"

It was only a matter of time before she asked this question. But she's entitled to know. "If we settle the case now, Jessie is still your guardian. So she will have great authority on how that money is spent. But I can petition to have her removed and appoint a different guardian and/or seek to have you declared competent. But, until then, Jessie's decisions regarding your money must be made in your best interests."

"That's pretty funny."

"What's pretty funny?"

"The only interests Jessie has are her own."

"That's really not being fair to your sister," I say, feeling the need to defend Jessie. I, after all, had been wrong about her masterminding the assault on me.

"Fair, *schmair*. As if lifting her guardianship would make a difference. She's going to do what she's going to do. Which means, if she wants my money, she'll make sure she gets it." *Click.*

I recognize how I keep going back and forth on the level of trust Jessie gets from me. I wish I could tell who's playing whom. My instinct has been to be protective of Nelly—after all, her injuries and her head trauma have left her impaired, not just once but twice. The trouble is, the worst thing a lawyer can be is ambivalent.

Show me an indecisive attorney, and I'll show you a weak-minded, confused, hesitant lawyer unfit to properly counsel his client.

Point made.

I've never been in this position before. So I feel much better knowing I'm on my way to see Roscoe now. He makes a living telling guys like me what to do in situations like this. Only he does it in his very special way.

But I never said that.

———————

I arrive at Roscoe's. He rents a single office in a large law firm across the street from the New York State Attorney Disciplinary/Grievance Committee, which is the body that sits in judgment of lawyers whose clients have made complaints against them. Here's what you need to know about it: if they're not ferreting out wrongs, then their existence is superfluous. Therefore, they keep themselves in business by making stretching-type efforts to find attorney misconduct. I'm not saying there is none, only I do employ the word "stretching" for a reason. Remember this, is all.

I step into the general reception area and note others there waiting. Quite likely for Roscoe.

How do I know? They're not looking happy, that's how.

"Go in. He's waiting for you," I'm told.

I glance over at the sinners sweating it out. Too bad, fellas, cutting the line is the only perk I get for repeat business.

When you enter Roscoe's office, what hits you in the face are the large framed pictures. It doesn't take long to recognize their common theme. Mets greats Dwight Gooden and Darryl Strawberry can be seen, each cuffed in prison garb for probation violations. Mike Tyson, also cuffed, wears a black vest without a shirt. Pete Rose, in a suit and tie, is waiting outside court, about to be slapped with his tax-evasion conviction.

Roscoe, a young, good-looking black man, is wearing his trademark hand-knotted burgundy bow tie and tiny round wire-rim glasses. His suit is three-piece and gray. He's only about ten years into his legal career, and already many prominent attorneys in the city, who find themselves with a disciplinary committee problem, retain him. There's a likable swagger to him, and he has his own, highly effective way of dealing with the problem set before him.

At the moment he's finishing a call. "Now," he's telling his listener firmly, "you must deny, deny, deny. And always remember, I never said that."

Down goes the receiver and up he looks at me. "Ignoramuses."

"Hi, Roscoe."

He gives me a disapproving head shake. "That Henry Benson will be the downfall of you yet."

"Maybe. There's logic to what you say. But let's get to business. Talk to me. What should I do here that you never said?"

He grins. "It's in your best interest to preserve your relationship with Benson and the fees it brings. The clients—what did you say their names were?"

"Jessie's the guardian and Nelly the injured. Jessie's the older of the two, and they're half sisters."

"I see, Jessie and Nelly. It has a nice ring to it. So, in your area of law, what we know is that it's unlikely you'll have repeat business from your clients. Therefore, it's imperative we subordinate their interests to yours. Now . . ."

"Roscoe," I cut in, "I appreciate that you're looking out for me. But the purpose of my visit, in part, is to protect Nelly."

"I see," he repeats. "So what we have then is a fundamental principle at play here—each is your client individually and together—meaning, your duty runs to them equally. They must be united in interests at all times. Once there's a divide, that's when your problems start. Understand rubber band?"

"Understood. Go on."

"First, let's analyze your concerns about Jessie acting in the best interests of her sister. If you take her to court, seeking her removal as guardian for cause—and lose—she'll then switch attorneys, and your legal fee will be on a midnight train to Georgia. You got that?"

"Got it. Go on."

"If you win and have her removed, the court is very likely to appoint a guardian of its own choosing, an ad litem since no other immediate family members exist. Then this court-appointed guardian will seek to have you discharged for cause and . . ."

"What cause would the ad litem have against me?" I interrupt. "I'm the one who will have brought the problem to the court's attention in the first place."

"The cause against you is either, or both, your conflict or incompetence. A good faith argument can be made that you represented these young women while knowing, or should have known, that the guardian breached her duty. Thus, given this, you should be disqualified and replaced by a more capable and competent attorney."

"What are you talking about?"

"You said you learned Jessie was spending Nelly's death benefit money against her wishes and that she, Nelly, couldn't do anything about it, right?"

"*Um,* . . . yes."

"Well, this happened under your watch, and you turned your cheek."

"But Jessie's actions—for the most part—occurred before I was retained."

"Define 'for the most part.'"

"On my watch, Jessie spent Nelly's money to take a trip to Florida—"

"Stop there. Did she take Nelly with her?"

"No. Nelly was still in the hospital."

"Slippery. Nelly couldn't protect her own interests, yet you, her lawyer, did nothing. You knew of her dipping and turned your cheek."

"Go on," I say, annoyed.

"Right, well, if the ad litem made that application—and it *will* be made so he might appoint an attorney of his own choosing to handle their case, a close friend no doubt—your legal fee will still be taking that midnight train since you're being discharged for cause.

"So, the way I see it," he goes on, "even though you're concerned that Jessie isn't acting in her sister's best interests, the trouble is, if you seek to remove her, you're risking your legal fee." Roscoe pauses here.

"Therefore, forget about protecting your injured client at the moment and protect your fee." He pauses again. "But I never said that."

"What do you mean, 'at the moment'?"

"Once you've settled her case and received your fee, if you still think there's a problem, then make the motion to have Jessie removed." He stops to look at me. "But I'd strongly advise against it."

"Why?"

"Because it may come out that you knew this all along and didn't make the removal application in a timely manner. That could cost you your license before the disciplinary committee, since your decision not to act was based on putting your interests before the clients'." Which of course is what he's "not" telling me to do.

"So, are you saying, never make the motion to have her removed?"

"That's what I'm saying. But I never said that. Want to move on to the other issues?"

"Yeah, okay," I say grimly.

"You say you have reason to believe Jessie was involved in the murder of Nelly's mother, who was married to her father, and that she was motivated by life insurance proceeds. You're basing this belief on the insurance adjuster's investigation, as well as the flashbacks that Nelly seems to be having, right?"

"Right."

"This is an easy one. A lawyer has no duty to advance the issue of law enforcement on prior crimes of their client. And you can tell anyone you want I said that."

"That's big of you."

"Ready to move on to the next issue?"

"Yep."

"Okay. You tell me you found some fibers on the IV flow-control clamp that you think are from clothing Jessie wore at this dentist's office and that she may be responsible for overdosing Nelly separate and apart from any acts of malpractice by this dentist. Do I have that right?"

"Yes."

"Give me a little more here."

"Okay," I begin, "the jeans Jessie wore have a decorative piece of blue fabric covering the zipper. The same blue color as the fibers I found on the controller. I had those analyzed, and they're a cashmere blend, which is what I believe that zipper-flap is made from."

"How do you know that?"

"I searched the brand on the Internet."

"Well, if Jessie did juice her sister, your legal fee will certainly be on that choo choo because then there *ain't* no case. Which means, keep your mouth shut." He waits a beat. "But I never said that."

"Fine. But I'm asking you, what's the right or legally appropriate thing to do here?"

"The right thing to do is preserve your motherfucking fee."

I give him a look.

"Okay," he replies. "But the right thing's in line with fee preservation anyway."

"Go on."

"Pursuant to Rule 1.6 a lawyer may, but is not required to, divulge confidential information to prevent the client from committing a fraud where the lawyer's services have been used to aid in its attempted perpetuation. However, you're only allowed to do social justice at the cost of a client when you have an extraordinarily high level of competent knowledge—which, in fact, you don't have. Google don't count. It would be quite another story if you had the fibers from her jeans analyzed, and it came up with a match. Then you'd have a real decision to make."

"Well, that's what I'm considering doing as my next move."

"Lose that thought now. Sometimes it's better not to know. Like infidelity."

"Wouldn't *you* want to know, Roscoe?"

"What she does on her time is her business. What I do on my time is mine. That's the first rule of marital ethics."

"No, not that. Wouldn't you have the jean fabric analyzed to see if the fibers matched?"

"Of course I would. But, by no means, would I ever tell anyone."

"Just so I understand this aspect of ethics law, let's say, hypothetically speaking, there was a match. Then would going forward on the malpractice case be a fraud on my part?"

"That sounds like an extraordinarily high level of competent knowledge to me. So I'd say, yes."

"And, if the fibers matched, wouldn't I also have a situation where the guardian attempted murder?"

"Sounds like you would."

"Then, hypothetically, what would I do?"

"Nothing. Because my firm advice—which I expect you would've followed—is not to have the fibers analyzed for a match in the first place. Are we done yet?"

"Last question."

He looks at his watch as if I'm starting to overstay my welcome. "Go on. Make it quick."

"What about a future attempt on Nelly's life? Jessie will be the sole heir of her sister's estate if Nelly dies. How do I guard against that? What do I do here?"

"Rule 1.6 also states a lawyer may, but is not required to, divulge confidential information to prevent reasonably certain death or substantial bodily harm. Again you have to have an extraordinarily high level of competent knowledge. Plus you also must be reasonably certain that, by revealing the information, you'll be preventing the death or harm. You've got none of that here and never will because you're not having those jeans analyzed."

He does his pause. "But, if Jessie does kill her sister, I never said that. This is some slippery shit."

"You're one of a kind, Roscoe."

"I'm just saying."

"Or not saying, as the case may be."

He grins.

"One last question."

"You already said that." He shakes his head. "Go on."

"What do I share with Nelly?"

"You have an obligation to keep the client reasonably in the know so they are able to make informed decisions. But, if I were you, I wouldn't tell her a thing—but I never said that. You see, if she makes waves, it could once again lead to your discharge."

"So, if I understand you correctly, I shouldn't do or say anything to anybody about any of this."

"Correct. Doing something could put your fee at risk. Besides, you just don't have the requisite level of certainty on any of this. It's all only stuff out there." He's wearing a suitably judicious expression. "Am I split-billing you and Benson on this?"

"No, I'll eat this one."

––––––––––

Now in front of Roscoe's building, I take out my phone. I have two calls to make. This first is one I need to handle delicately.

"Hello," Nelly says.

"It's me," I respond.

"I swear I didn't hit the Alert One button again."

"I know. I know. Listen, I was wondering, . . . those jeans you were wearing that my daughter liked, . . . you know, Jessie's?"

"What? Did she tell on me?"

I didn't anticipate this response. "Tell on you for what reason?"

"I don't know how, but I lost them."

Crap! Well, that settles that.

"And we've been fighting about it. She wants to buy another pair, and I just think they're way too expensive."

"*Um*, no, she didn't tell me."

"Then why are you asking about them?"

"Oh, . . . I was just wondering . . . if you thought Penelope was too young for me to get her a pair."

"Why are you asking me and not your wife?"

"No reason really."

"Okay, but, like I said, they're expensive. You may just want to wait a bit. Are her friends wearing them?"

"No."

"Then no problem really. At least until they become the rave in her school."

"Thanks. Sorry to bother you."

"No bother at all." *Click.*

Okay. Time now for call number two. I search my contacts and hit Dial.

"Hello, Tom Montgomery, Greater Life. How can I help you?"

"Oh, sorry. I thought I'd dialed Trudy Anderson's extension."

"You did."

"Oh. Well, may I speak to her, please?"

"Trudy is no longer with the company."

"Really?" Naturally I'm surprised. Her work was not only her job but, quite obviously, her passion.

"Yes, really. I'm handling all her files now. May I help you?"

"Sure. Can I have Trudy's contact number?"

"I don't have one, and, even if I did, company policy would prohibit me from giving it out. Is there something else I might help you with?"

"I'm not sure you can. I'll call back if I need you." *Click.*

Hmm. I need to get another copy of her scrapbook to make certain Henry doesn't think I'm totally nuts and also to get him on the same page regarding my Jessie concerns.

I send a text to Pusska, my private investigator:

> Pusska, I need you to get me the cell phone number and home address of a Trudy Anderson who used to work for Greater Life Insurance Company. Also see if you can find out why she was fired.

She immediately responds:

I'm running around Europe for a bit. Not sure when I'll be back. Met a sheikh at The W in Barcelona. Do you have a time frame here?

I reply:

The sooner, the better.

I head home early. This has been an extraordinarily crazy day. I need to recharge my batteries.

30.

n the door I walk. "Hi, honey," I say, as I pass Tyler in the kitchen. I'm heading for the sanctuary of my den.

"It's 4:30 p.m. Why are you home so early?"

"I'm exhausted."

She doesn't hesitate. "Good. I need you to pick up Penelope at dance at five. Bring her home. By that time, Connor should be done next door, and I'll need you to drive him and Brooks to get their haircuts at 5:30 p.m. It takes only a half hour, so I usually just wait there. Then, when you're back here, see if you can fix the printer. Brooks has to print out his book report, and he says it's not working."

"Didn't you just hear me? I'm completely beat."

"So, are you saying this exhaustion you're suffering from is compromising your ability to drive? Because you seemed to have made it home from the train station in one piece."

"No. I can drive. I just don't want to."

"*Ooooh.*" Sarcasm. "You don't want too. I understand that concept about not wanting to do things. But too bad. You're here, so you might as well help out. I've been chauffeuring them around all day long."

"*Um,*" I respond cautiously, "weren't the kids in school all day long?"

"Yes. But I took them there, and, after picking them up, each had activities all over town. What's your problem? I'm just asking for a little help, that's all."

At this moment I realize it's Wednesday. Crap! Here's the thing. We used to have a bit of a rendezvous on Tuesday nights. Not all, but, with any luck, every other. Yet what happened was that Tyler got invited to play on a desirable tennis team, and their matches are, you guessed it, Tuesday nights. So, what was once Tuesday Night Hand Job has now become Wednesday Night Hand Job.

Which means, I need to be on my best behavior or risk a cancellation.

"You know what, honey? You're right. I'm on it. Sorry for being so selfish."

"Great." She grabs her bag.

"Where are you going?" I inquire.

"For a massage and then I'm getting my nails done." And out the door she goes.

It's now later, and I've completed my errands-as-foreplay. Thus I find myself in the laundry room, staring at the printer. It's no secret I'm technologically challenged. And, if I don't get this thing to work, neither Brooks nor Tyler will be happy. I love my son and want him to do well in school. But right now—despite how immature this may sound—I'm more concerned about Tyler's happiness.

After all, it is Wednesday.

At least I admit it.

I employ my standard approach. I unplug the printer, count to five, then plug it back in. Nope. That didn't do the trick. I look at the information panel—which I should've done in the first place—and it reads Low Ink, Black Cartridge. *Duh.*

Opening the cabinet above the printer to get a new cartridge, I see something I've never seen before. A stack of folded clothing on the bottom shelf. Why would that be in here?

"Tacita!" I call out, hearing her just around the corner in the kitchen. "Tacita!" I repeat. A moment later, our live-in help—who's part of the family—appears.

"Yes, Mister?" she asks.

"What's this clothing doing in here?" I ask, motioning.

"Oh, *sí*, Mister. That's the lost and *founded*."

"The lost and found?"

"*Sí*, Mister."

"Why do we have a lost and found?"

"Because when kids have friends over, friends forget and leave clothes here. So I make it a lost and *founded*. See, I show you." Tacita opens the cabinet door farther. Taped on the inside surface is a handwritten sign Lost and Founded.

"That's very smart of you, Tacita." She smiles proudly. "Does Miss Tyler know you made a lost and found?"

"No. I no tell her."

"I see," I respond, thinking this clothing will never be *founded* by its rightful owners if Miss Tyler's not in the know.

"I have an idea," I say to her. "Maybe some of that clothing has name tags, you know, like you sew in the kids' clothing for camp. Why don't you look through it," I continue, handing her the stack, "and make one pile with name tags and one pile without. Then give Miss Tyler the ones with tags so she can contact the parents. But let her know too there's another stack in the lost and found."

Smiling, she says, "Oh, that's a good idea, Mister." And she proceeds doing just that as I change the printer cartridge.

Within moments each of us has completed our task.

Looking at the pile of clothes closest to me, I ask, "Is this the stuff without name tags that's going back into the lost and found?"

"*Sí*, Mister."

I pick up the pile—after pulling off the top article of clothing—and set the rest in the cabinet. Now fortuitously sitting on the counter is none other than Jessie's lost jeans. Jackpot! Or maybe not—depending on which ethics rules I embrace, Roscoe's or my own.

I immediately buzz Fred. He tells me he's leaving for Europe at six in the morning for two weeks; so, if I want him to analyze the fibers from the jeans against the fibers from the IV controller, he needs them tonight.

After phoning Trace, I run out the door—jeans in hand—and call Miss Tyler from the train. "Hi, hon."

"Where are you?" Instantly suspicious.

"Listen, I had to run out. I need to hand over something at Grand Central. It's important. But I'll be back in flash. I'm just making a round trip, that's all."

"Okay. But you don't need to rush home on my account."

Hmm. I don't like the sound of that. "Great. Thanks," I say, maintaining a positive demeanor. "But I'm sure I'll be back just in time for bed." There's a metered pause.

"By the way," she says, "I'm not sure I told you, but my tennis league ended last week. So we're switching back to Tuesdays."

"But last night was Tuesday."

"I know." *Click.*

I exit Grand Central on the Lexington Avenue side, and the Impala is parked at the curb. Trace gives it some juice to tell me he's there, as if such notification were necessary. I approach the driver's side as his window slowly lowers.

"No music, Trace?"

"Nah, man, meditating."

"You meditate?" I ask with a surprised tone.

A bothered look crosses his face. "Yeah. Why you saying it like that?"

"It just never would've occurred to me that you meditate, that's all."

"Why?"

"The truth?"

"The truth."

"'Cause you're a big black dude who wears tough-guy shades, rides around in a muscle car blasting gangsta music, and packs a gun under his leather, just to name a few."

"What's that have to do with meditation?"

"Nothing, I guess," I say, giving a shrug. "You're right. I'm guilty of profiling. Here." I hand him Jessie's jeans—against sound legal advice, I should add.

"A'ight."

"But tell Fred I don't want to hear his findings. You got that? He knows to analyze the fibers—but I forgot to tell him I don't want to find out what he learns. Ever. Unless of course I ask him. We cool?"

He studies me.

"What's the matter?" I ask. "I thought that was a pretty good 'We cool.' So, we cool?"

"We cool."

"Good. Now who's guilty of profiling?" A hint of a smile emerges as his window goes up.

31.

Since leaving Roscoe's office two weeks ago, I've come up with forty-seven additional ethics and conflict questions. I haven't called him though. What's the use? His directive was clear—do nothing. Yet I did do something.

At the moment I'm waiting for the sisters again in front of defense counsel's building. Brad Miller has assured me he has acceptable money to close Nelly's case. However, it seems there's an unorthodox exercise to go through first.

A taxi pulls up, and they get out as I pay the cabbie. Turning around, one thing's obvious from their body language—they're fighting again. Which, in fact, is confirmed the instant I approach.

"Screw that! You've got to help out," Jessie blasts.

"Nice, real nice," Nelly replies. "There's no way. Dr. Furman told you that. And you can see for yourself my problem walking."

"Ladies," I say firmly, "this has got to stop. Today's going to be a big day. Relax."

"Big day for her," Jessie snaps. "But what about me?"

"I'll tell you. You're a healthy, vibrant young woman. Waitressing is only temporary. It's time you start thinking about a career or going to college maybe. The thing is, you need to support each other at this juncture. However, for now, we need to focus on today. When we get upstairs, you guys just sit tight. I'll do all the talking."

The elevator ride atmosphere is angry, tense, and quiet. It's certainly not how I imagined their attitudes would be on the day they—or, should I say, Nelly—would become a multimillionaire. And what is Jessie planning on doing anyway, once the death-benefit money—that Nelly will use to support the *both* of them—runs out? She's acting jealous, like her sister's winning the lottery rather than being compensated for the losses that occasioned her brain injury, a reality she'll have to cope with the rest of her life.

As we enter defense counsel's office, the receptionist greets us, hits a button, and whispers into the phone. Moments later Brad Miller comes out.

"May I talk to you for a second?" he asks. "In private."

"Sure. I'll be right back," I tell the girls.

As we step into the hallway, I say, "We both know how unusual it is having the defendant present for a settlement mediation in a malpractice case. Especially so since you've told me you have settlement money."

"I know," he replies. "But Grad insisted on it before we offered a penny more. He's really quite a nice man. But clearly I view this as a bad liability case for us."

"Does that view have anything to do with Nelly's tonsils?"

He clears his throat. "Thanks for sending over those records. They provided useful leverage with the insurance company when it came to additional money. They also didn't make me look very good."

"Yeah, well, . . . sorry about that. The truth is, I appreciate all your efforts. It's rare that a defense attorney acknowledges how bad things are for his client."

He nods. In this instant I think what a scumbag lawyer I am. If Fred should ever tell me that the fibers from the jeans match the fibers from the controller, it will lead to only one conclusion.

The thing is, I don't plan on asking. I've decided I'm going to follow the advice of my lawyer.

"Without guys like you," Brad says, "I wouldn't have a job.

Someone needs to bring a lawsuit before I get hired to defend it. And I believe in what legitimate guys like yourself do."

Definitely not asking Fred.

"Anyway," Brad continues, "the reason I called you out here is to tell you that Dr. Grad has an agenda. He wouldn't share it but demanded we resolve the case in front of a mediator. This is to allow him to say a few things to the sisters in front of a quasijudge. Grad's day in court, so to speak. So, if you could encourage them to listen, I'd appreciate it. The case will be settled right after, I'm confident of that."

"It's highly unusual. But if it gets done what's to be done, fine."

When we return, I request that Nelly and Jessie be prepared to tolerate whatever it is Grad has to say. I don't know what it is, but please, I beg them, just listen and keep quiet.

We enter a large conference room and take our positions. Sitting on the other side of the table between his lawyer and a representative from his insurance carrier is Grad. I look at the mediator, who's ready to start.

Unfortunately, before he gets a word out, my phone goes off. So he waits. My caller ID reads The Other Fred Sanford.

Crap. What could he want?

"*Um*," I say apologetically, "I've got to grab this real quick." I hit the Answer button, wishing I hadn't.

"What's up, Fred?" I whisper. He responds. "No, Fred, no. I told Trace to tell you that I didn't want to know. Please, Fred, I don't want to know," I murmur, looking at defense counsel and Dr. Grad, "but if I ever change my mind, I'll be sure to call you. I don't mean to be impolite, but I'm in a meeting, and everybody is looking at the rude lawyer on his phone. Good-bye." *Click.*

I look up from stuffing my phone away to be met by six pairs of inquiring eyes. "Sorry," I say, offering no explanation. "Go on, Mr. Mediator, sir."

"All right," he begins. "I understand the need for my services is limited here, so I'll just act more as a moderator." He glances over at Grad.

"Doctor," Mr. Mediator says, "I understand that, first, before we proceed, you have something you'd like to say to these girls."

"Yes," Grad says, "thank you." He looks across at us, teary eyed, like a grandfather whose grandkid suffered an injury on his watch. "Good morning, Jessie, Nelly, and Mr. Wyler. I'm sorry to have inconvenienced you all by calling for a conference—or mediation, I should say—but bear with me as this case will be over momentarily."

He takes a deep breath, letting out a relieved sigh. "Not that it matters," he continues, "but I want you both to know that this is the first time I've ever been sued. Obviously I don't like it, but I have to say I was looking forward to my day in court because I just believe deep down in my heart that I did nothing wrong."

"Oh, please," Jessie blurts out.

"I appreciate how you feel," he says. And his tone strikes me as in every way sincere. "But kindly allow me to finish."

"You promised to sit quietly," I whisper, leaning over to Jessie. "Now do so, then we can resolve this and get out of here."

Grad offers a grateful nod. "As I said," he continues, "I was looking forward to a trial because it was so important to me to prove I did nothing wrong."

I look over at Jessie, now under control.

"But," he says, "after the passage of time and a lot of reflection, proving I'm right just doesn't seem important anymore. What's more important at the present, Nelly, is that you remain on your road to recovery without having the stress of financial concerns."

Tears are gathering, I can see, in Nelly's eyes. Grad's are trickling. Jessie's crying too. It's a bittersweet moment.

"When this happened," he goes on, "everybody changed the way they viewed me. My patients—people I've known for decades—well, they just stopped coming. And I lost many friends over this too. My wife and children, even they look at me differently, although I know in my heart I have their support. I guess that's why it was so important for me to prove my innocence. I'm sorry this happened to you, Nelly, very sorry. Therefore, I want to make sure you're fairly compensated for your injuries. I've directed Medical Liability to tender my primary and excess policies to you. Again I'm sorry for all you've been through."

He stands and walks toward the door, with the gait of a defeated man. He got to me is all I can say.

"Dr. Grad!" Nelly calls out.

He turns to her. "Yes, dear?"

"I want you to know that I accept your apology. I'm going to be all right. Don't you worry about me." Nelly's face takes on that look specific to her flashbacks, as my heart sinks. She's about to pull one of her disconnected utterances from that place—*oh, no,* I think—when her expression suddenly shifts back to normal.

"I know that was hard for you, Dr. Grad," she continues. "It would be hard for anybody to say what you just said. In some strange way," she pauses, glancing at Jessie, who seems withdrawn from the moment, "I also feel you did nothing wrong."

I should've let Fred say what he called to say.

But I'm glad I didn't.

32.

t's been seven months since that emotional day. Not only did Nelly accept Grad's apology but also the defense's offer. I was happy because the only alternative would've been to get a jury verdict in excess of insurance and have the sheriff enforce a judgment, seizing the Painless Dentist's house and assets. But, you know, I've never gone after anyone personally—above their insurance coverage—and I never will.

I asked Nelly, before putting her in a cab, what she meant when she told Grad she agreed he did nothing wrong. She hesitated, turned to Jessie, back to me, then just shrugged. I've thought about asking her that question again one day—without Jessie around—but never have.

What Fred Sanford had reported to me during his brief call was that the analysis of the fibers from Jessie's pants against those of the IV controller came to a finding within a 99 percent degree of accuracy. However, because I cut him short, I don't know whether that meant there was or was not a match. And looking in the mirror is becoming easier since ending the conversation before he could present his conclusions.

Initially all I saw in the mirror was a big ambivalent lawyer stuck dead in the middle of a professional and moral conundrum. I also saw a guy afraid to know the very important truth about a critical piece of information so he wouldn't have to deal with it and its repercussions if the circumstances demanded such.

What this reflection showed was a weakness in my character.

At least I admit it.

Yet, according to my lawyer, my conduct was proper. Thank you, Roscoe.

I think.

As I've indicated, Dr. Grad's personal agenda made this case unique. It marked the first time a doctor I sued had ever apologized, despite making it clear it was not an admission of guilt. The only time I ever saw an apology, coupled with an admission, in a malpractice claim was in Adora's case. But that came from Monica Lucas, who's a nurse, not a doctor.

As for Jessie, she moved back to Yonkers to live with her mother and is helping at Fritzi's. Just after the settlement, Juanita and Jessie tried to get Nelly to put money into the business. The idea being it would be both a "good investment" and "in her best interest"—the operative words necessary to release the funds. I intervened, however, putting the kibosh on it because the sum being asked seemed excessive and the timing wrong.

What it did was help me see, for the first time, Juanita's true colors. Meaning, the ones in which Henry had painted her for me.

Henry Benson and I whacked up the sizable legal fee—fifty-fifty—as always. He gave me grief on the expenses though. The Alert One monitoring device was a chunk of change, and he wanted me to eat it. He called it a "discretionary expense" instead of a "necessary one."

The truth is, there's no such distinction in our field, despite what Henry might think or try to have me believe. When I was firm about that not happening, he suggested Nelly foot the expense because she's still wearing it as a matter of medical necessity, owing to her risk of seizure. I said no to that too, and eventually we agreed that we'd share the expense up until Nelly received the settlement proceeds. At that point, she'd assume responsibility for the payments. Or at least I thought that's what we agreed.

Next thing I knew, Henry insisted on haggling with the company and somehow wangled Nelly six free months of monitoring. Following this small triumph, he turned adamant on still taking the value of that savings as an expense on the file, which I reluctantly went along with. He spent so much time on it that he started dating Nelly's Alert One account manager, Melissa.

With regard to Nelly's share of the money, I set up a meeting for the girls with my structured settlement guy, Brian Levine. That was the day everything was formalized and the last time the sisters actually saw each other. Nelly was advised to put the money into a structured settlement, which is a tax-free annuity where monthly sums are deposited directly into the guardian account for her jointly with Jessie. Such an arrangement prevents the guardian from stealing one big lump sum all at once. Yet, despite my insistence, Nelly wanted the money in toto, at which juncture I had the pair of them sign a document stating they were taking the money immediately in one lump sum against the advice of counsel. And the court, which must approve the terms of the settlement, did just that.

Approved it.

Against my documented advice.

A structured settlement was the one vehicle that could've afforded Nelly full protection from her "Jessie concerns." And yet she knowingly snubbed it. Despite how she felt about her sister, in addition to the $50K Jessie received as a fee for her guardianship services, the court approved a transfer of $200K to Jessie for miscellaneous services. It was very generous of Nelly to support it—ridiculous of the court to approve it.

I again voiced my strenuous objections, outside the presence of Jessie of course.

Me, I'm just glad the case is over.

I inhale the aroma, then take another sip of my morning coffee, thinking how I love that this case settled minus the blowback that I was so freaked out about before closure. I also love staying home late on Mondays when the rest of the world is rushing off to work. I take a deep breath in and exhale, as I readjust myself in my den recliner. Reaching over, I give Otis, my big Labradoodle, a pat on his head. He looks at me with his serene eyes. Man and his dog.

Just as I'm about to take another deep inhale . . .

"Honey!" Tyler yells from the kitchen. "Put on Channel 2. Quick!"

I grab the remote and turn to CBS where I see Dr. Grad. He's standing in front of the Bronx County Courthouse, hands cuffed behind his back.

What's this all about?

Todd Davis, a news reporter, is speaking:

> The DA's office has decided to prosecute Dr. Michael Grad for Reckless Endangerment in the First Degree, for engaging in conduct which created a grave risk of death to his patient when he overdosed her on anesthesia during a routine procedure which he employed without license to do so. He will also be prosecuted on a lesser related charge for giving false testimony under oath in a civil matter arising out of this same occurrence. He faces a maximum jail sentence of two to four years, if convicted. This is Todd Davis reporting from the Bronx County Courthouse. Back to you in the studio, Jim.

I hit the Off button, thinking that explains why Jack Herring from the DA's office subpoenaed my file after the settlement. But Nelly told me she'd spoken to him, asking that Grad not be prosecuted. She said he'd agreed not to, just like he'd told me I'd be the first call should he decide to go forward. A man of his word he is not.

And so much for a settled case without blowback and a quiet Monday morning.

"Shit!"

"Yeah, shit," Connor, my nine-year-old, repeats entering the room.

"Please don't curse, son."

"But you did."

"I know I did. But do as I say, not as I do. Besides, I had a reason to curse."

"What was your reason, Dad?"

"I may be partly responsible for a man going to jail—and the thing is, he may be innocent."

"That's bad. You should just call up the police and tell them he didn't do it."

"I wish it were that simple. I truly wish it were that simple."

33.

On my way to the office riding the Metro North, I start boiling down what my choices are. The way I see it, what's before me are different trajectories. I can do nothing and let a man, who may be innocent, go to jail for some horrible act Jessie might've committed. Or else I can come forward with what I know and let the chips fall where they may. I should add here that one of those chips will be peppered with my taking insurance money on a case I had reason to believe was a fake.

According to Roscoe, that wouldn't be enough to subject me to a proceeding, criminal or otherwise. What he said was that you're only allowed to go for "social justice" at cost to the client—meaning, choosing truth and the public good over your client's interests—when you're unable, in conscience, to act otherwise, based on an extraordinarily high level of competent knowledge. Not listening to Fred's conclusions gets me off this hook.

Instantly a decision comes to me. Option three: a hybrid approach between options one and two.

Before I act on this insight, I need to phone Fred and find out what this 99 percent certainty pertains to. Is it a match, making Jessie the overdose culprit? Plus would clear Dr. Grad of the malpractice finding as well as the impending wrongful criminal prosecution. At the same time making me guilty of swindling a bundle on a case without merit.

Or is there no match?

I planned on never making this call.

I take out my phone and get a disapproving look from the guy across from me. We're not supposed to phone in the "quiet car" on the commuter train. Unfortunately this is an emergency, buddy, so bear with me. Just then, it vibrates. I look at the ID.

Well, what do you know about that? I hit Answer.

"It's a match," Fred says. "Same type of blend, similar color, and similar microscopic characteristics."

"Thanks. But how'd you know? I told you nothing about the case, not my clients' names nor even the dentist's name."

"I'm a rocket scientist."

"Thanks, Fred." *Click.*

So that answers that question. Now it appears for sure Jessie tried to kill Nelly. But what was her motive? If I go with Trudy Anderson's answer, that would be the remaining monies of the death benefit, plus the monies to come on the property damage claim, plus the monies and possessions left to Nelly in her mother's estate. Altogether it adds up to be a significant sum. And that doesn't even include any monies Jessie would have received from Nelly's wrongful death lawsuit had Jessie succeeded with her plan. Factor into that how Jessie likes to spend money she doesn't have, along with her seeming resistance to work for a living, and it might just add up.

Still I question if it's enough to motivate Jessie to kill her sister. Yet I can't ignore it. People have done bad things for much less.

And is Nelly right now in harm's way, with her sister the perp? If I reveal Fred's analysis, the criminal focus will shift from Grad to Jessie, with Nelly being the sole witness. She'd told me she recalled her sister standing over her just before she lost consciousness, but this never came out at her deposition. Further, any motive for Jessie to off her sister is now higher than ever because of several millions in settlement money of which Jessie is Nelly's sole heir. Lastly, I also know an innocent man will go to jail unless I do something.

Still, keeping myself out of a cell is equally a priority.

Roscoe would call this slippery.

And, speaking of Roscoe, I don't give a damn what he says the legal standard is. The fact is, I had more than enough reasons to doubt, and that's plenty for any hotshot prosecutor looking to take down an injury lawyer. We're prime targets. Besides, my lack of knowledge on the fiber match was technically self-manufactured.

Time to implement Hybrid Plan Forty-Seven. Forty-seven is my utility number I assign to covert operation schemes such as this.

I arrive at my office, having made a self-promise that I wouldn't implement said plan until noon, following three further hours of thorough thought. As I pass Lily, I say, "Hold my calls, please."

"Did you see the news?"

"Saw it."

"Nelly's—"

"No time to talk," I say, without missing a stride. I enter my own office and finish Lily's sentence—"waiting to see you."

So much for my three-hour window of contemplation.

"Hey, Nelly. What's up?"

"Are you saying you don't know why I'm here?"

"Dr. Grad's criminal matter?"

"Correct. I don't want him to go to jail. He doesn't deserve to."

I don't know how to take that statement. Does she mean he doesn't deserve to because he's innocent or because he's suffered enough already from this tragedy? I'd know the answer if I'd pursued what she meant on settlement day—when she said she didn't feel he did anything wrong. But it was easier to stick my head underground than to man up.

At least I admit it. But who cares now?

Anyway I have an idea. A real lawyerlike one. Time to exercise the prerogative of creative legal thinking.

"What do you mean, he doesn't deserve to go to jail?"

"What I mean is, I don't believe he did anything wrong."

"Understood. I'm just curious, . . . what exactly are you saying?"

"You heard me. What I said, that's all."

"But it's obviously not all. What gives?"

She sighs, then shakes her head. "My flashbacks. They're not just about the fire. They're also about what happened in Dr. Grad's office. And other stuff too."

"I'm listening. Why don't you go ahead and tell me about the dental office."

"Okay, *um*, . . . it's still a little hazy, . . . but, just as I was under the effects of anesthesia, . . . as I was sitting there, light-headed, . . . after I was checked on by one of the assistants . . . I remember seeing Debbie come in to look me over, leave the room, then Jessie grabbing the pole and messing with the IV. . . . She looked really angry. . . . I couldn't respond, . . . couldn't move, not at all. I don't know what she did, . . . but seeing her do that is the last thing I remember."

She breaks down, crying.

I quickly move around my desk and take her hands. "Easy, Nelly, easy," I say, trying to comfort her. "I know this is difficult for you."

She looks up with tears rolling down her cheeks.

"You'll never know how difficult this really is." Now she's sobbing. "My own sister, trying to kill me. And I never had any memory of the fire, which was a good thing. Just as I was in full acceptance of the loss of my parents, and life was beginning to be good again, Jessie does this, and stuff comes back. Things I didn't even realize I knew. About the night of the fire."

She stops, and I wait. "About the murder," she says softly.

"Tell me, Nelly, like what?" I ask. Oh, boy, we're way past Dr. Furman's directive and deep into another visit to Roscoe Jenkins. But no turning back now.

"Well, first, my mother wasn't murdered, like I said. I think that night she planned to die," Nelly continues. Her face is all teary. "I know it, I just can't remember how I know it. She was terminal. I mean, if she didn't die that night, still she had only a week or two to live. And she was on a morphine pump, . . . and I think she was planning on overdosing herself sometime soon."

She pauses. "Oh, I'm so confused that I'm not sure."

"Go on, Nelly. Please. I want to hear this. Just go on with what you think."

"Okay, *um*, . . . I believe she was dead before the fire was started. There was this plan, I think. That's what I'm saying. What I remember." She shuts her eyes. "We said our last good-byes, all of us there. It was horrible. Then Mom told us to go downstairs. . . . Juanita, . . . she was going to help with the pump, to overdose Mom. . . . They'd become, like, friends near the end and—"

"Wait a second," I break in. "Juanita was there that night?"

"Yes. She planned it—with my mom, that is—to get the insurance money, . . . to have it look like an accidental death from the fire. But my father wasn't supposed to die that night, only my mother from the morphine, . . . and I'd get the life insurance money . . . "

Her face contorts. "It was something my mother wanted to do for me."

"What do you mean, your mother wanted to do this for you?" Like, we're on total memory overload here. Holy crap.

Nelly now unleashes a torrent. "She felt she'd been a bad mother for so many reasons—too many to name. And then the criminal proceedings were always happening, . . . but, most of all, she just felt she never did anything good for me. So, you see, she wanted me to have the money from her death as a gift, . . . because she was going to die soon anyway."

She looks at me. "At least, that's what the plan was. But, somehow that night, I got locked in my room. And my father died too. He wasn't even supposed to be there."

My head's spinning, I gotta tell you. But we've gone this far, and I need to know everything. I'm also worried about the effect this unloading will have on Nelly. . . . "Did your dad know about the plan?" is what I go with next.

"No," she says with conviction. "He didn't. He didn't know. I'm certain about that. It was my mother's idea with Juanita. They'd become close when Mom took sick. That's when things turned really bad between my parents. She hated my dad at the end. Juanita hated him too. But then she always did."

She pauses, chewing her lip, tears smeared on her face. "He used Mom's illness as an excuse to get bail, you know, saying he needed to take care of her and us. But he didn't."

She shakes her head angrily. "Instead doing ugly stuff, like bringing tramps back to the house to party while Mom was dying upstairs. But he never knew about Mom's and Juanita's idea because they thought, if he did, he'd try to steal the insurance money from me and blow it before going back to jail.

"Mom told me Dad didn't even know she had the insurance. She told me I was the beneficiary and that, when she died, the money would automatically go into a trust she set up for me so he couldn't get to it."

Worn out by all this explaining, she stops talking and begins hysterically crying.

Crap. Shit. But I know I have to stay in charge here.

Boy, do I need to think.

"Take a moment to gather yourself," I tell her. "I'll be right back." More than anything, I'm praying she doesn't have a seizure.

I walk into my conference room and sit down. She's got it wrong. Nelly has it wrong. Stella Rivera never received any life insurance. I know that for a fact. I saw her denial in the scrapbook. My phone vibrates. It's Henry.

Crap! I was trying to avoid him until I had things fully thought out. Instead it's getting more complicated by the second. "What's up?"

"Don't you 'What's up' me. Didn't you see the news?"

"I saw it and . . . " I say, trying to act casual.

"And you better keep your mouth shut. Just in case you need a reminder, you're Jessie's attorney, which means you have an obligation to your client to keep your mouth shut. That crazy notion you had running through your head about her somehow being involved better just stay a theory. Got that?"

"It's no longer a theory. My expert came up with a positive match between the fibers on the IV clamp and those from Jessie's jeans. It's proof positive."

"How did you get a hold of her jeans?"

"They were in the 'lost and *founded*' at my house. But that's not important."

"I'll tell you what's important! Keep your mouth shut, or I'll see that you have your license taken away for breaching your fiduciary duties. You got me, Counselor?"

"I hear what you're saying, but you do realize, Henry, we're now coconspirators in covering up an attempted murder. And if Grad goes to jail, I'll be responsible. But you know what? I couldn't live like that. Not to mention the topping on the cake is that Jessie tried to kill Nelly before this by locking her in her room the night of the fire."

"That's nonsense. You don't know what you're talking about. Keep your mouth shut!" *Click!*

I hate that guy sometimes.

I walk back into my office, where, thank God, Nelly now seems more composed.

"Do you think I'm crazy?" But she doesn't wait for my answer. "I think I'm going crazy. I mean, this can't be happening—so, really, I must be going crazy."

"You're not crazy, believe me. You're not crazy at all, and you're not going crazy. Actually you seem clearer to me right now than you've ever been."

"Why are you saying that? This all sounds so crazy. I know it does."

So, right about now, I have a decision to make. Do I tell her what I know about the fiber match, which would validate her? Or do I keep it in the vault along with what I learned from the scrapbook? I haven't had three hours to think about it yet, but my gut's telling me to share the information.

"Listen, Nelly. You don't sound crazy, and here's why. Because I had some fibers from the IV analyzed, and it came up with a match to ones on your sister's jeans. The ones she wore to Grad's office."

She looks at me strangely. "What are you talking about? I lost those."

"Well, I found them. You left them at my house. Anyway I went to the DA's office and inspected the controller device and found some weird fibers on it, . . . and I tried to put it all together and see what could be proved."

No response. Not at first.

She looks utterly shocked. "When did you find this out?"

And at this moment—with the instant replay in my head—I regret the beans I've just spilled. I should never have opened my mouth.

"The match I found out today. My suspicion that your sister tampered with the IV flow-control clamp I've had for a long time."

"How long ago was that?"

"A while ago, after we won your Motion for Summary Judgment."

"Why didn't you tell me sooner?" she demands. "I kept telling you I didn't feel safe around her! Now it turns out I was living with someone who'd tried to kill me. And my own lawyer knew it and didn't tell me. What the hell is with you?"

I stay calm. "I had to make a judgment call regarding the strategy of your case." This was true. "It was difficult. I even had to consult another lawyer about it. And, if I'd let anyone know I suspected such, I most likely wouldn't have been able to represent you because of a conflict. At which point the information itself could've cost you the whole lawsuit, and you'd have walked away with nothing. I made a judgment call in your best interests."

"So, are you saying you settled my case while at the same time having a suspicion my sister, not Dr. Grad, was responsible for overdosing me?"

"That's what I'm saying. But, in my own defense, my obligation was to you, not to Dr. Grad and not to the district attorney's office."

The hostile look on her face softens. But only just a bit. "I guess I should say thank-you then."

"Not a problem. I was just doing my job really. Now I need to know something, something important."

"What?"

"How much detail from the fire flashbacks has Jessie been aware of?" I ask her.

"Not much. She acted as if I was wacko when I first started having them."

"So she doesn't know you're now aware of your mom's plan?"

"No, or about having been locked in my room," she adds.

"Does she have any knowledge at all about your recollections of that day in Grad's office? Meaning, is she thinking you might suspect she tried to kill you?"

"No."

"You never said a thing to her?"

"Not a word. What was I supposed to say? 'Hey, Jessie, why'd you try to kill me?'"

"Good point."

There's a lull in our conversation. It's all pretty insane. But I sense Nelly has something more on her mind. Well, why wouldn't she? I wait, and I'm not surprised by what she comes out with. The reason she came here in the first place.

"I don't want Dr. Grad to go to jail," she says. "So now what?"

"Let me finish mulling it over. I have a plan—a middle-ground approach, so to speak. And I think it still works—that is, if you've told me everything." I pause. "So, have you told me everything?"

"I think so. Did I say Jessie knows you were snooping around about her at Fritzi's?"

I roll my eyes, certain that can't be good. "No. Anything else?"

"That's it."

"Okay. Good."

If Jessie's aware of my suspicions, I can't underestimate her. Especially since she seems to have little reservation about striking first and taking advantage of whatever opportunity is before her.

Hybrid Plan Forty-Seven may need some slight modifications.

34.

One week later and things are getting worse for Grad. Only he's too stubborn and righteous to know it. He's been telling the media that he doesn't need a criminal defense lawyer because he's innocent. What an idiot! Nice guy but an idiot nonetheless, because, for certain, he committed perjury—and I can't help him with that one. In the interviews, he's also explained that the reason Nelly's civil case had been settled was because she was injured while under his treatment. Thus, he wanted to make sure that she was taken care of, regardless of fault—the same thing he'd said at the mediation.

I take a deep breath, sitting in the comfort of my den, hoping all will go according to plan. Today's the day Nelly is going to Jack Herring's office. Remember, he's the district attorney handling Grad's prosecution. Hybrid Plan Forty-Seven, as modified, is in motion.

So far I've kept the specifics of this plan to myself. Which was smart because it's been in flux, owing to incoming new information, which, of course, results in my need to tweak it. Still, however I arrived at it, forty-seven is a miracle of creative legal thinking. Here it goes: Nelly's going to say that she now remembers the second person who came to check on her inadvertently and unknowingly knocked into the IV pole as she was leaving the room. This caused Jessie to jump up from her chair, rush over, and catch the top of the falling pole. Somehow then she must've accidentally opened the IV flow controller, causing the overdose.

Nelly's bringing Jessie's jeans with her and is going to tell Jack Herring that she remembers me telling her that I saw some dark fibers on the control clamp during my inspection. That it meant nothing to her then, but, just the other day, when Jessie wore these jeans, she complained how they were still shedding after zippering up. And, when Jessie showed Nelly a handful of dark fibers, she made the possible connection. She's going to suggest to Herring that he see if matching fibers are on the controller. Forced and contrived, yes. But it has to be done. If Herring does what he's supposed to—what he should've done in the first place—he's going to see the clamp in the open position covered with dark fibers and match them up to the jeans.

Nelly will further insist that Grad can't be held responsible for the overdosing, and, that she, as the victim, does not want him prosecuted. Moreover, if Herring's determined to go forward, she'll come into court as a witness against the prosecution to tell her version. He'll then lose the case and blemish his reputation, presenting a strong deterrent against proceeding further for any aspiring prosecutor.

If Herring decides to call me to discuss the matter, I'll play dumb. Tell him I didn't know any of it or that she was even going to see him. I'll support the credibility of what she's saying, reminding him to be aware that, as time passes, more and more recollections are surfacing in Nelly's mind. I will also advise him that it would be inappropriate—as well as a miscarriage of justice—to prosecute Grad for an accident caused by one of his dental assistants and that I intend to do everything in my power to see an innocent man isn't sent to jail.

The modification of my original plan is: Nelly will phone Jessie, saying she's on her way to the Bronx DA's office to try to stop the prosecution of Dr. Grad. She is also to tell her sister not to answer any calls from anyone until they have a chance to talk. The corollary to this is that Nelly plans to speak to Jessie personally tomorrow to explain everything. And, for good measure, that she loves her very much for being the best sister ever.

Pacification.

Because I regard Jessie as dangerous. Both before she had any knowledge of my snooping and even more so now when she does. Once the moment comes when I can tell her we know everything—and I mean *everything*—I'll promise to be quiet unto eternity. That is, unless she misbehaves.

I've also directed Nelly to phone me as soon as she leaves the DA's office to confirm all has proceeded according to plan.

You understand, it was the best I could fabricate, given the circumstances. And despite the high level of creative legal thinking, it's not a thing of beauty.

At least I admit it.

The primary benefit: it protects everyone involved.

Nelly keeps her money.

Grad doesn't go to jail for a crime he didn't commit.

Jessie doesn't get prosecuted for attempted murder and is deterred from any future misconduct because we now know what she's about.

Jack Herring doesn't lose a case.

Benson, well, . . . Benson is Benson.

Me, I escape scrutiny on all fronts. I'll do anything to keep my unblemished reputation for truthfulness in the pursuit of justice. Even lie if I have to.

At least I admit it. Again.

It's now two o'clock in the afternoon and sunny. So I go outside to play with the dogs. Next thing I know, after lounging around my den and binge eating, it's 5:30 p.m. I should've gotten Nelly's call by now. I didn't want to buzz her in the event she was still at Jack Herring's office—but, at this point, it's time to find out what happened.

I pick up my phone to walk outside. Tucker and Otis follow. A rush of emails scrolls across the screen. None from Nelly. No missed calls either.

Why don't I like the way this feels?

I try her phone, get voice mail, and hang up. I call four more times. On my sixth attempt, I leave a message. But it's a cryptic one in the event Jack Herring took possession of her phone for some crazy reason. "It's me. Call me back, please." *Click*. But I'm not satisfied. I need contact, and I need it now.

My mind starts playing games.

What if they put her in that interrogation room and shone a bright light into her eyes? What if they're trying to coerce a confession out of her? That's what those guys do. No one really confesses voluntarily, do they?

"Yes, Mr. Herring," she agrees, giving up, "this whole thing was my lawyer's idea. He concocted it all. He even gave it a name, Hybrid Plan Forty-Seven, so I could keep my money, and he could keep his fee. Oh, yeah, and his license too."

Next she tells him, "I'll come to court and testify to this. You want me to put it down in a written statement, you say? Okay, why don't you write it out the way you want it to read, and I'll sign it, as is. Then can I go home?"

Crap! Maybe this wasn't such a good idea. I mean, she has a brain injury, a fact I keep losing sight of. I take a few steps toward the door and Otis follows. Tucker, who's at a distance, sees us heading in and begins a playful charge. In his attempt to beat Otis to the door, Tucker slams into me, taking my legs out. As I awkwardly fall, my phone flies from my hand.

Ringing.

As I succumb to gravity, the right side of my face smacks down onto our bluestone entry path, as does my phone. I hear the screen crack. Getting up, I see blood on the stone and retrieve my phone. I go to the missed call log, hoping it was Nelly.

"Crap!" I scream out.

Alert One. Not good. I hit Call Back. "Hello, this is Melissa Freeman at Alert One. How can I help you?"

"Hi, Melissa, I got a call from you guys. Check the account of Nelly Rivera, please."

"One moment. Yes, we received an emergency signal from Alert One subscriber Nelly Rivera. The special instructions on this account direct that we call 917—"

"Yes, Melissa, that's my number. I missed the call."

"Yes, but we also called—"

"Never mind that, Melissa," I say, losing patience. "Where did the emergency call come from?"

"The transmission received from our satellite indicates an origination site of Route 9 in—"

"Yonkers. Got it, Melissa, thanks."

"Do you want us to dispatch emergency services?"

"I don't think it'll be necessary. Thank you."

Route 9 is where Fritzi's is located. Why did Nelly go there without me? Hadn't I told her we'd make our trip in the morning, to confront Jessie together? I hit her number, but it doesn't connect. Oh, great. Perhaps it's not 100 percent after its impact with the bluestone. I hit Speed Dial again and listen. *Whew.* It's ringing. But there's the voice mail again. Crap!

I run into my house, stuff my wallet in my pocket, grab a pair of sneakers, throw on my gray hoodie, and bolt into the garage. As I open the door of my SUV, I see my reflection in the window. Getting in, I check myself in the rearview mirror. The right side of my face is a bloody, swollen wreck.

Ten minutes into my drive, I try Nelly again. My phone's dead. At least I got the Alert One call out of it. Now, a half hour later, I'm approaching Fritzi's. The place is closed.

Pulling into a parking space, I contemplate my next move. I decide to look inside. It looks empty. Okay, what now?

What's ticking in my head is an arrow in fact. Like the kind you see on highways when there's a lane switch. And I got to tell you, where that big flashing arrow is pointing is to the old Rivera family home.

In truth, it's the beginning of all this and very likely the end as well.

It doesn't take me long to get there. I pull up to the house—off on its own, at the end of a dark cul-de-sac—and park. Time to see if anybody's home.

I enter and absorb the unusual vision. Scattered moonbeams shine in through the roof holes. It's the only source of light. Which is to say, not much. I walk guardedly, scoping out the first floor. Living area, kitchen, Nelly's and Jessie's rooms—all empty. Standing at the foot of the stairs back at the entry, I look up.

The first two steps leading to a small landing are fine. The rest though are shot. Because it's mostly dark inside, I'm moving super-cautiously but make it up to the second floor safely. One thing I noted is, six steps from the top is a serious weak spot.

Ahead are two doors on the right. I walk toward the far one, fists clenched. Taking hold of the knob, I turn it slowly and open the door to the master bedroom.

Holy shit!

In the center of the room is Nelly. Aided by moonlight, I see she has a gag in her mouth and is tied to the chair where she's sitting, staring at me wide-eyed.

"Nelly," I say, pulling off her gag, "are you okay?"

"We've got to get out of here! Now!" she shouts.

"No shit!" I hurriedly begin untying her. "Fill me in!"

"Jack Herring bought the story. It went like you planned. But then," she goes on, "I needed to take care of other family stuff, which didn't involve you."

"I told you," I remind her, "we'd come here together for the next phase!"

"I know. I know. I should've listened." She looks on with impatience as I struggle with the ropes to free her. It's a crazy tie-job, knot after knot. "I went to Fritzi's and told Jessie everything. She kept insisting I'm crazy. How could I ever believe she'd tried to kill me? Seeing and hearing us argue, Juanita closed early so we could hash out family matters in private."

I'm making progress, but knots are still left. "Juanita thought I was crazy too when I went on about someone having locked me in my room that night."

"But how did you end up here?"

"Finally Juanita told Jessie to drive me to the train station. I said I wanted to stop by the old house, thinking it might bring some more memories, but Jessie refused to drive me here. So I hit my Alert One button and was going to stall for time until you got here. On my way to the car, I'm slammed in the back of my head. The next thing I know, I'm here, tied up."

"When I'm finished with these loony knots, can you make a run for it?"

She nods. And suddenly she's standing. As I reach out to help steady her, I spot a notepad on the floor.

"Let's go!" I lead the way, bolting down the hall. It's hard to see where we're going—and *wham!* It gets much harder when I'm struck on my head.

Lights out.

35.

At some point, I'm coming to.

"You're so fucking crazy!" I hear Jessie scream.

"Stop calling me crazy!" Nelly retorts. "I'm *not* crazy! You just want me to think I am!" I edge my head painfully to the right. Jessie's kneeling behind Nelly in the same chair I found her in, untying her with the same trouble I was having with those knots. But wait! Didn't I already do that?

"You *are* crazy!" Jessie reiterates. Halting for a moment what she's doing, she stands up with authority, marches over, stops in front of where I'm lying on the floor, wrists and ankles tied, and berates me.

"You're supposed to be my lawyer!" she yells at me. "Why the fuck did you fill her head with lies? Why did you do that?"

At first I'm too groggy to answer. And the shouting isn't helping my throbbing head.

"Answer the question!" Jessie insists.

I look up. She's dimly lit from the moonlight. "Because the physical evidence implicated you. The fibers from the zipper flap on your jeans were on the IV clamp controlling anesthesia flow, that's why. And Nelly," I add, nodding in her direction, "had flashback recollections where she saw you standing over her next to the pole. Plus the device was in the full-flow position, and Grad, with his experience, would never have set it at that."

She stares at Nelly, then back to me. "A flashback? Wow. That's too much. So you actually do believe I did something," she says, amazed.

Her disbelief is rather convincing. Still, I give her a cold stare in support of my allegation.

Addressing her sister, now out of the chair, she orders Nelly, "Help me." They get me up and set me in the chair. I'm feeling woozy.

"Would you mind untying me?" I ask.

"Yes! Stand there next to him." Nelly complies. "Let me make myself clear to you two," Jessie begins, glaring at us both. "I was in that room, and everything I've ever said is the truth about what happened that day. But there's one detail I did leave out. Something I didn't know had any importance until this very moment."

"Go on," I challenge. "Tell us because I can't wait to hear how the fibers of your jeans got onto the IV controller."

She gives me an angry squint, the kind given when a strong retort is on the horizon. She looks at Nelly. "Tell him, Nelly! Was anybody else that day wearing the same label jeans? Tell him!"

"*Um*, I'm not sure."

"Are you sure that you're not sure? Think, Nelly! Who else?"

"*Um*, . . . Debbie, the receptionist?"

"Finally we're getting somewhere!"

She's certainly got my attention. I'm the attorney who failed to rule out other fiber sources, after all.

"You remember two people coming into the room, don't you?"

"Yes," Nelly replies.

But now I have something to say. "Listen, Jessie, you testified only one person checked the IV. I remember that clearly. That was the only difference in testimony between the two of you."

"That's right. I said only one person came in to check because that's the truth. But Debbie had entered the room too."

What the fuck? I think. So I ask, "Why would a receptionist leave the entry area and come into a patient exam room?"

"Because," she begins, "my stupid phone had fallen out of my stupid bag. Debbie saw it on the floor where we had been sitting and was returning it to me."

"But how does handing your phone back translate into fibers making their way onto the IV controller?"

"You remember her sweater, right?" she asks of Nelly.

"The one with the big wood buttons?"

"Yes. The one with the big wood buttons," Jessie confirms.

She turns back to me. "As she passed Nelly on her way out, the IV line snagged around a button. She started dragging the pole without realizing. I jumped up and stopped her. Then she unhooked her button, seemingly without harm. But she must've hit that controller thing you're talking about. She rolled the pole back where it belonged, and out the door she went."

I look at Nelly, and she's unresponsive. Last question on this topic. "Why didn't you tell me about Debbie's entanglement with the pole?"

"Because it never occurred to me it was of any significance. But also I didn't want to get Debbie in trouble. It was her second day on the job, and she'd already been yelled at right in front of us for dressing unprofessionally. In jeans!"

"But I specifically asked you."

"What you specifically asked me is how many times someone came into the room to check on Nelly. And my answer is still the same. Once. Debbie came in to return my phone."

I feel like a total ass at this moment. I look to my right, and, from the expression on her face, Nelly feels like one too. And I acknowledge what a fine line there is between fact and fiction as this scenario parallels my contrived Hybrid Plan Forty-Seven.

Worse yet Henry Benson was right.

But I still need answers. "There's the other stuff."

"I'm listening," Jessie tells me, still on her high horse and very pissed. "What other stuff is there that leads you to believe that I tried to kill my sister? Twice!"

Oh, man. At this point, the only thing I was right about was a dental assistant having an encounter with the pole—and that I had made up to prevent Grad from being wrongfully prosecuted. Still worse, what I'm about to say is based on the flashback rants of my brain-injured client. What's the matter with me? How did I end up in this situation? Am I just another egomaniac trial lawyer who thinks he's never wrong?

Nelly, I can see, has an uncertain look on her face. I mean, why wouldn't she? The person she thought had attempted to kill her—not once but twice—instead, by quick action, saved her life at the dental office and just now has unknotted a rope, setting her once again free. Once again? What is going on here? Who knocked me out?

"Should I give the money back since Grad did nothing wrong?" Nelly asks.

"No!" Jessie and I chorus. An issue we can both agree on. "Grad's legally responsible for the conduct of his employees," I add. "And Debbie's conduct—unknowingly dragging an IV pole around a room she had no business being in and opening the controller—counts as negligence in my book. Besides, if Grad had been in the room, and had there been reversal agents, this never would've happened to you."

"But look here," Jessie demands. "What's the rest of your conspiracy theory against me?"

Nelly is ready for this and defends herself. "Well, I know you were in on the plan to make Stella's death look like an accident to collect the life insurance proceeds."

Jessie erupts. "You know, it was a lot simpler when you were suffering from post-traumatic amnesia!" She shakes her head. "Did you think he could ever understand it? You idiot!" She now glares at me.

My confusion is still a factor, however. But I address Jessie, striving for an even tone. "Nelly believes you locked her in her room so you could have all the money from her mom's scheme."

"Great," she says. "So we're back to that. Is this what you really think?"

"Well," Nelly starts off, "I know I was locked in my room during the fire and—"

"Your door was stuck! Your door was stuck! I almost died trying to get you out of there! I mean, the smoke or heat or something sealed your door, expanded the wood, melted the paint, I don't know. Your room is underneath where the fire was, and it burned through. Look!"

She points to a gaping hole in the floor. "No one realized that would happen, just like we didn't realize Dad was home. Or would die. Jesus, he wasn't even supposed to be here!"

A thought strikes me at this moment. "Jessie," I say, "why was the plan to make Stella's death look accidental to collect life insurance proceeds when her life wasn't insured?"

Jessie gives me a look like I don't know what I'm talking about. But this time I actually do.

"Of course she was," she answers me with certainty. "Nelly collected the money from the insurance company."

"No, that's not so. The money paid out was based on your father's death. He was the only one insured. Stella had been denied coverage because of her medical condition."

A confused look crosses her face. And Nelly's too.

"What are you talking about?" Jessie demands excitedly. "That's not right!"

"I know what I'm talking about. Though I understand you may find that difficult to believe at this point. The money Nelly received was your father's death benefit. It's complicated, but I know that for certain."

"No, it isn't right," Jessie repeats.

"But it is. I've seen the documentation to prove it."

"How?"

"I met with a lady named Trudy Anderson, the claims adjuster."

"Trudy Anderson?" Jessie looks at Nelly.

"Yes."

"But she's completely, certifiably crazy. She went to the nuthouse after Nelly got her money. She fought tooth and nail against the payout."

"Well, I don't know anything about her certifiable craziness, but I read the policy. Roberto owned the policy and was the insured."

"But he wasn't even supposed to be home. All of us were fed up with him and all his horribleness, and we didn't want him there when Stella left us. . . . That wasn't part of the plan." Hearing her own words, Jessie's face pales from a horrid realization.

"Oh, my god! Oh, my god! We've got to get out of here!" Jessie now shouts, as she feverishly unknots me.

"What? What?" Nelly's yelling too. "What's going on?"

"Figure it out!" She looks up for an instant. "If Stella didn't have life insurance, then Roberto's death was no accident. Don't you see it?"

"Help me here," Nelly answers. "I'm kinda lost. . . . You mean, they killed him?"

"That's exactly what I mean!" Jessie takes a deep breath. "They both were in on it. Your mom and mine."

Nelly gasps.

Jessie continues. "Stella hated him for bringing his women around while she was on her deathbed. He had used her sickness to get bail, but she understood he would be incarcerated for life. She wanted to take care of you, so much so she was willing to die for it. And kill for it. Plus we know Juanita despised him for divorcing her when she was in jail, leaving her penniless. We've got to get out of here before she gets back."

"Before who gets back?" I break in.

"Yeah, before who?" Nelly adds. "I thought it was you who knocked me out and brought me here."

"No! I didn't—Juanita must've! Who else? When I left the bathroom at Fritzi's to take you to the train, you both were gone. I drove past the station, but you weren't on the platform. So I figured you persuaded Juanita to bring you here. Juanita must be running scared, thinking it's all going to come out. That she killed Roberto—just like that crazy insurance adjuster tried to prove."

Untied, I stand. I realize I'm feeling a bit steadier. "Come on!" I order them. "Juanita knows I'm aware the payout was for Roberto, so we're *all* in danger here!"

We rush to the stairs. "One at a time," I say.

Nelly goes first, slowly and hesitantly. "Come on! Hurry up!" she urges now, as Jessie descends.

"Hurry up! Hurry up!" they plead. I nod and start my way down, praying the stairs can hold me one last time. Remembering the weak spot, I move left, then . . . BOOM! My body shoots through the staircase, which creates a hole around my torso. I stop my motion by extending my arms with my lower body dangling in the space beneath the stairs.

Jessie starts up.

"No! Don't! Stay there! This can't take any more weight. I'll get myself out." Which, after great effort, I do, surprising myself.

As I reach the landing, I order, "To the door! Go!" At the moment Jessie reaches for the knob, it swings in, knocking her backward. She hits the floor with her head at my feet. Blood's running from a giant gash above her eye. She lets out a moan.

I look up, and the dark shadowy outline of a figure moves directly toward us. As I step to pull Nelly out of harm's way, an object catches her across the head. When she falls, I pivot and bolt down the hall. That object appeared to be the butt of a rifle, so my flight response kicked in, to the exclusion of my fight. For it's me who she needs out of the way first, before dealing with the girls.

To my surprise, Juanita doesn't give chase. What's the story here? I expect to hear Jessie or Nelly screaming, but all is silent. I'd like to get back to them, but I have to stay alive first.

I hide in the darkest corner of Nelly's bedroom, crouching, and ready to lurch forward. I'll have one run at her.

I hear steps approaching in the hall—slow steps, patient steps, and guarded steps.

Now the footfalls come to a standstill within the doorframe. Enough moonlight shines through to see the outline of a person holding a rifle for sure.

She steps in, halts, and lifts her weapon, scanning the room methodically, using the barrel as her pointer. She makes another forward movement, then turns to her left.

Now we are facing, but only I seem to know it. Yet that doesn't matter much because what's pointed right at me can produce instant death.

If I leap forward now, I'm just a bigger target. Anyway she's not close enough. *Come on,* I think to myself, *just turn the other way.* I see the shadow of her fingers move about the trigger. Oh, man!

I hear a *click*—then *bang!*

Her body topples forward, landing facedown.

It must've backfired.

"Are you okay?" Henry asks.

"Jesus, where did you come from?"

"Dating Nelly's care coordinator at Alert One has its benefits."

"The girls?"

"They're in my car. Not at their best after being attacked. Scared and upset obviously."

I approach Henry. He regards my face carefully, as if he's taking an inventory of my injuries.

"You look like hell, boy, even in this light."

No need to share that the assailant mostly responsible was my playful puppy.

I turn to take stock of the body, limp in the darkness.

Just then at the doorway the girls appear. Out of breath, Jessie says, "We heard a bang and—"

"Mom! Mom! You shot my mom!" Jessie screams, seeing the mound in the darkness.

"Jessie, take it easy," Henry says. "That's not your mother. She's at home. Safe. Waiting for my call."

A confused look crosses Jessie's face, similar to the one the rest of us wear.

Henry steps toward the inert figure as Jessie switches on her phone flashlight. He takes the tip of his boot and wedges it under the body's shoulder, flipping it over. A little moan escapes.

"Who the hell is that?" Nelly asks.

"Trudy Anderson," I answer.

36.

S o now we're outside—except for Trudy—waiting for the
authorities and an ambulance. Juanita has just arrived.

"Why'd she kidnap me?" Nelly wants to know.

"To coerce a statement out of you" is my answer.

"Really?"

"Well, a notepad is upstairs. I don't know what else it'd be for."

As Henry turns, he and Juanita share stares. "You're going to
hear me out," she tells him.

"I'm listening," Henry replies. So are Jessie and Nelly. Me too.

"Stella told us she had life insurance and wanted to make her
death seem accidental so Nelly could get the money—a parting
gift," she begins. "It was her dying wish."

"Go on," Henry says smugly.

"She called us up to her room as planned. Right, girls?" she says,
turning to them.

They nod.

"Jessie and Nelly made their last good-byes. Which were a fast
kiss and hug, unlike you'd expect in such a situation. But it was the
end of a week of good-byes, and Stella was firm that this last one
would be short and sweet with no drama. The girls then went to
their bedrooms, ready for the next act."

She pauses, then continues. "Stella was brave and ready to end her suffering. She pressed the button on her machine, distributing the regulated dose of pain medication, and then it was up to me to inject into her port the giant dose she'd, over time, stockpiled from the hospice nurse. Just as I was about to do this, a phone rang from behind her bathroom door. A ring tone I knew all too well."

Her face clouded. "The plan had been for Roberto to be out. I said this to her, but Stella corrected me. 'Not my plan,' she said."

Jessie's and Nelly's attention fixes on her with expressions of disbelief. Turning to them and looking weepy, Juanita goes on.

"I never intended to share this with you girls. But now, well, I don't see that I have a choice. Behind that bathroom door lay Roberto. Dead. Stella had killed him. By injection." She sighs and looks over at me.

"It all made sense only when you said it was Roberto's death benefit. Anyway," she continues, "when I came out of the bathroom, Stella was unconscious with an empty syringe sticking out of her port. And she had started the fire. The room quickly became a raging inferno. I ran downstairs to let the girls know. The plan—to make it real—was that they were to sustain mild smoke inhalation. But the fire spread faster than anyone could've anticipated. Jessie and I were pushing on Nelly's door. Though it was stuck, like heat-sealed. Overwhelmed by the smoke, we rushed out, and Jessie called 911. We stood there praying the fire department would arrive in time to save Nelly."

She sighed—with sadness, despair, regret. Then shook her head. "End of story."

"Not quite" is Henry's only response, as the sound of sirens is heard in the distance. When you've put in the call for emergency services, you should feel a sense of relief as their approaching presence is made apparent. Not this time.

"Listen up," Henry orders in his authoritative manner.

Heads turn.

"Every family has a secret." He pauses, then gives me the nod to take over. I say my line.

"This is yours."

37.

start my SUV and glance at my rearview mirror. There they all are. Standing where I left them minutes ago.

Except for Henry, that is.

He'd given his statement to the police—the agreed-upon one, that is, an explanation resembling the truth—then quickly took off.

Typical.

His last words to me were the familiar "See you later, litigator."

I should mention here too how Trudy Anderson's eyes were heavy with defeat as they wheeled her past me on a stretcher. A mixed-up lady and a determined one, her righteousness had been her undoing.

I head out, taking one last look. Juanita's now lighting two cigs, passing the second to Jessie. Nelly's holding an ice pack from an EMS tech to her head. They look weary. I'm beat too.

As I drive away, I can't help thinking over a missing detail of what's gone down. I mean, how can I not wonder if Henry had any idea of Stella's murderous insurance fraud scheme? For he—and only he—possessed the knowledge that the payout had been for the death of Roberto, not Stella. A fact he never bothered to share with anyone.

By the time I'm nearly home, distracted by everything that's happened and barely noticing the traffic, I have one final thought.

Which is this: Nelly's malpractice case—straightforward enough to start with, even given its few extra twists—had sparked an unforeseeable chain of events, including the resurfacing of memories, ones that otherwise would've remained dormant forever. Unfortunately those memories had consequences.

My phone vibrates. I'm sure it's Tyler, calling to find out where the hell I am. I peek at the screen. Tug Wyler—supersleuth—is wrong again. What's there is a reminder on my calendar popping up. I have an appointment tomorrow.

With the dentist.

ACKNOWLEDGMENTS

Michele Slung—best editor ever—thank you for everything. You add clarity to my words and thoughts. Denise Barker and Cynthia Bushmann, your editorial services, encouragement, and guidance are invaluable. Erin Mitchell, thank you for taking the reins and making Rockwell Press happen. Renata Di Biase, your artistic excellence in book design is unmatched, thank you. Fauzia Burke, thank you for your support and marketing expertise.

Numerous individuals have influenced my writing in some way, shape, or form. Too many to mention out of fear of forgetting someone—but you know who you are. These people consist of my family and friends, trusted business associates, and those hardworking special people who make up my law firm. And . . . my brave clients.

To my children, Blake, Cooper, and Phoebe: Thank you for loving me, inspiring me, and entertaining me. I love you guys so much. More than you could ever imagine. And to my wife, Randi: As always, I knew it would piss you off to be the last person acknowledged. That's why I did it. Again. Consider it foreplay. In the next book I'll acknowledge you right up front. But I'm pretty sure it won't create the same vigor. Anyway, you inspire me, incite me, annoy me, and put up with me—as I do you. But that's what provokes the intense energy that makes our marriage work. For now. Just kidding. I love you dearly, and I always have. Well, most of the time. Kidding, again.

BEHIND THE BOOK

When a guy's been practicing law in New York City for thirty years and has written several novels, you don't look at him and think, "Hey, in high school, they kept him in remedial reading through eleventh grade." But it's true. There I was, meeting three times a week with five other students in a room with a solid wooden door and a tiny window set up high to prevent kids from peeking. By junior year though, everybody was tall enough to look in.

From that classroom came my earliest identification with the underdog. Okay, I may have had more going on for me than the rest of the kids in there, but I'd been one of them. I knew what it felt like to be at a distinct disadvantage.

All things turn out to be connected. After I began practicing law, I quickly realized the little guys of this world—the ordinary joes unable to stand up for themselves—most needed my legal expertise and fighting spirit to take on large and powerful insurance companies.

Justice is something you shouldn't have to compete for, but it is.

It's common to diss personal injury lawyers—ambulance chasers they call us. But just remember: anyone, in an instant, can become a victim. Even you.

ABOUT THE AUTHOR

Andy Siegel maintains a special commitment to representing survivors of traumatic brain injury in his practice of law. He is on the Board of Directors of the New York State Trial Lawyers Association and of the Brain Injury Association of New York State. His many trial successes have regularly placed those outcomes among the "Top 100 Verdicts" reported in the state annually. A graduate of Tulane University and Brooklyn Law School, he now lives outside of the greater NYC area.

ABOUT THE SERIES

Tug Wyler will thrust readers headfirst into the emotionally charged high-stakes arena of medical malpractice law. At the center of each book lays the rush to cover up genuine wrongs. What keeps Tug digging deeper and deeper into the circumstances is his compulsion to make the system work for people at a disadvantage with their life situation stacked against them. Tug is unswerving in his dedication because justice is an outcome the big insurance companies—through their high paid lawyers—vigorously resist.

Suzy's Case

When Henry Benson, a high-profile criminal lawyer known for his unsavory clients, recruits Tug to take over a multimillion-dollar lawsuit representing a tragically brain-injured child, his instructions are clear: get us out of it; there is no case. Yet the moment Tug meets the disabled but gallant little Suzy and her beautiful, resourceful mother June, all bets are off. When his passionate commitment to Suzy's case thrusts him into a surreal, often violent sideshow, the ensuing danger only sharpens his obsession with learning what really happened to Suzy in a Brooklyn hospital. Did she suffer from an unpreventable complication from her sickle cell crisis that caused her devastating brain injury? Or, did something else happen . . .

Cookie's Case

Cookie, an angel in stiletto heels, is by far the most popular performer at Jingles Dance Bonanza. To her devoted audience, she's a friend, therapist, and shoulder to cry on, all rolled into one. While meeting an old pal at the club, Tug doesn't expect to pick up a new client but quickly realizes the gallant Cookie—dancing in a neck brace, each leg kick potentially her last—is in need of a committed champion. Believing that Cookie is the victim of a spine surgeon with a sloppy touch, Tug takes her case. But as he seeks both medical cure and a fair shake for Cookie, he realizes—a tad too late—that sinister sights are now trained on him.

Nelly's Case

Nelly Rivera, when Tug first sees her, lies helpless in a hospital bed. Once sassy, active and ambitious, she's now a young woman with an uncertain future and a present seemingly tied to dependency. Discovering exactly what happened to her in a dental office while under anesthesia and who was responsible, however, is just one of Tug's goals. For he soon enough learns Nelly has recently inherited a hefty sum from her late father's life insurance. Which definitely complicates matters. The closer Tug, committed as always to gaining justice, gets to the truth, the more elusive it becomes.

Elton's Case

Wrongfully locked up for a crime he didn't commit, the wheelchair-bound Elton Cribbs's immediate situation soon goes from bad to tragic. Could it have happened that, while in custody and being transported with less than suitable care in a police van, he suffered the injuries which rendered him a paraplegic? Certainly, ever since then—for the past decade—he's led the life of an aggrieved victim, seeking justice while rejecting pity. Retained now to litigate Elton's case even as the clock's ticking, Tug finds himself caught in the unlikeliest of conflicts. After all, what's he supposed to think when the defendant, otherwise known as the City of New York, begins offering him millions to settle while at the same time maintaining its allegation that Elton's case is a phony one?

Jenna's Case

A teen-aged girl can be among the most vulnerable of human beings. And the preyed-upon young woman at the dark center of Jenna's Case is certain to win the heart of readers. Believing Jenna Radcliff to be the victim of a Brooklyn doctor willing to put greed above his oath to do no harm, Tug takes on her case with deeply felt zeal. Yet what he quickly comes to understand is that his new client—once an obviously bright, outgoing girl (and ace neighborhood jump-roper)—is now a nearly mute shadow of her former self. As he proceeds to amass evidence against the conscienceless and defiant surgeon who'd willfully mutilated Jenna, Tug unfortunately soon discovers that the forces set against him are not only more numerous than he'd imagined but also more deadly.

Turn the page for an excerpt from the next book in the Tug Wyler Mystery Series, *Elton's Case*.

Visit **andysiegel.com** for more.

elton's
case

A TUG WYLER MYSTERY

ANDY
SIEGEL

When nothing's straightforward about a personal injury case, maverick New York attorney Tug Wyler is the ever-ingenious, hard-charging fellow to turn to. But what happens if, as in Elton's case, the biggest surprises aren't the ones he's himself springing?

Wrongfully locked up for a crime he didn't commit, the wheelchair-bound Elton Cribbs immediate situation soon goes from bad to tragic. Could it have happened that, while in custody and being transported with less than suitable care in a police van he suffered the injuries which rendered him a paraplegic? Certainly, ever since then—for the past decade—he's led the life of an aggrieved victim, seeking justice while rejecting pity.

Retained now to litigate Elton's claim even as the clock's ticking, Tug finds himself caught in the unlikeliest of conflicts. After all, what's he supposed to think when the defendant, otherwise known as the City of New York, begins offering him millions to settle while at the same time maintaining its allegation that Elton's case is a phony one?

Stumped but fascinated, and struggling to untangle fact from fiction—not to mention the good guys from the bad—Tug once again shows himself as a stubbornly crusading hero unlike any other.

THE UNFORTUNATE EVENT

S low down!"
"Shut up!"
"I'm being knocked around back here."
"I said, shut your face, inmate! You're bugging me."
The driver—a corrections officer—grumbles a few choice words.
He ups the static on the portable radio duct-taped against the
windshield. The signal's weak, interfered by the downpour pelting
the roof of the jail transport van.

The right front tire hits a pothole splash-curling a wave toward
a row of abandoned warehouses. Again the passenger is tossed like
a rag doll. He's defenseless, unrestrained—except for a three-point
shackle binding his handcuffs to a belly chain. He crash-lands awkwardly on the unforgiving steel bench.

"Please!" he implores as the van rumbles along the dark,
deserted way dotted with rain-filled potholes. "Come on, man!" he
pleads as he's slammed about in the tiny square cage constructed
for transport isolation. "You didn't belt me in!"

"Seat belts are overrated" comes the mocking reply.

Bam! goes the van, hammering a rear shock, while up pops the
sole passenger.

"You're gonna break my back! Please!"

"You don't like to follow directions, do ya now?" Chuckling,
the driver hits the gas pedal—the engine roars. The van veers left

across a faded double-yellow line toward a flooded crater. The prisoner's eyes go wide with fright. "What the fuck you doing?" No response. Only a smirk that he can't see.

Just as the tire plunges in, the driver jams on the brakes, catapulting the passenger violently up and forward. His broad chest smashes into the cold metal cage. At the same instant the engine growls, thrusting the van forward and pitching him into the hind bars of the enclosure.

"Ugh! My back!"

A satisfied smile appears on the CO's face, reflected in the rearview mirror.

But there's more to come.

"No! Stop!" shrieks the inmate now as he realizes what's about to happen. "You're gonna kill me!"

The driver heads straight for a light pole. Impact in three, two . . .

At the last second, he yanks the wheel, causing the van to sideswipe the fixture. The passenger's sent flying headfirst into the corner of the cage and is knocked unconsciousness. The driver looks at his rearview. The man is slumped over. Motionless.

The corrections officer turns off the radio, an act signaling his mission has been accomplished. He readjusts his seat position, seemingly satisfied. Now the engine runs at a quieter purr. The rain lets up, and the clouds above abruptly break, giving way to moonshine that reflects off the wet pavement ahead.

All is calm.

The din of wet tires traveling along asphalt is the only sound to be heard. The driver takes a second glimpse in his mirror at his passenger—Elton Jerome Cribbs. His body position is awkward, half off the back-row bench with his face jacked up against the cage.

"Now that's more like it, fella. But don't die on me. Those reports are a bitch to fill out."

40313806R00179

Made in the USA
Middletown, DE
25 March 2019